The dashing, mysterious rogue must pay for toying with Victoria's heart...
But this game of seduction may prove more dangerous than the lady ever imagined!

Nathan moved slowly toward her, like a jungle cat stalking his prey.

Surprise flashed in Victoria's eyes, then she drew herself up and raised her chin another notch, meeting his gaze unflinchingly. If Nathan had not been so irritated with her, he would have admired her pluck. She might be a thorn in his side, but she wasn't a coward.

"You'll never find it," she insisted. "It's hidden in a place where you will never locate it."

Nathan allowed his gaze to wander slowly down, then up her form. When his eyes once again met hers, he said softly, "You're wearing it. The question is, is it tucked into one of your garters, or"—he glanced down at the swell of creamy skin rising from her bronze bodice—"nestled between your breasts?"

"You'll not bully me into giving you the note," she said, her voice not displaying the slightest tremor.

Nathan planted a hand on each wall, bracketing her in. "I've never had to bully a woman into giving me what I want, Lady Victoria."

By Jacquie D'Alessandro

NOT QUITE A GENTLEMAN
LOVE AND THE SINGLE HEIRESS
WHO WILL TAKE THIS MAN?

Jacquie D'Alessandro

Not Quite A Gentleman

AVON BOOKS
An Imprint of HarperCollinsPublishers

This is a work of fiction. Names, characters, places, and incidents are products of the author's imagination or are used fictitiously and are not to be construed as real. Any resemblance to actual events, locales, organizations, or persons, living or dead, is entirely coincidental.

AVON BOOKS
An Imprint of HarperCollins*Publishers*
10 East 53rd Street
New York, New York 10022-5299

This book is dedicated with my love and gratitude to my sister-in-law Brenda D'Alessandro, who is not only World's Greatest Shopper, but also World's Greatest Hairdresser. Thanks for making me laugh and for wielding your magic scissors.

And to Erika Tsang, for being such a great editor. Thank you for helping me bring this story to life and for loving it so much. And for forcing me to clean my house by coming to visit (my family thanks you for this as well).

And as always, to my wonderful, encouraging husband Joe, for always being my perfect gentleman, and my makes-me-so-proud son Chris, aka Perfect Gentleman, Jr., who I know will grow up to be the same sort of terrific gentleman as his dad.

Acknowledgments

I would like to thank the following people for their invaluable help and support:

The wonderful people at Avon/HarperCollins for their kindness, cheerleading, and for helping make my dreams come true, especially Michael Morrison, Mike Spradlin, Brian Grogan, Carrie Feron, Debbie Stier, Pamela-Spengler Jaffee, and Jamie Beckman.

My agent, Damaris Rowland, for her faith and wisdom.

Jenni Grizzle and Wendy Etherington for keeping me going and always being up for champagne and cheesecake.

Thanks also to Sue Grimshaw, Kathy Baker, Kay and Jim Johnson, Kathy and Dick Guse, Lea and Art D'Alessandro, and Michelle, Steve, and Lindsey Grossman.

A cyber hug to my Looney Loopies Connie Brockway, Marsha Canham, Virginia Henley, Jill Gregory, Sandy Hingston, Julia London, Kathleen Givens, Sherri Browning, and Julie Ortolon, and also to the Temptresses.

A very special thank you to the members of Georgia Romance Writers.

And finally, thank you to all the wonderful readers who have taken the time to write or e-mail me. I love hearing from you!

Prologue

Cornwall, 1817

*N*athan Oliver gripped the worn leather cache of stolen jewels to his chest and leaned back against the rough bark of the towering elm to catch his breath. *A king's ransom . . . almost there . . . almost done.* He had only to cross the moonlit clearing, deliver the goods to the man waiting on the opposite side of the woods, then it would be finished. And he'd enjoy financial security for the rest of his life.

He dragged a long, slow, deep breath into his burning lungs, allowing his racing pulse to slow. His heart thundered in his chest, he could hear its beat in his ears, feel it in the hollow pit of his stomach. All familiar reactions he'd experienced the dozens of times he'd done this before, but this time all those sensations were heightened— for reasons he ruthlessly shoved aside. Damn it, his conscience certainly chose an inconvenient time to rouse itself. Still, in spite of his best efforts to prevent their intrusion, the second thoughts and guilt that had plagued him since agreeing to this particular commission continued to claw at him. *Forget it. What's done is done. Just finish this.*

He cautiously peered out from behind the tree, senses on alert. The moon slipped behind a cloud, drenching him in darkness. A cool, sea-scented breeze rustled the leaves, mingling with the night songs of crickets and a nearby owl. Nothing seemed amiss, yet his gut tightened in warning—an instinct that had served him well in the past. He remained perfectly still for another full two minutes, gaze scanning, ears straining, but detected nothing out of place. Anchoring his bundle more firmly under his arm, he drew another deep breath, then ran forward.

He'd almost reached the protection of the copse of trees on the opposite side when a shot rang out. Nathan dove forward, hitting the ground with a skidding thud that jolted pain through his ribs. Another pistol report came in quick succession, followed by a cry of surprised pain, then, "Watch out!"

Everything in him froze. Bloody hell, he recognized that voice.

Pushing himself up, Nathan dashed toward where he'd heard the cry. As he rounded a curve in the path, he saw the masculine form on the ground. With all his attention focused on the fallen man, he didn't hear the noise behind him until it was too late. Before he could react, he was shoved, the blow catching him squarely between the shoulder blades. Thrown off balance, the pouch containing the jewels propelled from his grasp. A black-gloved hand snatched up the cache, then the shadowy figure dashed into the woods.

For the space of one stunned heartbeat, Nathan lay on the path, watching the figure melt into the darkness, clutching that which seconds ago had belonged to him. Then, with sharp talons of dread urging him on, Nathan rose and ran to the fallen man. Dropping to his knees, he looked into the pain-filled eyes of his closest friend.

"Damn it, Gordon, what the hell are you doing here?" Nathan asked, his voice rigid with fright while he began a hasty examination. When he touched Gordon's shoulder, he encountered the slick warmth of blood.

"Was going to ask you the same thing," Gordon ground out.

"Were you hit only once?"

Gordon winced, then nodded. "Second shot got me. Hurts like hellfire, but only clipped me. Don't know if Colin was as lucky. Saw him go down with the first shot."

Nathan froze at the mention of his brother's name. "Where is he?"

Gordon jerked his head to the left. Nathan turned and saw a pair of boots protruding from beneath a hedge. The sight hit him like a physical blow and he had to clamp his jaws together to contain the agonized *Nooooo!* that roared into his throat. Whipping out his handkerchief, he set the linen to Gordon's wound, then pressed Gordon's opposite hand on it. "Keep as much pressure on that as you can." He then jumped up, grasped the boots, and, as gently as he could, slid the body onto the dirt path, his mind reverberating with a single prayer: *Don't let him die. Don't let my greed have killed him.*

The instant Colin was free of the bushes, Nathan knelt beside him. Colin looked up at him and groaned, and Nathan released the pent-up breath trapped in his lungs. His brother was alive. Now if he could only keep him that way.

"Colin, can you hear me? Where are you hit?" He pushed the words through clenched teeth, his medical training cleaving through the panic, forcing him to remain calm, to concentrate on the task at hand.

"Leg," Colin rasped.

Nathan located the bleeding injury in Colin's thigh, and after a brief examination, said tersely, "There's no exit wound." He unwound his cravat and applied pressure to stem the blood flow. "I need to remove the lead ball as quickly as possible. Then Gordon needs to be stitched up. We have to get back to the house. Do you have horses?"

"No," said Gordon from directly behind him. "And why the hell do you think I'd allow *you* to stitch me up?"

Nathan glanced over his shoulder and noted Gordon standing, glaring down at him. His friend's hand remained pressed to his upper arm, but even in the dim light, Nathan could see the blood dripping from between his fingers. Just as he could see the anger glittering in Gordon's eyes.

"Perhaps because I'm the only doctor in your immediate vicinity and you both require immediate medical care."

"Seems to me that you're a bit more than a doctor this evening, Nathan." Gordon's gaze swiveled to Colin. "I told you something foul was afoot." He shifted his glare back to Nathan. "Why? Damn it, why did you do it?"

The carefully fabricated lie that was supposed to protect him lodged in Nathan's throat then unraveled like poorly woven cloth in the face of tonight's debacle. His brain, normally so nimble, felt incapable of thought at the sight of his best friend bleeding and his brother felled by a pistol shot. Clearly, Gordon believed him guilty of something—and with good reason. Yet, based on Gordon's tone and frosty glare, he also clearly believed the worst.

Nathan slowly turned back to Colin, then stilled. As much as Gordon's words had cut him, it was the look in Colin's eyes that struck Nathan like a blow to the gut. And the heart. Their gazes met and held, and Nathan's insides cramped at the doubt and accusation so eloquently evident in his brother's eyes.

"Nathan?"

Only one word. But the way he said it, the look in his eyes, was enough to drive a stake through Nathan's heart.

One

Today's Modern Woman should never allow a gentleman to take advantage of her, toy with her affections, or to view her as a mere plaything to be discarded after a pleasurable interlude. If a gentleman makes the mistake of doing so, she should retaliate by treating him in a similar dismissive fashion. A deed once avenged can then be buried in the past.

A Ladies' Guide to the Pursuit of
Personal Happiness and Intimate Fulfillment
by Charles Brightmore

"What is that you're reading so intently, Victoria?"

With a guilty start, Lady Victoria Wexhall slammed shut the slim leather-bound *Ladies' Guide* resting in her lap and looked across the carriage at Aunt Delia, who, for the past hour, had been napping, but was now peering at her through pansy-blue eyes alight with curiosity.

Heat rose in Victoria's cheeks and she prayed she did not look as red-faced as she felt. She slid the book onto the gray velvet squabs then quickly covered the volume with a flick of her forest-green spencer. Aunt Delia would no doubt be horrified if she discovered her reading the book whose explicit and provocative contents had recently whipped up a tornado of scandal in London. And she had no doubt at all that her aunt would be horrified to know what she planned to do once they arrived in Cornwall, thanks to her reading of the book.

" 'Tis just one of the books I purchased at Wittnower's Book Emporium before we departed London." Before her aunt could question her further, Victoria hastily asked, "Are you feeling refreshed after your nap?"

"Yes." Aunt Delia grimaced and stretched her neck from side to side. "Although I'm relieved we'll finally arrive in Cornwall today and no longer be confined to this coach."

"I agree." Their trip from London had been long and arduous, a journey Victoria normally never would have undertaken. If someone had suggested to her that she would willingly leave the comfort, glamour, and social whirl of London Society—especially as the Little Season was about to commence—to trek to the uncivilized wilds of Cornwall, she would have laughed herself into a seizure. But then, she hadn't realized she would be handed this perfect opportunity to avenge a past wrong on a man who so richly deserved it. Armed with her well-read copy of the *Ladies' Guide* and a clear plan, she was prepared. Still, the timing of the trip was not to her liking. "I still cannot credit it that Father insisted we make this journey *now*. Surely waiting a few weeks would not have mattered."

"You will learn, my dear, that even the most jovial of men are, at heart, utterly vexatious creatures."

"And vexing this timing is," Victoria said. The irritation that had bubbled under her skin ever since she'd been unable to convince Father to delay this trip erupted once again. For reasons she could not decipher, she'd been unable to budge her normally indulgent father. When it became obvious he would not bend, she'd finally consented to his timetable. She didn't wish to unduly upset or disappoint her father, who rarely asked anything of her. And neither was she willing to forfeit this opportunity to finally put the past to rest, as this would surely be her last chance. If all went according to her carefully constructed life's plan, by this time next year she would be a married woman, her future secured. Perhaps she'd even be a mother.

"When I think of all the soirees I'm missing . . . I simply do not understand what Father was thinking."

Aunt Delia's brows rose. "Do you not? Why, I'm surprised, what with you being such a bright gel. Clearly, your father wishes for you to marry."

Victoria blinked. "Naturally. And I intend to do so. But that cannot be his reason for sending me to *Cornwall*. Especially *now*. In the last month alone both Earl Branripple and Earl Dravensby have initiated conversations with Father regarding marriage. With the Little Season about to commence, affording me with numerous opportunities to further my acquaintances with the earls, and meet even more marriageable gentlemen, he'd have been much better served had I remained in Town."

"Not if the gentleman he wished you to meet was in Cornwall, my dear." Her aunt pursed her lips. "I wonder which of the Oliver men your father is leaning toward—the widowed earl or his heir Colin, Viscount Sutton? Or perhaps even the younger son, Dr. Nathan Oliver?"

Victoria forced her features to remain impassive at the mention of *his* name. "Surely none of them. I've only briefly met Lord Sutton—once, three years ago—and as for the earl, surely Father wouldn't encourage me to marry someone so *old* as Lord Rutledge."

"I believe *old* Earl Rutledge is a year younger than me," Aunt Delia said in a dust dry tone. Before Victoria could apologize for her faux pas, her aunt continued, "But you forgot Dr. Oliver."

If only I had . . . if only I could . . . but I shall. After this visit he will be exorcised from my mind. "I didn't forget him, I just didn't think it necessary to comment, as neither Father nor I would ever consider such a lowly match. Especially when two earls have expressed interest."

"I don't recall you mentioning a *tendre* for either Branripple or Dravensby, my dear."

Victoria shrugged. "Both are highly sought-after, fine gentlemen from well-respected families. Either would make an excellent match."

"It is well known they both seek to wed an heiress."

"As do many peers with lofty titles and depleted purses. I've always known I would be sought for my fortune. Just as I've always known I would have to marry well to secure my future. I certainly cannot count on Edward being generous once Father is gone." Victoria suppressed a sigh at the mention of her older brother. As much as it pained her, there was no denying that Edward—currently on the Continent doing heaven knows what—was an irresponsible, unreliable, gambling, drinking womanizer who would most likely cast her out after Father passed away. Naturally, Father would provide financially for her, but she wanted a family. Children. And a firm place in Society.

"You've no preference between Branripple or Dravensby?"

"Not particularly. They are of similar age and temperament. I'd planned to spend more time with them in London during the Little Season to help me decide."

"So you're certain that you will marry one of them?"

"Yes." Why didn't her heart soar with joy at the prospect? Marriage to either man would provide her with a life of luxury at the pinnacle of Society. Clearly her mind was preoccupied with the task she'd set for herself in Cornwall. Surely her enthusiasm for her suitors would manifest itself once she'd completed her objective.

Aunt Delia sighed. "I'm so sorry, my dear."

"Sorry? Whatever for?"

"That you haven't fallen in love."

"Love?" Victoria laughed. But even as she did so, an inner twinge pinched her. She used to harbor such silly fantasies, as most girls did. But then she'd matured and wisely put such foolishness aside. "You know as well as I that love is a poor basis for a marriage. Especially when family names, titles, fortunes, and estates are involved. Mother and Father's marriage was not based on love." An image of her mother's face rose in Victoria's mind's eye, the image she carried in her heart, of her mother smiling and beautiful, before the illness had stolen her vitality and then her life.

"Perhaps not, but their affection for each other eventually blossomed into love," Aunt Delia said. "Not every couple is so fortunate. *I* was not so fortunate."

Victoria gently squeezed her aunt's hand in a show of sympathy. Her widowed aunt's decade-long marriage hadn't been a happy one.

"As I understand it," Aunt Delia continued, "the reason your father insisted you come to Cornwall was to expand your horizons. See more of the country other than your usual haunts of London, Kent, and Bath. Open your mind, and heart, to new experiences, new people."

"I suppose. But surely Father cannot be expecting a match in *Cornwall*. He would have told me so."

"Would he? I think not, my dear. As you will learn, men are often annoyingly secretive creatures."

She couldn't argue that, especially where her father was concerned. "Why wouldn't he tell me?" Yet even as the question passed her lips, Victoria realized the answer. "He wouldn't tell me because he knows I would never consent to living so far from Town. So far from . . ." She waved her hand to encompass all the green nothingness. ". . . civilization. How could I not live in the city during the Season? And for summer, certainly nowhere more than several hours from London—just far enough away for proper rusticating, yet close enough to enjoy the social swirl of Town, the shops, and keep abreast of the latest fashions and *on dits*."

She sat up straighter. Could Aunt Delia be correct? If so, Father was to be sorely disappointed, for no matter how charming the earl and viscount might prove to be, she would never consent to entering into a marriage that would bind her, by law, to a man who could—and most likely would—relegate her to the desolate wilds of Cornwall. A shudder ran through her at the mere thought.

"I recall that we met Viscount Sutton in London several years ago," Aunt Delia said. "Handsome young man."

"Yes." Exceptionally handsome. Yet it was Lord Sutton's younger brother who had so thoroughly unsettled her. "But it wouldn't matter if he were the most comely man on the planet. I am not interested."

"We met his younger brother on that occasion as well," Aunt Delia said, her brow creasing. "Dr. Oliver. Bit of the devil in that one, you could tell at a glance."

The image she'd tried so hard to banish from her memory instantly materialized in Victoria's mind. A tall, broad-shouldered young man with thick, wavy sun-streaked brown hair, intriguing, flirtatious hazel eyes, and a wicked smile that had inexplicably—yet undeniably—fascinated her the instant they'd met in London three years ago at the Wexhall town house. Even now her heart seemed to skip a beat—no doubt a result of the severe irritation the mere thought of Dr. Oliver brought.

With the image of him now firmly in her mind, the haunting memories of that night three years ago assailed her. She'd recently celebrated her eighteenth birthday and had been flush with feminine confidence from her fabulously successful first Season, confidence that had soared even higher at the unmistakable interest that flared in the eyes of her father's sinfully attractive guest. Her imagination had immediately cast Dr. Oliver as a swashbuckling, rakish pirate who absconded with her and brought her back to his ship to kiss her and . . . well, she wasn't quite sure what else, but certainly whatever it was that brought a fierce blush to her maid Winifred's cheeks whenever she mentioned Paul, the handsome new footman.

Victoria's instantaneous attraction to Dr. Oliver had been heady, and breathtaking, unlike anything she'd previously experienced, although it had frankly confused her for she'd certainly seen handsome gentlemen before—handsomer gentlemen. His own brother, Lord Sutton, who'd stood not ten feet away from her, was by far the handsomer of the two, and appeared much more gentlemanly and proper.

Yet while she was at a loss to explain her reaction to Dr. Oliver, there was no denying it. There'd been something about him . . . perhaps his hair was a bit too long, his cravat just a bit mussed, the hints of mischief lurking in his gaze and the corners of his lovely mouth that had captured her fancy. Made her want to touch his hair, smooth his cravat, and ask what he found so amusing.

But mostly it was the way he'd looked at her that had set her heart fluttering and arrowed heated tingles of pleasure to her toes. He'd gazed upon her with a combination of warm amusement and an unabashed flirtation that skimmed the borders of propriety. She should have been appalled, but instead was entranced. He was unlike anything or anyone she'd ever before experienced, and when he suggested that she give him a tour of the portrait gallery, she'd instantly consented, rationalizing that it wasn't really improper. Her aunt and Lord Sutton would be in the next room. The adjoining door would be ajar. . . .

Once alone with him, however, Victoria's normal aplomb deserted her. To her horror, her efforts to impress Dr. Oliver with her maturity, new gown, and conversation went completely awry. She found herself chatting in a breathless, nonstop manner she couldn't control. Everything she'd ever learned about deportment seemed to flee her head and she babbled like a river overflowing its banks, unable to stop the nervous torrent of words bubbling from her. Her mind told her mouth to cease, to raise her chin and gift him with nothing more than a long, cool stare, but for reasons she couldn't understand, her lips continued to move and the words to spill out. Until he'd silenced her with a kiss.

Heat coursed through her at the memory of that kiss . . . that incredible, heart-stopping, breath-stealing, wits-robbing, knee-weakening kiss that had ended far, far too soon. She'd opened her eyes and found him looking at her with a crooked smile. "That did the trick," he'd murmured in a husky rasp. When she'd remained mute, he cocked a brow and said, "Nothing more to say?" To which she'd managed to whisper one word: "Again."

Something dark and delicious had flared in his eyes, and he'd obliged her with a different sort of kiss. A slow, deep, lush melding of mouths and breath, a stunningly intimate mating of tongues that awakened every nerve ending in her body. She'd clung to him, filled with a desperation and longing she didn't understand, other than to know that she wanted more, wanted him to never stop. But stop he did, and with a groan he'd untangled her arms from around his neck and set her firmly away from him.

They'd stared at each other for several long seconds. Victoria had tried to interpret his intense expression, but it was impossible, as she was so very dazed. Then his lips had tilted in a devilish smile and he reached out. With a flick of his long, strong fingers, he adjusted her bodice, which she hadn't even noticed was shockingly askew, then brushed the pad of his thumb over her still tingling lips. He looked as if he were about to say something when his brother had called from the adjoining room. Dr. Oliver had raised her hand to his mouth and pressed his lips against her fingers. "A most unexpected, pleasurable, interlude, my lady," he'd whispered, then, after a rakish wink, had swiftly left the room.

Afraid to face her aunt before she'd gathered her wits, Victoria raced to her bedchamber. Standing in front of her cheval glass, she'd been stunned by her own reflection. Her perfect coif was wildly mussed, her gown wrinkled, her skin flushed, her lips red and puffy. But even without those outward manifestations of her passionate exchange with Dr. Oliver, the look of wonder and discovery shining in her eyes would have given her away in a thrice.

Her common sense demanded that she be appalled at her shocking behavior, at the liberties she'd allowed him, but her heart was having none of it. How could she be expected to think clearly when, for the first time in her life, all she wanted to do was *feel*? She hadn't allowed any of the numerous gentlemen who'd sought her favor during the Season to kiss her. She'd dreamed of her first kiss—indeed had carefully planned the entire scenario, as she did with everything in her life—it was to take place in the formal gardens, after the gentleman had asked for and been granted her permission. But in an instant all her plans evaporated into a wisp of steam. Never in her wildest imaginings had she conjured up anything like the incredible, magical moments she'd shared with Dr. Oliver. She couldn't wait to see him again, and after what they'd shared, she knew he would contact her.

She had never been more wrong in her life. She'd never seen nor heard from him again.

Now, looking out the carriage window at the endless verdant hills dotted with thatched roof cottages marking yet another small village, Victoria closed her eyes and inwardly cringed at how foolish she'd been, at the idiotic expectant hope that had ruled her for weeks afterward. She had searched for him at every soiree, waited impatiently for the daily delivery of letters, jumped every time the brass door knocker sounded, announcing a caller. The truth she'd been too blind to see didn't finally hit her until one morning at breakfast, six weeks after Dr. Oliver had stolen that kiss, when she casually brought up his name to her father. In a single sentence Father had squashed all her hopes. Dr. Oliver had returned to Cornwall the morning after visiting the town house and had no intention of returning to London.

She still vividly recalled the fever of humiliation that had scorched her. What a fool she'd been! Here she'd hinged all these romantic, heroic ideals on a man who was nothing more than a cad! A man who had kissed her senseless with no intention of ever even speaking to her again. A man who had stolen her first kiss, a kiss that to this day she'd never been able to erase from her mind, whereas he no doubt would not even recall the exchange. It was the first time in Victoria's life she had ever been so summarily dismissed, treated so shabbily, and she had not liked it one bit. Rude, insufferable man. He may have been born a gentleman, but clearly his education and moral fiber were severely lacking, for he possessed no manners *at all*.

Well, by the time she left Cornwall, he would remember her. She'd been young and dazzled, and he'd clearly been experienced enough to know he was taking advantage of her naiveté. He'd toyed with her in a way she surely would have forgiven and accepted the blame for if only she'd been able to forget him. The idea of revenge had never occurred to her until this unwanted trip at her father's request had come up, coupled with her recent acquisition of the *Ladies' Guide*. But thanks to both, she would now see to it that Dr. Oliver was forgotten. The *Ladies' Guide* advised avenging such cads, then burying them in the past where they belonged, and she had every intention of doing so. She would flirt with him and kiss him as ruthlessly as he'd done to her, then abruptly depart, leaving *him* with memories that haunted the long, dark hours between nightfall and dawn. She'd blithely return to London and marry one of her earls, the entire Dr. Oliver episode finally behind her. Yes, it was an excellent plan.

Aunt Delia's voice pulled her attention away from the scenery. "According to your father, Dr. Oliver is a very fine physician, an assessment I'm sure is correct."

"Why is that?"

Her aunt's eyes twinkled. "'Twas obvious he'd have an excellent bedside manner. Your father also mentioned Dr. Oliver's interest in scientific matters."

Victoria barely suppressed the grimace that tugged at her lips. Most likely he enjoyed pinning the wings of insects to boards and such. And as for his profession? Humph. Just further proof that he wasn't a true gentleman, for no true gentleman would pursue a trade.

The coach slowed to a crawl, and the coachman's deep, booming voice rang out, "Ye can see the side view of Creston Manor, beyond those tall trees on the right, my ladies. Just need to follow this road around to the front. We'll be arriving within the quarter hour."

The conveyance then resumed a brisker pace, and Victoria and her aunt craned their necks to look out the window. As they moved past the trees, an impressive manor house came into view. The brick facade, faded to a delicate creamy rose, appeared to glow in the soft gilding of golden, late afternoon sunshine. Nestled amongst soaring trees and emerald lawns, Creston Manor looked at once inviting and imposing. From her advantageous side view, Victoria could see the formal gardens and stables in the rear, and a sparkling blue pond in the front that reflected both the surrounding trees and the house, the building's austere design softened by the rippling water.

A movement near the stables caught Victoria's attention, and she leaned forward. Two men stood near the open stable doors. One of them, a gentleman with dark hair, was dressed in riding attire. He seemed to be speaking to the other man, who was clearly a servant, as he was shirtless and held what appeared to be a hammer.

Victoria's gaze fastened on the man's bare back, which even from a distance she could see was broad and gleamed with a sheen of sweat. Warmth crept up her cheeks, and although she tried to force herself to look away, her suddenly stubborn gaze refused to move. But certainly only because she was scandalized. Of course. The servants at her family's country estate would never go about their chores half naked. She couldn't help but wonder what the man looked like from the front, given that the rear view was so very . . . captivating.

Aunt Delia raised her quizzing glass. "I do believe the dark-haired gentleman is Lord Sutton."

Victoria forced her gaze back to the other man, then nodded. "Yes, I believe you are correct."

"And the other man," Aunt Delia said, leaning so close to the window her nose was nearly pressed against the glass, "good heavens, none of my servants look like that *at all*. 'Tis enough to make one want to do nothing more than think of excuses to summon the dear shirtless boy."

Victoria's lips twitched at the outrageous comment. "That's one of the things I love most about you, Aunt Delia. You speak your mind—even when your thoughts are . . ."

"Naughty? My dear, that is precisely when it is the most fun to express your thoughts."

"I'm sure he dons a shirt before entering the house," Victoria said, still trying to pry her gaze away and keep the wistful note from her voice.

"Pity. But I suppose he would." Their carriage rounded a corner and the man was no longer visible. After they'd leaned back in their seats, Aunt Delia said, "I imagine he's left a trail of broken hearts in his wake."

"I imagine so," Victoria murmured, instantly sympathizing with those women, as she knew precisely how they felt. But thanks to the *Ladies' Guide* and her well-thought-out plan, she was going to see to it that her heart—and pride—no longer lay in the dirt.

Two

Today's Modern Woman must recognize that once she asserts herself, she will face many temptations. Sometimes this temptation takes the form of a delectable gown, or a delicious confection, which, depending on her financial situation, she should perhaps resist. However, sometimes this temptation takes the form of a delectable, delicious gentleman, in which case she should never resist.

*A Ladies' Guide to the Pursuit of
Personal Happiness and Intimate Fulfillment*
by Charles Brightmore

Nathan hammered another nail into place, banging on the small metal head with a satisfying thump.

"Pounding out your frustrations?" asked a deep voice from behind him.

Nathan tensed at his brother's question. He then drew a deep breath and forced his shoulders to relax, wondering when, or if, the awkwardness between him and Colin would ever dissipate. After exhaling, he whacked the nail head with a final grunting stroke, then looked over his shoulder. Impeccably dressed in riding attire, immaculately groomed, and exuding the image of a perfect gentleman that Nathan had long ago given up emulating, his brother regarded him with his usual inscrutable expression.

Nathan turned and grabbed his rumpled, discarded shirt to wipe his damp forehead. The sun warmed his bare back, and he welcomed the cool, sea-scented breeze that brushed over his heated skin. "Pounding out my frustrations," he repeated. "Yes, as a matter of fact, I am."

"Based on the amount of hammering I've heard all morning, you must be frustrated indeed." Colin jerked his chin toward Nathan's handiwork. "Quite the animal pen you're building."

"In case you haven't noticed, I arrived at the estate with quite a number of animals."

"Would have been damned difficult not to notice, what with all the mooing, baaing, clucking, barking, meowing, quacking, oinking, and . . . what sort of noise does that goat make?"

"*That goat* has a name. It's Petunia."

Colin pinched the bridge of his nose and shook his head. "I find it nearly impossible to understand why you think it necessary to keep such a menagerie, and even more impossible to comprehend why you would bring it—them—all the way to Cornwall. But what I truly cannot fathom is why you would burden the unfortunate beast with a name like *Petunia*."

"I didn't name her. Mrs. Fitzharbinger, my patient who gave her to me, named her Petunia."

"Well, clearly Mrs. Fitzharbinger possesses no sense of smell whatsoever because never in my life have I ever caught a whiff of anything that less resembled a flower than that filthy beast."

"I'd mind my words if I were you, Colin. Petunia is sensitive to insults and fond of butting the arse of those who speak ill of her." He shot a glance at his goat, who, upon hearing her name, lifted her pale brown head from the patch of flowers upon which she munched and stared at him through obsidian eyes. Telltale purple flowers and stems protruded from the sides of Petunia's mouth as her scruffy chin worked back and forth. "She has a particular fondness for petunias, thus her name."

Colin looked skyward. "If she were named by her favorite foods, then she also could have just as easily been dubbed 'Handkerchief,' 'Button,' 'Vellum—'"

"Yes, she loves to eat paper—"

"As I discovered this morning when she ingested a note I'd tucked in my waistcoat pocket. At which time I also lost a button." He sizzled a heated glare at Petunia. Petunia continued to chew in an unconcerned fashion.

"What about your handkerchief?"

Colin's eyes narrowed. "That was yesterday. Doesn't that beast know she's supposed to eat *grass*?"

"Actually, goats prefer to eat shrubs, bushes, leaves, and gorse."

"Seems to me she prefers to eat anything that isn't nailed down. At every opportunity."

"Perhaps. But she won't appreciate you saying so. I'd watch my arse if I were you." Nathan cocked a brow. "Your note must have been from a young lady. Petunia harbors a great appetite for love letters."

"Because she can *read*, I'm certain."

"In truth, I wouldn't be shocked to discover she could. Animals are much more intelligent than we give them credit for. I've discovered that Reginald can differentiate between apples and strawberries. He does not care for strawberries."

"I'm certain Lars and the entire gardening staff will breathe a collective sigh of relief at the news, especially given the current sad state of the petunias. And which of your brood is Reginald? The goose?"

"No, the pig."

Colin's gaze shifted to where Reginald lay sprawled on his side in porcine glory, beneath the shade of a nearby elm. "Ah, yes, the pig. Another gift from a grateful patient?"

"Actually, he was *payment* from a grateful patient."

"A patient who most likely thought he'd provided you with a feast of pork, ham, and bacon."

"Most likely. How fortunate for Reginald that I'm not overly fond of bacon."

"Or beef, either, by the looks of that cow."

"Daisy. Her name is Daisy." Nathan jerked his head toward the black and white bovine munching grass near Reginald. "I know you like to think of yourself as impervious, but look at her. One glance from those huge, liquid brown eyes and even you couldn't think of her providing anything other than fresh milk."

Colin shook his head. "Good God, you're a candidate for Bedlam. Petunia, Daisy," he muttered. "Are all your pets named for flowers?"

"Not all of them. The mastiff's name is B.C."

"Based on the size of the beast, short for Bone Crusher, no doubt?"

"No. Boot Chewer. Consider yourself forewarned."

"Thank you." There was no missing the sarcasm in Colin's tone. "B.C. is payment from another grateful patient?"

"Yes."

"As I suppose the ducks, geese, cat, and lamb were."

"Correct."

"You are aware that *money* is the normal compensation for a physician's services?"

"I receive that as well. Occasionally."

"By the looks of your menagerie, *very* occasionally."

Nathan shrugged. He'd never convince Colin or their father that he was perfectly content living in a cottage that could fit, with room to spare, in Creston Manor's drawing room. Or that his mismatched animals were his friends. His family. And as such, he needed them here, to help him through the ordeal he suspected awaited him just around the corner. "I'm paid enough to keep a roof over my head and keep my furry and feathered friends fed."

"Quite a bit tamer than the old days," Colin said.

Instantly the wall between them that they'd skirted around since Nathan's arrival yesterday could no longer be ignored. Yet he had no desire to talk about the past. "Much tamer. And that's just the way I like it."

"This was your home, Nathan. You didn't have to leave."

How was it possible that such softly spoken words could hit him so hard? "Didn't I?" He couldn't keep the edge of bitterness from his own words.

Colin studied him for several long seconds through green eyes that were so like their mother's they inspired another wave of memories Nathan had to fight back. Finally Colin turned his head and stared into the distance. "You could have made different choices."

"I don't see how. Even if I'd wanted to stay, Father demanded I go."

"He spoke in anger. So did you. He's since written to you, inviting you to come home."

"True. But by then I'd already settled in Little Longstone." He raked a hand through his hair. "While our relationship is civil, there remains an . . . awkwardness between Father and I that I'm not sure we'll ever breach." He didn't need to add *as there remains between you and I.* The words hung between them like a dank fog.

Colin nodded slowly. "You hadn't intended to return."

Nathan's gaze inadvertently flicked to the wooded area behind Colin. He jerked his head in a tight shake. "No."

"Yet you're here."

"Lord Wexhall's letter left me little choice."

"I'd have thought you'd embrace the chance to clear your name."

"Believe me, the opportunity to do so is the only reason I agreed to come here." Guilt pricked Nathan when Colin's jaw tightened, but it was better he told the bald truth. There were already enough lies between them.

"Evidenced by the fact that you haven't been home in three years," Colin murmured.

Yes, three years. Three years since his life had changed so drastically. Three years of burying memories and striving to find peace. Of finding a place where he belonged, where the past didn't linger around every corner. "I've written."

"Infrequently."

"My time was consumed with finding a place to settle. Establishing myself."

"Which happened to be three hundred miles from here."

"Yes. In a place where no one knew me. Where no one knew what happened."

"Leaving as you did only made you look more guilty."

"Everyone believed me guilty anyway, so I cannot see that it mattered."

They exchanged a long, measuring look. Then Colin said, "I was surprised that you gave up so easily. That you didn't fight to clear your name. You'd never before been a quitter."

"Well, I guess you didn't know me as well as you believed."

"Apparently not."

"Or I you." Another look passed between them, then Nathan said, "At least at a distance of three hundred miles I'm not subjected to the whispers and stares. Which is one reason my 'beasts,' as you call them, are so important to me. They care nothing of my past. They do not judge me. They can't hurt me."

"And that is how you wish to live? Feeling nothing?"

"Avoiding rejection and pain is not the same as feeling nothing."

"It's been three years, Nathan. It's time for you to move on."

"I have."

"I meant more than geographically."

"And I have. It's just that this place . . . being here is . . . difficult." His gaze dropped to Colin's leg, which he knew bore scars. "Have you so easily forgotten?"

"Of course not. And neither has Gordon. But neither Gordon nor I have allowed what happened to rule us."

Nathan nearly flinched at the name. Gordon . . . Earl of Alywck . . . boyhood friend and neighbor. Another man who'd almost lost his life, whose body bore scars because of that final disastrous mission for the Crown. *Because of me . . .*

"Neither of you were accused of stealing the jewels. Neither of you lost your honor. Your reputation." *Lost everything.* "Neither of you were responsible for . . ." Nathan's voice trailed off and he clenched his jaw so tight his teeth ached.

"You saved my life, Nathan. Gordon's as well."

A bitter sound erupted from Nathan. Yes, he'd succeeded in repairing the physical damage, but he'd failed in so many other ways. Ways he had no desire to think about or relive. He'd never forget the accusing doubt in Colin's eyes. And it was no less than he deserved.

Determined to steer the conversation back onto lighter topics, he said, "I suppose our guests will be arriving today."

Colin stared at him for several seconds, then slowly nodded, clearly taking the hint. Excellent. Nathan had endured all the reminiscing he could stand for one day.

"Yes. Lady Victoria and her aunt are expected today," Colin agreed. "Lady Victoria . . . can't say that I recall her very well, other than a vague remembrance that she was remarkably pretty."

Years of practice allowed Nathan to keep his features perfectly composed. He remembered Lady Victoria only too well. "Probably you don't remember her because on the occasion we were together you abandoned the chit to me while you spoke to her aunt, Lord Wexhall's sister."

"Hmmm, yes. No doubt you're correct. Lady Delia was quite an entertaining character as I recall."

"Not that I would know," Nathan said with a pointed look, "as I was the one with Lady Victoria foisted upon him."

"Foisted? Odd, I seem to recall that you rather commandeered her and asked her to show you the ghastly family portraits." Colin nodded slowly, and Nathan well recognized the gleam in his brother's eyes. And it suddenly struck him how much he'd missed it. "I also recall that your feathers were quite ruffled after your, um, conversation with the lovely Lady Victoria."

Nathan slammed the door on the flood of memories that demanded entrance. "Nothing of the sort. I simply did not enjoy conversing with a supercilious child." He dispassionately marveled at his ability to still lie so effortlessly. Clearly some things never changed. Yet, the hollow ache in his gut indicated that perhaps the lying wasn't achieved so effortlessly after all.

"Conversing? Is that what you were doing in that dimly lit room that rendered your hair mussed? And at eighteen, Lady Victoria was hardly a child," Colin said, the gleam glowing brighter.

"She certainly behaved like one, chattering inanely about the weather and fashion."

"Well now, at twenty-one, even by your standards she is a child no longer. And Lord Wexhall is sending her here. According to his note, he expects you to look after her. How very interesting."

"And how precisely would you know what my note from Lord Wexhall contained?"

"I read it."

"I don't recall giving you permission to do so."

"I'm certain you meant to, as you left it lying on a table in the library."

"I'm certain I did no such thing." Damn Colin and his superior pickpocketing skills. Well, he might be light-fingered, but an expert cipher he was not. Even if he'd studied Lord Wexhall's missive at length, he wouldn't have been able to decode the secret message it contained. Guilt pricked Nathan for not sharing the hidden contents of Lord Wexhall's note with Colin, but he wanted to wait until he had further information before doing so. No point in dragging Colin into a situation that could potentially be dangerous until he knew exactly what the situation was.

Colin waved his hand in a dismissive gesture. "Perhaps it was a table in the drawing room. How did Lord Wexhall put it in his letter? Oh, yes. 'I expect you to take care of Victoria and see that no harm comes to her,' " he recited in a sonorous voice. "I wonder what sort of harm he believes might befall her?"

"Probably thinks she'll wander off and fall from a cliff. Or overspend in the village shops."

Colin cocked an eloquent brow. "Perhaps. Note how he said *you*. Note how I was not mentioned *at all*. The chit is completely *your* responsibility. Of course, if she's as lovely as I recall, I perhaps could be persuaded to assist you in looking after her."

Nathan blamed the heat that scorched him on the unseasonably warm afternoon. Bloody hell, this conversation was bringing on the headache. "Excellent. Allow me to persuade you. I'll give you one hundred pounds if you'll watch over her," Nathan offered in a light tone completely at odds with the tension consuming him.

"No."

"Five hundred."

"No."

"A *thousand* pounds."

"Absolutely not." Colin grinned. "For starters, given the fact that you're routinely paid with farm beasts, I doubt that you have a thousand pounds, and unlike you, I've no wish to be paid with things that make 'mooing' sounds. Then, no amount of money would be worth giving up seeing you do something you so clearly do not wish to do, as in acting as caretaker to a woman you think is a spoiled, irritating twit."

"Ah, yes, the reasons I stayed away for three years all come rushing back."

"In fact," Colin continued as if Nathan hadn't spoken, "I'll give *you* a hundred pounds—in actual currency—if you're able to carry out your duty to Lady Victoria without me witnessing you fighting with her."

Well accustomed to Colin's tricky nature, Nathan said, "Define fighting."

"Arguing. Exchanging words in a heated manner. Verbal altercations. I'm assuming you would not enter into any physical altercations."

"I've no intention of getting within ten feet of her," Nathan said, meaning every word.

"Probably for the best. She's unmarried, you know."

He stilled. No, he hadn't known. Not that it mattered. He shrugged. "Can't say as I'm surprised. I pity the poor bastard who finds himself leg-shackled to that puffed-up bit of talkative goods."

An image rose in his mind of silky dark hair and laughing blue eyes, and a plush, delicious mouth. In spite of being fully aware that she was testing out her newly minted feminine wiles on him, he'd found himself charmed by her combination of innocence, flirtatiousness, and nervousness in his presence, and had been unable to resist stealing a kiss. He'd meant it to be nothing more than a teasing way to end her nervous chatter, but it flared into an inferno, stunning him. Virginal Society misses barely free from the schoolroom had never been to his taste, and he hadn't counted on his reaction to that kiss. Or her reaction. Both had taken him by surprise, and he wasn't a man who liked surprises.

But those few stolen moments were in the past, and as he'd learned, memories and regrets were best buried in the deepest crevasse one could find. Over the past three years he'd convinced himself that Lady Victoria had matured into nothing more than a peer's typical empty-headed daughter, able to converse about nothing save fashion and the weather. A nose-in-the-air hothouse flower reeking with self-importance and affected manners. A woman who pouted and sulked to get her way—indeed, he'd firmly categorized her as the exact sort of woman he could not abide.

And now he would be forced to endure her company. To protect her. But from what? Whom? And for how long? According to Lord Wexhall's encoded letter, he'd secreted information in Lady Victoria's luggage—information that would answer those questions and that could help him solve the mystery of the missing jewels that had plagued him and his conscience for the past three years. Recover the jewels. And regain everything he'd lost.

"Even if he believes her in danger, it's odd Wexhall would send his daughter all the way to Cornwall," Colin said. "I think he's likely trying to get her away from some unwanted suitor. Probably hopes to marry the chit off, in which case it seems he's chosen *you* as the victim, er, lucky man."

Nathan simply stared. "Impossible. He would want her to marry the heir, not a second son." Especially one whose reputation was tarnished. He wondered how much Lady Victoria knew about his past—how much her father might have told her, or if he'd been the subject of gossip in London. "And I cannot imagine Lady Victoria wanting anything less for herself." Nathan's brows rose and he shot his brother a speculative look. "Yes, indeed, perhaps he *is* hoping to rid himself of the chit. In which case, *you* would certainly be the intended victim, er, lucky man."

"Yet his wishes are for *you* to look after her. And I've no intention of allowing you to fob her off on me."

"Given your status as the heir and mine as the poor, second son who is paid for his doctoring services in farm beasts, I'm certain I won't need to fob her off at all. I suspect she'll run directly in your direction."

"How fortunate that I am fleet of foot."

"And how fortunate that I have neither the title nor estates that would lure an heiress, or even make marriage necessary, as I've no need to produce an heir. I'm afraid all the family marriage hopes fall on you, Lord Sutton."

"You would need to marry if the title was yours."

"But it's not, thank goodness."

"Yet it would be if I failed to produce an heir."

"Only if you died, and you appear to be in excellent health. And if that should change, luckily I am a superior physician and I shall see to it that you live to a ripe old age. And marry. And produce many children." Nathan smiled. "All while I remain a carefree bachelor."

"Do you recall how I used to toss you in the lake, little brother?"

"I do. It's how I learned to swim." He gave Colin a pointed head-to-toe look. "You'll note I'm not so little anymore. You'd have one hell of a time throwing me in that lake now."

"Perhaps." Colin nodded toward the pen. "Are you nearly finished?"

"Another hour or so should do it." He looked at Colin's pristine white shirt, brocade waistcoat, Devonshire brown jacket, buff breeches, and polished boots. "I don't suppose you'd care to lend a hand?"

"I don't suppose I would. I'm off to Penzance to meet a lady. A lovely lady, who, unlike your Lady Victoria, would never be described as a supercilious child."

"She is not *my* Lady Victoria."

Colin merely laughed. "I'll be home in time to join everyone for dinner this evening." Then, with a wave, he entered the stables, leaving Nathan to stare at his back, with an odd lump tightening his throat.

God, he'd missed his brother. Hadn't allowed himself to think about how much, but seeing Colin again brought it all roaring back. Those hints of the camaraderie they'd once shared made his chest ache with loss, but also gave him a ray of hope that this visit might, if nothing else, mend the rift with his family.

With a sigh, Nathan picked up another nail, set it in place, then hit it sharply with his hammer. The vibration radiated up his arm, and he repeated the action, while he speculated what the upcoming weeks might bring.

When he'd left the Crown's employ under a dark cloud of suspicion and his reputation in tatters three years earlier, he'd vowed that nothing would entice him back into the fold—except the opportunity to clear his name. Yet when he made that vow, he hadn't suspected that the opportunity would ever arise. He'd buried the past, built a new life in a new place, and existed in peace—a marked difference to the life he'd left behind. Yet now that the opportunity had arisen to possibly recover the jewels and restore his reputation, his feelings were more than a little ambivalent. Someone had once told him to be careful what he wished for as his wish might come true. He hadn't truly grasped the meaning until now. To add to this sudden wrinkle in his peaceful existence was the fact that he'd have to see Lady Victoria again.

Well, his interaction with her would be minimal. Indeed, he had the entire scenario planned. He'd secure the information she carried with her, then, as soon as possible, send her back to London. He'd hopefully clear his name, then return to his peaceful cottage in Little Longstone and resume his calm existence. Yes, it was indeed an excellent plan.

Three

After finally finishing the animal pen, Nathan introduced his menagerie to their new, temporary home. He bestowed encouraging pats to Reginald's solid girth, and was rewarded with snuffling oinks. Petunia gently butted his thigh, and he fed her a handful of her favorite flower. "Do not, under any circumstances, tell the gardener," Nathan warned, running his palm over the goat's pale brown coat. After making sure his friends were comfortable, Nathan shrugged into his shirt, then walked across the lawns toward Creston Manor. His arms and shoulders ached with fatigue, but it was a sensation he relished, as it kept his mind from wandering to areas he wished to avoid.

As he walked in the long, cool shadow of Creston Manor cast by the waning late afternoon sun, he heard the indistinct sound of a feminine voice. As he neared, he was able to make out the words.

"The roads were simply frightful due to the rains."

Nathan paused near the corner of the house. Leaning his back against the brick facade, he swallowed a groan. Even though it had been three years since he'd heard it, there was no mistaking that voice.

Lady Victoria had arrived.

His heart performed the most ridiculous leap, and his brows snapped down in a frown. What the hell was wrong with him? Something, obviously. Perhaps a lack of sleep. Yes, that must be it. For there was no other explanation for such an idiotic reaction. He closed his eyes and thumped the back of his head twice against the stone—lightly, for as tempting as it was to render himself unconscious, there was no point in prolonging the inevitable. The sooner he found out what he needed to know from her, the sooner he could send her back to London.

He looked down and a grin pulled at the corners of his mouth. Lady Victoria would no doubt swoon at the sight of his dirt-streaked breeches, damp, untucked shirt, and scuffed boots. He cheered considerably. All the better to encourage her to depart Cornwall as soon as possible. He supposed he should nip around to the back of the house and change clothes, but with Colin off and Father visiting the village, the duty of greeting the guests fell to him.

He pushed off from the wall and strode around the corner. A well-appointed coach painted glossy black and bearing the Earl of Wexhall's family crest stood in the curved drive. A pair of wilted-looking female servants who were clearly the ladies' maids waited beside a second carriage bearing more luggage. The heavily mud-splattered exteriors and wheels gave testament to the foul road conditions. Two sets of matching grays stood patiently while Langston and Mrs. Henshaw, Creston Manor's butler and housekeeper, directed servants on the unloading of the trunks. As he approached, Nathan scanned the group.

A woman he recognized as Lord Wexhall's sister Lady Delia was talking to Mrs. Henshaw. Dressed in a dark blue spencer over a cream muslin gown creased with travel wrinkles, and wearing a lace-trimmed bonnet, Lady Delia appeared exactly as Nathan remembered her from their last meeting three years earlier. Twenty years ago she would have been described as beautiful. Today the word still could apply, although her maturity lent itself more to "handsome."

He continued forward, craning his neck, and caught sight of the back of a frilly, ivory bonnet, its wearer nearly hidden amongst the throng of hovering servants. At that moment Lady Delia stepped aside and Lady Victoria's profile came into view. His footsteps slowed and he studied her.

Dressed in a pale pink muslin gown and a deep rose spencer, she stood in a swatch of bright golden sunlight, looking like a delicate spring flower. A brisk, sea-scented breeze courtesy of Mount's Bay threatened to dislodge her bonnet. She reached up a cream lace-gloved hand to hold in place the ridiculous bit of frippery, which he supposed was the latest French fashion. In spite of her efforts, several dark curls escaped and blew across her cheek. He had the ridiculous thought that she resembled a Gainsborough portrait, captured in the breeze and sunshine, her features partially cast in shadow from her upraised arm and bonnet. All she needed to complete the image was a field of wildflowers. And perhaps a gamboling puppy. At that moment she turned and their eyes met.

His footsteps faltered, then stopped completely as he was hit by the same punched-in-the-gut sensation he'd experienced the first time he laid eyes on her three years ago. The breeze pressed her gown against her in a way that suggested the curvaceous, feminine form that had fit so perfectly against him would do so still. A golden shaft of sunlight highlighted her in a halo of brilliance that made her look like an angel, but he vividly recalled the deviltry that had danced in her smile.

Unmistakable recognition flashed in her eyes, followed by a flash of something else that he couldn't fully decipher, but that erased any doubt that she recalled the passionate kiss they'd shared. Then her features wiped clean of all expression and her eyes filled with a cool indifference that crept his brows upward. Clearly he'd not made a favorable impression on Lady Victoria. He wasn't certain if he found that more annoying or amusing.

Her gaze flicked over his clothing. Her lips pressed together and one of her brows inched upward with an eloquence that indicated she found his appearance about as appealing as something she would scrape off the bottom of her dainty shoe. Excellent. She'd been here less than two minutes and he'd already ruffled her feathers. He hated to be the only one thrown off balance.

Suppressing a smile, he moved forward. "Greetings, ladies," he said as he joined the group. "Delighted to see you've arrived safely. Your journey was pleasant, I hope?"

Lady Delia raised an ornate quizzing glass and peered at him. "Dr. Oliver, a pleasure to see you again after all these years."

"The pleasure is mine, Lady Delia," he said, offering her a smile and a formal bow.

Her sharp-eyed gaze took in his disheveled appearance. "It appears some manner of catastrophe has befallen you."

"Not at all. Merely the result of a project by the stables which proved rather dirty work. I was just returning to the house to make myself presentable for your arrival, but I fear it is too late."

"By the stables?" Lady Delia's eyes widened. "Were you there a quarter hour ago? Hammering something?"

"I was. If I'd known your arrival was so imminent—"

"Nonsense, dear boy. Wouldn't want you abandoning your project on our account." Lady Delia graced him with a dazzling smile, then said, "I'm not sure if you recall meeting my niece, Lady Victoria—"

"Of course I remember Lady Victoria. I pride myself on never forgetting a face." *Or a passionate kiss.* He turned toward her and found himself the subject of Lady Victoria's bland regard. Certainly not the warm reception he'd received the last time they met. Probably upon reflection she'd relegated him a cad for stealing that kiss and regretted not slapping his face. Well, fine. That would make their interactions even briefer.

He made her a formal bow, then rose to his full height. He recalled she was slightly taller than average, although the top of her head still only reached his shoulder. Now that he was closer, he noted her flawless complexion, which was stained with a becoming rosy hue. Indeed, she looked rather flushed. Probably very warm in the carriage. In spite of what he knew had to have been an arduous journey, she surprisingly showed no outward signs of fatigue. No, she appeared fresh and lovely. Prim, proper, coolly elegant, and altogether ladylike. Still, he didn't doubt she'd suffer from the vapors like most ladies of her station and swoon about on every chaise Creston Manor had to offer at her first opportunity.

His gaze took in her eyes, noting their vivid blue shade, made all the more outstanding by the crescent of dark lashes surrounding them. The last time he'd seen those eyes they'd been drooped at half-mast and glazed with arousal. And then there was her mouth . . . so lush and full. Everything about her demeanor and dress was perfectly prim and proper, but there was nothing proper about those lips. He instantly recalled how delicious they'd tasted, how plush they'd felt beneath his. She'd grown even lovelier in the last three years. Except he no longer detected that glitter of mischief in her eyes, that impish curve to her lips, and he idly wondered what had brought about the change. Probably had wisely decided that kissing strangers in the gallery was not a good idea. Not that he cared. No indeed. He had his own problems to worry about. She'd all but knocked him on his arse once before—he wouldn't give her opportunity to do it again. Give him a warm, sweet-natured, plain woman over a cool, nose-in-the-air hothouse beauty any day.

"How do you do, Lady Victoria?"

She lifted her chin and somehow managed, in spite of their height differences, to peer down her nose at him, as if she were a bloody princess and he the lowly hired help.

"Dr. Oliver." Her gaze again flickered over his dirty attire and her nose twitched. Catching a pungent whiff of Reginald and Petunia no doubt. When their eyes met again, she said, "You are precisely as I recall."

Surely he should have been insulted by her insinuation that when last they'd met he'd been dirty, unkempt, and smelled foul, but instead he found himself unexpectedly amused. "I'm honored that you remember me, my lady. Our meeting was . . . brief."

She muttered something that sounded suspiciously like not brief enough, then said, "I was expecting your father or brother to greet us."

"Neither are home at present, although they will both return for dinner this evening. In the meanwhile, Langston and Mrs. Henshaw have everything in order for your visit."

"Excellent. Naturally we are both anxious to get settled and refreshed after our journey."

"Naturally." Although what she needed to refresh, he couldn't imagine, as she appeared perfectly crisp. He extended his arm toward the house. "Follow me, please."

Victoria gathered her skirts, fell into step behind Dr. Oliver and breathed a sigh of relief that she was no longer forced to look into those intriguing gold-flecked eyes that saw too much, knew too much. No longer had to see that lovely mouth that had so thoroughly initiated her into the wonders of kissing. Botheration, she felt overheated and positively breathless, and as much as she longed to blame the condition on the strain of the journey, she'd done nothing more strenuous than sit and her conscience wouldn't allow such a blatant lie.

No, Dr. Oliver was the source of her discomfort, and a more vexing situation she could not recall. What on earth was wrong with her? The man looked *dreadful*. Dirty. Unkempt. Completely ungentlemanly. And he smelled as if he'd spent the day mucking out the stalls and engaged in hard labor. Without his shirt . . .

Her gaze settled on his broad back and heat crept up her neck. She now knew what his rumpled, dirty shirt covered, or at least as much as she'd been able to see at a distance. If only that distance hadn't been so great—

She chopped off the disturbing thought before it could take root and fill her mind with images she did not wish to . . . imagine. It seemed that ever since she'd read the *Ladies' Guide*—a half-dozen times—her thoughts had increasingly veered toward things of *that* nature. But of course, that was the point of the book—to encourage women to change the way they viewed themselves and men. To encourage Today's Modern Woman to take her destiny in her own hands and not allow it to be determined solely on the basis of her gender. She'd taken its teachings to heart. And thus far she was deservedly proud of her performance. She'd managed to not allow her lips to run amok, although it had required some effort, as she tended to babble when unsettled, and damnation, the man unsettled her.

Victoria raised her chin and straightened her shoulders. She was a Modern Woman. And as such, she would gather her fortitude, recall with whom she was dealing, and put her plan into action. She was not the same naive girl Dr. Oliver had met three years ago. Her inner voice warned her that unfortunately *he* was the same devastatingly attractive man *she'd* met. But she could easily resist him. She knew the sort of cad he was. And he would soon know she was not a woman to be trifled with. She took comfort in the fact that she was going into battle well-armed with her *Ladies' Guide* and a foolproof plan.

The gravel drive crunched beneath her shoes, yanking her from her thoughts. She jerked her gaze away from Dr. Oliver's back to look up at the majesty that was Creston Manor and could not deny her surprised pleasure at the grandness of the house. Two impressive stone stairways curved gracefully downward, appearing like welcoming arms to embrace any and all who approached the massive double oak doors. The windows gleamed, reflecting gilded sunshine, and the aged brick and soaring white columns lent the structure an air of old world charm that appealed to Victoria's sense of proportion.

Settling her hand on the glossy black, wrought-iron banister, she climbed the stairs behind Dr. Oliver. She looked up and found herself staring at his backside. One would have had to been blind—and her eyesight was exceptionally keen—not to notice how his breeches hugged his muscular legs. How those muscles flexed with each stair tread he climbed. The trimness of his hips. The broadness of his back. The fascinating shape of his . . . bottom.

How utterly aggravating that he looked as marvelous from the back as from the front. How incredibly irritating that in spite of being filthy, sweaty, and smelling as if he'd spent the day cavorting in a dirty barn, she still had to grip the banister tighter to quell the overwhelming desire to reach out and touch him.

And how completely unsettling and frustrating that her heart had stumbled into an erratic beat the instant she'd seen him. Just as it had the first time she laid eyes on him three years ago. Botheration. What on earth was wrong with her? Clearly the long journey had addled her wits, for Dr. Oliver's unkempt appearance alone proved that he was no more of a gentleman than when they'd last met. Well, once she'd had a bath, changed her clothes, and enjoyed a hot meal and a good night's rest in a proper bed, she'd be set back to rights.

But, there was no denying that Dr. Oliver was still devilishly attractive. Perhaps more so. 'Twas fortunate that she knew what sort of ill-mannered man he was, lest her head might have been turned. Yet, during those few seconds when they'd studied each other, she'd noted that there was something different about him . . . something in his eyes that she hadn't noticed before. Shadows . . . of hurts, perhaps. Or secrets. If it had been anyone else, she would have felt sorry for the person. Indeed, a fissure of sympathy had nearly worked its way into her heart before she'd squashed it like a bug. If he had hurts, he no doubt deserved them. And as for secrets, well, that was fine. She had some secrets of her own.

She looked up and was once again treated to the sight of Dr. Oliver's backside. Left, right, left, right, flex, flex . . . heavens, how many steps were there? She yanked her gaze away from his far too fascinating bottom and noted with relief that only five steps remained. When he reached the top, Dr. Oliver turned and paused, clearly waiting for Aunt Delia, who was maneuvering the stairs at a slower pace. Victoria stopped as well, and was disconcerted to find herself standing no more than three feet away from him. And the fact that she was disconcerted only added to her irritation. How was it that despite his dishevelment she couldn't seem to pull her gaze from him? Certainly if she were dirty, rumpled, and smelled like she'd cavorted in the barn no one would mistake *her* for attractive.

"Are you all right, Lady Victoria?" he asked. "You look flushed."

She gifted him with one of the cool, detached looks she'd diligently practiced in the cheval glass for just this occasion. "I'm fine, Dr. Oliver."

"I hope climbing the stairs wasn't too taxing for you." The corner of his mouth twitched, and she realized he was making sport of her. Obviously believed she was nothing more than a hothouse flower. Arrogant beast.

"Certainly not. I'm perfectly fit. Indeed, I daresay I could sprint up these steps without losing my breath." She fought the urge to clap her hand over her mouth. Damnation, she'd meant to say nothing more than *certainly not.*

He cocked a single dark brow and appeared wholly amused. "A feat I look forward to witnessing, my lady."

"I was speaking metaphorically, Dr. Oliver. As I cannot imagine a scenario that would lead me to sprint anywhere, let alone up the stairs, I fear you shall witness no such thing."

"You might sprint if you were being pursued."

"By whom? The devil himself?"

"Perhaps. Or perhaps an ardent admirer."

She laughed, and mentally applauded the carefree sound. "None of my admirers would act in such an undignified, ungentlemanly manner. But even if, for some bizarre reason, they should, I'm confident I could outrun them, as I'm very agile and fleet of foot."

"What if you didn't wish to?"

"Didn't wish to what?"

"Outrun him?"

"Well, then, I suppose I would be—"

"Caught?"

Victoria stilled at the intense expression in his eyes, which was at complete odds with his lighthearted tone. She pressed her lips together to stem the torrent of nervous words that pooled in her throat and noted how his gaze flicked to her mouth. Heat snaked through her and she had to swallow to find her voice. "Caught," she agreed, thankful her voice was steady. "But not captured."

"Indeed? That almost sounds like a challenge."

Triumph rippled through her. *Tantalize him with a challenge* . . . Excellent! The first step of her plan was already in motion, and she'd only just arrived. At this rate she would accomplish her goal in record time. Why, she might even make it back to London before the Little Season ended.

Lifting her chin a notch, she said, "You may take it however you wish, Dr. Oliver."

Whatever he might have replied was silenced by Aunt Delia's arrival. "This way, ladies," he murmured, leading them to the door.

You may lead me into the house, Dr. Oliver, but rest assured, 'tis I who intend to lead you on a merry chase. Then blithely walk away, as you did three years ago.

Four

Today's Modern Woman must rebel against the
notion that a lady should conceal her intelligence
from men. Embrace knowledge and strive to learn
something new every day. Rejoice in your intelligence, do not keep it a secret. Only a foolish man
would desire a foolish woman.

*A Ladies' Guide to the Pursuit of
Personal Happiness and Intimate Fulfillment*
by Charles Brightmore

Nathan sat at the mahogany dining room table feeling
very much like the prodigal son. Actually, the prodigal son
science experiment who dwelled beneath a microscope
with five pairs of eyeballs trained upon him. Every time he
looked at anyone, he discovered their gaze already upon
him. And all that while trussed up like a fatted goose in the
damned formal clothes dinner in the dining room demanded. The instant this meal ended he was going to rip
the confining cravat from his throat and toss the damn
neck cloth into the fireplace. But of course, he first had to
get through this interminable, awkward meal.

A footman topped off his wineglass and he took a grateful sip, barely squelching the urge to toss back the entire glass in a series of long gulps. He chanced to glance around the table and was relieved to note that for the first time since he'd sat down he wasn't the cynosure of all eyes. Lady Delia, who sat on his right, was engaged in a lively discussion with his father, who was seated on her right at the head of the table.

His gaze then flicked to the trio who sat across from him—Colin, Lady Victoria, and Gordon Remming, who'd come into his title since Nathan had seen him last on that fateful night three years ago and was now the Earl of Alwyck. Gordon's shining golden blond head was bent close to Lady Victoria, as if she imparted some diamond of wisdom he couldn't bear to miss. Lady Victoria, who sat between Gordon and Colin, appeared to be enjoying herself immensely, smiling, chatting, laughing. No doubt because both men were showering her with compliments and attention. Bloody hell, one would think neither of them had ever seen an attractive female before. And all this for the woman *he* was supposed to watch over. Well, the instant he'd satisfied his obligation to her father, Colin and Gordon were welcome to her.

His gaze settled on Gordon, and the guilt and regret he'd strived so hard to bury catapulted to the surface. Gordon's greeting had been reserved, but when Nathan had extended his hand, Gordon accepted the gesture, albeit after a brief hesitation. Nathan clearly read the lingering suspicion in Gordon's eyes, but he hadn't expected anything less.

"I saw the animal pen you constructed, Nathan," Father said, jerking his attention away from the laughing trio across the table. "Impressive bit of work."

"Thank you," he replied, surprised and pleased by the praise.

"Of course, it wouldn't be necessary for you to dirty your hands in such a manner if you were paid properly for your services."

Nathan merely shrugged off the backhanded side of the compliment. "I enjoy working with my hands. Keeps my fingers nimble."

"They won't remain nimble if you smash them with a hammer," Father said, "or if one of those beasts bite you."

"Animal pen?" chimed in Lady Delia, her eyes alight with curiosity. "Beasts?"

"Since settling in Little Longstone, I've accumulated a bit of a menagerie," Nathan explained. The conversation on the opposite side of the table ceased, and he again felt the weight of those stares. One vivid blue one, in particular, he felt most aware of.

"Cats and dogs?" asked Lady Delia.

"More like a pig and hens, but I also have a dog—"

"Who is the size of a pony," broke in Colin.

"—and a cat—"

"Which is a kitten who has already required being rescued from a tree," Colin added. "Not to mention a cow, a lamb, a pair of ducks, I'm not certain how many geese, and an incorrigible button-eating goat—most of which are named after flowers. They are loud, smelly, fond of chasing one about the grounds—when they're not chewing off one's buttons or decapitating the flower beds—and Nathan loves them as if they were his own children."

"Thank you for that edifying description . . . *Uncle* Colin."

Colin shook his head. "I refuse to be an uncle to that beastly goat."

"Petunia is very fond of *you*."

Colin glared. "She ate my button. And my personal correspondence."

"Only because she loves you," Nathan said very seriously. "And I didn't hear you complaining this morning when you feasted on eggs courtesy of Daffodil, Tulip, and Guinevere."

Colin lifted a brow. "Guinevere? I suppose you have a rooster named Lancelot?"

"No, but that is an excellent suggestion and one I plan to follow up on as soon as I return to Little Longstone so as to increase my flock. Three hens will produce an average of two eggs per day. That means to get a dozen eggs a day, I would need—"

"Eighteen hens," said Lady Victoria. Everyone turned toward her but she seemed unaware of their surprised looks, her gaze resting on Nathan. "You must be very fond of eggs, Dr. Oliver."

Was that a whiff of sarcasm in her voice? Nathan returned her steady look. "Actually, I am, however, even I couldn't hope to consume however many eggs that would produce in a year."

Lady Victoria blinked twice, then said, "Four thousand three hundred and eighty."

Everyone chuckled at her quick wit for tossing out a random number—except, Nathan noticed, Lady Delia, who, from the corner of his eye, he could see was simply nodding in an approving manner. He performed a quick calculation, and to his surprise realized Lady Victoria had been correct.

"At the rate Nathan collects animals, he'll most likely accumulate that many chickens before the year is over," Colin said, shaking his head.

"Why would you want so many eggs, Dr. Oliver?" Lady Victoria asked.

"No doubt to throw from his window at unsuspecting passersby," Colin said dryly. "I was his victim a time or two when we were lads. Had the most dastardly accurate aim." He rubbed the back of his head and winced, as if in remembrance.

"I still do," Nathan said to his brother, although his gaze remained steadily on Lady Victoria. "And I never pelted you unless you deserved it."

"*I* never hit *you* with an egg."

"Because you couldn't." He pulled his gaze from Lady Victoria and smirked at his brother. "Your aim is such that you could not hit water if you fell out of a boat. Which, by the way, is precisely why I pelted you with eggs on one occasion—you pushed me out of the rowboat."

"And did you hit the water?"

"Obviously."

"Ah. Thereby proving that I can indeed hit water."

"Yes—when *I* fell out of the boat—*I* who possess not only flawless aim, but a trio of egg-laying hens."

The ghost of a smile hiked up one corner of Colin's mouth and a look born of many shared memories passed between them. "Touché," Colin murmured. "I'll think twice before pushing you from the rowboat again." He grinned. "Actually, I thought about it twice the last time I did it, and both times it seemed a capital idea."

Everyone chuckled, then Lady Victoria said, "But you never said why you would want so many eggs, Dr. Oliver."

Nathan shrugged. "I've a number of neighbors with large families who could make good use of them."

"Why on earth do you keep such a barnyard of animals," Gordon asked, "and why bring them here?"

"The question we have all asked, I assure you," Father muttered.

"I wasn't certain how long I would be away and I didn't wish to impose such responsibility on my neighbors. Nor did I wish to split the animals up, sending some to one neighbor, some to another. They're all quite accustomed to each other. Besides, the animals are really no trouble. In fact, I greatly enjoy their company."

"They *smell*," Colin said. He turned to Lady Victoria. "You'd be wise to give those beasts a wide berth, Lady Victoria. Especially the goat. If you see the beast, I recommend running in the opposite direction."

"Actually, running will only tempt her to chase you," Nathan said, looking at Lady Victoria over the rim of his wineglass. "While I recall you saying that you are a capable sprinter, I fear you would not be able to outrun a goat as easily as a persistent suitor."

"I imagine you must have dozens of persistent suitors to outrun," Gordon said to Lady Victoria with a warm smile, which for some reason irked Nathan.

A mischievous smile that brought back a flood of memories curved her lips. " 'Tis how I became such a proficient sprinter, my lord."

Everyone chuckled, although Nathan's laughter felt a bit forced. He vividly recalled her looking at him in that precise same way three years ago. It was a look that had led to a kiss he'd hadn't, to this day, been able to erase from his mind.

"But the sprinting is about to end, is it not, my dear?" Lady Delia asked.

A rosy blush bloomed on Lady Victoria's cheeks, but before she could answer, Gordon pressed his hand to his chest as if mortally wounded, then, in a teasingly dramatic fashion said, "Please don't say you're betrothed."

"I'm not—"

"Excellent news," said Gordon, smiling.

"—yet."

"And like that . . ." Gordon snapped his fingers. ". . . the news is not so excellent. So tell us, who is the lucky gentleman to whom you are not betrothed . . . yet?"

"Either Lord Branripple or Lord Dravensby."

Nathan's brow crept upward. "Egad. Branripple and Dravensby? They're still alive?"

Lady Victoria sent him a glacial look. "You must be thinking of their fathers, as I believe Lord Branripple is actually a year younger than you, Dr. Oliver. And Lord Dravensby only several years older."

"Ah. So they've both offered for you, have they?"

"They've both approached my father, yes."

"Well, as worthy as those two gentlemen are, since you are not yet engaged," Gordon said, "you should consider that there are eligible noblemen right here in Cornwall."

Nathan barely repressed the urge to look heavenward. Bloody hell, Gordon might as well have said *there are eligible noblemen right in here Cornwall, right here in this very room, sitting right next to you*. A becoming blush flooded Lady Victoria's cheeks, and Nathan decided he knew precisely how a cat felt when it was petted the wrong way. Right after it had been tossed into a tub of water.

"Yes," Colin added, with an unmistakable gleam in his eye, "there are eligible noblemen right here in Cornwall."

Humph. Obviously both Gordon and Colin had fallen under whatever sort of spell Lady Victoria weaved. More fools they—although it clearly wouldn't be difficult at all to foist Lady Victoria off. Surely that realization should have pleased him immensely. Instead it was accompanied by an unsettling sensation that resembled a cramp. And suddenly Nathan realized for the second time that day that a man should be careful what he wished for, as he might just get it.

He picked up his wineglass, focused his attention on the smooth claret, and firmly shoved aside the inexplicably irritating image of Colin and Gordon vying for Lady Victoria's attention. Their houseguest had in her possession information he needed. It was time for him to retrieve it so as to determine exactly what he was dealing with—aside from an irritating hothouse flower who was supposedly in danger.

When the meal ended, the party moved to the drawing room for cards and postdinner drinks. After assuring that everyone was comfortably ensconced and occupied, Nathan claimed a headache and retired. Indeed, his head was aching from watching Colin and Gordon vie for Lady Victoria's favor—and from witnessing Lady Victoria's flirtatious response to both of them.

He walked down the thickly carpeted corridor, passed by his own bedchamber, and quickly continued on. When he stood in front of Lady Victoria's bedchamber, he pressed his ear to the door. Satisfied by the silence that her maid was not inside, he entered. After silently closing the door, he leaned back against the oak panel and allowed his gaze to sweep over the room. Mrs. Henshaw had given Lady Victoria the blue guest chamber that had always been his favorite, as the color reminded him of the sea, especially during the summer when the pale aqua of the shallows near the beach slowly deepened into indigo near the horizon.

Even though she'd only arrived a few hours ago, Lady Victoria had already established her presence in the spacious room. A half-dozen books were stacked on the bedside table. An ornate jewelry case rested on the mahogany dresser, alongside a polished silver hairbrush and a delicate glass vial, no doubt containing perfume. The thought of her perfume had him drawing a deep breath. A tantalizing, elusive whiff of her fragrance clung in the air, but it was enough to bring a vivid image of her into sharp focus. Roses. She smelled of roses, but in the most subtle, delicate of ways, as if instead of dabbing on perfume she'd merely brushed the velvety flower petals over her soft skin.

His gaze riveted on those feminine accoutrements, and, as if in a trance, he crossed the Axminster rug to the dresser. Unable to stop himself, he carefully lifted her hairbrush and slowly ran the pad of his thumb over the bristles. Several long strands of her dark hair remained entwined in the coarse bristles, and he stared at them, instantly recalling the sensation of her lustrous locks slipping through his fingers while his mouth explored hers.

After replacing the brush, he slowly lifted the glass vial. The instant he removed the stopper, the delicate scent of her filled his head. A groan rose in his throat and he squeezed his eyes tightly shut, but it proved a weak defense against the intense memory slamming into him. Of skimming his lips over her satin smooth skin, breathing in the subtle scent that could only be detected when mere inches separated them. Since that night three years ago, every time he'd smelled roses, he instantly thought of her. Every bloody damn time. He quickly discovered, to his annoyance, that England was apparently overrun with roses.

He inhaled again and this time couldn't suppress his groan. Luscious curves pressed against him . . . her slim fingers gliding through the hair at his nape . . . the delicious, seductive taste of her against his tongue—

Muttering an obscenity he rarely allowed to cross his lips, Nathan snapped his eyes opened and jabbed the stopper back into the vial. He set the glass back on the dresser as if it had burned him, then quickly withdrew his handkerchief to wipe away any remnants of her fragrance that might have clung to him. As the memory of her and their kiss clung to him.

He shot a scowl at the offending vial, then, after slipping his handkerchief away, resolutely turned toward the wardrobe to begin his search for the note Lord Wexhall had indicated he'd concealed in Lady Victoria's luggage. He eyed the two trunks stacked in the corner, but didn't change course. Wexhall had indicated in the coded letter that he would utilize Lady Victoria's portmanteau to secrete his note.

As he passed the bedside table, he paused to look at the books, unable to resist learning what sort of reading material Lady Victoria preferred. Lifting the two top volumes, he perused the titles. *Letter to the Women of England on the Injustice of Mental Subordination* by Mary Robinson and *A Vindication of the Rights of Woman* by Mary Wollstonecraft. His brows shot upward. He'd expected nothing more strenuous than Mrs. Radcliffe's novels. It appeared Lady Victoria harbored some bluestocking tendencies. He picked up the remaining three books and noted with an inward smile that two of them were indeed novels by Mrs. Radcliffe, and the third Shakespeare's *Taming of the Shrew.* Nathan's lips twitched. How apt.

He replaced the books, intrigued in spite of himself by Lady Victoria's eclectic choices in reading materials. He had assumed she thought of nothing more profound than which gown to wear to her next social engagement. Shaking off the thought, he resumed crossing to the wardrobe.

Grasping the brass handles, he pulled open the oak doors. Instantly his senses were wrapped in the delicate scent of roses that clung to her garments. Gritting his teeth, he firmly told himself that he detested roses and knelt down. He pushed aside the colorful array of gowns. In the back left corner he spied a portmanteau. He pulled the soft-sided leather case toward him and quickly opened it, scanning the upper edge. He immediately saw where clumsy stitches had repaired the lining, and a frown yanked down his brows. Wexhall must be losing his touch to leave such sloppy work behind. Not bothering to take care, as a rip could always be easily explained away, he tore the brown satin lining and slid his hand into the opening. A thorough examination of the space yielded nothing.

Damnation, where was the bloody note? He felt around again, but nothing. Frustrated, he slid his hand out then thrust it into the interior of the bag. His fingers encountered what felt like a book, and he quickly pulled it from the bag. Tilting the slim volume toward the light cast by the fire burning in the grate, he read the title: *A Ladies' Guide to the Pursuit of Personal Happiness and Intimate Fulfillment* by Charles Brightmore.

Again his brows rose. Even living in the small, secluded village of Little Longstone, he was aware of the scandal this explicit treatise on women's behavior was currently causing. He found it fascinating to discover such a book hidden in Lady Victoria's luggage. Fascinating, and titillating.

He flipped through the pages to ascertain that Lord Wexhall's note wasn't tucked between the pages, and wasn't surprised to discover it was not. He flipped through the book again, then paused when the word "lovemaking" caught his eye. Opening to the page, he scanned the paragraph.

Today's Modern Woman must realize that lovemaking is not something to be enjoyed only by men and simply endured by women. Be an active participant. Tell your partner what you want. What feels good. Do not doubt that he will be delighted to oblige you. And do not be afraid to touch him—most especially in the ways that you yourself would like to be touched. And the best way to ascertain how you like being touched is to touch yourself to discover what you find pleasurable. After doing so, Today's Modern Woman would then certainly tell her gentleman what she'd learn. Or better yet, show him.

Heat engulfed Nathan, and before he could control his runaway thoughts, his mind filled with an erotic fantasy of her, naked, standing in front of a mirror, slowly running her hands down her supple body. Watching her reflection, he stepped up behind her, slid his hands around her waist, then up, to cup her full breasts. Her eyelid drooped and she laid her hands on top of his. Leaning back against him, she whispered, *Let me show you what pleases me. . . .*

Bloody hell. He shook his head to rid himself of the image, but the effects lingered. His body ached and he felt as if someone had set his breeches on fire. With a disgusted exclamation, he yanked at his cravat, which felt as if it were strangling him. But that was a mere discomfort compared to the strangulation occurring in his breeches. He shoved the book back into the bag, refusing to consider that she'd read those words. Refusing to wonder what affect they'd had upon her. It mattered not. All that mattered was finding Wexhall's damn note—and since it wasn't in this portmanteau, there must be another portmanteau. He again shoved aside the yards of material comprising her gowns and reached into the far recesses of the wardrobe. It had to be here—

"I cannot wait to hear the explanation as to why you are searching through my luggage."

Five

Today's Modern Woman knows there is often a great chasm between what she should do and what she wants to do. Naturally there are times when duty's dictates must take precedence. However, there are other times, notably when an attractive gentleman is involved, when she should throw caution to the wind and do what she wants.

A Ladies' Guide to the Pursuit of Personal Happiness and Intimate Fulfillment
by Charles Brightmore

Victoria planted her hands on her hips and stared down at Dr. Oliver, who appeared frozen in place, his expression unreadable—although she did not detect even a hint of the guilt that any decent person would have felt being caught in such a manner.

Hiking a disdainful brow, she said, "I cannot deny that on more than one occasion I've wished you on your knees, but in my thoughts you always knelt before *me*—not my portmanteau."

Without taking his gaze from hers, he slowly rose. Instead of appearing in the least bit abashed, he had the audacity to wink at her. "Ah. So you have thought of me."

"Not fondly, I assure you."

He winced. "You wound me, madam."

"No, not yet." Her gaze flicked with unmistakable significance to the fire poker. "But that could be arranged."

He shook his head and made a *tsking* sound. "I'd no idea you harbored such violent tendencies, my lady. As for kneeling before you? I fear that is a sight you shall never see."

"Never say never, Dr. Oliver."

He made a dismissive gesture with his hand. "I'm certain that's no huge loss, as you're undoubtedly quite accustomed to men playing your adoring slave."

Victoria heard a muffled sound and realized it was her shoe tapping against the carpet. She forced her foot to remain still, then fixed her most glacial stare upon him. "My admirers are none of your concern, and do not think for a moment that your transparent ploy to divert my attention from your outrageous behavior has worked. Why were you rifling through my things?"

"I was not rifling."

"Oh? And what would you call it?"

"I was merely looking."

"For what?"

For an answer, the insufferable scoundrel cast a meaningful glance down at her portmanteau, which rested near his feet. "Interesting reading material you conceal in your luggage, Lady Victoria."

Heat suffused Victoria's face until she was certain she emitted a glow. Before she could recover herself to issue him the set-down he so richly deserved, he said in a silky voice, "I thought girls like you only read torrid novels and simpering poetry."

Again Victoria forced her foot to remain still—but this time so that she did not give him a swift kick. "Girls like me? My my, a thief *and* so charming. And in case you've failed to notice—not surprising since your powers of observation are clearly not all they should be—I am no longer a girl. I am a woman."

Something flashed in his eyes. His gaze dropped to her feet, then roamed upward in a slow, assessing perusal no decent gentleman would ever bestow upon a lady. A tingly warmth that surely was outrage began in her toes then worked its way upward in tandem with his gaze until even the roots of her hair felt hot. When he finished, their gazes met. The heated glimmer in his eyes hitched her breath.

"There is nothing wrong with my powers of observation, Lady Victoria. However, I am finished with these games." His eyes narrowed. "Where is it?"

"Where is what?"

"Stop being coy. You know what I am talking about. The note that was secreted in the lining of your portmanteau. The correspondence belongs to me. Hand it over. Now." He extended his hand in an imperious manner, and she fisted her fingers in the soft material of her gown to keep from slapping it away.

"Of all the unmitigated gall. Breaking into my bed-chamber—"

"The door was unlocked."

"—touching my personal items—"

"Only very briefly."

"—then accusing *me* of stealing something from *you*! Why didn't you retrieve this note you claim is your property the first time you searched my chamber?"

His gaze instantly sharpened and he lowered his hand. "The first time? What are you talking about?"

She glanced heavenward. "I thought you'd said you were finished with games. Is my meaning not obvious?"

He erased the distance between them in one long stride then clasped her upper arms. "This is no game. Are you saying that your room was searched earlier today?"

The heat from his hands seemed to burn her through the thin material of her gown. Victoria jerked herself free from his grasp then took a step back. "Yes, that is what I am saying, as if you didn't know." Her anger almost made her forget the heated sensation of his hands on her. Almost. "Tell me, do you impose upon all your guests in this unseemly manner, or am I the only fortunate one?"

"How do you know your room was searched?" he asked, ignoring her sarcasm as well as her question.

"It is my habit to be very precise about how and where I place my possessions. 'Twas obvious my things had been disturbed, and my abigail Winifred was not responsible. I'd assumed a Creston Manor maid was to blame—until I caught you red-handed."

"If you suspected a Creston Manor maid, why did you not report the incident?"

"Because nothing was missing. I saw no reason to instigate an inquiry that would most certainly end in disciplinary action against someone who was merely curious."

Although his expression didn't change, she sensed his surprise at her words. Determined to make the most of that small advantage, she lifted her chin. "I've answered your questions and I demand the same courtesy of you— although I suspect that the word 'courtesy' is lost upon you."

"You haven't begun to answer my questions." He jerked his head toward the wardrobe. "That portmanteau—is it the only one you own?"

"Certainly not. I've half a dozen."

"Where are they?"

Pretending to give the matter serious consideration, she tapped her chin and frowned. "Two are at the London town house, and three at Wexhall Manor. Or are there three in London and only two in the country—"

He made a low noise that sounded like a growl. "*Here.* Do you have any others with you *here* in Cornwall?"

Victoria barely suppressed a smile at his frustration and made her eyes go round with innocence. "Oh. No. That is the only one I brought to Cornwall."

Without shifting his gaze from her, he reached down and behind him. Holding the open case against his chest, he pointed to the ripped lining. "How did this happen?"

"Surely you should be the one explaining that to me."

He advanced a step and Victoria had to fight the urge to back up. His eyes glittered in the firelight and a muscle jerked in his cheek.

"Lady Victoria," he said in a deceptively soft, silky voice, "you are severely testing my patience."

"Excellent. I would hate to think I was alone in being irritated."

He pressed his lips together and she could almost hear him counting to ten. "When I arrived, this lining had already been ripped, then very sloppily repaired." He said the words slowly, pronouncing each syllable very precisely, as if he were speaking to a child—a fact that raised her hackles even further. "Do you know anything about how that came about?"

"As a matter of fact I do."

Nathan stared at her, waiting for her to elaborate, his patience, normally so even and reliable, straining dangerously close to the end of its tenuous tether. She stood before him, chin raised, brows hoisted up, lips pursed, looking as impatient as he felt, which of course was impossible, as he would have laid odds that at this moment he was the most impatient individual in the entire bloody country. Which further served to annoy him, as he was not an impatient man, in any facet of his life. But something about this woman brought out the worst in him.

After taking a slow, deep breath, Nathan said in a perfectly calm voice, "Tell me what you know."

"I'm afraid I do not respond well to imperious orders, Dr. Oliver," she replied in a haughty tone. "Perhaps if you couched your request more politely . . ."

Her words trailed off, and Nathan swore his teeth would be reduced to nubs before this interview was over. "Please," he forced out between his clenched lips.

"Much better," she said in a prim tone. "Although I'm not certain you deserve an explanation after insulting my sewing abilities."

"*You* sewed the lining?"

"I did."

"When?"

"Earlier this evening." She paused again, but clearly whatever she read in his gaze wisely compelled her to continue without further prodding. "After freshening up from our journey, my aunt and I took a turn around the gardens—which are lovely, by the way."

"Thank you. Go on."

"Hmmm. Some politeness, although rather brusque. As I was saying, we walked the gardens. When I returned to my bedchamber to prepare for dinner, I realized someone had been in my room. The disturbances were subtle—a wrinkle on the counterpane, my perfume bottle not precisely where I'd left it, the wardrobe door closed rather than open several inches to aid in the airing of my gowns, the latch of my trunk open. If only one thing or one part of the room had showed signs of being tampered with, I would have simply attributed it to a servant, but it was all about the room. My things had been unpacked and put away before I left for the gardens, so there wouldn't have been any reason for anyone to touch the wardrobe or my trunk."

"So you conducted a search of your own to see what, if anything, was missing."

"Yes. And nothing was missing. Not even from my jewel case. But during my search, I discovered a faulty seam in my portmanteau, which very much distressed me, as the bag had belonged to my mother and is a favorite of mine. Upon closer examination, it was clear that the stitches were extremely amateurish. Certainly not the work of any reputable tailor or my mother, who was very accomplished with a needle and thread. My curiosity was aroused and I pulled out the stitches. When I finished, I felt around in the space behind the lining."

"You discovered a letter." It wasn't a question.

"I did."

Bloody hell. "Did you read it?" Not that it would matter, as naturally Wexhall would have written it in code.

"Really, Dr. Oliver, I think the pertinent question here is: How did you know a letter was secreted in the lining of my luggage?"

Nathan studied her for several long seconds. Damn it to hell, this was a complication he didn't need. Or want. Indeed, he hadn't wanted or needed any of this. He should be in Little Longstone, tending to his patients, caring for his animals, enjoying the peaceful existence he'd worked so hard to achieve. Instead he stood facing a veritable termagant who had his note and by the stubborn look of her wouldn't give it up easily.

A half-dozen lies rose to his lips, but a sudden overwhelming weariness washed over him. God, he was sick of lying. And why should he? His service to the Crown was completed. He was no longer sworn to secrecy. How easy and refreshing it would be to simply tell the truth.

Watching her carefully, he said, "I knew the letter was there because it was meant for me."

"And why would a letter meant for *you* be hidden in *my* portmanteau?"

"Because as you were traveling to Cornwall, it was the most expeditious way to get the note to me."

"If that is so, then why was it hidden? Why couldn't I have simply been given the note with instructions to hand it over to you when I arrived?"

"Because it contains top secret information that is meant for my eyes only."

"Top secret? You make this sound like some sort of spy adventure."

When he did nothing to deny or confirm her statement, her eyes narrowed and she studied him. Finally she said, "Are you implying that you're some sort of . . . spy?"

"I'm not implying anything. I'm stating it outright."

She blinked. "That you're a spy."

"*Was* a spy," he corrected, in keeping with his new policy of honesty. "I retired from my service as an operative three years ago, but have been temporarily reactivated."

She stared at him for a full ten seconds. Then her lips twitched. "You must be joking," she said, unsuccessfully trying to disguise her laughter.

"I assure you I am not," Nathan said stiffly.

She laughed outright. "Surely you don't think I would fall for such a Banbury tale."

"Actually, I can't fathom why you wouldn't believe me."

"For starters, you're clearly hard of hearing. Whoever heard of a spy with afflicted hearing?"

"My hearing is perfectly sound."

She uttered a distinctly snortlike sound. "I entered the room and walked right up to you, yet you still didn't know I was there until I spoke."

Bloody hell. Because of that damn *Guide* and the erotic images it had inspired. "I was, er, distracted." Before she could launch into more reasons, he said, "I was involved in a mission three years ago that failed and resulted in my resignation. That note contains information that could afford me the opportunity to reverse the mission's failure." *And to retrieve what I lost.*

Clearly still amused, she nodded encouragingly and made a rolling motion with her hand. "Oh, please do continue. This is more entertaining than any torrid novel a girl like me might read."

Nathan took a second to wonder if he'd ever met a more aggravating woman and knew without a doubt that he had not. Narrowing his gaze, he dropped her bag to the floor then took a step toward her, taking perverse delight in the sudden flicker of uncertainty that flashed in her eyes.

"You want the torrid tale?" he asked in a silky tone. "I'd be delighted to tell you. From both a military and smuggling perspective, this estate is located in a very advantageous location. During the war, I was recruited by the Crown to perform various tasks, which included spying on the French and retrieving goods being smuggled in and out of England. Three years ago I was assigned to recover a cache of jewels, but the mission did not . . . go as planned and the jewels went missing. I left the Crown's service shortly thereafter. Recently, new information regarding the jewel's possible whereabouts came to light. Since I was most familiar with the case, I was asked to return to Cornwall to help recover them. The new information regarding the jewels is in the note you found—a note which, as I'm sure you now understand, belongs to me." He crossed his arms over his chest, gratified to see that she no longer looked amused. She did not, however, look entirely convinced. "As I trust I've satisfied your curiosity, I would appreciate it if you would now return the note to me."

"Actually, you've only succeeded in whetting my curiosity, Dr. Oliver."

"A pity, as that is all the explanation I'm prepared to give you." He held out his hand. "My letter, if you please, Lady Victoria."

Instead of complying, she commenced pacing in front of him. He could almost hear the gears turning in her head as she considered all he'd said. With a resigned sigh, he lowered his hand and watched her. The firelight cast her in a soft, gilded glow, highlighting her shiny hair. Her gown, a burnished bronze silk that accentuated her blue eyes while complimenting her creamy complexion, swirled about her ankles as she turned.

His gaze settled on the delicate curve of her slender neck, left enticingly bare by the upswept Grecian knot in which her hair was arranged. He found himself fascinated by the spot where her neck met the gentle slope of her shoulder . . . by that delicate hollow formed at the juncture of the base of her throat and her collarbone. His fingers and lips suddenly itched with an overwhelming desire to touch her there. Taste her there. Experience the silky smoothness of that vulnerable spot. Breathe in the elusive rosy fragrance he knew would be clinging to her skin.

She turned again and pursed her lips, drawing his attention to their rosy plumpness. In spite of the passage of three years, he recalled every exact detail of those lips. Their smooth texture. Their lush fullness. Their delicious taste. The sensuous glide of them against his mouth and tongue. He'd kissed his fair share of women before that stolen moment with Lady Victoria, but those few minutes with her in the gallery had effectively wiped his memory clean of those previous encounters.

He'd also kissed his fair share of women after that stolen moment with Lady Victoria. To his profound puzzlement—and annoyance—he'd discovered that while other lips might feel nice and taste fine, no other lips felt quite like hers. Tasted quite like hers. Indeed, the need to prove to himself that he was wrong on this score had turned into something of a quest—until he'd started feeling like the prince in the Cinderella fairy tale, only rather than trying to discover whose foot fit the glass slipper, he attempted to find a set of lips that suited him as well. The prince had eventually succeeded. Unfortunately, he had yet to be so lucky.

Perhaps because you've been looking in the wrong places, his inner voice whispered. *Kissing the wrong women. Perhaps you should look no further than this very room. . . .*

Nathan consigned his damn inner voice to the devil then clenched his hands at his sides to keep from reaching out to snag Lady Victoria as she paced by him again, to snatch her into his arms and kiss her. Prove to himself that he'd attached far too much significance to a meaningless kiss. It couldn't have been *that* good. Yes, he'd obviously blown the entire episode out of proportion. And there was one sure way to prove that.

Before he could move, however, Lady Victoria ceased pacing and swirled to face him. "If this tale you've related is true," she said, eyeing him with the sort of ripe suspicion a mouse would cast upon a hungry tabby, "then my father must somehow be involved."

Damn. He'd known she might add two and two and arrive at the correct sum. He'd hoped she would not, gambled that like many women of her station, her head would be filled with nothing more than gossip and fashions. Clearly Lady Victoria wasn't a fool. A denial rose to his lips, but he somehow couldn't bring himself to voice it. Instead he found himself fascinated to hear what she'd say next.

She obliged him by rushing on. "Even if Father wasn't the person who hid the note in my bag, he must have known of its existence. He was *most* emphatic that I travel to Cornwall. *Too* emphatic, now that I ponder upon it." She slowly shook her head, her frown growing more pronounced as her gaze shifted to the flames dancing in the grate. "It would explain so much. . . ." she murmured.

Nathan kept his features completely impassive—a talent left over from his spying days—and simply watched her. After nearly a full minute of silence, her gaze swiveled and bore into him. "My father works for the Crown."

The words were a statement rather than a question, and said in an utterly flat tone.

Nathan saw no point in prevaricating. "Yes."

A humorless sound escaped her. "It's all so clear now . . . the late night clandestine meetings in his study, his frequent absences, the worried look in his eyes when he thought himself unobserved." She blew out a long breath and shook her head. "I knew, in my heart, that he wasn't being truthful, that there was more going on than just the gambling and male frivolity he used as excuses, but I never pressed him." Her expression changed to one of profound hurt, and the area around his heart seemed to collapse in on itself at that distressed look. "I thought he had a mistress and was merely being circumvent and discreet for the sake of my sensibilities."

"I'm afraid secrecy goes hand in hand with spying."

"Secrecy? You mean lying."

He could see she was floundering, trying to assimilate her emotions, and seeing her struggle affected him in a way he couldn't name. Walking to her, he lightly grasped her upper arms.

"I mean saying and doing what is necessary to keep your association with the Crown concealed so as to carry out your duty to protect this country's interests. To keep yourself, your friends, your family safe."

Her gaze searched his, then she asked, "That night you came to our town house to see my father . . . was that about the mission involving the jewels?"

A muscle ticked in Nathan's jaw. "Yes."

"My father was involved?"

Up to his bloody damn neck. "He was." He released her, and then, after a quick debate with himself, decided there was no point in not telling her. "Your father coordinated the mission. He is the person who recruited us."

She absorbed that, then said, "So Father is more than simply a spy. He's a . . . boss of other spies?"

"Correct."

"And who besides you is included in this 'us' he recruited?"

"My brother and Lord Alwyck."

She nodded slowly, her gaze never leaving his. "So at dinner this evening I sat between two spies and across from another one."

"*Former* spies. Yes."

"Was your father also a spy?"

"No."

"Your butler? Housekeeper? Valet?"

One corner of his mouth hiked up. "Not that I'm aware of."

"How refreshing. But let us not forget my absent-minded, genial father who I clearly do not know at all." Her voice trembled on the last word, and she lowered her chin to stare at the floor.

Nathan again experienced that hollow feeling in his chest. Touching a single finger under her chin, he gently urged her head up until their gazes met. "The fact that he is regarded as absentminded and genial worked greatly to his advantage. The work he coordinated saved hundreds of British soldiers' lives. In order for him to do that, there were aspects of his life that he couldn't share with you, or anyone else."

She swallowed, her slender throat working, her eyes brimming with questions. "I can understand that," she finally said. "But what I don't understand is why send this note to you with *me*? Why not send one of his spy people? Or summon you to London?"

Before answering, he slid his finger from beneath her chin, allowing its tip to trail over her skin for the merest fraction of an inch. Soft. Bloody hell, she was so soft. His hands all but twitched with the need to touch her again. The desire was so intense, he had to move away from her to ensure he wouldn't give in to the need.

After walking to the mantel, he stared into the glowing flames and engaged in a quick internal debate. Then he turned to face her. "Your father sent you to Cornwall because he believes you're in danger. He wanted you out of London and the information brought to Cornwall, so he accomplished both goals with one journey."

"Danger?" she repeated, her tone expressing both doubt and surprise. "What sort of danger? And why would he think such a thing?"

"He didn't say specifically, but he clearly believes some harm might befall you. As to why, I would guess that he has either received a threat against you or he has himself been threatened and therefore fears you might be harmed in the melee. Perhaps both."

Her face paled. "You believe my father is in some sort of danger?"

"I don't know." He shot her a significant look. "I'm certain that the letter he sent me via your portmanteau contains the answer to your question."

"I read the letter. There was no mention of danger. Indeed, it read only of—" She snapped her lips together. After a pause she said, "It did not mention danger."

"Not that you or any other lay person would be able to discern. Your father would have written to me in code."

A long, strained silence stretched between them. Finally she lifted her chin, her eyes troubled. "What if Father is hurt—or worse—while I'm so far away?"

The worry in her eyes unsettled him in a way he couldn't explain. All he knew was that he wanted that look to vanish. "Your father is an extremely clever and resourceful man," he said quietly, "with great resources and manpower at his disposal. I've no doubt he will outwit whoever challenges him."

A strangled sound emerged from her throat. "That does not sound at all like my father, but obviously you know him far better than I." Some of the worry faded from her gaze, replaced by speculation. "'Tis clear you're more than the simple country doctor you pretend to be."

"I've never pretended to be a doctor. I am one. A damned good one." He inclined his head. "'Tis clear you're more than the empty-headed heiress you pretend to be."

"I've never pretended to be an heiress. I am one. Nor have I ever been empty-headed—that is just your arrogance and unfounded assumptions talking."

"I want that note, Lady Victoria."

"Yes, I know. How unfortunate for you that it is in my possession."

"I cannot hope to protect you without knowing what danger your father fears is imminent."

"You? Protect me?" she said in a scoffing tone. "You who are as deaf as a post? What is your plan to protect me—order your hens and ducks to nibble into submission 'he who would threaten my safety'?"

Good God. Had he ever considered her attractive? Surely he was mad. She was infuriating. And clearly toying with him. Bloody hell, she was nothing more than . . . an infuriating toyer-wither. And his patience had officially been stretched to its limit.

With his narrowed gaze steady on hers, Nathan demanded, "Why are you refusing to return the note to me?"

"I haven't refused."

"Then you'll comply with my request?"

"No . . . at least not yet."

"I'm not the sort of man to dance to your merry tune, Lady Victoria."

"I never said I wanted you to dance to a merry tune."

"Good. But clearly you want something."

"I do."

"How fortunate I am not prone to swooning at hearing shocking statements. What do you want?"

"I want to be included. I want to help you."

"Help me what?"

"Accomplish the mission my father assigned to you. To recover the jewels."

Luckily his jaw was attached to his face or it would have landed on his boots. As it was, he couldn't contain a bark of incredulous laughter. "Absolutely not."

She shrugged. "Well, then I'm afraid I cannot give you your letter."

"Why would you want to involve yourself in something that is not only none of your concern, but could potentially be dangerous?"

"Seeing as how both my father and myself may be in danger, and that that letter is the reason I was dispatched to this godforsaken end-of-the-earth place, I believe this is very much my concern. It is now clear to me that I have been subjected to lies and secrecy for more years than I care to contemplate. I refuse to be subjected to them any longer." Her expression hardened, turning angry. And resolute. Two expressions that would put any man immediately on his guard. "Do you know what it's like to be lied to, Dr. Oliver?"

He did. And he had not enjoyed the experience. He inclined his head to acknowledge she'd scored a point. "But you cannot be so foolish as to harbor anger because your father did not tell you things that would have compromised the security of this country."

"No, although I cannot deny feeling foolish—and resentful—that I clearly know very little about the man I grew up with, who I thought I knew and understood extremely well. I am, however, very angry that he did not tell me he might be in danger."

"I told you—he can take care of himself. And more efficiently if he wasn't distracted by worrying about the safety of his daughter. He wanted, needed, you to leave London. He obviously thought you would not if you knew the truth."

"He took away my choices," Lady Victoria said hotly. "I deserved to know. To be given an opportunity to help him. To know the real reason why I was being sent away. To know *I* might be in danger as well." She huffed out a breath. "At least that would have granted me the opportunity to prepare myself. To raise my guard. But no, instead I was patted on the head and toddled off to the wilderness to be looked after by a man I barely know and whom I haven't seen in three years, as if because I'm a woman I'm helpless." Her entire demeanor exuded stubborn determination. "Well, he made an error. I am a Modern Woman. I will not be shunted aside and treated as if I am a feeble nitwit. I have devised a plan, and unlike you and my father, I am willing to be honest and share it with you. It is a simple plan, one even you won't have trouble understanding: I have your note. I will return it to you if you agree to include me in your mission."

"And if I refuse to agree?"

She smiled brightly. "Then I shall not return it to you. See? I told you it was simple."

Nathan stepped away from the fireplace and moved slowly toward her, like a jungle cat stalking his prey. Her smile faded and she slowly backed away from him. He kept pace with her retreat, shifting so as to maneuver her toward the corner—exactly where he wanted her both physically and strategically. She took another step back and her shoulders bumped into the vee where the two walls met. Surprise flashed in her eyes, then she drew herself up and raised her chin another notch, her eyes wide but meeting his gaze unflinchingly. If Nathan had not been so irritated with her, he would have admired her pluck at realizing she was trapped and braving her way through it. She might be a thorn in his side, but she wasn't a coward. Surprising, as he'd have wagered the word "danger" would have sent her running for the hartshorn.

"You'll not bully me into giving you the note," she said, her voice not displaying the slightest tremor.

Nathan planted a hand on each wall, bracketing her in. "I've never had to bully a woman into giving me what I want, Lady Victoria."

Her gaze flicked to his arms, positioned near her head, before returning to his face. "You'll never find it."

"I assure you I shall."

"No. It's hidden in a place where you will never locate it."

Nathan hid his triumph at her inadvertent admission that the note was still intact and that she hadn't destroyed it. He allowed his gaze to wander slowly down then up her form. When his gaze once again met hers, he said softly, "You're wearing it. The question is, is it tucked into one of your garters, or . . ." He glanced down at the swell of creamy skin rising from her bronze bodice. ". . . or nestled between your breasts?"

Her startled expression, coupled with her furious blush, confirmed the accuracy of his guess.

"That was the most ungentlemanly scrutiny I have ever been subjected to," she said, sounding as if she'd just darted up a flight of stairs.

He brushed a single fingertip slowly over her cheekbone, memorizing the silky texture of her warm skin and the sound of her quick intake of breath. "If you think I'll believe this crimson stain is the result of mere maidenly outrage, you underestimate me, Lady Victoria, and that would be a mistake."

She swallowed, hard, then said, "Of course I am outraged. And since you clearly are not aware, a gentleman asks for permission before touching a lady."

"I've never claimed to be a gentleman." Because he couldn't resist, he glided the pad of his thumb over that enticing blush once more before resettling his hand against the wall. "I prefer to ask for forgiveness afterward—if it's necessary—than to request permission beforehand."

"How convenient for your conscience—although I'd wager you do not possess one."

"On the contrary, I do. In fact, right now it is instructing me to ask if you would have granted me permission to touch you."

"Certainly not."

"Ah, then you can see why my method is much more preferable."

"Yes—for you."

"Then I shall ask for your forgiveness."

"Denied."

Nathan blew out a long put-upon breath and shook his head. "It appears you are determined to deny me in all matters this evening." He moved a step closer to her, then leaned down so his lips hovered just above her ear. The subtle scent of roses filled his head, and his hands fisted against the silk wall covering. "You'll have to remove your clothes eventually, my lady. And now you've given me a great incentive to make certain that I'm present when you do."

She sucked in a hissing breath. He leaned back, cursing the alluring scent of her now branded in his mind. "That will never happen, I assure you."

"Never say never, Lady Victoria."

Six

Today's Modern Woman must realize knowledge is equal to power. It is therefore essential to discover everything she can about a gentleman, be he friend, enemy, or lover. The more she knows, the more power she will be able to wield in the relationship, and the less likelihood that she will be taken advantage of.

A Ladies' Guide to the Pursuit of Personal Happiness and Intimate Fulfillment by Charles Brightmore

Gritty-eyed from a troubled night filled with much thinking, exhaustive pacing, and little sleep, Victoria requested a breakfast tray in her bedchamber. After a light repast of tea, toasted bread, and eggs—eggs she glared at wondering if they came from *his* hens—she rose. Wanting to be alone with her thoughts, she didn't summon her maid, and dressed herself in her favorite forest-green riding habit. After ensuring that the much contested letter was safely concealed, she set off for the stables. A brisk ride always helped clear her mind and improve her mood, and heavens knew she needed both.

And it was all *his* fault. That doctor posing as a spy posing as a doctor. No wonder he hadn't given her or their encounter three years ago a second thought. He no doubt had women in every town, village, and hamlet. She'd provided nothing more than a momentary diversion to an accomplished scoundrel. Recalling how she'd flirted with him at their one meeting, she inwardly cringed. He'd no doubt been highly amused. Well, she had no intention of amusing him again.

After Dr. Oliver had departed her bedchamber last evening, she'd locked her door—and shoved a chair beneath the knob for good measure—then spent hours poring over the letter, trying to find some secret meaning, some hidden pattern of words or letters, but could find nothing. How could a letter that spoke of nothing but art, museums, and the weather translate into a tale of danger and jewels? She finally admitted defeat when the words swam before her eyes from fatigue. But she would make another attempt after she returned from her ride, renewed and refreshed.

Even more frustrating than her failure to decipher the note, however, was the unfamiliar disquiet she felt. She couldn't recall a time when she'd been so bombarded with conflicting emotions. Indeed, until this journey where she'd discovered the note in her luggage and then Dr. Oliver in her bedchamber, her life had consisted of a pleasant but unbroken pattern of Seasons in Town, summers in the country, and yearly holidays in Bath. With the exception of that stolen kiss three years ago, nothing extraordinary had ever happened to her, and her life had progressed precisely on the course she'd set for herself.

But now it felt as if she were being buffeted on storm-tossed waters, her emotions awash in turmoil. Worry for her father's safety warred with a sense of confusion, disbelief, and betrayal at learning of his secret life. Thrown into the seething tempest of her emotions was her anger at Father for treating her like a child. Dozens of questions buzzed through her mind, and by God, she intended to demand answers from him the instant she returned to London. How long had he been involved with the Crown? Had Mother known? Most likely not. Victoria could only imagine that such a revelation would have been met with a case of the vapors that spanned months.

Yet underlying all that was the undeniable thrill and pride she felt at asserting herself and standing her ground with Dr. Oliver. The teachings she'd absorbed from the *Ladies' Guide* had served her well, and although she had to alter her plans to accommodate the new turn of events, she'd managed to set up a challenge for Dr. Oliver while still affording herself the perfect opportunity to exact her revenge on him. Forcing him to accept her help in his mission would ensure they'd spend ample time together so she could entice him to kiss her again. Then she would return to London, marry one of her earls, and take her place in Society as she'd always planned. Only this time she'd make certain it was a kiss, an encounter, Dr. Oliver wouldn't soon forget.

For a brief, heart-stopping moment last night she'd thought he meant to kiss her. The way he'd bracketed her against the wall . . . his arms so strong, his chest so wide and solid in front of her. That same sense of warm giddiness she hadn't experienced since that night three years ago had raced through her. Her heart had pounded, not with fear, but with exhilaration at his nearness. The clean scent of him, linen and starch and something else she couldn't define but found heady and pleasing, had filled her head. His body had emanated an intoxicating heat that made her press her back more firmly against the wall to keep from moving closer to absorb his warmth. She'd felt utterly surrounded by him, his tensile strength. It was all that, and the compelling look in his eyes, that kept her captive far more than his arms.

And his touch . . . that gentle sweep of his finger over her flaming face had forced her to lock her knees so as not to slither to the floor. And his outrageous suggestion that she would ever remove her clothes in front of him . . . another wave of heat washed over her. *That will never happen, Dr. Oliver, although I intend to make certain that you want it to.*

Right now she had the upper hand in their dealings, like a chess game where she'd put his king in check. Next, she needed to outmaneuver him into checkmate before he could regroup and plan a defense. She needed information—about him and this failed mission. Her eyes had been opened wide last night, filling her with a determination she'd never before felt. No longer would she permit anyone to treat her like a child to be pacified with a pat on the head then sent on her way. Lady Victoria Wexhall was a Modern Woman and a force to be reckoned with. *Brace yourself, Dr. Oliver. Your citadel is about to be seized.*

She exited the house through the rear terrace, surveying the grounds from her vantage point as she crossed the spacious flagstone patio. The gardens stretched to her left, an array of perfectly trimmed hedges and colorful blooms. They appeared to be at least as large as the gardens at Wexhall Manor—a pleasant surprise. Beyond the gardens rolled an expanse of verdant lawn, sparkling with a silver dusting of morning dew. The lawn gave way to soaring trees that rose up to spear a sky still stained with fading mauve traces of dawn.

She paused for a moment before walking down the wide, curved terrace steps. A slight breeze teased the tendrils of hair surrounding her face, brushing welcoming, cool air over her skin. She lifted her face, closed her eyes, and drew in several deep breaths. The air smelled so different here . . . clean and fresh as country air was wont to smell, but with an intriguing underlying hint of salty tang from the sea. She'd make certain her morning's ride included a view of the water.

Deciding she'd best be off before anyone else in the household awoke, she was about to start down the steps when a soft mewing sound arrested her. Victoria looked down and saw a tiny kitten rubbing against the hem of her skirt.

"Well, hello," she crooned, crouching down to scratch the ball of fluff behind its minuscule ears. "What are you doing out here all alone? Where's your mama?"

For an answer, the kitten let out the most pitiful sounding mewl Victoria had ever heard. "My my, that is indeed sad." She scooped up the kitten and cradled it against her chest, where it set up an immediate purr.

"Aren't you a charmer." She smiled and tickled her fingers under the animal's soft chin. The kitten was pure black, except for the tips of its four paws, which were snowy white.

"You look as if you were dunked in a bucket of paint," Victoria said with a laugh. A delighted purr rattled in the kitty's throat, and it stretched out a white-tipped forepaw to rest along her sleeve. "I wonder if you might be the little devil who was stuck in the tree."

"Yes, she is," came a deep, familiar voice from directly behind her.

Victoria turned swiftly. Dr. Oliver stood not six feet away, his arms casually crossed over his chest. Her heart lurched, surely just the result of his unexpected company, while her stomach jittered—no doubt due to the eggs. Her gaze traveled over him, noting his mussed dark hair, as if he'd combed his fingers through the shiny strands, leaving several locks drooping onto his forehead. Her gaze dipped lower and she was instantly riveted by his shirt, or rather by the way he wore the garment. No cravat graced his neck, affording her an unimpeded view of his tanned throat and a tantalizing glimpse of muscular chest before the white linen thwarted her view. He'd rolled back his sleeves, revealing strong forearms roped with muscle and dusted with dark hair. He looked nearly as devastating wearing a shirt as he had when she'd viewed him shirtless yesterday.

Camel-colored breeches hugged his long, muscular legs in a way that made her wish she could halt time for several moments just to give her the opportunity to study his fascinating limbs in minute detail. His black boots were clearly old favorites, as they looked as if he'd walked across England wearing them. How had he managed to cross the stone terrace without her hearing him? He must move like a ghost. An annoying, irritating, arrogant ghost. Still, no matter what else she might think of him, she could not deny that he was attractive. In an uncouth, ungentlemanly sort of way. With an effort, she pulled her gaze upward. The speculative look in his eyes indicated she'd been caught staring, and her face heated. Thank goodness spies couldn't read minds.

He offered a bow that somehow managed to seem polite and mocking at the same time. "Good morning, Lady Victoria."

She inclined her head in her most regal, prim fashion. "Dr. Oliver."

"Did you sleep well?"

"Marvelously."

He cocked a brow. "Indeed? Based on the shadows beneath your eyes, I would have guessed you'd remained up all night, most likely attempting to decipher *my* letter."

Victoria couldn't decide what irked her more—his eerily accurate guess, or the fact that he'd intimated she looked tired. "Why, thank you. I'm certain I don't know when I've been the recipient of such a flowery compliment."

Instead of looking abashed, he smiled, his teeth flashing white. "You're heading toward the stables?"

"Yes. I enjoy an early morning ride."

"I'm on my way there as well. Shall we walk together? In spite of our meeting last evening, I'm certain we can make it to the stables without inciting an argument."

"Yes—if we both remain silent."

Another grin flashed, then he indicated the steps with a flourish of his arm. "Shall we?"

As this was a perfect, albeit unexpected, opportunity to learn more about him, Victoria said, "By all means."

They descended the wide, curved stairs, then struck out across the immaculately manicured lawn. Instead of remaining silent, Dr. Oliver nodded toward the kitten who had drifted off into a purring sleep. "It seems you've found a friend. Look at her, sleeping like an angel." He shook his head and laughed. "I nearly broke my neck rescuing that imp, and do you think she was the least bit grateful?"

"Of course not," Victoria said, running her index finger

over the kitten's warm fur. "You ruined all her fun. I'm certain she stuck her nose in the air and flounced away."

A slow smile tilted one corner of his mouth, creasing an intriguing dimple in his cheek. "Typical female," he murmured.

Choosing to ignore that lest an argument ensue, Victoria asked, "What is her name?"

"Boots."

She couldn't help but grin. "Boots . . . 'Puss in Boots.' *'Le Chat Botte.'* A very apt name. And one of my favorite fairy tales."

Surprise flickered in his eyes. "It is a favorite of mine as well."

Victoria's brows shot up. "Fairy tales? A fearsome spy like you?"

"Believe it or not, I once was a child. For my eighth birthday, I received a copy of Perrault's *Histoires ou contes du temps passé, avec des moralités: Contes de ma mère l'Oye.* It instantly became my favorite book. It is to this day."

"*Stories or Tales from Times Past, with Morals: Tales of Mother Goose,*" Victoria translated. "Your French is perfect."

"Thank you. A handy talent when one is employed spying on the French."

"I have two later editions of the book, one French, one translated into English, which I treasure, but I would dearly love an original."

"Mine is a first edition."

Victoria turned to stare at him. "A 1697 first edition?"

"I don't know of any other year a first edition would have been printed."

"Oh, I am green with envy! I have wanted one for years,

but it is impossible to find." She eyed him. "Would you consider selling yours?"

"I'm afraid not."

"What if I were to make you an outrageous offer?"

His eyes filled with an unreadable expression that she supposed had helped him enormously during his career as a spy, but which she found utterly vexing. "An outrageous offer meaning a large sum of money, Lady Victoria? Or outrageous in an altogether different way?"

Heat suffused her all the way up to her hairline. "Money, of course."

He shook his head. "I'm not interested in selling it, for any sum. It was the last gift I received from my mother before she died. My attachment to the book has nothing to do with its monetary value." His gaze raked her face. "That surprises you."

"Actually, yes. I didn't think men were so sentimental."

"Men in general, or me in particular?"

Victoria shrugged. "Both, I suppose."

Silence fell between them, and Victoria found herself undeniably curious about this man who, based on what his brother had said, could have used the money, yet wouldn't consider selling a very valuable book because it had been a gift from his mother. Botheration, when she'd set out to find out more about him, she hadn't anticipated discovering anything, well, *nice*.

"I'm intrigued that 'Puss in Boots' is your favorite tale from Perrault's collection," Dr. Oliver said. "I would have thought 'Cinderella' more to your liking."

"Indeed? Why is that?"

"A handsome prince, a glittering ball . . . they seem like things most ladies would like."

"Oh, I enjoyed the story, especially the magical aspect

of the fairy godmother and the romantic way the prince pursued the woman who had stolen his heart. But the fiendishly clever Puss in Boots enchanted me. His ingenuity made me wish he were real so I could match wits with him. I even attempted to fashion a pair of boots for my own cat."

"Having recently seen an example of your sewing ability, I'm guessing that the boots were not a smashing success."

Victoria shot him a mock glare. "Unfortunately they were not, but most of the blame rests upon Buttercup, who simply refused to wear them."

"You named your cat *Buttercup?*" He twisted his face into a comical look.

"From what I've heard, you are hardly one to cast aspersions on the names of anyone else's pets."

"I suppose not, although in my defense, I've only named Boots and my dog. All the others came to me with names."

"You could have changed the names, you know."

"Would you like it if someone changed your name?"

"No, however *I* am not a barnyard animal."

He touched his finger to his lips. "Shhhh. They don't know they're barnyard animals," he said in an exaggerated whisper. "They think they are visiting royal dignitaries."

Victoria fought back a smile at his nonsense. "I admit I know what you mean. *I* belong to Buttercup. She allows *me* to live in *her* house."

"Yes, that's the way it was with Boots the instant I brought her home. Settled right in and took over my favorite chair. Someone once told me that dogs have owners and cats have—"

"Servants," she finished with a laugh. "Completely true. Was Boots a gift?"

"A patient offered as payment a kitten from his cat's latest litter. I looked over the group, but I knew immediately that this little devil was the one."

She glanced down at Boots. "I can see why it was a case of love at first sight. She's darling. She reminds me of my Buttercup."

"Buttercup is black and white?"

"Oh, no. She has the stripes of a tabby, but her fur is golden in color."

"Ah, yes, I can see how she would remind you of Boots. The resemblance is striking."

Victoria couldn't help but laugh at his arid tone. "I meant because Buttercup enjoys being held in just this same way, and she falls asleep within minutes of being scratched behind her ears."

"Something many animals enjoy, as it is a difficult spot for them to reach themselves."

"Tell me, Dr. Oliver, why was 'Puss in Boots' your favorite tale?"

"Like you, I greatly admired the cat's cleverness. My favorite part was always when he instructed his master to bathe in the river, then he hid his clothes under the rock and told the king not only that his master was drowning, but that thieves had stolen his clothes."

Victoria chuckled. "Quite a sight for the king and his daughter to witness."

"Indeed. And a clever way to ensure that his master's ragged clothes weren't seen by the royals. Although, I've always wondered if the princess fell in love with the master because he looked so handsome wearing the rich clothing her father lent him—or because she'd seen him naked."

Victoria tried to smother a laugh but wasn't entirely successful. She looked up at him and saw the glittering mischief in his eyes. Before she could think of a suitable reply, he said, "And the moral of the story always resonated with me."

She considered for several seconds, then quoted, " 'There is great advantage in receiving a large inheritance, but diligence and ingenuity are worth more than wealth acquired from others.' "

He looked mildly surprised at her recitation, then nodded. "Suited my situation as the lowly second son rather well," he murmured. "I found those words . . . inspiring."

An odd feeling she couldn't name washed through Victoria. Before she could figure out what it was, he added, "The other moral I admit I found quite shallow—that one's clothes and appearance and youth play a role in matters of the heart."

"Shallow, perhaps," she conceded, "but true nonetheless. I believe it is human nature to be attracted to that which is beautiful. After all, not only was the master very handsome, but the princess was described as the most beautiful young lady in the world."

"True. However, beauty is in the eye of the beholder. Would the princess have fallen in love with the handsome hero if she'd seen him wearing his poor man's clothes?"

"I don't know." Some inner devil made her add, "But if your theory holds true, she fell in love with him because she saw him wearing *no* clothes."

He laughed. "Yes. But it does beg the question: If all the accoutrements of wealth and privilege were stripped away, leaving nothing but the true person exposed, would that person still be loved? Admired? Sought after? I think not."

"A rather cynical view."

"No, merely a realistic one. Take yourself as an example, Lady Victoria. You father is currently entertaining offers from not one, but two earls. If either man was suddenly stripped of his wealth, position, and title, would you still consider marrying him?"

There was no mistaking the challenge in his gaze, and a fissure of irritation wound through Victoria. "You make it sound as if there is something wrong with a woman wishing to marry well."

"Not at all. I'm merely challenging the definition of 'well.' Has it more to do with one's title, wealth, and position, or with one's character, honor, and integrity?"

"Surely those things are not exclusive to each other. One can be titled and wealthy and still possess honor and integrity."

"Naturally. But if faced with choosing one or the other . . . an interesting dilemma. Personally, I think that if the fairy tale's most beautiful princess in the world had seen the master in his ragged clothes and hadn't been tricked into believing he was wealthy, she would never have given him a second glance."

"One can hardly fault a princess for that."

"I suppose not. But it was still the master's outward appearance that she fell in love with—not the man himself. Therefore, the story makes a case for the theory that appearances do indeed play a role in matters of the heart."

There was something in his tone that aroused Victoria's curiosity, and she suddenly wondered if there was a woman who owned his heart. The thought unsettled her in a way she couldn't define, then a frown burrowed between her brows. If he were committed to someone, that could wreak havoc with her plans.

"I gather that means that when you choose a wife you shall do so with a blindfold tied around your eyes," she remarked lightly, watching him closely. "Or have you already chosen someone?"

He shook his head and grinned. "No blindfold—I might mistakenly choose a potted gardenia, thinking the lady smelled nice and was delightfully reserved. And no, I haven't settled on a wife. I don't even know if I shall marry at all. Since I'm not the heir nor in need of securing an heiress to pay off gambling debts or things of that sort, I've no reason to marry—except for love."

In spite of her relief at his single status, Victoria's brows shot up. "Love? I wouldn't have thought spies were so . . . sentimental."

"I don't know where you've gotten these notions about spies, Lady Victoria. Torrid novels, perhaps? My reason has just as much to do with logic as sentiment. Since I do not need to produce an heir nor add to the family coffers, why would I consider pledging my life to one woman unless I loved her?"

"How very . . . unfashionable."

"In the exalted circles in which you socialize, yes, I'm certain it is. However, 'tis quite common once one steps away from the glitter of Society. Besides, I care nothing for what's fashionable. Never have. I would never allow the capricious rules of Society to dictate with whom I spend the rest of my life." He shook his head. "I actually pity Colin the marital responsibilities being the heir forces upon him. I have freedoms he will never know."

Victoria digested his words with no small degree of surprise. She'd never before considered that a younger son wouldn't envy the heir his title and position. Before she could give the matter full consideration, however, she noted that they were nearing the stables. Her gaze settled on the structure he'd built alongside the stables for his animals. And her eyes widened.

A pair of ducks flapped through the open door, then

waddled quickly toward them. They were followed by a cow, an enormous pig, and a goat—a goat that had what appeared to be pigeon perched on its back. The entire group broke into a trot. Victoria halted and stared. Dr. Oliver kept walking, then looked over his shoulder and laughed.

"I wish you could see your face, Lady Victoria. Your expression is priceless."

"It looks as if they're about to attack you."

"Not at all. They're simply saying good morning—enthusiastically, as I am the one who feeds them."

Victoria remained exactly where she was, preferring to observe from a distance and cuddle Boots. She watched in amazement as Dr. Oliver was "greeted" by the group of animals. The ducks quacked noisily and pecked at his boots, while the pig rubbed against his legs much like a cat. The cow let out a plaintive *moooooo*, then swiped Dr. Oliver's hand with a huge tongue, causing Victoria to wrinkle her nose. The goat gently prodded Dr. Oliver's backside toward the pen, while the bird seated on the goat's back, which Victoria realized was indeed an enormously fat pigeon, cooed and ruffled its feathers.

Dr. Oliver patted them, chatting as if they were children rather than beasts—beasts, who by the ripe scent wafting toward her, were all in dire need of a bath.

"Come along," he said to the group, leading them back toward Victoria. "Allow me to introduce you to Lady Victoria—"

"That isn't necessary," Victoria said hastily, backing up and warily eyeing the goat, who was showing a great deal of interest in the lace ruffles adorning her wrists.

Dr. Oliver halted and, damnation, she could see he was wholly amused at her expense. "After your impressive performance last evening, I hadn't thought you a coward, Lady Victoria."

She raised her chin and, due to the gamey odor in the air, breathed in through her mouth. "I am *not* a coward. I am simply not fond of animals that . . . outweigh me. And smell . . . peculiar." She lifted Boots up a bit. "I'm simply more of a cat person than a goat person."

"Are you fond of dogs?"

"As a matter of fact, I am."

"Excellent, as you are about to meet B.C."

"Who is—*eeeeyiiiii!*" Victoria stumbled forward when she was firmly nudged right in the center of her buttocks. After regaining her footing, she whirled around and found herself facing the most massive dog she had ever seen. Light brown, with darker markings and a black, jowly muzzle, the monster stood regally, observing her through wide-set, dark brown eyes that bore an alert but hopefully kind expression. The top of the giant's head reached her chest. She forced herself to remain perfectly still while the beast raised his head to sniff the air, his nose quivering.

"Lady Victoria, may I introduce B.C."

"Wh-What does B.C. stand for?" she asked, guessing that the the B was for either "behemoth" or "buttocks."

"Boot chewer. Consider yourself forewarned, although I must say it is his only bad habit."

"D-Delighted," she murmured, slowly backing up several steps, alarmed when B.C. kept pace with her. She hit something solid and stopped. Large hands clasped her upper arms from behind and she realized that the something solid she'd hit was Dr. Oliver.

"I thought you said you liked dogs," came his amusement-laced voice directly next to her ear.

Warmth from his hands eased down her arms, a stunning contrast to the tingling sensation his rich, deep voice so close to her ear invoked. Her shoulder blades brushed against his chest and she had to lock her knees to keep from leaning back fully into him.

"I do like dogs," she said, her gaze locked on the massive beast in front of her. "But that is not a dog. That is more like a small . . . bear."

He chuckled, his warm breath brushing over her neck, awakening sensitive nerve endings on her bare skin. He released her, then moved to stand beside her. Although he no longer touched her, the heated imprint of his hands lingered, and she gave thanks that she still held Boots, lest she brush her fingers over the warm spot where he'd held her. B.C. immediately trotted to his master, his tail wagging.

After patting the dog's massive head, Dr. Oliver said, "Let's do this properly, shall we, boy? Sit." B.C.'s bottom instantly hit the grass. "Shake." The dog raised a forepaw the size of a plate. "He wishes to formally make your acquaintance."

Victoria eyed the dog suspiciously. "He's gentle?"

"Like a lamb."

"Sadly I, um, have no experience with lambs to know if they're gentle or not. Oh, they sound gentle, but for all I know, they might be snarling, snapping beasts—"

"B.C. is extremely gentle."

"He looks as if he could eat my torso for an hors d'oeuvre. Tell me, are all your animals so very *large*? Have you nothing smaller?"

His lips twitched. "Not in a dog I'm afraid."

Determined to wipe the amusement from that grinning mouth, Victoria swallowed her trepidation, then extended her hand to shake the proffered paw. After she released the massive paw, B.C. lowered it to the ground, leaving her hand perfectly intact. In truth, he was a handsome animal and seemed friendly enough—a bit too friendly, based on the buttocks bump he'd treated her to—but his sheer size rendered him intimidating.

Another pungent whiff of barnyard beast roused her from her frozen position. Deciding she'd gained enough information for one morning, she slowly sidestepped toward the stables, her wary gaze fixed on Dr. Oliver's herd. "If you'll excuse me, I'm going to go for my ride."

"Aren't you forgetting something, Lady Victoria?"

Good Lord, that goat was staring at her again. She quickened her pace. "Er, I don't believe so." To her dismay, Dr. Oliver, his handsome face creased with a wicked grin, started toward her. As if that weren't alarming enough, his pungent herd promptly fell into step behind him.

"My Boots," he said.

Her gaze flicked down to his scuffed footwear. "They're . . . very fine. Need a bit of polish, but—"

"I meant my cat, Lady Victoria." He continued moving toward her, his animals behind him—except the cow, who'd paused to munch on a bit of grass.

"Your *Boots*," she said, coming to a reluctant halt and feeling foolish. She looked down at the sleeping kitten, curled so sweetly in the crook of her arm, and was swamped with a feeling of unreasonable, ridiculous possessiveness.

Dr. Oliver stopped directly in front of her. He shot her a look of complete understanding. "Wriggle their way right into your heart, do they not?"

"I'm afraid so." He reached out and she carefully set the kitten in his hands. Her fingers brushed his, jolting her pulse in the most ridiculous way. Once assured that Boots was securely transferred, she snatched her hands away. He tucked the tiny animal against his chest then nodded toward the stables. "Shall we?"

"Shall we what?"

"Go for a ride, of course. I need to feed the animals, but I can do that while Hopkins saddles our horses."

"I don't recall extending an invitation for you to join me, Dr. Oliver."

"An accidental oversight, I'm sure."

"Actually, no. I would prefer to ride alone."

"How unfortunate, as I will be joining you."

"I fear that is impossible, as I am without my chaperone."

He waved her words aside. "It is not as if we will be in an enclosed carriage or confined area, Lady Victoria. We shall be outside, each riding our own horse, for all the world to see, should anyone care to—perfectly respectable behavior here in Cornwall. Now, tell me," he continued in a conversational tone, "have you reconsidered returning my note to me?"

"I told you my terms last night. Those terms have not changed. Have you reached a decision regarding my proposition?"

"I gave you my decision last night, Lady Victoria."

"And you'll not reconsider?"

He shook his head then grinned. "I'd prefer to wait until you take off your clothes."

Victoria pressed her lips together and willed away the heat prickling her face. "If you'll excuse me . . ." She made to move around him, but he stepped to block her progress.

"Let us not argue," he said. "It's a lovely morning for a ride. I'll play the charming host and show you a path that leads down to the beach."

"Charming?" She uttered a sound dripping with disbelief. "No, thank you."

"I'm afraid you have no choice, Lady Victoria. Your father instructed me to protect you. Since you won't give me the note so as to determine precisely what his concerns are, you leave me with no option but to follow you about day and night. From sunup to sundown. Every minute of the day, from when you awake . . ." He moved a step closer to her and smiled. ". . . until you slip between the sheets at night."

Seven

Today's Modern Woman should apply the simple rules of fishing to catching her gentleman. First, bait the hook with a tempting morsel, such as a low-cut gown. Then cast the lure in the form of flirtatious conversation and suggestive looks. Reel in the prey with "accidental" brushings of her body against his, then drag him onto the shore and leave him gasping for breath with a slow, deep, sensual kiss.

*A Ladies' Guide to the Pursuit of
Personal Happiness and Intimate Fulfillment
by Charles Brightmore*

𝒩athan looked at the blush spreading riotous color on Lady Victoria's creamy smooth complexion and forced himself not to reach out and touch that bewitching color. Her blue eyes snapped with outrage and she all but bristled at his improper comment. Indeed, she resembled a firework about to explode.

"If that arrangement is not suitable to you, my lady, you need only to give me my note. Otherwise I fear I shall have to stick to you like green to lettuce. Like yellow to daffodil. Like red to tomato. Like—"

"I quite understand your meaning." She pressed her lips together and he found himself staring at her mouth, anticipating her releasing the pressure so he could watch it resume its plump fullness. "Clearly you think that by making a pest of yourself—not a difficult feat, by the way—I will find your constant company so odious, I will gladly hand over the note."

"That is my fondest wish, yes."

"Then you've underestimated me and my determination."

"On the contrary, I can see how stubborn you are."

"There is a difference between determined and stubborn."

"I'm sure you think there is. And I'd be delighted to hear your theory on the subject during our ride." He raised his brows. "I should think you'd want me to go with you so as to ensure that I'm not searching your bedchamber in your absence." He allowed his gaze to wander down her form, then met her eyes and slowly grinned. "Unless you fear that I'll find the note on your person."

She raised her chin in that obstinate, haughty, prim, look-down-her-nose fashion that for some idiotic reason he found highly arousing. "Certainly not."

"Excellent. Then it is settled. Follow me." He walked toward the stables, and she fell into step alongside him. Watching her from the corner of his eye, he suppressed a grin at the furtive glances she threw over her shoulder at his animals who followed directly behind them.

They entered the stables and he called out, "Hopkins, are you about?"

"Right here," came a muffled voice. The first stall door on the left swung open and a rugged man with a swatch of fiery red hair and a matching beard shouldered his way through the opening carrying a large pail in each hand. "'Mornin', m'lady, Dr. Nathan." He held up the buckets. "Just about to fill yer brood's troughs. The hens left ye a gift of three fat eggs."

Nathan smiled. "Thank you, Hopkins. Bring them up to the kitchen and have Cook prepare them for you."

"Thank ye." He shot a narrow-eyed look at the goat, pig, cow, and ducks who hovered in the doorway. "Out with the lot of ye. Yer grub is comin'." He looked at Nathan. "Will ye be needin' horses saddled, Dr. Nathan?"

"If you'll feed the animals, I'll take care of the saddling for Lady Victoria and myself."

Hopkins jerked his head in a nod, then headed outside, followed closely by the herd. As he disappeared from sight, his voice drifted back into the stable. "Git yer bloody snout out o' my arse, ye damn impatient beast."

Pretending he didn't hear a thing, Nathan said, "Just let me settle Boots." He set the sleeping kitten in the first stall then latched the door. When he returned, he said to Lady Victoria, "Are you a proficient rider?"

"Yes."

"Good. I think Honey will be a fine mount for you. She's spirited, but gentle." He led the way to the last stall, where the mare, named for her pale golden mane, nickered at the sight of him.

"She's beautiful," Lady Victoria exclaimed when he led the mare from the stall. He watched her stroke the horse's neck and velvety nose.

While Lady Victoria and Honey became acquainted, he outfitted the mare with a sidesaddle, listening to Lady Victoria croon soft, complimentary words to the horse. He then saddled Midnight, a pure black gelding, for himself.

After seeing Lady Victoria safely settled in the saddle, he swung up onto Midnight and led the way out of the stables. Curious as to whether she truly was a proficient rider, he struck out at a brisk trot toward the huge copse of elms at the far edge of the lawns, purposely avoiding the other direction, where the haunting memories from that night three years ago waited to ambush him. When they neared the trees, he slowed their pace, wandering slowly along the wood-scented trails dappled with pale skeins of early morning sunlight. Birds twittered, leaves scrunched underfoot, and a soft sea-scented breeze filled his head. Memories assaulted him from all directions. He'd ridden and walked and run these paths countless times during his youth, and even after such a long absence it now felt as if he'd never left.

He wasn't certain how long they rode in silence before she said, "The grounds here are lovely. Do you visit Creston Manor often?"

He wondered if something had shown on his face to prompt her question. "I haven't been here in three years."

Her brows shot upward. "You mean since that last mission?"

"Yes."

"Why haven't you returned?"

He turned and faced her directly. The sunlight glimmered on the dark brown curls framing her face, coaxing cinnamon highlights. Her dark green riding costume complemented her creamy complexion. And her lips . . . bloody hell, her lips looked like they were fashioned from plump, moist, succulent peaches. Perhaps going riding with her hadn't been a good idea after all—

"Lord Nathan? Why haven't you returned?"

Bloody hell, he'd completely dropped the conversational ball. He quickly debated telling her the truth, then decided, why the hell not? It's not as if her opinion of him mattered. "After the mission failed, I had a falling out with my father and brother. It was best for all concerned that I left."

Her gaze searched his, then she said softly, "That must have been very difficult for you."

Whatever he'd expected her to say, it hadn't been that. He'd expected her to pry, to look scornful, to be curious. Instead she offered him sympathy, as if she understood such estrangement. He found it confusing. And unsettling. Damn it, he didn't want to discover anything *nice* about her.

"I imagine that being here again brings back many memories," she said, again disarming him with her uncanny ability to understand precisely what he was thinking.

"Yes. This trail we're on right now was always my favorite. It splits about a quarter mile ahead, with the right fork heading toward the beach and the left to a small private lake at the far edge of the property."

"So this particular spot is filled with happy memories?"

He nodded slowly, a smile tugging at his lips as some of those memories slipped through his mind. "Yes, it is."

"Would you care to share some with me?"

He shot her a look. Her expression revealed only interest. "You realize that if we converse, we run the risk of arguing."

"We won't converse," she said with a smile. "You can talk, and I shall simply listen to your stories of your misspent youth. So tell me, why was this spot your favorite?"

He hesitated several seconds, allowing the atmosphere of the surroundings to infuse him with nostalgia. The twittering birds, the soaring trees bathing them in dancing ribbons of shade and gilded sunshine. The scent of fresh earth, clean air, and always, that underlying tang of the sea that made him think of home. "My two favorite spots on the estate were the lake and the sea. Every day, no matter what the weather, I walked this path, debating the entire way which body of water I would visit that day." He laughed in remembrance. "The decision was agonizing."

"How agonizing could it be? Why not simply solve the dilemma by alternating destinations every day? Or better yet, visiting both?"

"Excellent suggestions, however, visiting both never seemed viable, as I do not like to rush, and once I arrived at one location I hated to leave. Therefore, much had to be considered when choosing my daily destination. Such as the weather."

"What did the weather have to do with your choice?"

"I always chose the sea route if it was storming. The drama of the waves crashing against the shore, the roar of the churning water spraying up onto the rugged cliffs, enthralled me. I also chose the sea path directly after a storm, as the shore always held a new selection of debris to look over and shells to collect."

"I love collecting shells," Lady Victoria said, her eyes shining. "I keep them in an enormous glass jar at Wexhall Manor which I add to every year during our holiday in Bath."

"Then you'll certainly enjoy the beach here."

"I gather, then, that you took the lake route on fair-weather days?"

"Usually, as I enjoyed swimming in the lake. Sometimes I came alone, enjoying the solitude of just floating on the water, staring at the sky, watching the clouds. Most of the time, however, Colin, Gordon, and I were together, making some sort of mischief, playing pirates or the like."

"Gordon . . . do you mean Lord Alwyck?"

"Yes. We've known each other our entire lives." *And used to be the best of friends.* Nathan shook off the thought, then continued, "Of course, Wednesdays were always devoted to the lake, regardless of the weather."

"Why is that?"

"Because that is the day Hopkins bathed in the lake. We would skulk down there and wait until he was fully submerged, then nip off with his clothing."

Her eyes widened, then she pressed her gloved fingers to her lips to hide her smile. "You did this to the poor man every Wednesday?"

"Without fail."

"Did he not retaliate?"

"Oh, yes. It became a battle of the wits. Hopkins took to hiding his clothes in different places, we found them. He'd bring an extra set, but we caught on to that as well. He hid a towel in the bushes, we located it. We always left his clothes in the stable, neatly folded, with a note that read 'Till next week, the Got Yer Arse Bared Clothes Thief.' " A smile eased across Nathan's lips. "When he was around us, he always pretended that he didn't know it was us. But we would hide in the woods and watch him emerge from the lake, dripping wet, cussing and swearing, promising vengeance against those 'young hooligans'—although his words were decidedly saltier than that and not ones I would repeat to a lady."

She tried to look stern, but there was no mistaking the amusement in her gaze. "Did Hopkins never get the better of you?"

"Oh, yes. One time he filled our boots with horse manure." He made a face, then laughed. "The expression on Colin's face when he shoved his foot into his boot is one I shall never forget. Another time Hopkins nipped off with our clothes, which I can't say we didn't richly deserve. We nearly made it into the house undetected through the servant's entrance, but as luck would have it, we ran into two maids delivering fresh linens to the bedchambers. And I mean literally ran into them. Sheets and pillowcases flying in the air, naked, red-faced boys, gaping, gasping maids. And to make it worse, Father came upon us—it was quite the spectacle. Received an ear-blistering set-down from Father, forbidding us to swim in the lake ever again."

"And did you heed him?"

"Of course not." He grinned. "Where is the fun in that?" He reined Midnight to a halt and pointed. "There is the fork. Which direction do you choose?"

When she tapped her finger to her pursed lips and considered, he said, "Now you understand my agonizing. Imagine, if you will, that your two favorite shops in London were *giving away* merchandise, but only for a single afternoon, and at the exact same times. Which would you choose to go to?"

"I wouldn't choose at all. I'd go to one location and send a servant to act in my stead in the other."

Nathan couldn't help but laugh. "But then you would miss the thrill of choosing the items yourself."

"But I'd still have items from both stores." She smiled. "As today is Wednesday and I've no wish to interrupt Hopkins's bathing routine, I prefer the beach and shell collecting."

He bowed deeply. "As you wish." They started down the path, which narrowed, making it necessary for them to travel single file. Nathan led, allowing visions of the past to flow around him. These were the paths of his boyhood, filled with countless memories, all now conspiring to resurrect the dull ache of homesickness he'd thought he finally buried. In an effort to keep it at bay, he said, "The sea is just ahead." He kept Midnight to a slow pace, allowing the anticipation to build, knowing the exquisite view that awaited him.

He rounded the curve and reined Midnight to a halt as the vista from their high vantage point hit him like a stunning blow. Cerulean skies, dotted with cottony clouds melding at the horizon with sun-dappled, white-crested water that graduated from the deepest sapphire to pale blue in the shallows at the beach below. Dark cliffs rose majestically, at once mysterious and forbidding, and, as Nathan well knew, a treasure trove of hiding places for smugglers.

A brisk, salty breeze cooled his skin, and he lifted his face, briefly closing his eyes and deeply breathing in the scent that had always brought him both a sense of peace and a longing for adventure. The screech of gulls captured his attention, and he reopened his eyes to watch a group of the gray and white birds float on the wind, suspended for several seconds, wings spread wide, before swooping downward to capture a morsel from the sea.

"Oh, my . . . this is spectacular."

Nathan turned to look at Lady Victoria. Her eyes glowed with delighted wonder as her gaze slowly scanned the panorama spread before her. It occurred to him that her eyes were the identical intriguing shade of blue as where the sea and sky met. He watched her raise her face toward the sun, close her eyes and draw a deep breath, exactly as he had done. Then she opened her eyes and looked at him with a bemused expression. "I'm not certain what I expected," she said in a breathless voice, "but it wasn't . . . this."

He watched, fascinated, as a slow smile spread across her lovely face. Even when she frowned, she was lovely, but her smile utterly dazzled him. That same fierce tug of attraction he'd experienced the first time he laid eyes on her seized him with stunning force.

"I've never seen anything like this," she said softly, moving her hand in an encompassing arc. "The sheer beauty of the colors, the majesty of the cliffs and sea from this height . . . truly magnificent. You should have prepared me for what I was about to see, as the sight stole my breath."

His gaze dropped briefly to her moist lips. "I think there are some things you cannot prepare yourself for, Lady Victoria. They simply . . . happen. And steal your breath." He forced his gaze back up to her eyes. "As many times as I've rounded that corner and seen this very same view, I'm awed each time. Not only because it is so beautiful, but because it is so unexpected."

She nodded slowly. "Yes, that describes it perfectly. It makes me wish I'd brought along my watercolors, although this is clearly a scene whose drama and vibrant colors are more suited to oils."

"You paint?"

A splash of rose colored her cheeks, as if brushed on by an invisible artist. "Not well, I'm afraid, although I enjoy the hobby immensely. I've never attempted oils, but I brought my watercolor supplies to Cornwall."

"Then by all means you must try to capture this scene before you return to London."

Her gaze shifted to the stretch of golden sand below. "How do you access the beach?"

"There is a path about a mile ahead. Follow me."

Victoria set her mount into motion, then reluctantly dragged her gaze away from the panoramic view to turn her attention to the trail ahead. Her gaze settled instead on Dr. Oliver's broad back. His white linen shirt stretched across the expanse of golden skin and sleek muscles she so vividly recalled seeing from the carriage yesterday. Skeins of sunlight showered down between the leaves and branches of the trees, gleaming through the strands of his dark hair. He handled his mount expertly, and a shiver of awareness worked its way through her at the sight of his powerful legs straddling the saddle. The way he moved— from the fluid ease with which he rode to the smooth, almost predatory way he walked—had her swallowing to relieve the sudden dryness in her throat. Heavens, old Dr. Peabody, who had been her family physician for years, didn't look like that, move like that. No, he stomped through the house with all the grace of an elephant.

But there was nothing graceless about Dr. Oliver. With an effort she pulled her gaze away from him, concentrating on the beauty of her surroundings, the sound of the gulls and the surf, the brisk refreshment of the sea-scented air, the glimpses of white-capped blue through the trees. Still, no matter where she looked, she was very much aware of him riding ahead, and she wondered what he was thinking.

They continued on for a quarter hour before he halted near a small pond and dismounted. "The path to the beach is just ahead. We can leave the horses here so they can drink and rest while we're exploring." Midnight immediately went to the pond for water while Dr. Oliver approached her. When he stood beside Honey, he wordlessly raised his arms to help her dismount.

Her heart performed the most ridiculous somersault and Victoria inwardly frowned. Numerous gentlemen had helped her dismount in the past without causing any such reaction. But the thought of Dr. Oliver's large hands gripping her waist, a man whose hands had once caressed her in a manner that proved he was not quite a gentleman, unsettled her in a way that she couldn't name other than to know that it . . .

Excited her.

Whatever part of her sensible self that warned her she shouldn't allow him within ten feet of her was wholly overridden by the emerging daring part of herself that wanted him to touch her.

She looked down at him and easily read the amusement and challenge in his eyes. "I don't bite, Lady Victoria. At least not very often."

"A relief to be sure," she said lightly. "However, are you certain that I don't bite, Dr. Oliver?"

His eyes seemed to darken and his gaze dipped to her mouth. "As I recall, you do not. However, it is a risk I am willing to take."

There was no mistaking his meaning, and she barely resisted the urge to fan herself with her gloved hand. Clearly he recalled their kiss, possibly in more detail than she'd suspected. Well, if that was the case, excellent. It could only help her cause, something she'd lost sight of for a few moments.

Reaching down, she rested her palms on his shoulders. His hands grasped her waist and he lowered her. But not in the quick, efficient manner other gentleman had. No, instead she found herself being lowered with a deliberate lack of haste that dragged her torso down the hard length of his. Mischief and something else, something that accelerated her heartbeat, glittered in his eyes. By the time her feet touched the ground, her face felt flushed and her breathing was erratic.

Instead of releasing her, his hands tightened on her waist, and her fingers flexed in response on his broad shoulders. She inhaled sharply and her head filled with the scent of him. Clean linen, sunshine warmed skin, mixed with a hint of sandalwood. Only inches separated their bodies. The last time she'd stood this close to him, the room had been dimly lit, but today ribbons of sunlight embraced them. Looking up at him, Victoria admired the intriguing dark gold flecks in his eyes, eyes that even up close remained maddeningly unreadable. Noted the faint pattern of lines that radiated from the corners of his eyes, as if he were accustomed to laughter. The golden texture of his skin, smoothly shaven, stretched over his high cheekbones and firm chin. And then there was his mouth . . .

His lips, like everything else about him, had fascinated her the instant she'd seen them. Surely men were not supposed to be blessed with such beautiful mouths. His lips looked simultaneously firm and soft, as if they could issue harsh commands yet yield at the same time. Perhaps it was due to the perfect, precise shape of his upper lip, which contrasted so unexpectedly with the sensual fullness of his lower lip. It was a mouth that commanded attention, and Victoria knew she couldn't have been the only woman to be held so enthralled by it. As she well remembered, he knew how to use that mouth.

And it suddenly struck her that she wanted him to kiss her again. Wanted to know if the magic she'd experienced three years ago had been real or just a figment of her overactive, girlish imagination. She'd come to Cornwall armed with the intention of sharing another kiss with him, but it hadn't occurred to her that she would actually *want* to kiss him for more than mere revenge. A frown furrowed between her brows. Damnation, *wanting* him—in any manner—was not part of her plan at all. He was the one who was to want her.

Jerking her attention upward, their gazes collided and Victoria inwardly groaned. He'd obviously caught her staring. Bad enough, but even worse was the absence of any hint of desire in his eyes. No, he simply stared at her with an utterly blank expression. Definitely not boding well for her revenge plan.

Clearly this wasn't an optimal time to try and entice him, as he appeared quite . . . unenticeable. Well, no matter. She would have plenty of opportunities during her visit, although she couldn't deny she was irked that he'd so unsettled her while her nearness had obviously not affected him at all. Slipping her hands from his shoulders, she backed up several steps, further annoyed that her knees felt less than steady. His hands slid from her waist, and although he no longer touched her, she swore she still felt the imprints of his palms on her midriff.

Several seconds of silence stretched between them, then he cleared his throat. "Shall we continue to the beach?"

"Please." She fell into step beside him, and had to grudgingly admit that he was politeness itself, offering his hand in spots where the path was a bit steep, holding back stray branches so she could pass unharmed, catching her arm when she stumbled once. Of course, he certainly should have caught her, as it was entirely his fault she stumbled. If she'd been concentrating on the path rather than the brush of her shoulder against his upper arm, she wouldn't have missed her step.

But holding onto any semblance of annoyance was completely impossible as they neared the beach. A band of golden sand stretched before them, filling her with the desire to spread her arms and run across the unspoiled grains. The sea breeze caught at her bonnet, and she pressed a hand to her head.

"Most likely a lost cause," Dr. Oliver said, indicating her bonnet with a nod. "We're about to leave the protection of the trees, and the wind can gust quite strongly."

Victoria kept her hand clapped onto her head as they ventured onto the sand. The wind seemed to have died down, and she lowered her hand. Almost instantly a salt-misted gust snatched the bonnet from her head. "Oh!"

Dr. Oliver shot her a quick grin that clearly said, "I told you so," then he took off in pursuit of her runaway bonnet, sprinting toward the water. Watching him dash across the sand filled her with the overwhelming desire to do the same. Grasping her skirts, she lifted them to her ankles and ran after him.

The leather ankle boots she'd worn for riding sank into the soft sand, slowing her progress, but the wind whipped at her hair and gown, the sun gleamed on the azure water, and the scent of salty freshness filled her lungs, instilling her with a heady sensation of freedom unlike anything she'd ever known. A delighted laugh escaped her, then another, and she ran faster, kicking up golden grainy arcs of sand behind her.

She ran on toward the water, watching Dr. Oliver reach down twice for her bonnet, only to be eluded both times, before finally capturing the elusive hat by one of its long dark green satin ribbons. He was brushing sand from it when he caught sight of her running toward him. He stilled, watching her approach. She halted several feet away from him, laughing, breathless, and invigorated.

"You rescued my hat," she said, her words coming out in breathy pants, her chest heaving. "Thank you."

He handed her the runaway bonnet. "You're welcome. Although I would have returned it to you. There was no need to exhaust yourself."

"I'm not exhausted. I'm invigorated!" She threw her arms wide and spun around twice. "I have never been anywhere as refreshing as this beach. It seems as if the air is vibrating with energy. Yet, it somehow manages to also feel... serene." She made a dismissive gesture with her hands, then laughed. "I'm afraid I cannot explain what I mean."

He looked at her intently. "There's no need to explain, as I understand precisely what you're saying. It is a place that simultaneously inspires excitement and infuses the soul with peace."

"Yes! That's it exactly."

A slow smile curved his lips, speeding up her heart in an altogether different way than her impromptu run. She felt bewitched by his gaze, captivated by the way the breeze ruffled his hair and how the sunlight bathed him in golden warmth. She managed to force her gaze downward, only to find herself again transfixed by the way the breeze molded his linen shirt to his chest and torso, offering a teasing hint of his masculine form that was at once entirely too much and not nearly enough.

Determined not to be caught staring again, Victoria turned her head, and her gaze fell upon a shell in the sand. She quickly pulled off her gloves, then bent down. "My first treasure," she said as she rose, holding up the delicate pearly white shell.

"Lovely," he murmured. She glanced at him and noted that he wasn't looking at the shell, but at her, with that same unreadable expression. What might wipe that expression from his eyes and fill them with something easily decipherable, such as . . . desire?

She wasn't certain, but she realized she wanted very badly to know.

Eight

*Today's Modern Woman must master the art of
kissing, especially the hello kiss and the good-bye
kiss. The hello kiss because it sets the tone for her
encounter, essential when it comes to enticing and
enthralling a gentleman. And the good-bye kiss
because she wants to leave him with something to
think about—namely her.*

*A Ladies' Guide to the Pursuit of
Personal Happiness and Intimate Fulfillment*
by Charles Brightmore

After fashioning a basket of sorts by tying her bonnet
strings together, Victoria set her shell in her makeshift
carrier, then looped the ribbons over her arm like a reticule. No sooner had she done so than she spied another
shell several feet away. She pounced on the treasure, ex-
claiming over the unusual find. "I've never seen shells
such as these," she said, scooping up several more.

"And we haven't even reached the best location this
beach offers," Dr. Oliver said.

Victoria shaded her eyes with a sandy-fingered hand

and looked up at him from her crouched position. "You cannot mean that there is a better place than this?"

"That is precisely what I mean. Would you like to see it?"

"Do ducks *quack*?"

He laughed. "As the owner of two ducks, I can attest that they do indeed quack. Often very early in the morning when you're not particularly eager to hear it." He extended his hand. "Come. I'll show you a magical place, and you may fill up your bonnet on the way."

Victoria slipped her hand into his and allowed him to help her to her feet. Their palms only touched for several seconds before he released her, but the impact reverberated through her. His hand was large and strong and warm. She'd detected the hard roughness of calluses on his palm, an intriguing texture she'd never felt before, as none of the gentlemen of her acquaintance would ever build an animal pen or ride without gloves.

With her bending down every few seconds to pick up another shell, their progress was slow, but even if she hadn't been adding to her collection, she couldn't have rushed. The sound of the waves crashing against the sand and cliffs offered a hypnotic background to the dramatic scenery. After absorbing the sound for several minutes, she said, "May I ask you something?"

"Yes, although based on your tone, it sounds like a topic that might incite an argument—a pity, as we're doing so well thus far."

"Not an argument, but the topic is . . . personal."

"Ah. Well, ask away, and I shall endeavor to satisfy your curiosity."

"You said earlier that after your last mission failed, you had a falling out with your father and brother and that it was best for all concerned you left here."

He looked straight ahead and a muscle ticked in his jaw. "Yes." He turned and his gaze bore into hers. "I suppose you want to know what caused our estrangement."

"I cannot deny I am curious, but what I actually wondered was if your return meant that the rift between you was now healed." When he continued to simply look at her, she fell into her hated habit of babbling when unnerved. "I only wondered because I know how hurtful the severing of family ties can be. My mother was estranged from her sister and I witnessed firsthand how harmful the situation was to both of them before Mother died. I was merely hoping that your situation had been resolved." Her words came out in a rush, and she had to physically press her lips together to stop the torrent.

A frown pulled down his brows, and he turned to once again stare straight ahead. "The rift is still there, although we're all maneuvering carefully around it, as if it's a pile of something we've mucked from the stalls and don't wish to step in. I don't know if the break can ever be completely healed. Trust, once broken, is difficult to repair. And words, once spoken, cannot be unheard."

"True, but there is great power in forgiveness, for both those who extend it and those who receive it."

"Then I shall hope that someday my brother and father can forgive me."

Forgive you for what, she wanted to ask, but managed to hold her tongue, hoping he would volunteer the information. Nearly a minute of silence passed before he said, "The failure of that mission rests on my shoulders. Colin and Gordon were both shot and easily could have died. The jewels disappeared. It was believed that I betrayed the mission in order to secure the jewels for myself."

"Who believed that?"

"Everyone who mattered." The words sounded flat, bitter. "Nothing was proved against me, but the rumors were damaging enough."

"Did you do it?"

He turned to face her, and she found herself pinned by his intense scrutiny. "Do you think I did?"

"I hardly know you well enough to say."

"And I hardly know you well enough to admit to committing a crime."

Victoria nodded slowly, noting that he didn't proclaim his innocence. "So the note from my father provides information about these jewels. Information that could either reunite you with your supposed ill-gotten gains—which I'm guessing are worth a great deal . . . ?"

"A king's ransom," he agreed.

"Or provide you with a way to clear your name—also worth a great deal."

He raised a brow. "Or even better, perhaps a way to accomplish both tasks."

"Since my father sent you this information, it seems clear he believes you innocent."

"Does it? That's a rather naive deduction, Lady Victoria. It is equally possible he has other reasons."

"Such as?"

"Such as a plan to entrap me. Or perhaps to have the jewels recovered for his own financial or political gain."

He clearly read the outrage that flooded heat into her face because before she could speak, he said, "I'm not making any accusations or even a suggestion. I'm merely pointing out that things are not always as they seem and that there is usually more than one reason or explanation for any set of circumstances."

"That reeks of making excuses, which sounds like a

convenient method for you to explain away any past indiscretions."

Instead of looking offended, a devilish gleam sparkled in his eyes. "Surely something everyone is guilty of at one time or another. Even you, Lady Victoria."

"I've done nothing for which I need to make excuses."

"Never? A beautiful woman such as yourself? Come come, now. Surely at one soiree or another some impertinent rogue was smitten by your charms and convinced you to part with a kiss." He tapped his finger to his chin. "Hmmm. Perhaps your suitors Lords Bransby or Dravenripple?"

"Branripple and Dravensby," Victoria corrected in a cold voice at complete odds with the heat of embarrassment creeping up her neck. "And that is none of your business."

"And surely afterward," he continued, taking no note of her icy tone, "you blamed your behavior on any number of excuses rather than accepting the actual reason."

"And what reason would that be?"

"That you found the gentleman as attractive as he found you. That you were as curious to know the taste and feel of his kiss as he was to know yours."

Victoria often cursed her inability to think up a suitable reply until hours or days after the fact, and never more than she cursed it now. Chagrin burned her cheeks for she knew perfectly well that he referred to the passionate kiss they'd shared. And the fact that he so accurately pinpointed that she'd made excuses for her scandalous behavior only served to fluster her further. He paused to pick up a perfectly formed small conch shell which he then held up for her examination. "Shall we add this one to your collection?"

Grasping the opportunity to change the subject, she held out her bonnet and said, "It's lovely. Thank you."

"Something to remember me by," he said, placing the treasure in her bonnet.

The last thing Victoria wanted was something to remind her of Dr. Oliver when her entire purpose in coming here was to erase him from her memory. But she certainly wasn't going to tell *him* that. Instead, she looked at the soaring stone cliff rising before them and said, "We're almost at the end of the beach. Are we nearing this magical place you mentioned?"

"We are. In fact, it is directly ahead of us."

"The cliff?"

Instead of answering, he smiled and held out his hand. "Come. Let me show you the magic."

Unable to resist the intriguing invitation, Victoria settled her hand against his. His long, strong fingers closed over hers, shooting a warm tingle up her arm. When they neared the jutting stone cliff a moment later, it looked as if he intended to walk right into the rough surface. Victoria tried to slow her pace, but he urged her onward. To her amazement, he led her into a cleverly hidden narrow crevice in the stone, so narrow they had to turn sideways to navigate it.

"Careful," he said, moving slowly. "The rocks can be sharp in places."

She followed his lead, stepping carefully on the hard-packed sand, avoiding brushing against the craggy black rock. The air in the narrow passage was still and cool, and the farther they walked, the dimmer the light became. The sound of the waves receded to a distant echo. The passageway widened enough to allow them to walk single file, but by then they were swallowed in complete darkness. He was no more than a foot in front of her, yet she couldn't see him at all.

He must have felt her apprehension because he whispered, "Don't be alarmed. We're almost there.

She sensed they turned a corner and was relieved to note what looked like a wan patch of light ahead. They rounded another corner, and Victoria suddenly found herself standing in a circular cavern approximately twelve feet in diameter. A swatch of pale light dimly illuminated the area, and she looked up. A small piece of blue sky was visible through an oblong opening in the stone far, far above her head.

"What is this place?" she asked, setting down her bonnet then turning in a slow circle.

"A favorite haunt of mine. I discovered it as a boy, quite by accident during one of my endless explorations. I dubbed it Crystal Cave."

"Why Crystal Cave? I don't see any crystals."

"Only because a cloud is obviously obscuring the sun. Run your finger over the wall."

An odd request, but Victoria skimmed a fingertip lightly over the rough surface. He clasped her hand and brought it to her lips.

"Taste," he said softly.

An even odder request, but with her gaze locked on his, Victoria touched her tongue to her fingertip. "Salty," she said.

He nodded. "This cavern fills with water at high tide— something I discovered the hard way and nearly didn't live to tell the tale. But it is like this at low tide. When the sunlight hits the accumulated dry salt crystals . . ."

His voice faded as a shaft of bright sunlight illuminated the cave. Victoria gasped as the dark walls suddenly shimmered with sparkling light. "It's like being surrounded by glittering diamonds," she said, delighted and awed by the spectacle. She again rotated in a slow circle. "I've never seen anything like it. It's . . . dazzling."

"Yes. I'd almost forgotten just how dazzling."

She stopped turning and looked at him, then stilled when she discovered his gaze resting upon her. Her heart jumped in that ridiculous manner it seemed to whenever she found herself near him. "I suppose you and your brother and Lord Alwyck enjoyed many adventures in here."

He shook his head. "I never told them about this place." He leaned his shoulders against the wall and regarded her with an enigmatic expression. "I've never brought anyone here. Until now."

His softly spoken words seemed to echo off the glittering walls. Leaning against the rock, a shadowy contrast to the shimmering crystals, he looked dark, a bit dangerous—very much like the rakish pirate she'd once imagined him—and very delicious. Her heart slapped against her rib cage so hard she wondered that the sound didn't reverberate off the sparkling walls.

"I suppose I should then be flattered that you brought me here," she said, proud of the light tone she achieved. Still, her curiosity made her ask, "Why did you?"

Nathan watched the glittering play of light shimmer over her, coating her in ribbons of sparkles, and any good intentions he may have harbored fled. She looked like a princess bathed in diamonds, her silky curls in glorious windblown disarray, her full lips glistening, tempting him like a siren's call. Pushing off the wall, he slowly approached her. "I could offer any number of plausible reasons, such as I wished to play the polite host and thought you would enjoy it. Or, I'd a strong desire to visit the cave myself and since I couldn't very well leave you alone on the beach, I brought you with me. And while those are true, if I offered them, I would be blaming my behavior on excuses rather than accepting the actual reason." When only two feet separated them, he reached out and captured her hand. Her eyes widened slightly, but she made no move to stop him. Instead she moistened her lips with the tip of her tongue, clearly an unconscious gesture on her part, but one that shot liquid heat straight to his groin. Bloody hell, he didn't stand much chance of being immune to her kiss when she rendered him so painfully aroused before their lips even met.

"What is the actual reason?" she whispered.

"Are you certain you want to know?" At her nod, he said, "I'm curious to know if the kiss we once shared would be as enjoyable the second time around." He settled her hand on his chest, right above the spot where his heart thumped as if he'd run a race, then lightly clasped her waist and drew her slowly closer. When only inches separated them, he said, "Are you willing to admit you want the same thing?"

He stood perfectly still, waiting for her response, wondering if she would display the same courage she had the previous evening or if she would hide behind a false curtain of prim, maidenly reserve. She leaned into him, raised her face and whispered, "I want the same thing."

Thank God. Nathan bludgeoned back the nearly overwhelming primitive desire to simply yank her against him and devour her and instead slowly lowered his head toward those tempting lips that had haunted countless hours. At last he would know if he'd just imagined how good that long ago kiss had been.

He lightly brushed his lips over hers, a tantalizing whisper of a touch. A breathless sound escaped her, and he feathered his lips over hers again, teasing, searching, tasting. He ran the tip of his tongue over her plump lower lip, an invitation she accepted by parting her lips. With a groan he couldn't hold back, he drew her tightly against him and settled his mouth on hers. And instantly knew what had gone through the mind of the prince in the Cinderella tale when he'd finally found the foot that fit the glass slipper: *It's about bloody damn time.*

Desire seared him with the intensity of a flash fire, and as it had the last time he'd held this woman in his arms and kissed her, he lost all sense of time and place. There was only her, the luscious taste of her silky mouth, the erotic friction of her tongue mating with his, the satin of her hair sifting through his fingers, the delicate scent of roses rising from her skin, the lush feel of her feminine curves pressing against him, the arousing sensation of her hands gliding up and down his back.

Damn it, he felt . . . unhinged. Desperate. In a way that would have appalled him if he'd had any control over his reaction to her. The last time he held her, he'd been very much aware that his brother and her aunt sat in the next room. But there was no one else here now . . .

Hauling her up against him, he stepped back until his shoulders hit the wall. With a deep groan, he spread his legs, planted his boots firmly in the sand, and drew her into the vee of his thighs.

Lost . . . he was totally, utterly lost. No woman had ever felt like this, tasted like this. Yet, it wasn't simply the way she fit so perfectly in his arms or the delicious flavor of her that affected him so powerfully. It was also her ardent response to his kiss, to his touch. He doubted he'd have had a prayer of resisting her under any circumstances, but the fact that she kissed him, touched him, with a fervor equal to his own all but brought him to his knees.

She moaned and shifted restlessly against him, and his hands wandered down her back, to cup the enticing curve of her buttocks. He settled her more firmly against him then slowly rubbed himself against her. His erection jerked and he knew he stood in real danger of losing all control. Desperate to slow things down before he disgraced himself in a way he hadn't since he was a green lad, but unable to stop this madness, he somehow found the strength to abandon the silken delights of her mouth, to trail his lips over her soft cheek, then along her jaw.

But he found no relief there, as her skin inundated his senses with the elusive hint of roses. He ran the tip of his tongue over the delicate shell of her ear, absorbing her sharp intake of breath, which melted into a husky groan when his teeth gently grazed her earlobe. He nuzzled the sensitive skin behind her ear, and she arched her neck to afford him better access, all while her hands smoothed over his chest and shoulders. He touched his tongue to the throbbing hollow at the base of her throat, absorbing the frantic beat.

Stop . . . he had to stop . . . but every halfhearted rational thought fled when she fisted her hands in his hair and dragged his head up.

"Again," she whispered against his mouth, not a plea, but a command filled with impatience. If he'd been capable of doing so, he would have laughed at the autocratic demand, which was the same one she'd issued him three years ago. He hadn't denied her, or himself, then, and he'd be damned if he was capable of it now.

Their mouths melded in a lush, deep kiss, his tongue

stroking in an imitation of the act his body ached to share with hers. Wild hunger, unlike anything he'd ever before experienced, roared through his veins. His hands glided up her back, then forward to cup her breasts. Her beaded nipple grazed his palm through the material of her riding costume—material that had to go. He slipped off her lace fichu, then glided his fingers over the satin swells of her full breasts. Bloody hell, she was so soft. Her warm skin quivered beneath his hands, and his fingers slid beneath the edge of her bodice.

She leaned back, breaking off their kiss. "Wh-What are you doing?" she panted against his lips.

Questions? She expected him to be able to answer questions? His fingers brushed over her nipple and he groaned.

"*What* are you doing?"

He had to swallow to find his voice. "Surely that is obvious."

Shoving against his chest, she pulled out of his embrace and backed up several paces. With her chest heaving, hair mussed, bodice askew, color high, and lips moist and swollen, she looked aroused and as if she'd just left her lover's arms. Until he looked into her eyes. Then she looked like glaring Fury about to sizzle him where he stood with a lightning bolt.

"Yes, it is obvious," she said, her eyes spitting anger as she grabbed at her bodice. "You're looking for your letter."

Nine

Today's Modern Woman will hopefully in her search for intimate fulfillment meet a gentleman who can render her aroused and weak-kneed with a mere look. While it is always delightful to find such a man, she must remain on her guard with this man at all times for he, by virtue of her strong attraction to him, wields power over her.

A Ladies' Guide to the Pursuit of
Personal Happiness and Intimate Fulfillment
by Charles Brightmore

Nathan stared at her, nonplussed, ragged breaths puffing from between his lips for several seconds. Then he shook his head and laughed. "Well, hell. That's actually what I *should* have been doing. Unfortunately it never occurred to me."

She sent him a withering look. "Surely you don't expect me to believe that of an accomplished spy."

"After three years of not using my spy skills, I'm afraid they're a bit rusty. And you're not giving your charms nearly enough credit. I never once thought of the letter." *As if I could have*. Damn it, if she'd asked him to state his own name he would have been hard pressed to recall it. He sucked in a deep breath and shoved back his hair with hands that still weren't quite steady. "However, now that you've brought up the subject of my note, I want it back." He pushed away from the wall and approached her. Her eyes widened, but then she straightened her shoulders, lifted her chin and stood her ground. When only two feet separated them, he reached out and gently traced the backs of his fingers against her flushed cheek.

"Please, Victoria . . ." Her name rolled off his tongue, and he knew that after what they'd just shared, he'd never want to address her formally again. "Give me the note. After everything I told you today, surely you can see that it's important to me."

She blinked, then her eyes narrowed. "Dr. Oliver—"

"Nathan. We're rather past the formal use of titles, don't you agree?"

"Nathan . . . I cannot decide if you're sincere or trying to trick me. Spies are known to be very crafty, you know."

"I can't deny that I can be crafty on occasion. But in this case I'm sincere."

She studied him for several seconds, then said, "I want to give you the note, but I insist it be done on my terms. I want to help in this search for the jewels." Stepping away from him, she paced the narrow confines of the cave, then paused to face him. Her features remained resolute, but her eyes—those huge blue eyes that reminded him of the sea—beseeched him. "Nathan, I've been cosseted and coddled my entire life, but ultimately always dismissed as nothing more than a decorative piece. I am simultaneously admired and ignored. Men hear me when I speak, but they do not *listen* to me. Do you have any idea how frustrating that is? I've nearly always managed to suppress these feelings, but lately . . ."

She blew out a long breath and her bravado seemed to wilt. "Lately, I've experienced an unprecedented, unsettling sense of discontent that urges me to stop accepting things that I do not like. Things I think are unfair. And these feelings came to a head with the discovery of my father's secret occupation. For years he lived an adventurous life while I was lied to and relegated to an existence that was as exciting as watching a blob of paint dry." Her chin dropped and she looked at the ground. "Until you brought me to this cave, the most exciting moment of my life was when you kissed me in the gallery."

That admission, whispered so softly, slammed into him with the force of a blow to the chest. He touched his fingers beneath her chin, urging it gently up until their gazes met. To his alarm and dismay, her eyes shimmered with moisture. "You're not going to cry are you?"

"Certainly not. I'm not the weepy sort."

"Good. Because I'm not the sort of man who is swayed by feminine tears." His conscience kicked him squarely on the arse for that bold-faced lie. Damn it, if she'd railed at him, demanded her way, he could have fought her, but this show of vulnerability sliced him off at the knees. Of course, he'd be damned if he'd let *her* know that.

A flash of anger glittered in her eyes and she pulled away from him. "And I'm not the sort of woman who resorts to false tears to cajole a man into giving me what I want."

"No, I can see that you're more the type to bludgeon a man with your demands."

"I am simply sick and tired of being treated like an empty-headed nitwit because I'm a woman."

"I don't think you're an empty-headed nitwit. Indeed, I think you're far too clever."

She seemed to recover herself. "Er, thank you. Far too clever to give up the note without you agreeing to my terms."

"All right."

"I'll not compromise on this."

"Very well."

"Do not think that I'll fall victim—" She squinted her eyes at him. "What did you say?"

"I've agreed to your terms."

"That I'll assist in the search for the jewels?"

"In exchange for my letter. Yes. However, I have some terms of my own."

"Which are?"

"As I am experienced in these matters and you are not, I will expect you to heed my advice."

"So long as you agree to not dismiss my ideas out of hand, that is acceptable to me. Anything else?"

"Yes. There is a possibility that there may be some danger involved in this matter. Your father has sent you here for safekeeping, and it is my duty to see that you remain unharmed. I'll insist on your word that you will not take any risks or wander off by yourself."

She nodded. "I've no wish to place myself in danger. You have my word. So . . . we've struck our bargain?"

"Yes. Well, except for the final thing."

"And what might that be?" she asked in a suspicion-laden tone.

"We must seal our bargain as all spies do."

"Oh. Very well." She held out her hand.

"With a kiss."

She snatched back her hand and narrowed her eyes at him. "What nonsense is this?"

"Spies seal bargains with a kiss." When he stepped toward her and she hastily backed up, he made a *tsking* noise. "Here we are, mere seconds into our agreement, and already you are reneging, Victoria. We agreed that as I am the expert in spy-related matters, you would heed my advice." He took another step toward her, which she answered with another step backward.

"And I shall gladly heed your advice when you are not spouting Banbury tales. Kiss to seal a bargain indeed. Next I suppose you'll expect me to believe that you sealed bargains with my father, your brother, and Lord Alwyck with kisses."

Another step forward for him, another retreat from her. "Of course not. Male spies use secret handshakes with each other. Only bargains between male spies and *females* are sealed with kisses. It's all written down in the Official Spy Handbook."

"Official spy handbook?" She made a snorting sound of disbelief. "You're joking."

"I'm perfectly serious. There are very exacting rules to spydom, you know, and they had to be written down somewhere. Thus the handbook."

"And you have a copy?"

"Of course."

"You'll show it to me?"

He smiled and took another step toward her. "My dear Victoria, I would be delighted to show you anything of mine you might wish to see."

She swallowed, retreated another step, and her back hit the sparkling wall. She lifted her chin. "I have a feeling that this 'seal the bargain with a kiss' is merely a ruse to insinuate your hand into my bodice again."

"As tempting as that thought is, I will prove my sincerity." Nathan stepped forward once more, stopping when less than a foot separated them. Reaching out, he slowly placed his palms on the stone wall on either side of her head. "See there? I won't even touch you. My hands will remain exactly where they are. Now, shall we seal our bargain?"

Victoria stood with her back pressed against the rough stone wall and desperately tried to summon the outrage she should be feeling at him for trapping her like this a second time. But instead of outrage, deep yearning and a purely feminine thrill shivered through her. Had less than an hour passed since she'd wondered what his eyes would look like filled with desire? Well, now she knew. They glittered with a combination of hunger and arousal that made her feel as if her skirts had caught fire. Even though he wasn't touching her, she could feel the heat emanating from him. Smell his warm skin, the subtle fragrance of sandalwood, starched linen, mixed with the fresh crisp scent of the sea. She'd yet to fully recover from his last devastating kiss. She wasn't at all certain her legs wouldn't buckle from another kiss. But certainly Today's Modern Woman would want to find out. . . .

His dark head descended toward hers. Her eyes slid closed and she pressed her fisted hands against the wall in preparation for the frantic onslaught.

But it never came. Instead, he brushed light, airy kisses, as gentle as butterfly wings, over her brow. Her temple and cheeks. Her closed eyelids, the line of her jaw, the corners of her mouth. His warm breath, scented with something spicy that reminded her of cinnamon, caressed her skin with the same gentle touch as his lips. By the time his mouth brushed over hers, her heart pounded so hard she could feel the frenzied beat throughout her body . . . in her temples. At the base of her throat. Between her thighs.

Eager with anticipation, she again braced herself for the demanding onslaught of his kiss, but again he surprised her by barely touching his lips to hers. A slow, gentle brush, followed by a leisurely drag of his tongue across her bottom lip. Her lips parted, and he kissed her slowly, softly, with a complete lack of haste that simultaneously melted and maddened her. Her body ached to be pressed against the hard length of his. To feel his hands skimming over her, to run her hands over him. Heat swept through her, settling low in her abdomen. She pressed her trembling legs together in an effort to relieve the tingling pressure between her thighs, but the friction only served to frustrate her further. She wanted, needed, more. Yet the instant she slid her hands around his waist to urge him closer, he stepped back. A groan of protest rose to her lips and her hands fell back limply to her sides. She could only be grateful for the solid wall at her back which prevented her from slithering to the sand in a boneless, breathless heap.

She dragged her heavy eyelids open and noted with no small amount of pique that *he* appeared not in the least bit undone, while she felt completely unraveled. While she remained propped against the wall, fighting for breath and willing her pulse to slow, he gathered up her discarded fichu. Without asking her permission, he settled the delicate blond lace around her neck, nimbly tucking it into the top of her gown, then adjusting her bodice with a deft tug and practiced ease that indicated he was well acquainted with the intricacies of ladies' clothing. Heat gushed through her and she wondered if he would be as adept at removing a woman's clothes.

With his gaze, once again indecipherable, resting on hers, he said, "Our bargain is sealed, Victoria. My note, if you please."

The way he said her name, in that deep rasp, had her pressing her lips together to keep from asking him to say it again. "I will give it to you once we return to the house."

One dark brow quirked upward. "If it is your modesty you seek to protect, may I remind you that I am already acquainted with what's inside your bodice."

Fire scorched her cheeks. Still, she was grateful for his words, as they served as a much needed reminder that this man was an arrogant blight on her peace. "The note is not hidden in my bodice. I shall return it to you once we're back at Creston Manor."

He studied her for several seconds, and Victoria returned his speculative look with a cool regard of her own. Finally he nodded. "Very well. Then let us be off."

He picked up her shell-filled bonnet, tucked the bundle under his arm, then extended his hand. Wordlessly, Victoria slipped her hand into his and allowed him to lead her from the cave. The instant they exited the narrow passage between the stones, he released her and she forced away the absurd sense of disappointment that flooded her. There was no reason to be disappointed. Indeed, she should be ecstatic. She'd only arrived in Cornwall yesterday and already achieved her objective—she'd given him a kiss he wouldn't soon forget. Of course, she was now faced with the indisputably annoying fact that she'd also given him a kiss *she* wouldn't soon forget. Botheration, that hadn't been part of her plan at all.

Then another disturbing thought hit her. *Had* she given him a kiss he wouldn't soon forget? While there was no denying that he'd been physically aroused by their encounter, how could she be sure he wouldn't forget their kiss five minutes from now? Perhaps he'd already forgotten.

She peeked at him from the corner of her eye as they

crossed the beach, and her lips pressed together with a combination of dismay and annoyance. He strode along as if he hadn't a care in the world, his face lifted toward the sun, the wind ruffling through his dark hair. Bending down, he picked up a small, perfect ivory conch. A smile played at the corners of his mouth. He looked altogether unperturbed, unconcerned, and certainly not in the throes of brooding over their time in the cave.

Unable to keep from asking, Victoria said, "May I ask your thoughts?"

He rubbed his hand over his stomach. "I was wondering what Cook planned for lunch. Hopefully something hearty. I'm famished."

Food. The blasted man was thinking about food. Clamping her jaw shut to prevent her from asking any other questions to which she didn't want to hear the answers, she remained silent for the remainder of their journey back to the house. As they neared the stables, she noted Lords Sutton and Alwyck standing in the wide doorway, watching them approach. Both men were looking at her intently, and she realized what a disaster her hair must look from the brisk breeze. *And Nathan's long-fingered hands*, her inner voice added slyly.

Humph. The wind had wreaked havoc with her coiffure long before Nathan had touched her. Indeed, she was grateful for the gusty wind, for without it she would have no other explanation for her disheveled state.

Sitting astride Midnight, Nathan observed his brother and Gordon watch Victoria approach and decided he didn't like what saw. Gordon looked at her as if she was a delectable confection and he'd suddenly developed a sweet tooth. Colin's expression was equally rapt. By the looks of it, neither man would object to taking over his duty of protecting Victoria. A decidedly unpleasant sensation, which he told himself was hunger, gripped his gut.

Nathan's jaw tightened as he noted that Victoria had barely reined in Honey before Gordon greeted her with a wide smile. "How fetching you look, Lady Victoria."

She laughed. "You are either excessively gallant or dreadfully nearsighted, Lord Alwyck, for I know I must look a fright. The wind at the beach stole my bonnet, and I fear my coiffure as well."

"I'm not the least nearsighted," Colin said, joining them and smiling up at Victoria, "and I agree, you look most fetching. Did you enjoy your visit to the beach?"

"Very much. The scenery was breathtaking and I filled my runaway bonnet with the most lovely shells."

"I enjoyed myself as well," Nathan said dryly, reining Midnight next to Victoria's mount.

"But where is your chaperone, Lady Victoria?" Gordon asked, casting a disapproving glare at Nathan.

"Since when is a chaperone required for a horseback ride in broad daylight?" Nathan cut in, looking at Gordon with a cold expression that dared him to suggest either he or Lady Victoria would act in an untoward fashion. "The rigorous ride and walk to the beach would have been exhausting for Lady Delia."

Both Gordon and Colin returned their attention to Victoria. Gordon helped her dismount, and Nathan grimly noted that his hands remained on her waist a fraction too long. And that a becoming blush stained Victoria's cheeks as a result.

He swung down from the saddle. Colin, who held Honey's reins, handed them to him as if he were a stable hand. Disgruntled in a way he couldn't ever recall feeling before, Nathan led both horses into the stable, the sound of Victoria's delighted laughter as she basked in the attention of her two new admirers following him into the shadowy interior. It appeared he'd have to pry her away from Colin and Gordon to get her back to the house to fetch his note. It suddenly occurred to him that if Colin had accompanied Victoria to the cave, his brother's talented fingers most likely could have already relieved her of the note, but damn it, the thought of Colin putting his hands on her did not set well at all.

"Enjoy your ride, Dr. Nathan?" Hopkins asked, coming from the tack room to greet him.

"It was . . . stimulating." *And intriguing.* He inwardly winced. *And painfully arousing.*

"Stimulating, eh?" Hopkins nodded thoughtfully. "A ride with a beautiful woman is often just that." He jerked his head toward the doorway where Colin, Gordon, and Victoria were engaged in a lively conversation. "Seems like there's some competition fer her attention."

Nathan's shoulders tensed. "I'm not in competition for her favors."

" 'Course yer not. She's got eyes only for you."

Nathan's head whipped around to face Hopkins. "What do you mean?"

Clearly his voice was sharper than he'd intended because Hopkins eyed him with a combination of hurt and surprise. "Beg yer pardon, Dr. Nathan. Meant no disrespect. 'Tis just we used to always speak plainly to each other."

Nathan dragged a hand through his hair and silently cursed his thoughtlessness. Hopkins had been with his family since before he was born, and he'd always viewed the kindly man who loved horses as much as he did as a friend. "We still can speak plainly," Nathan said, clasping the older man's shoulder. "Forgive me. It's just that your words startled me."

Hopkins acknowledged the apology with a nod, then said, "Surprises me, that does. Usually yer keen observant. Ye didn't see the way she looked at ye?"

"As a matter of fact I did. She looked as if she wanted to skewer me then roast me over a slow flame."

"Yep, that was the look." Hopkins chuckled. "Got it bad fer ye, she does." He narrowed his eyes at Nathan. "Wonder if she noticed the way ye look at her?"

"As if I wanted to toss her into the first coach leaving Cornwall?"

"No, like she were a ripe peach ye wanted to pluck. Then feast on."

Damn it all, when had he become so bloody transparent? Before he could voice a denial, Hopkins chuckled. "And ye don't look happy about it, either. No point in denyin' it. Been able to read ye like a book since ye were a lad." He squinted toward the now empty doorway. Obviously the trio had walked away. "A well-favored filly, Lady Victoria is. Spirited—I can tell. And a fine rider. Still, a pampered London diamond . . . not the sort of lady ye used to fancy. And would be my guess that yer not the sort of man she usually takes a shine to."

"Oh? And what sort of man am I?"

" 'Tis more the sort of man yer not. Yer not one of them fancy London swells with yer nose hoisted in the air traipsing from party to club to gamin' hell and back again. Yer a decent, hardworking man. No offense meant to the lady, but I doubt she's ever looked twice at someone as lowly as a doctor. Understandable. But she's lookin' now." He shot Nathan a pointed look. "And yer lookin' back."

"You seem to have divined an awful lot in a short amount of time," Nathan said.

Hopkins shrugged. " 'Tis my nature to study folks."

Before Nathan could make any further reply, a commotion was heard outside, followed by a loud cry that unmistakably came from Victoria. "Oh! What are you doing? *Stop!*"

Nathan raced toward the doors, Hopkins directly behind him. When he emerged, he skidded to a halt, his gaze raking over the tableau before him. Gordon and Colin, both looking chagrined, knelt next to Victoria, who was crouched down and clutching her hem of her gown. Her face was devoid of color. All three were staring at Petunia, who stood near them, her fuzzy chin working back and forth as she chewed.

Nathan strode forward and crouched next to Victoria, alarmed at her pallor. Grasping her upper arms, he asked tersely, "Are you all right? What happened?"

"That idiotic goat of yours is what happened," Gordon said, his tone dripping with disgust. "Not only did the beast scare poor Lady Victoria to death, it gnawed a hole in her riding costume. That animal is a menace. Why, it could have bitten her."

Nathan's gaze shifted to Petunia, who flicked her tail then sashayed toward the pen. Returning his attention to Victoria, he said, "You're not hurt, are you?"

After she shook her head, he rose, helping her to her feet. "My apologies. Petunia is famous for nibbling on things she shouldn't. I'm sure your riding costume can be repaired. If not, I'll see that it is replaced."

"It is not my riding costume that concerns me," she said in a choked voice. She stared up at him with stricken eyes. "It is your note."

"What about my note?"

"Your goat just ate it."

Ten

Today's Modern Woman should never waste the opportunity to view a superior male specimen, particularly if he is in some state of undress. If faced with such a stroke of good fortune, she should not allow modesty to dictate that she squander such a lucky turn of events. Enjoy the moment, look your fill, and be prepared for what might happen next.

A Ladies' Guide to the Pursuit of
Personal Happiness and Intimate Fulfillment
by Charles Brightmore

*H*er stomach churning with disbelief and dread, Victoria watched Nathan's eyes narrow. She expected him to shout, but instead he said with quiet, icy calm, "I beg your pardon?"

She swallowed. "Your note. It was eaten. By your goat."

"Please tell me that is just a hideously bad rhyme."

"It is a hideously bad rhyme. But true, nonetheless."

His gaze dropped, arrowing in on the ragged spot of forest green hem she still clutched in a white-knuckled grip. "You'd sewn it into your hem."

"Yes."

His gaze jumped back to hers, pinning her in place. "You led me to believe it was in the house."

"I never said that. I said I would return it to you once we were back here."

"Why didn't you simply return it at the beach? Knowing your sewing abilities, it surely wouldn't have been too difficult to rip open a few sloppy stitches."

Victoria flung down her ruined hem, planted her hands on her hips and narrowed her eyes right back at him. "If certain people didn't find it necessary to keep secrets from me and hide letters in my luggage, and other people refuse to let me help—"

"If you're referring to your father and me—"

"Of course I'm referring to my father and you. If the two of you weren't so pigheaded, it wouldn't have been necessary for me to sew the note into my hem. Where it was perfectly safe, until *your* goat ate it."

"So it's *my* fault the note is gone?"

Victoria lifted her chin. "Partially, yes. Although I am willing to accept a portion of the blame."

"How incredibly generous of you."

Before Victoria could respond to his sarcastic reply, Lord Alwyck broke in. "Will someone please explain what you're talking about? What note?"

Nathan sent her a warning look, but she ignored him and turned her attention to Lord Alwyck. "My father secreted a note for Dr. Nathan in my luggage. Unfortunately for him, I found it before he could retrieve it. Even more unfortunately for him, his goat just ate the note out of the hem of my skirt where I'd hidden it."

Lord Alwyck shot Nathan a piercing look. "Why was Wexhall sending you a secret note?" When Nathan's only reply was an unreadable steady stare, Lord Alwyck said slowly, "The fact that you've returned here . . . a note from Wexhall . . . this has something to do with the jewels." The words rang like an accusation. "Why didn't you tell me?"

Nathan's gaze didn't waver. "If Wexhall had wanted you to know, he'd have told you. Or perhaps I would have told you, depending on what instructions he gave me in the note. But now that the note is gone, I don't suppose we'll know. At least until I am able to contact him to tell him what happened." His gaze swiveled to Victoria. "Which, needless to say, is an extremely inconvenient delay."

Lord Alwyck turned to Lord Sutton. "Did you know about this, Colin?"

Lord Sutton nodded. "Yes. I'd planned to tell you about it during today's ride." He turned to Nathan. "Gordon had every right to know."

"I never said he didn't. However, I would have preferred to have all the information from Wexhall's letter before telling anyone anything."

"Still good at keeping secrets it would seem," Lord Alwyck said to Nathan. His voice sounded calm, but it was obvious to Victoria by the frigid look in his eyes that he was very angry. "You had no right to keep me in the dark."

Nathan hiked a brow. "Why would you care? It wasn't your reputation that suffered."

"Perhaps because I was shot during the failure of the mission the last time out. Or had you forgotten?"

A tension-laden silence filled the air. Victoria pressed her lips together to prevent herself from spewing any nervous babble to fill the void. A muscle jerked in Nathan's jaw, and she noted his hands were clenched.

"No, I hadn't forgotten," he said in a flat tone. He turned toward Victoria, and she stilled at the utterly bleak look in his eyes. A curtain then seemed to fall over his expression, leaving complete blankness where only seconds ago shadows and pain and regret had dwelled.

"You read the note, examined it, did you not?" he asked her tersely.

"Yes."

"Good. You'll come with me to the house and write down everything you can remember while I compose a letter to your father. *Now.*" Without waiting for a reply or so much as glancing at his brother or Lord Alwyck, he turned on his heel and strode toward the house.

Lord Alwyck muttered something that contained the words "rude" and "autocratic," then said aloud, "It appears you need an escort to the house, Lady Victoria. May I have the honors?"

Victoria yanked her gaze from Nathan's retreating back and noted that Lord Alwyck's eyes still reflected anger, while Lord Sutton stared after his brother with a troubled expression. "Thank you, but I don't wish to delay your ride. If you will both excuse me . . ." She hurried away before either gentleman could stop her.

Walking as swiftly as she could without resorting to running, Victoria tried to settle her jumbled emotions before she faced Nathan again. Part of her felt horribly guilty that her actions had led to the destruction of the note. Another part of her itched with irritation at Nathan for the dictatorial manner in which he'd flung commands at her. Good Lord, one minute the man was kissing her—

She cut off that thought immediately. This was no time to think about that kiss. That mind numbing, glorious, dazzling kiss—

Enough. Later. She would think on it later. Right now she was annoyed with him for tossing orders at her as if he were a general and she a lowly foot soldier. But tempering her annoyance was the deep pull of sympathy she'd felt right down to her core when she witnessed that flash of desolation in his eyes. The depth of the naked pain she'd seen had shaken her and filled her with an overwhelming urge to wrap her arms around him, to offer him comfort from whatever had caused that look. How was it that she wished to simultaneously cuddle and cosh him? The man roiled her emotions in a way no one else ever had. And she was quite certain that she didn't like it one bit.

When she entered the house through the French windows leading to the terrace, a footman greeted her. "Dr. Nathan asked that you please meet him in the library, my lady." He cleared his throat. "He specified that I should stress the word 'please.'"

In spite of herself, Victoria's lips twitched. "Thank you."

"He said that you would no doubt wish to change clothes first, and that he'd arranged for a meal to be sent to your bedchamber."

Victoria couldn't hide her surprise at his show of thoughtfulness. Of course she'd had every intention of changing her clothes before joining him, but a private meal would be most welcome.

"Please tell Dr. Oliver I will join him as soon as I have eaten and made myself presentable."

"Yes, my lady."

Victoria hurried to her bedchamber. When she looked in the cheval glass, she gasped. Good Lord, her hair resembled a bird's nest. But it wasn't the disheveled state of her coiffure that stunned her as much as her face. Pink stained her cheeks and the bridge of her nose, a souvenir from not wearing her bonnet on such a sunny day, which would no doubt cause her to skin to freckle. Her eyes appeared huge and . . . glowing. And her lips . . .

She leaned closer to the glass and tentatively touched her fingertips to them. There was only one way to describe her reddened, swollen mouth: thoroughly kissed. Her eyes slid closed and in a heartbeat the thoughts she'd tried to hold at bay invaded her mind. The dizzying way he'd held her, touched her, the thrilling hardness of his body pressing into her, the delicious feeling of running her hands over his strong torso and back. In spite of all she'd learned from reading the *Ladies' Guide,* never in her life had she imagined what she'd shared with Nathan in the cave. He said he'd been curious to discover whether the second time around could be even better than the first. She wouldn't have believed it possible that the magic he'd introduced her to three years ago could be surpassed, but it had been. And God help her, she hadn't wanted him to stop.

Straightening, she scowled at her reflection. "Be careful of this man and do not underestimate him," she whispered to the wide-eyed woman staring back at her. The plan was to make herself unforgettable to him—not the other way around. If she and Nathan were to share another kiss, she would make certain it was on her terms.

That decided, Victoria opted not to ring for Winifred, knowing that the sharp-eyed abigail would instantly note her unsettled manner and kiss-swollen lips. Instead, she simply removed her riding habit, used the basin to freshen up, then set about detangling her hair. After arranging the unruly curls into a simple Grecian knot, she donned her favorite pale blue muslin day gown. She'd just slid her feet into the matching slippers when a knock sounded on the door.

At her bid to come in, a smiling young maid entered,

bearing a silver tray that she set on the cherrywood table next to the bed. An enticing aroma floated from beneath the dome-covered dishes, and Victoria's stomach rumbled in anticipation. "It smells wonderful."

"One of Cook's specialties, my lady. A rich hearty stew made from an assortment of local seafood. Cook made it especially for Dr. Nathan, as it's his favorite."

Considering the fact that Nathan refused to eat the animals given to him as payment, it didn't surprise her that his favorite meal was fish. After the maid withdrew, Victoria dipped her spoon in the rich mixture and sampled a bit of broth with a small chunk of flaky white fish. She had to fight the urge to roll her eyes in ecstasy. She'd never tasted anything so delicious. Two fluffy rolls accompanied her stew, and she used them to soak up the last drops of the savory meal. Clearly the sea and salt air affected her appetite, for she couldn't recall enjoying a meal more. Indeed, she looked into the empty bowl and heaved a forlorn sigh.

Laying aside her linen napkin, she made her way to the foyer, where Langston escorted her to the library.

Victoria stood in the doorway and allowed her gaze to wander around the well-appointed room. Sunlight poured in from the floor-to-ceiling windows that lined the center half of the back wall, the sparkling glass flanked by dark wood bookcases filled with leather-bound volumes. A huge desk stood in front of the windows, catching the natural light. Another full wall of bookcases soared from the floor to the twenty-foot ceiling, delighting Victoria and filling her with the urge to explore the wondrous room. The cheerful blaze burning in the grate of a huge marble fireplace occupied the opposite wall, bathing the room in gentle warmth. A blue and maroon Axminster rug covered the floor, and overstuffed chairs were placed in cozy groupings around the room. The brocade settee angled in front of the fireplace beckoned one to curl up with a favorite book. She breathed in and briefly closed her eyes at the familiar and much-loved scents of leather, aged parchment, and beeswax. When she opened her eyes, she realized she was alone. Where was Nathan?

Deciding to sit while she waited, she crossed to the fireplace. As she rounded the settee, she halted. Nathan's mastiff, B.C., lounged on his side on the hearth rug, his body taking up the entire length, canine snores emitting from his snout. What had Nathan said B.C. stood for? Boot chewer? Behemoth Canine was more apt, if you asked her. Never in her life had she seen such a tremendous dog.

Just then the beast's nose twitched, as if he'd caught the scent of something. His eyes blinked open, and heavens, for such a large animal, he was very fast, on his feet in seconds, staring at her—hopefully not as if she were a savory pork chop.

"Nice doggie," Victoria murmured, taking a cautious step back. "Nice big huge doggie. Go back to sleep."

Instead B.C. walked slowly toward her. Recalling from some distant childhood lesson that one shouldn't run from a dog, as it encouraged them to chase you, and praying that Nathan had been correct when he'd said the beast was gentle, Victoria remained perfectly still. B.C. halted in front of her. After giving her gown a nose twitching sniff, he sat on his bottom, then lifted his massive right forepaw toward her.

Victoria blinked. "Shaking hands are you? But, er, we've already met." Clearly B.C. didn't care, because he kept his paw extended. Praying this wasn't a precursor to chewing off her arm, she hesitantly reached out and shook his paw. The instant she released him, he stood and bumped her hip with his muzzle. Then he pushed his cool, damp nose against her wrist and licked the back of her hand with a tongue that was larger than her shoe.

She gave his head a tentative stroke then scratched behind his dark ears. This set up an immediate tail wagging that threatened to sweep an end table clear of its Staffordshire vase. "Ah, so that's what you like," Victoria murmured, continuing to scratch while moving around to sit on the settee in an effort to save the vase's life. B.C. followed her, and once she was seated, her other hand joined in. With her seated and B.C. standing, they were just about on eye level with each other. She scratched vigorously, and laughed at the dog's rapturous reaction. His tail wagged, tongue lolled, and a blissful humming sound rumbled in his throat.

"Why, you only *look* like a big, ferocious dog," she scolded with a laugh, moving her ministrations down to the straight, coarse coat on B.C.'s fawn neck. "Inside you're just a little sweet puppy."

B.C. grunted and moaned, as if to say, "Finally . . . someone who understands me!"

So engrossed was she in rubbing down the dog, she didn't realize she was no longer alone until a familiar deep voice said, "I see you've made a new friend."

Victoria turned. Nathan stood in the doorway, one shoulder casually propped against the jamb, his arms folded across his chest. He regarded her with his usual unreadable expression.

"Are you speaking to me or the dog?" Victoria asked, continuing to rub B.C., her words slightly breathless—due to her exertions, of course.

"You, but clearly the statement could apply to either of

you." He pushed off from the doorway and walked toward her. "He likes you."

She sent him an arch look. "You needn't sound so surprised."

"Actually, I am."

"Why, thank you. I can't recall ever hearing a more delightful compliment. Truly."

"I meant it as one. B.C. is normally more reserved with strangers."

"Perhaps because strangers tend to be reserved with him? His size *is* intimidating, you know."

"I suppose so. You realize that he'll now want you to rub him like that every time he sees you. In fact, I'd wager that he'd give you a fortnight to stop it."

"A fortnight?" She smiled. "And then what?"

"Oh, then he'd get very nasty and probably smother you with wet dog kisses." He halted next to the sofa, then reached down to pat B.C.'s back. "You like all this attention, boy?"

B.C. barked. "That means yes," Nathan translated. His glance slid over her, and warmth that had nothing to do with her vigorous rubbing of the dog crept up her neck. "You changed your clothes. Fixed your hair."

"I thought it best. Otherwise B.C. might have been tempted to bury me in the garden. As it was, I think my hideous hair situation scared five years from your footman's life."

"Not at all. Everyone looks like that after a windy day on the beach."

She refrained from pointing out that *he* hadn't looked hideous. On the contrary, he'd looked utterly masculine and devastatingly attractive. Like a tall, ruggedly handsome pirate, his dark hair windblown from the sea air. She noted that he'd changed his clothes as well, donning a fresh linen shirt and midnight blue breeches. He'd again forgone a cravat, and her gaze settled on the golden tanned column of his throat. He was completely out of fashion—indeed, some circles would label his attire as scandalous. But even so, she couldn't deny that she very much liked that tantalizing glimpse of his skin.

"Your hair wasn't hideous, by the way."

His voice jerked her from her rapt contemplation of his throat and her gaze flew upward to see him studying her hair. Warmth rushed through her and a shaky laugh pushed from between her lips. "You're right. Horrifying is probably a more apt description."

He shook his head. "No. That's not the word I would use at all."

She drew in an exaggerated breath. "All right, I've braced myself. What word *would* you use?"

His gaze met hers. "Exquisite."

That single softly spoken word stunned her. Before she could even think of a reply, he gave B.C. a final firm pat then rose. Striding toward the desk, he said, "I've set out vellum, a pen, and ink for you."

"Th-Thank you," she said, keeping her attention on the dog while she struggled to regain her balance, which Nathan had so effectively shifted. "And thank you for the meal you had sent to my bedchamber."

"Did you enjoy the stew?"

"It was delicious. I gobbled it down with embarrassing gusto."

"There's no need to be embarrassed with me, Victoria. Ever."

Those huskily spoken words jerked up her gaze and

their eyes met. "The sea and salt air tend to increase one's hunger," he said. "Personally, I admire a woman who isn't afraid to indulge her appetite."

Victoria suddenly wasn't so certain they were still discussing meals. And no doubt in two days' time she would think up some witty response. Now, however, her mind remained stubbornly blank.

"I suppose it's too much to hope that you remember much of the letter?"

Letter? She blinked and recalled herself, clearing her throat. "Actually, since I studied it at length, I believe I'll be able to reproduce it quite accurately."

"Excellent. Shall we get started?"

"Of course." After a final scratch to her new friend, Victoria rose and crossed to the desk. B.C., she noted with a smile, trotted along at her heels.

"I've never seen such a large desk," she said, running her fingers over the smooth walnut surface and the polished brass fittings adorning the edge. "It actually looks like two desks joined at the front."

"That's precisely what it is. It's called a partners desk and is for two people so they can work while facing each other. It's very convenient for my father when he's going over accounts with his steward." He pulled out a maroon leather chair. Victoria sat and murmured her thanks as he pushed in the chair for her, all the while keenly aware of his nearness. With his one hand resting on the back of the chair and his other on the leather arm, she felt surrounded by him. She turned her head, intending to indicate she was quite well settled, and found herself staring directly at the front of his breeches, which were no more than a foot away.

Oh, my. She stared, transfixed, her avid gaze riveted on his muscular thighs and his . . .

Oh, my my my.

Heat whooshed through Victoria as if her gown had been set afire, and her imagination flamed out of control. Even though the *Guide* had described in detail that which his breeches covered, she still couldn't quite fully picture it in her mind. And here, literally right before her very eyes, was what clearly appeared to be a perfect specimen. If only his blasted breeches didn't thwart her view—

"Are you ready, Victoria?"

She snapped her chin up and found him watching her with a speculative look—one that left little doubt that he was fully aware she'd been ogling his . . . that which his breeches covered. More heat, this time from mortification, rushed into her face. "Ready?" she repeated, horrified that her voice came out in weak squeak.

"To replicate my note . . . unless there's some other activity in which you'd prefer to engage?"

His tone was innocence itself, but his eyes glittered in a way that flared a scorching blush all the way to the soles of her feet.

"Replicate. Note. Right." She grabbed the quill pen as if it were a lifeline tossed to a drowning victim and bent her head over the vellum.

He made a noise that sounded suspiciously like a laugh disguised as a cough, and she pressed her lips together to stem the tide of nervous babble that rose in her throat. Good lord, this would never do. What on earth was wrong with her? She felt as if she teetered on a slippery ledge and was about to lose her balance and plunge over the edge. Never before had she felt so utterly lacking in poise. Since she didn't have any problem talking to other gentlemen, clearly this unusual behavior was all *his* fault. Well, the sooner she completed the task before her, the sooner she could depart his unsettling company.

Yet as soon as the idea entered her mind, she realized that the thought of departing his company did not in any way settle her. Rather, the prospect left her . . . forlorn. Good lord, she'd taken leave of her senses. She dared not voice these concerns out loud lest she be relegated to Bedlam.

Peeking up from beneath her lashes, she saw him sit in a leather chair identical to her own on the opposite side of the desk. Four feet of polished walnut separated them, certainly enough of a buffer, yet she was painfully aware that she had only to reach out to touch his hands.

His hands . . . for a woman who had never before taken particular notice of any man's hands, she suddenly found herself fascinated by his. Large and long-fingered, they looked capable, steady, and strong. The perfect hands, she imagined, for a doctor. The sun had tanned his skin, yet lightened the dusting of hair to a tawny gold. Although she couldn't see his palms, she knew they bore the calluses of physical labor, something she shouldn't have found appealing, yet did. Despite their size and strength, she knew his hands could be gentle . . . magically so, as he'd proven when he slowly sifted his fingers through her hair. Brushed his fingertips over her lips. Yet they could also be demanding . . . thrillingly so, as he'd demonstrated when he held her tight against him. Explored her curves and—

Good heavens, her thoughts had once again run amok. Yanking her attention back to the blank ivory vellum, she dipped the pen tip in the well of indigo ink and forced herself to concentrate on the letter she'd studied so thoroughly last night. The salutation rose in her mind: *To my very good friend Nathan . . .* and she set to work. She paused occasionally, closing her eyes to summon an image of the letter when a word proved elusive. Nathan, she noted, busily scratched his pen across his own vellum.

Nathan paused in writing his letter to Victoria's father to consider his next sentence. All thoughts of words, however, fled his mind when he looked across the desk at Victoria. Her eyes were closed, a frown puckered between her brows. His gaze was drawn to the way she worried her full bottom lip between her teeth, and instantly he recalled the bewitching feel of that plump mouth beneath his. When her tongue peeked out to moisten her lips, he found himself mimicking the gesture, vividly recalling the luscious taste of her, then profoundly wishing this blasted desk didn't separate them. Still, he had only to reach out to touch her hands, and he suddenly found himself gritting his teeth in an effort to keep himself from doing just that.

When had he ever been so drawn to a woman's *hands*? The simple truth was he hadn't. Indeed, his absorption with Victoria's bordered on the ridiculous. They were the lily white hands of a pampered aristocrat. But that pale skin, those slim fingers, enthralled him, and he didn't need to search very hard for the reason. It was because he knew how gentle those hands could be, how achingly hesitant as she'd tentatively touched him. And how incredible those hands felt brushing over his skin. And how they smelled of roses. And how they could become impatient with want, fisting in his hair as she demanded he kiss her again.

She resumed her writing, and he was helpless to do anything save watch her, unreasonably entranced by the sight of her fingers gripping the quill. As his gaze roamed over her hand, he noted a thin scar near her wrist. Unable to stop himself, he reached out and brushed his fingertip over the inch-long mark. She stilled and her head jerked up. Their eyes met and a rosy blush stained her cheeks. He decided that rose-hued blush was very apt, as she smelled so perfectly of that flower.

He traced the scar again. "How did this happen?"

Her gaze lowered to where his finger stroked her, and he looked down as well. Her pale, slender hand and soft skin contrasted starkly to his darker, rougher skin. Bloody hell, the sight of him touching her aroused him to the point that he had to shift in his seat.

"I cut myself," she murmured in a husky voice.

"How? When?" he asked, slowly caressing her.

"I . . . I was twelve," she said, and he decided he very much liked the breathless way she sounded. "I was digging in mud and unearthed a sharp stone that cut my hand."

"Digging in mud? Fond of gardening, are you?"

"Yes, but I wasn't planting when I was injured."

"What were you doing? Hunting for buried treasure?"

"No. I was making a mud pie."

Nathan pulled his gaze away from their hands to look into her eyes. "A *mud pie*?"

"Yes."

"By mud pie you mean a pie made from mud?"

"I hardly mean a pie made from apples and honey."

"And what would an earl's daughter know about making mud pies?"

She lifted her chin. "Quite a lot actually, as I used to make them frequently. The dirt from the lower gardens at Wexhall Manor was far superior to that in the upper gardens. But the soil near the pond was the best of all."

Nathan shook his head. "I simply cannot imagine you playing in the mud. Getting . . . dirty. Why did you do it?"

She hesitated, then said, "I loved the pies our cook made and I wanted to learn how to bake them. But Mother forbade me from spending time in the kitchens. Therefore I had to pretend."

"You weren't allowed in the kitchens but you were permitted to dig in the mud?"

"No. Mother would have flown into the boughs if she'd found out. Actually, the day I received the cut that left that scar was the day she found out. After I was properly bandaged, Mother treated me to an extremely long-winded lecture on the proper decorum of young ladies—one part of which is that they never, *ever* make mud pies."

"And did you ever make another one?"

Her lips twitched and a whiff of mischief crept into her eyes. "Hmmm. I'm not certain I should answer that question."

"Why not?"

"You might well be scandalized. Besides, I'd hate to dispel your exalted opinion of me as a hothouse-flower earl's daughter who would never deign to dirty her hands in the mud."

"After the things I've seen in my profession, I assure you, nothing could scandalize me. And as you've already managed to poke a number of holes in my perception of you, you might as well poke another."

"Very well. Yes, I did make more mud pies. Many more. Mother never found out, and those hours I spent pretending to be the finest baker in all of England were amongst the happiest of my childhood."

An image of her preparing her culinary mud delights popped into his mind, bringing with it a warm feeling he couldn't put a name to. "Did you ever learn how to bake a real pie?"

She gave a short laugh. "No. It was merely a silly childhood wish."

Nathan studied her for several seconds, then said, "Just when I think I've pinpointed the sort of person you are, I discover something else about you, such as a fondness for mud pies, that . . ." *Enchants me. Bewitches and beguiles me. Intrigues and fascinates me.* ". . . surprises me."

"I could say the same about you—except for the mud pies, of course. Unless you were fond of them yourself?"

"I'm afraid not. Not that I didn't relish getting dirty at every opportunity, but growing up near the sea, it was always sand castles for me."

Her eyes sparkled with interest. "A castle made from sand? The sort of castle a princess would live in?"

"Good God, no. The sort fearless warriors resided in as they prepared for battle." He looked up at the ceiling with an air of exaggerated manly exasperation. "Princesses. Heaven help us."

"Well, if I were to build a castle from sand," she said with a haughty sniff, "it would be for a princess."

He couldn't help but grin. "This does not surprise me, what with you being so very *girlish.*"

"I suppose I cannot help that, as, since it has apparently escaped your notice, I *am* a girl." She shook her head and made a *tsking* sound. "For a spy, you really are shockingly unobservant."

Her gaze dropped and he looked down, as she was, at their hands. His finger still brushed lightly over the faint scar. He wanted nothing more at that moment than to lift her hand and press his lips to that mark. Something strange happened to the area around his heart, a weak sensation that felt as if the moorings holding it in place in his chest shifted. Damn it, he'd noticed she was a girl. The instant he'd set eyes on her three years ago. Only now she was no longer a girl, but a woman. A beautiful, desirable woman. And every nerve and cell in his body was screamingly, achingly aware of that fact.

She cleared her throat, then gently slid her hand away from his to dip her quill tip in the ink. "You say you wish me to replicate your letter, Dr. Oliver, yet you've distracted me from doing so. I'd best return to the task." She bent her head over her vellum.

He'd distracted *her*? Damn it, *she* was the distracting one. "Nathan," he said, a note of irritation creeping into his voice.

She looked up only with her eyes. "I beg your pardon?"

"You called me Dr. Oliver. I prefer simply Nathan."

She nodded. "Very well. May I *now* return to this task which you set me upon?"

"Yes," he said, feeling inexplicably annoyed. She applied herself to her writing, and Nathan forced himself to do the same, and pretended he didn't know she was close enough to touch.

Eleven

As most gentlemen are fond of gambling, Today's Modern Woman should take advantage of, or create, an opportunity to issue her gentleman a wager with a reward for the winner—but not money. No, a much more enticing prize is a kiss. Not only would both parties then win, but that kiss could lead to even more interesting rewards.

A Ladies' Guide to the Pursuit of Personal Happiness and Intimate Fulfillment
by Charles Brightmore

*A*fter rereading the note she'd written for a final time, and satisfied that she'd reproduced it verbatim, Victoria set down her quill and looked up to discover Nathan's intense gaze resting upon her.

"I've finished," she said, hating the breathless edge to her voice. She slid the vellum toward him. Reaching out, he turned the page so he could read it.

"How accurate do you think this is?" he asked, scanning the words.

"I'm confident it's an exact duplicate. I read the original

dozens of time last evening, examining each sentence closely. The wording was memorable to me because it was . . . unusual. Stilted. If I hadn't known the letter was from my father, I never would have believed it. I've often helped him with his social correspondence, and nothing has ever read like that letter." She frowned. "And the contents were so strange. Father has absolutely no interest in art, yet he goes on and on about a painting. If you give me another piece of vellum, I'll try to duplicate the drawing that was sketched at the bottom of the note."

His head snapped up. "Drawing?"

"Yes. Supposedly a rendition of the painting he wrote about. Based on the sketch he'd done, the painting is quite hideous."

"Why didn't you mention this before?"

"You didn't ask me before."

Muttering something under his breath that sounded less than complimentary, he pulled open a drawer in the desk, then pushed a new piece of vellum toward her.

"Thank you," she said primly, then set to work. A half hour later, after much thought, concentration, and toil, she pushed the vellum back toward him. "There you are."

He flipped the page around and scowled at it. "What the devil is that supposed to be?"

"I presume it is the landscape that he believed you might be interested in acquiring, although why on earth you would want such an ugly painting that consists of nothing more than a mass of untidy squiggles is beyond me."

He looked up from the drawing and pinned her with his gaze. "This is *exactly* what it looked like? The same size, the same number of squiggles, all the same length?"

"As near as I can recall. I fear I'm not an artist."

"An understatement if ever I've heard one."

She shot him a potent glare. "Even if I were Da Vinci himself, I fear I did not pay as much attention to the drawing as I did to the body of the letter itself. Do you recognize the painting?"

"No, but that isn't surprising. Clearly what your father drew, under the guise of a painting, was a map, one that would presumably contain the location of the jewels."

"Really?" A sense of excitement trilled through her. "Are you merely guessing because hidden maps are the sort of things spies do, or do you know for certain?"

"Hidden maps are our forte, of course," he said in a dry tone, "but I know for certain based on what I've decoded from your father's letter."

She leaned across the desk. "You've deciphered the note? So quickly? How did you figure it out? Will you show me how you did it? What does it say?"

His lips twitched at the barrage of questions. "Yes, I've deciphered it. I figured it out so quickly because not only was decoding my specialty, but I am unsurpassedly brilliant."

"Hmmm. I don't believe 'unsurpassedly' is a word, Dr. Brilliant."

He waved his hand. "It should be. As for showing you how I did it, I fear I cannot, for it quite clearly states in the Official Spy Handbook that a spy cannot, under any circumstances, no matter how he might be coaxed or tortured or kissed, reveal any code used by the Crown."

"Coaxed, tortured, or *kissed*?"

He heaved a heavy sigh. "It was all in the line of duty, I assure you. As for what the note said . . ." His voice trailed off and his expression sobered.

"What is it?" she asked, a fissure of dread snaking down her spine.

For an answer, he pushed a piece of vellum toward her. "This is the decoded message."

Victoria pulled the note closer and read the neatly written words.

Finally located Baylor. French found him first, he was near death. Gave unexpected information about jewels. That same night attack attempted on me. Believe this attempt related to another case. Am fine but want Victoria far away from me for her safety. Entrusting her to you. Don't allow her to leave there until directed. This is map Baylor sketched. He said it was rock formation that showed jewel's location on your property. Find jewels, get them to me, and we'll clear your name. Be safe. Keep my girl safe.

Her heart thumped in slow, painful beats and she looked up at him. "Do you know if my father truly is unharmed?" she asked, proud that her voice remained steady.

He studied her for several seconds before replying. "Truly? No. He claims he's fine, and I know your father, Victoria. He is the most resourceful man I know. Over the years, he has weathered several attacks against him."

She actually felt the blood drain from her face. "If you're hoping to reassure me of his safety, you aren't doing a very good job."

"I'm being honest with you. He knows how to take care of himself. Since he didn't indicate he'd been hurt, I'm sure he wasn't."

"How do I know this is actually what he'd coded into the note? That you haven't left something out?"

His gaze seemed to bore right through her. "You don't. If you continue with your insistence on helping me, I suppose you'll just have to trust me."

Trust him? A spy? A man who made his living by telling elaborate lies? A man who was no doubt searching for a way to find his cache of jewels without her? A man who could adversely affect her self-control with a mere look? A man who'd proven he would take advantage of being alone with her? She'd be mad to trust him. Yet . . . there was something about him that inspired confidence and faith. And as for being alone with her, well, her conscience demanded that she admit she'd taken just as much advantage of that situation as he had. And apparently her father thought him trustworthy. Surely he wouldn't entrust her care to him otherwise.

Heat crawled through her from his intent regard, and she dropped her gaze to the note. "How on earth did you decipher this message from Father's letter?"

"I told you, I am unsurpassedly brilliant."

"You mean your brilliance is unsurpassed."

"Why thank you."

"Who is this Baylor?"

"A man for hire, and he wasn't particular about who hired him—us or the French. He played both sides and gave his information to the highest bidder. He was one of the craftiest, most unscrupulous men I've ever run across. When I resigned from my service to the Crown, Baylor was being sought by the French and English alike."

"How did he have information about the jewels? Could he have been involved in their disappearance?"

He shrugged. "Possibly. But Baylor was like a rat,

sneaking around into crevices, ferreting out snippets of information, then selling them to interested parties. He might have come across the information inadvertently and was trying to make a sale when your father found him."

She looked at the drawing she'd made. "That doesn't look like any sort of map I've ever seen."

"You cannot recall anything else?"

She slowly shook her head. "No. I thought it was a picture of tufts of grass, but according to the decoded note, it's a rock formation."

"Yes, but which one? There're dozens on this estate."

"So where do we begin?"

"I'll draw a grid map of the property and we'll search one area at a time. And you're not to discuss this. With anyone."

She raised her brows at his peremptory tone. "What about your brother and Lord Alwyck?"

"No one."

"But why? They already know about the note. They know *I* know about it."

"Because your father requested it." He pointed to two words at the bottom of the note. " 'Be safe' was a secret code between your father and me. It means not to discuss the matter with anyone." His gaze bore into hers. "Unfortunately, with circumstances such as they are, you already know—something your father would not be pleased about, I'm sure. Of course, I'm also certain he wouldn't be thrilled to know that since your arrival in Cornwall you've resorted to kidnapping and blackmail."

"I've done no such thing!"

"Really? What would you call holding my letter hostage and demanding I accept your assistance before you'd return it to me?"

Victoria lifted her chin. "If I'd done anything less, I'd have once again been relegated to the corner with an indulgent pat on the head. As a Modern Woman, I refuse to be treated like that any longer."

"Bravely spoken words. However, you might want to keep such declarations under your bonnet once you return to London. I doubt either of your potential fiancés would be happy to hear them. Most likely the prospect of taking a Modern Woman for their wife would put them off the hunt."

Refusing to rise to his bait, she asked, "Why do you suppose Father requested secrecy, even from your brother and Lord Alwyck?"

An odd look passed over his face. "I've no way of knowing what was in his mind. Perhaps he suspects that someone in this area—including my brother or Gordon, or perhaps both of them—were somehow involved in the jewels' disappearance."

Victoria stared. "Do you think they were involved?"

"No." The word came out sharply, and he raked his hand through his hair. "No," he repeated in a milder tone, "but the point is, I wasn't to discuss this with anyone, so now I must have your promise that you will not do so."

"What if Lords Sutton or Alwyck specifically ask me?"

"Hmmm. Yes, that could present a problem. Best you avoid their company whenever possible. Pity, especially as they both seemed quite taken with you."

She couldn't tell if he was serious or jesting. "Avoid the company of two handsome, eligible men, especially when they both, as you say, seemed quite taken with me? I'm not enamored of that idea at all. Even if I were, given that I'm a guest in your family's home and Lord Alwyck is clearly a frequent visitor here, I couldn't very well avoid them entirely."

"Then if asked, change the subject," he said, sounding testy. "Claim the headache. Or the vapors. Lay your hand across your brow and call weakly for your hartshorn."

Insufferable man. Oh, he was attractive and sinfully well-versed in the art of kissing, but insufferable nonetheless. Before she could firmly inform him that she wasn't prone to headaches or the vapors, voices sounded in the corridor.

"I'll have your word not to mention this, Victoria." His voice was a low, deep command.

"Very well. Consider my lips sewn closed."

His gaze dropped to her mouth. "Now that would be a dreadful waste," he murmured, so softly she wasn't even certain he'd said the words. Before she could decide, he gathered the papers and slipped them from the desk. Seconds later a smiling Aunt Delia sailed through the open library doorway, followed by Nathan's father. "I cannot *believe* the duke would say such a scandalous—"

Her aunt's animated words cut off when she saw Nathan and Victoria. "There you both are," she said, heading straight for the desk. "I've the most wonderful news."

That would explain the rosy tint staining her aunt's cheeks, the glow in her eyes, and her wide smile. Aunt Delia loved nothing more than imparting news.

"While Lord Rutledge and I were returning from our stroll in the garden, we came across Lord Alwyck, who was returning to his estate," Aunt Delia said. "He has invited us all to dine with him this evening at Alwyck Hall. Isn't that marvelous? You simply must wear your new aqua gown, Victoria. You'll want to look your best, and the color is exquisite on you." She turned to Nathan. "You should see her in aqua, Dr. Oliver. It's a sight to behold."

Heat flared in Victoria's cheeks. Good Lord, what on earth was Aunt Delia saying?

"I shall count the hours," Nathan said solemnly, "although I'm certain that Lady Victoria wears every color well. As would you, Lady Delia."

A noise that could only be described as a girlish giggle came from Aunt Delia, and Victoria stared at her aunt in amazement. "Why, thank you, Dr. Oliver."

Nathan's father cleared his throat. "Speaking of attire . . ." he shot a pointedly raised brow at Nathan's lack of a jacket and cravat.

Nathan pushed back his chair and rose. "If you will all excuse me, I have some correspondence—"

"And a cravat," his father intoned.

"—to attend to. I'll see you all this evening." He bowed, then strode toward the door, the vellum papers now folded over in one hand.

This evening? Victoria watched him leave the room with the letter and map and wondered exactly what he planned to do between now and then.

Nathan sat in Gordon's drawing room after dinner and tried to concentrate on the inlaid chessboard set between him and his father, but his attention was focused on the same thing it had been all through the interminable evening.

Victoria.

The torture had commenced three hours and seventeen minutes ago—the instant he'd seen her walking down the stairs toward the foyer where he stood, alone, waiting for the rest of the group to gather to travel to Gordon's estate. Dressed in a pale aqua muslin gown with short, puffed sleeves and a low, square-cut neckline, her shiny curls twined with ribbon and arranged in a becoming Grecian knot, she moved slowly and gracefully down the wide staircase, as if gliding on air, like a gorgeous sea nymph from a Botticelli painting. She was precisely what her aunt had said she'd be. A sight to behold.

Their gazes met, and she hesitated on the steps, one gloved hand gracefully holding the oak banister while her other hand settled on her stomach, as if to calm a sudden fluttering there. Was it similar to the bewildering commotion the sight of her set up in his own stomach? Although he'd never considered himself a fanciful man, he swore that in that instant something passed between them. Something warm and intimate, and certainly on his part filled with a longing he could neither explain nor deny.

He watched her draw a slow, deep breath, his gaze drawn to the delicate hollow at the base of her throat, which deepened as she inhaled . . . that fascinating bit of vulnerable skin he knew felt like a swatch of velvet and was scented with the hint of roses. She blinked several times, breaking the spell that seemed to have been cast between them. She then resumed her descent, but had taken no more than two steps when Colin spoke softly from directly behind him. "Exquisite, isn't she?"

Nathan forced his posture to remain casual, but didn't bother to turn around. He didn't want to see the stark admiration he knew would be evident in Colin's gaze. And he refused to give Colin the opportunity to see the stark longing he suspected still lingered in his own gaze. "Exquisite," he murmured in agreement, as it was fruitless to deny anything so obvious.

"Pity she has those suitors in London," Colin whispered. "Of course, I wouldn't let that stop me."

Nathan turned around at that. Colin was staring up the staircase with an expression of rapt fascination.

"Stop you from what?" Nathan asked through clenched teeth.

"From going after what I wanted." He shifted his gaze from Victoria to Nathan. "And making certain I acquired it." With that, he stepped around Nathan and moved to the bottom of the stairs. Extending his hand toward Victoria, who'd nearly reached the bottom, Colin said, "Lady Victoria, how lovely you look."

It was not a promising beginning to the evening.

The torture had then continued during the carriage ride to Gordon's estate. Victoria had sat between her aunt and Colin, while Nathan and his father sat opposite the trio. Colin spent the entire ride regaling the group with some story about what, Nathan had no idea, other than to guess it was apparently quite humorous based on the ensuing laughter. No, he'd been too busy trying—with no success whatsoever—not to notice Victoria smiling at Colin. Her melodic laugh at something he said. The way Colin's thigh was pressed against hers in the close confines of the carriage. How his shoulder brushed hers with every bump in the road.

His stomach had clenched with an unpleasant sensation that couldn't be called anything other than what it was: jealousy. It had been some time since he'd experienced the emotion, and he wasn't happy that it was snaking through him now. And he especially didn't like that it was his brother inspiring these envious feelings. While he couldn't deny that he and Colin had occasionally competed while growing up, as brothers were wont to do, they'd rarely done so over anything other than racing their horses or a backgammon board, as their interests were so different. They'd never competed over a woman, as their tastes differed greatly in that area as well. Colin had always preferred aristocratic women, while Nathan's tastes ran more toward women who didn't put on Society's airs. He was attracted to women whose interests reached beyond fashion, gossip, and the weather. In truth, he'd always preferred to spend an evening conversing with a homely bluestocking than engaging in small talk with the most beautiful woman in the room.

Until now, it seemed.

Victoria, with her lofty position in Society and all that entailed, her expensive clothing, her beauty, her numerous suitors who undoubtedly hung on her every word, epitomized the exact opposite of the sort of woman he preferred. Yet, he couldn't take his eyes off her. Couldn't stop thinking about her. Couldn't squelch the remembrance of kissing her. Touching her. Couldn't control the deep ache of want and lust she inspired.

The torture hadn't lessened at all during dinner—in fact it worsened with the addition of Gordon, who was also clearly besotted with Victoria. And she seemed extremely flattered by his regard. While she basked in the glow of the attention both Colin and Gordon showered upon her, Nathan's father and Lady Delia kept up a lively discussion between themselves, leaving Nathan with a great deal of time to observe everyone and eat a meal that he supposed was delicious but tasted like sawdust.

And naturally the torture had continued when, after the interminable meal, the group retired to the drawing room for games. Nathan had been sorely tempted to fabricate an excuse to depart, but after Victoria, her aunt, Colin, and Gordon decided to play whist, Nathan's father had invited him to share a brandy and a turn at the chessboard. Given the tension between him and his father, the invitation had both surprised and pleased him, and he'd accepted. While he was in no mood for chess, the brandy had sounded extremely welcome, as did the opportunity to perhaps ease the awkwardness between them.

Yet now, working his way through his second brandy, and though he stared at the chessboard, all his attention remained focused on the laughing group across the room. Giving up all hope of concentrating on the game, he moved his rook.

Based on his father's raised brows, he judged he'd made an unwise move, which was proven seconds later when his father said, "You seem to have lost your skill for this game, Nathan."

"Er, not at all. I'm setting an elaborate trap from which you will not escape."

Doubt was written all over his father's face. Another burst of laughter came from across the room, and Nathan's gaze involuntarily shifted to the merry whist players. After he pulled his vision back to his own disastrous game in progress, he noticed that his father's attention remained fixed across the room with a speculative expression.

"Remarkable woman," his father said softly.

Nathan stilled, then barely controlled the urge to look heavenward. It appeared Victoria had made yet another conquest. How bloody delightful. "Remarkable?" he repeated with feigned indifference. "I find her rather . . . tiresome." He again resisted the urge to look heavenward, this time to see if a lightning bolt would smite him for uttering such an outrageous lie.

His father's surprised gaze flicked toward him then resettled again across the room. "I wasn't aware you'd spent enough time in her company to form such an opinion."

As far as his peace of mind was concerned, he'd spent

far too much time in her company, and before her visit to Cornwall was over, he'd be forced to spend much more time with her. And damn it, he couldn't wait.

"One need not spend days or weeks with a person to form an opinion, Father. First impressions tend to be fairly accurate." A frown pulled down Nathan's brow as he realized that his first impression of Victoria had been that she was utterly . . . charming. Too innocent for him, too aristocratic, but charming nonetheless.

"I completely agree," Father said, nodding.

Nathan pulled himself from his brown study. "You agree? With what?"

"What you just said. That it isn't necessary to know someone very long to realize they are . . . special."

"I said *that*?" Good God, he needed to stop drinking brandy. Immediately.

"Perhaps not in those precise words, but that was the idea, yes."

"You might not need to spend much time, but certainly at least a private conversation is necessary, Father."

"Again, I agree. We had a delightful chat this morning in the garden, then again this afternoon over tea. Can't recall the last time I was so delightfully entertained."

Nathan's brows puckered further. "I thought you spent this morning with Lady Delia in the garden."

"And so I did. As I said, a remarkable woman."

Nathan blinked. "You think *Lady Delia* is remarkable?"

His father looked at him strangely. "Yes. What on earth did you think I was saying? Has your hearing become afflicted along with your chess playing ability?"

No, but clearly his mental capabilities were not all they should be. "I thought you were referring to Lady Victoria," he muttered.

Father stared at him hard for several seconds. "I see. A man would have to be blind not to notice that Lady Victoria is comely."

"I never said she wasn't."

"No. You said she was tiresome. Chit doesn't strike me as such. Clearly, neither your brother nor Alwyck find her objectionable, either." He studied Nathan over the rim of his crystal snifter. "Not the sort of woman you used to be attracted to."

Damn it all, when had he turned into a book his father could read so accurately? "I wasn't aware that 'tiresome' was synonymous with 'attracted to,'" Nathan said, keeping his tone light.

"Normally it's not. However, sometimes . . ." Father's voice drifted off, then he added, "A woman of her rank is a much better match for Colin. Or Alwyck."

The bitterness he'd spent years holding at bay twisted Nathan's lips. "As opposed to an untitled second son who is a lowly country physician with a dubious reputation. I wholeheartedly agree."

His father's gaze hardened. "I harbor no objections to your choice of profession. Indeed, being a physician is respectable for a man in your position and far preferable to having you risk your life and your brother's life as a spy. But I neither approve of nor understand the decisions you've made regarding where and how you live and the way you left Cornwall."

Nathan hiked up one brow. "Little Longstone is a quiet, charming place—"

"Where people pay you with farm animals and you live in a shack."

"Cottage. It's a cottage. And not everyone pays me in

farm animals. And if you recall, I left here because you ordered me to go."

A tension-filled silence followed his tersely spoken words. A muscle ticked in his father's jaw, then he replied in a low voice. "Let's be honest, Nathan. Angry words were said on both our parts. Yes, I told you to go, but we both know you're the sort of man who wouldn't do something you didn't want to."

"I'm also not the sort of man to stay where I'm not welcome."

"Face the truth. You wanted to go. To escape the untenable situation your actions caused. I may have told you to leave Creston Manor, but it was *your* decision to run away."

An uncomfortable flush heated Nathan's face. "I've never run away from anything in my entire life."

"I know. That is why I found it, and continue to find it, so confounding that you did so in this instance. Your situation was difficult, yet instead of fighting for what you wanted, you left."

"I left to find what I wanted. What I needed. A peaceful place. Where no one whispered behind my back or stared at me with doubt and suspicion."

Another burst of laughter drew Nathan's attention across the room. Victoria was smiling at Gordon in a way that set Nathan's teeth on edge. Pulling his attention back to his father, he found himself on the receiving end of a troubled stare.

"If you believe a woman such as Lady Victoria will settle for the rustic way you live when she could be a countess and have all this," Father waved his hand to encompass the entire room, "then I fear you are destined for disappointment."

"As I agree that not only am I an unsuitable choice for a

lady like her, but that a pampered Society diamond such as Lady Victoria would be a disastrous choice for me, I do not fear suffering any disappointment. And now that that's settled, shall we resume our game?"

"Of course." Father reached out and moved his bishop. "Checkmate."

Nathan stared at the board and realized that he had indeed been vanquished. He looked across the room and his gaze collided with Victoria's, who was watching him over the fan of her cards. He felt the impact of her regard as if he'd been sucker punched, and he greatly feared he'd been vanquished in more ways than one.

Twelve

*Today's Modern Woman must realize the impor-
tance of fashion in her quest for intimate fulfillment. There are times to wear a fancy ball gown,
times to wear a negligee, and times to wear nothing
at all....*

A Ladies' Guide to the Pursuit of
Personal Happiness and Intimate Fulfillment
by Charles Brightmore

$\mathcal{V}$ictoria left her bedchamber early the next morning
with a determined step and a plan firmly in mind: locate
Nathan and make certain he did not escape as he had from
the library yesterday afternoon and from Lord Alwyck's
drawing room last evening. She'd not had the opportunity
to have a private word with him since he left the library
with the notes and map yesterday, a vexing situation to be
sure. Her heart had leapt and her stomach trembled when
she'd seen him standing in the foyer last evening before
the group departed for Alywck Hall. And certainly not because he looked so dashing and rakishly handsome in his

formal evening wear, or because of the heated, compelling look in his eyes. No, it was because she'd finally have a moment alone with him to find out what he'd been up to all afternoon. Yes, that was why.

But then Lord Sutton had appeared, followed quickly by her aunt and Nathan's father. There'd been no opportunity during the crowded carriage ride nor through dinner and then games in the drawing room, all while she pretended an enthusiasm for the attention both Lord Alywck and Lord Sutton showered upon her when what she actually felt like doing was pulling Nathan into a secluded alcove and kissing him. Er, questioning him.

He'd departed Lord Alwyck's home before the rest of the group, claiming the onset of the headache and stating that he wished to walk home, as fresh air usually helped relieve the condition. Sympathy eased through her, as he had indeed appeared out of sorts, and she'd wondered if his conversation with his father had been the cause. But then sympathy had turned to suspicion. Perhaps the entire headache claim had been a ruse and he'd spent the night out searching for the jewels. He might well be out this minute doing that very thing. Without her. The wretched man. She all but stomped down the corridor and entered the dining room. Then halted.

Or, he might well be in the dining room eating eggs and reading the *London Times*.

He paused with his fork halfway to his mouth and quirked a brow. "Ah, it is you, Victoria. With all that stomping about, I thought perhaps we'd been invaded by marching soldiers."

Oh, how droll. How humorous. And how irritating that she wouldn't think of a cutting set-down until sometime next week. And 'twas even more irritating that he looked so divine. Dressed in a snowy white shirt adorned with an obviously hastily knotted cravat, a cream waistcoat, and a Devonshire brown jacket that bore several wrinkles, he should not have looked so . . . perfect. Especially since his dark hair looked as if he'd combed it with nothing more than impatient fingers. Hmmm . . . what color breeches was he wearing? She found herself rising onto her toes in an effort to answer that question, but the mahogany table thwarted her view. Fawn, most likely, she decided, envisioning his muscular legs encased in light brown. Forcing the image from her mind, she touched her heels back onto the parquet floor.

"It appears we are the only early risers," Nathan said. He nodded toward the sideboard lined with silver warming trays. "Please help yourself. Do you prefer coffee or tea?"

"Coffee, please." The instant the words left her mouth, a young footman jumped into action to serve her beverage. After filling her plate with eggs, thinly sliced ham, and a flaky muffin the mere looks of which set her mouth to watering, she sat down opposite Nathan.

"Did you sleep well?" he asked, raising his china cup to his lips.

"Very well," she lied. She'd spent a miserable night tossing, fretting, alternately wondering if he was searching for the jewels without her and vividly recalling the taste of his kiss, the feel of his hard body pressed against her, wrapped around her. In desperation she'd retrieved the *Ladies' Guide* from her portmanteau, but reading the sexually explicit book had done nothing to calm her. Indeed, the sensual words had only served to further fuel her already heated imagination. "Did *you* sleep well?"

"No."

"Oh? Why not?" *Skulking about in the woods looking for jewels, were you, Lord of the Spies?*

"Do you really want to know, Victoria?"

Something about that silkily asked question and the steady gaze he'd pinned her with tingled a warning along her nerve endings. Pulling off a bit of biscuit, she raised her chin. "Yes, I do."

He nodded at the footman, dismissing the young man. After the door closed behind him, Nathan leaned forward on his forearms, cradling his delicate china cup between his large palms. "I didn't sleep well last night because my mind was too crowded."

"So you were here? In the house?"

"Of course. Where else would I—" His words chopped off and he leaned back. "I see. You thought I was out skulking in the woods, looking for the jewels without you."

His words so precisely mirrored her thoughts, a guilty flush heated her face. "Isn't skulking about in the woods what spies do best?"

"I can't deny it's something I'm good at, but it's not what I do best."

"And what do you do best?"

His gaze dipped to her mouth, then he shot her a mischievous grin. "Ah, an interesting question if I've ever heard one. Are you certain you want to know the answer, Victoria?"

Heat whooshed through her and her toes curled inside her shoes. God help her, yes, she wanted to know. Desperately. Especially since that gleam in his eyes made it clear the answer was something that would leave her breathless. But it wouldn't do to let *him* know that. Indeed, clearly the best way to deal with him was to play his game. Looking directly into his eyes, she asked softly, "Are you offering to tell me, Nathan?"

"Do you always answer a question with a question?"

"Do you?"

He laughed. "Sometimes. Usually when I'm stalling for time. Is that what you're doing?"

"Certainly not," she replied with a sniff.

"As for what I do best, I'd be delighted to tell you. Even more delighted to provide you with a demonstration."

Whoosh. Another wave of heat engulfed her. She attempted her most prim expression but wasn't certain she succeeded, as it was difficult to appear prim while sensual images danced through her mind. "Here? In the dining room?"

"Certainly not the most traditional of locations, but if that is your wish, I'm willing to forgo convention."

An unladylike snort escaped her. "You? Willing to forgo convention? Thank goodness I'm not prone to the vapors lest that statement would send me into a serious decline."

He waved his hand in a magnanimous gesture. "Feel free to succumb. As I am a physician, I could immediately set you back to rights."

"Immediately? So then doctoring is what you do best."

A smile that could only be described as wicked curved his lips. "No. Doctoring is what I do when I'm not doing what I do best."

Oh, my. Surely he didn't mean . . . but, oh yes, based on that devilish grin, he clearly did. Despite the knowledge she'd gained from reading the *Guide*, she suddenly felt woefully unprepared to continue this conversation. In an effort to regain the upper hand, she adopted the chilly tone that never failed to put people in their place. "How delightful for you. Now, what is the plan for today?"

"Plan?"

"To locate the jewels."

"I haven't the vaguest idea."

Victoria laid down her fork. "Haven't the vaguest idea? After thinking about it all night long?"

"What makes you think that pondering the location of the jewels is what filled my thoughts last night?"

"Because it should have been. If I'd lain awake all night it most certainly would have been what *I'd* pondered." Her conscience jumped up and shrieked with outrage. *Liar! You were wide-awake, and maps and jewels were the last thing on your mind!* She suddenly stilled. Was it possible that Nathan had suffered from the same sensual thoughts that had stolen her sleep? If so . . .

Whoosh. Good lord, it was *hot* in here. She barely refrained from fanning herself with her linen napkin.

"Then how unfortunate for our search plans that you slept so well," Nathan said in a dust dry voice. "I did study the drawing and the letter further, but was unable to glean anything more. I also drew the grid map of the estate. I suggest we begin in the northeast corner and work from there. In the letter I sent off to your father yesterday explaining, in code, how you lost the note—"

"You mean how your goat ate the note."

"—I requested that he send another drawing. Unfortunately, given the distances involved, by the time the note reaches him in London and a reply is returned, at least a fortnight will have passed. I'd hoped to have this matter settled by then."

"So you can return to your home in—where is it again? Little Longstone?"

"Yes." He tossed back the last of his coffee. "I'm certain you're anxious for this matter to be settled as well so you can return to London. To your parties and shopping excursions and your suitors. So you can choose your husband and plan an extravagant wedding."

"Yes, that's what I want," she said, a frown burrowing between her brows at the sudden hollow sensation in her stomach. She lifted her chin a notch. "You make it sound as if there is something wrong with that."

"Not at all. If that's what you want . . ." He shrugged.

Warmth crept up Victoria's cheeks. How had he managed to make her feel so . . . shallow? Superficial? Every girl dreamed of fancy parties, shopping sprees, suitors, and her own wedding—didn't she? Certainly all the girls she knew did.

Before she could inform him of that, however, he asked, "Tell me, did either my brother or Gordon question you last evening regarding your replication of the note?"

"Yes. Actually, they both did. After you departed."

"The three of you were together?"

"No. Lord Alwyck asked me when we had a moment alone."

His eyes narrowed. "And how did you happen to have a moment alone?"

Feeling much more in command of the conversation, Victoria enjoyed another bite of eggs before answering. "He gave me a tour of the music room."

"Where was everyone else during this tour?"

"My aunt and your father were engaged in a game of backgammon. Your brother had stepped onto the terrace."

"What did Gordon ask you?"

"How much of the wording of the note I'd been able to remember and how much you'd been able to decipher."

"And your response?"

"As promised, I revealed nothing. I played the part of the forgetful, foolish, giggling female."

"He believed you?"

"Without a doubt. Clearly he is accustomed to the forgetful, foolish, giggling sort."

"And my brother? I take it you found yourself alone with him as well?"

"Briefly, yes. After we arrived back here, as we walked up to the house. I used the same ruse with him."

"His reaction?"

Victoria considered for several seconds, then said, "He clearly believed me as well. But he also seemed rather . . . relieved. Of course, now both gentlemen think me a cabbage-headed nincompoop."

"On the contrary, I'm certain they think you girlishly charming."

"And a cabbage-headed nincompoop," she muttered. "Did they question you?"

"Yes. I told them that as you were a forgetful, foolish, giggling female cabbage-headed nincompoop, any search would be delayed until I heard from your father."

Deciding nothing she said would be pleasant, she applied her full attention to her breakfast. After generously slathering her biscuit with blueberry jam, she took a bite, chewed, then closed her eyes in rapture. "This is the most delicious jam I've ever tasted," she proclaimed, "and that is high praise, as I consider myself something of a connoisseur."

She ate in silence for a moment, then heard Nathan chuckle. "You have a sweet tooth and a hearty appetite, I see."

Heat crept into her cheeks for forgetting herself. She normally breakfasted alone, as Father tended to sleep late and therefore she was accustomed to eating a large meal—something a proper lady wouldn't do in front of a gentleman. "I'm afraid so."

"No need to sound so sheepish. I wasn't criticizing. Indeed, I find watching you eat very . . . stimulating. It inspires me to an idea."

Her ham-laden fork paused halfway to her lips and she looked across the table at him. He was watching her with a speculative look in his eyes while he slowly tapped his lips with the tip of his forefinger. She wasn't sure what idea she'd inspired in him, but the way his lips looked, so soft yet firm beneath his finger, was certainly inspiring *her* to an idea. Several in fact.

"What sort of idea?" she asked, inwardly cringing at how breathless she sounded.

"A picnic. I'll arrange for Cook to prepare a meal we can bring along so we do not need to interrupt our search by returning to eat. How does that sound?"

An entire morning and afternoon spent exploring the countryside in search of a cache of stolen jewels with a man who made her insides simultaneously tingle and tremble? Who excited and frustrated and challenged her as no man ever had? It sounded exhilarating. Exciting. And oh, so very tempting. Her mind issued a cursory caution about being alone with him again, but her heart instantly silenced all objections. She'd wanted an opportunity to kiss him again—on her terms—and he'd just handed her the chance.

And based on her brief conversation with Aunt Delia last night before they'd retired, she needn't worry about her aunt objecting to her riding alone with Nathan. Indeed, her aunt had encouraged her, saying, "Heavens, my dear, enjoy the lovely weather while you can. Just because I don't care for riding doesn't mean you should be deprived. Things are much less formal here than in London. Daylight rides in the country are perfectly respectable."

"That sounds perfect . . . ly acceptable."

"Excellent. I'll make the arrangements with Cook while you change into your riding clothes. Then we'll meet in, shall we say thirty minutes at the stables?"

"Fine."

He touched his napkin to his mouth, then rose. After a bow, he quit the room and Victoria heaved a long, feminine sigh.

His breeches were indeed fawn. And they did indeed fit him very nicely.

Nathan sat on a wooden stool in the massive kitchen, munching on a still warm biscuit, and watched Cook pack items into the worn brown leather saddlebag he'd retrieved from his bedchamber. Memories of other times he'd sat in this exact spot, eating a treat fresh from the oven, stole over him. Growing up, the kitchen had been one of his favorite places in which to escape, not only because of the delicious treats he procured, but because of the thrill of the forbidden—neither he nor Colin were supposed to ever visit the kitchen. Most improper, his father had decreed. But as this was where all the treats were, neither he nor Colin had paid the slightest bit of attention to that dictate.

"Just like old times, eh, Dr. Nathan?" Cook said, a wide grin splitting her jolly features, her round cheeks rosy from the heat of the stove.

He smiled back. Her name was Gertrude, but for the twenty-five years she'd been in charge of Creston Manor's kitchen, she'd simply been Cook.

"I was just thinking that very thing." He inhaled deeply. "Mmmm. I believe this is the best smelling spot in all of England."

There was no mistaking Cook's pleasure at his remark.

"'Course it is. And it's ashamed ye should be for stayin' away for so long. But now yer back and it's a veritable feast I've prepared for you and your young lady."

"She is not my young lady," he said, ignoring the odd tingle those words induced. "She is merely a guest. Who likes to eat. A lot."

"Oh, but that's the best kind of lady, Dr. Nathan. The sort wot don't mind eatin' in front of others and don't put on no airs. Can't abide by these ladies who peck at their food in the dining room then stuff themselves in their bedchamber." She waved her hands and wrinkled her nose. "Bah. False is wot they are. Ye can always tell wot sort of woman yer dealin' with by how she eats. This Lady Victoria has a hearty appetite ye say? Then she's one to keep, ye mark my words."

"She'd be a difficult woman to 'keep.'"

Cook nodded in immediate understanding. "Strong-willed is she?"

"Very. And opinionated."

"Both blessings, to be sure. Ye'd quickly tire of a chit who agreed with you all the time."

"Perhaps. But agreeing with me *once* would certainly be welcome," he muttered.

Cook laughed. "Oh, she's got you right disgruntled, she does."

"Because she is so very irritating." *And lovely. And amusing. And charming. And desirable.*

Cook chuckled and shook her head. "That's exactly what me and my William thought of each other at first. Couldn't decide if we wanted to cosh each other or kiss each other. Can honestly say that in three and twenty years together neither of us have ever been bored."

"And I'm happy for you," Nathan said, reaching for a towel to wipe his fingers. "But as I said, Lady Victoria isn't *my* lady. In fact, the sooner she leaves Cornwall, the better I'll like it."

Cook shrugged, but there was no missing the speculation in her shrewd dark eyes. "'Course you know wot's best for ye." She secured the saddlebag's flap, then pushed the parcel toward Nathan. "There ye go. And I expect it to be empty when ye return."

Nathan lifted the bag then pretended to stagger under its weight. "Empty? That could take a week."

"I doubt it. Ridin' somehow seems to give folks an appetite."

Her voice and expression were all innocence, but Nathan knew her well enough to realize they were anything but. He shot her a mock frown, which she blithely ignored.

"Thank you for arranging the meal," he said, slinging the bag over his shoulder and heading toward the door.

"Yer welcome. Have a pleasant afternoon."

"Doubtful," Nathan grumbled under his breath as he stepped outside. "But at least I won't go hungry."

He strode across the lawn toward the stables, a frown tugging down his brows. Damn it, he felt completely out of sorts, and he didn't like it one bit. His life in Little Longstone was peaceful. His life since he'd arrived in Cornwall was . . . the exact opposite of peaceful. He felt as if he were being pulled in half a dozen directions. His better judgment questioned the wisdom of spending the day with Victoria, but still his heart quickened at the prospect. He knew he should want nothing more to do with her, yet he wanted her with a growing desperation that threatened to overwhelm his common sense. In spite of the fact that his chances of finding the jewels and clearing his name were slim, he still felt compelled to try. And

even though part of him longed to return to Little Longstone, he couldn't deny that he'd missed Creston Manor.
He hadn't realized how strong the impact of being near the
sea and cliffs and caves would hit him. The ache of nostalgia they would invoke.

Shaking off his pensive mood, he looked ahead toward
the stables. To his surprise, he saw Victoria standing next
to the animal pen, her back turned toward him. When he'd
suggested they meet at the stables in thirty minutes, it
hadn't occurred to him that she'd not only be on time, but
early. His heart quickened in that ridiculous way it did
whenever he saw her, as did his footsteps.

She turned then and his steps faltered when he noted
she wasn't alone. No, she was with Petunia. And Victoria
and his goat appeared to be engaged in a tug of war over
what looked like a piece of white material. Undoubtedly
Victoria's handkerchief. Having had several such altercations with Petunia, he well knew who would emerge victo-
rious, and it wouldn't be the woman attempting to yank
that bit of material from a clearly determined goat.

He broke into a run, watching both Victoria and Petunia
dig in. As he neared, he heard Victoria huffing and puffing
with effort. "Not again," she said through gritted teeth,
straining backward. "You stole the note but you'll not
have my favorite handkerchief. Why can't you eat shrubs
like normal goats?"

Nathan set down the saddlebag and started forward.
Petunia caught sight of him and instantly abandoned her
grip on the material and trotted toward him, clearly expecting an even better treat. Fortunately, that freed Victoria's handkerchief. Unfortunately, it also freed Victoria.
With a surprised cry, she stumbled backward and landed
with a resounding plop on her bottom.

Nathan raced forward and dropped to one knee beside her. "Are you all right?"

She turned to him. Crimson stained her cheeks and her skin glistened from her exertions. Her bonnet was askew and one long brunette curl bisected her forehead, resting on the bridge of her nose. Ragged breaths puffed from between her parted lips. Triumph gleamed in her eyes.

"I won." She raised her gloved hand, in which she clutched a wrinkled, non-too-clean linen handkerchief that was missing a piece of lace around one edge.

Relieved that she obviously wasn't hurt, he said, "I'm not certain that the one with the mussed hair and disheveled bonnet and who's sitting on her bottom in the dirt can be declared the winner, but I'll bow to your assessment."

She blew a puff of breath upward to dislodge the curl resting on her nose, but the silky skein resettled itself in the exact same position. "It matters not who is on the ground. She who holds the spoils of war is the victor." She shook her fist gripping the handkerchief for emphasis.

"Are you hurt?"

"Only my pride." She cast a woeful glance at her clenched fist. "But I fear my handkerchief is grievously injured."

"What on earth were you doing?"

She turned back toward him and hoisted a brow. "Was it not obvious? I was attempting to rescue my property from that four-legged handkerchief thief."

"How did she manage to get it in the first place?"

"She sneaked up on me. I was feeding bits of bread to your ducks when I felt something nudge me. When I turned, your goat was chewing my handkerchief."

"An animal that weighs at least *ten stone* sneaked up on you?"

She raised her chin and shot him a haughty look. "She's shockingly quiet for one her size."

"Why were you feeding the ducks? I thought you didn't like . . . what did you call my animals? Oh yes, farm beasts."

"I never said I didn't like *ducks*. I said I didn't care for animals that outweigh me. Both your ducks, you'll notice, are considerably smaller than me."

"Where did you get the bread?"

"From the dining room."

"I see. So you pilfered food from my family home then attempted to bribe my ducks with stolen goods."

An unmistakably guilty flush stained her cheeks, and something inside him shifted at the realization that she'd attempted to befriend his ducks. But rather than appear abashed, she hiked up her chin another notch and met his gaze without a flinch. "I could certainly find a more delicate way to describe the events, but in a nutshell, yes, that is what happened. And I'll have you know that the ducks and I were getting on swimmingly until *you-know-who* sneaked up on me."

The sight of her, so disheveled and indignant, had him pressing his lips together to stifle a grin. Her eyes instantly narrowed. "You're not *laughing*, are you?"

He coughed to cover a chuckle. "Certainly not."

"Because if you *were* laughing, I fear it would bode very poorly for you. Very poorly indeed."

"Oh? What would you do? Toss me onto *my* bottom? Swat me with your laceless handkerchief?"

"Both tempting scenarios. However, one should never reveal one's plan for revenge, especially to the person upon whom the revenge shall be wrought. Surely a spy would know that."

"Ah, yes. I believe it is mentioned in the Official Spy Handbook."

After muttering something that sounded suspiciously like "aggravating man," she shot him a glare, one rendered considerably less potent by the curl bisecting her nose, then struggled to stand. Nathan rose and offered his hand, but she pushed it aside. Once she stood, she planted her fisted hand on her hip and raised her other arm to point an imperious finger at Petunia, who sat, perfectly relaxed, under the nearby copse of elms.

"That goat is a menace."

"She's actually very sweet. Her only fault is being insatiably curious."

"And sadly lacking in discernment when it comes to snacks."

"Yes, that, too."

She eyed his clothing. "How is it that your attire doesn't seem to be missing buttons or have any teeth marks upon it?"

"I learned very quickly, right after I lost not one but two waistcoat buttons, that while Petunia *likes* clothing-oriented snacks, she *loves* carrots and apples. It clearly states in the Official Spy Handbook that one tends to fare much better against one's foes when the foes are offered what they want."

"So you saved your clothing with—"

"Carrots and apples. Yes."

She brushed at a streak of dust marring her skirt. "You might have mentioned that helpful hint prior to now."

"You didn't ask. Besides, it hadn't occurred to me that you would arrive at the stables before me."

"I wanted to make certain you didn't try to sneak off without me."

Her words had the effect of a splash of cold water and his shoulders stiffened. "We struck a bargain. I'm a man of my word," he said in a cool voice.

Silence stretched between them. Reaching up, she tucked the stray curl into her bonnet and studied him. "Then I suppose I owe you an apology."

He merely inclined his head and waited.

Another silence followed. Finally she said, "I'm not happy about the condition of my handkerchief."

He stared at her, nonplussed, then shook his head. "Well, *that* was the worst apology I've ever received."

"What do you mean? I admitted I owed you an apology."

"Actually, you said you 'supposed' you did."

"Exactly. What more do you want?"

"It's not an apology without the actual words, Victoria." He folded his arms across his chest and raised his brows.

Again she studied him for several long seconds, a strange expression on her face. Then she cleared her throat. "I'm sorry, Nathan. We struck a deal and you've given me no reason to doubt that you're a man of your word." She pressed her lips together, and he couldn't help but chuckle.

"It killed you not to add the words 'so far,' didn't it."

"It required an effort, yes."

"Well, I accept your apology. And in the spirit of fairness, I offer one of my own. I am sorry that my goat wreaked havoc upon your handkerchief. I realize that this is a poor substitute, but . . ." He reached into his waistcoat, withdrew a folded square of linen and presented it to her with a flourish. "Please accept mine as a replacement."

"That isn't necessary—"

"But I insist," he said, pressing the cloth into her hand. "And let us be grateful that Petunia didn't nibble upon your shoes instead, as I fear mine would be much too large to offer as a replacement."

Her lips twitched. "Hmmm. Yes. Especially as you already have one pet who is named for munching upon footwear." She tucked both his handkerchief and her ruined one in the pocket of her riding habit, then extended her hand. "Truce?"

He shook her hand, but after doing so, some inner devil made him raise her hand to his lips. But suddenly touching his lips to her gloved fingers wasn't enough, so he turned her hand to expose the thin band of bare inner wrist visible between her glove and the sleeve of her riding habit. Keeping his gaze locked on hers, he touched his lips to that soft bit of pale skin. And immediately regretted it.

An elusive whiff of roses teased his senses, instantly filling him with the urge to bury his face against her soft skin so as to breathe her in. But it was her reaction that had him swallowing a groan of pure want. A quick intake of breath, followed by a long, slow, exhalation. Eyes that widened slightly then drooped to half mast. The tip of her tongue moistening lips that remained parted. She looked flushed and aroused and . . . bloody hell, the effect this woman had on him was absurd. She'd all but brought him to his knees by doing *nothing* save look at him. God help him should she ever deliberately attempt to entice him.

Damn it all, he should have let her stay angry with him. Should have strove to keep that bit of distance between them. It would have been much easier to resist her if she weren't speaking to him. Challenging him. Looking at him with those big blue eyes. But no, he had to accept her offer of a truce. Instead, he should have insisted she cover herself with a burlap sack.

And now he was about to embark on an entire afternoon

in her company. Where he'd be forced to visit the place where the worst night of his life had taken place.

God help him, he wasn't sure what frightened him more—the thought of the afternoon beginning or of it ending.

Thirteen

Every Modern Woman deserves to experience one grand passion in her life, but unfortunately not every woman is blessed with finding someone who inspires such desire. If she is lucky enough to meet the man who makes her heart pound and her knees quake and her insides shiver, she should not allow anything to stand in her way of grabbing happiness with both hands.

*A Ladies' Guide to the Pursuit of
Personal Happiness and Intimate Fulfillment*
by Charles Brightmore

Nathan slowed Midnight as they neared the curve in the shady, tree-lined path.

"Is this the place?" asked Victoria, riding beside him on Honey.

"Just around this curve." He pulled in a deep breath and braced himself, but it did nothing to stop the onslaught. The instant he rounded that curve, the memories he'd fought so hard to hold at bay assaulted him, laying siege to the carefully built fortifications he'd constructed to ward off the guilt, remorse, and self-condemnation that had threatened to consume him from the inside out. He'd known he'd have to revisit this spot, but he'd hoped, prayed, that the images would have faded. Instead they impaled him like a knife in his gut.

Reining Midnight to a halt, Nathan's gaze fell upon the spot where he'd come upon Gordon, then shifted to the hedge from which he'd pulled Colin. He squeezed his eyes shut. Vivid images cut through his mind, slashes of pain, each one stinging like the lash of a whip, deepening the scars of regret that already marked him. His chest and throat tightened, and he opened his eyes, his gaze scanning the ground. Three years worth of rain had washed away all traces of Colin's and Gordon's blood. If only he'd been able to wipe his memory as clean.

He felt a touch on his arm and turned his head. Victoria's gloved hand rested on his sleeve and she was looking at him with unmistakable concern. "Are you all right, Nathan?"

No. I'm not all right. Everything that mattered to me was lost. Right here. And I've no one to blame but myself. "Yes, I'm fine."

"You don't look fine."

He forced a half grin. "Thank you, although I must warn you that such honeyed words are apt to swell my head."

No trace of amusement lit her features as her gaze searched his for what seemed like an eternity. Finally she said quietly, "It is painful for you to be here."

He swallowed the humorless sound that rose in his throat and nodded, not trusting his voice.

"Will you tell me what happened?"

An immediate *no* rose to his lips, but her voice and eyes

were filled with a compassion that beckoned him. And suddenly he couldn't think of one compelling reason *not* to tell her.

"Based on information I'd received from an informant, I retrieved the cache of jewels from a ship anchored in Mount's Bay."

"How did you retrieve them?"

He shrugged. "Let us just say I am a strong swimmer and handy with a knife." Her eyes widened, but before she could question him further, he continued, "I was to deliver the jewels here that night, but just as I arrived, shots rang out. I discovered Gordon lying injured in the path. When I started toward him, I was struck from behind and dropped the jewels. Before I could recover myself, my attacker grabbed them and disappeared into the forest."

"You didn't give chase?"

"No."

"Why not?"

Another guilt-filled memory hit him with a visceral punch. "Because seeing if Gordon was alive was more important. Then I realized Colin had also been shot."

"Who were you supposed to deliver the jewels to?"

He hesitated. He'd never told anyone, in spite of the fact that he was no longer under any obligation to remain silent. Yet even though his instincts warned him to continue to keep the information to himself, they also told him that he could trust this woman. And that she had a right to know.

"I'll need your word that you won't repeat what I'm about to tell you."

"Very well."

"I was supposed to deliver the jewels to your father."

Her hand slowly slipped from his sleeve and she frowned. "My father?" she repeated in a confused tone. "I don't understand. He was here? In Cornwall?"

"Yes. When I heard the shots, my first thought was that your father had been waylaid. I was shocked to learn it was Gordon and Colin who'd been hurt."

"Why?"

"Because they knew nothing about the mission. The only people who knew were me and your father. To this day neither Gordon nor Colin know it was your father I was to meet, and I want it to stay that way. At least for now."

"But why were they not included in the mission? And if they weren't, what were they doing here that night?"

"Your father was in charge of the mission and only wanted one other operative involved. As to why he chose me rather than Colin or Gordon, the reason came down to money. A huge reward was offered for the recovery of the jewels. As heirs, both Colin and Gordon were financially set for life. I, on the other hand, could not say the same thing. By assigning the task to me, your father offered me the chance for financial security."

"I . . . see," she said, although it was clear she still had questions. "What happened to my father that night? Was he injured as well?"

"I was, of course, very concerned about him. I'd just finished treating Colin and Gordon when I received a coded message from your father informing me that he was waylaid shortly after leaving the inn where he'd been staying and asking what had transpired. I wrote back an explanation, to which he replied that he intended to return to London and instructed me to say as little as possible to Colin and Gordon regarding the mission and insisted I not mention his involvement. I'd managed to forestall questions from Colin and Gordon while I treated their injuries, but I knew I couldn't avoid them much longer. When they did finally demand answers, my vague responses failed to satisfy them. Rumors about the missing jewels and my involvement ran rampant almost immediately—no doubt thanks to tidbits the servants overheard. The next thing I knew, I was being officially questioned. Nothing was ever proven against me, but it was clear that few believed me innocent. Every day fresh bits of gossip surfaced. Whispers and stares followed me around the village. And at home as well."

"Your family thought you guilty?"

"Neither Colin nor my father ever flat-out accused me, but neither did they proclaim my innocence. A blind man could have read the doubt in their eyes." The image of Colin that was burned into his brain—staring up at him with doubt and suspicion—flashed in his mind, bringing a sharp jolt of pain. Blinking away the memory, he continued, "As for my best friend, Gordon, he flat-out accused me."

"What evidence did he have?"

"None. There was none. Only innuendo and speculation, but that can be just as damaging, I'm afraid. Gordon, among others, thought it very convenient that I had been the only one to escape the debacle uninjured."

"How did you respond to that accusation?"

"I didn't. It was obvious that nothing I said would sway him." And damn it, that had hurt. Nearly as much as Colin's doubting him. He refocused his attention on Victoria, and he could almost see the wheels turning in her mind. How long before she asked him if her father thought he was guilty? How long before she realized the implications that if he and her father were the only two people who knew of the mission, and he wasn't guilty—

"You say your brother and father didn't proclaim your innocence. Did *you* proclaim it?"

Nathan pulled his gaze from hers and looked into the dense forest. "I told them I hadn't betrayed my country, but it fell on deaf ears. Colin felt deceived by and suspicious of my continued secrecy. My father, who was shocked to discover that his sons had been working for the Crown, accused me of being responsible for Colin's injury. Colin could have died, he said, as if I didn't know that. As if that wouldn't eat at me every day for the rest of my life. A terrible row followed. Angry, hurtful words. They felt duped and betrayed, and I felt . . ." His voice trailed off.

"What did you feel?" she asked softly.

"Guilt. Remorse. Gutted. My father told me to leave, and I did so."

"That must have been very painful."

He turned to look at her, searching her gaze for signs of condemnation, yet detected nothing but sympathy. Somehow that made him feel worse than if she'd looked at him with censure. "That's putting it . . . mildly. After moving about for more than two years, I finally discovered Little Longstone. Everyone there accepts me simply as Dr. Nathan Oliver. No one knows of my exalted family connections or my past as a spy or my tarnished reputation. I've embraced the profession I love and live the way I've always wanted. The way I've always felt most comfortable. Simply. Peacefully."

"Perhaps peacefully, but you're not really at peace."

An immediate denial sprang to his lips, but the words died at the warm compassion, the gentle tenderness, so obvious in her gaze.

"I can see it your eyes, Nathan," she said softly. "The

shadows. The hurt. I knew as soon as I saw you again that you weren't the same man I'd met three years ago."

Damn it, how did she manage to sneak beneath his guard like this? She made him feel . . . vulnerable. Defenseless. And he didn't like it. "I'm sure you mean that in the nicest way," he said in a dust dry tone.

"I mean I knew that something had changed you. Now I know what. And I'm sorry for you that it happened."

"Because you liked me so much the first time we met."

He said the words with unmistakable sarcasm, but she surprised him by answering in a dead serious tone, "Yes." Then she smiled. "Surely that was obvious to a master spy such as yourself. I believe you liked me as well."

God, yes, he had. Liked the look of her. The twinkle in her eyes. Her alluring smile. The sweet innocence mixed with mischief overlaid with delicate beauty. Her charming nervous chatter, which had led him to silence her with a kiss. Then the delectable taste of her. The delicious feel and scent of her. Nothing, no one, had fired his blood or affected him so profoundly before or since.

"Yes, Victoria," he said softly. "I liked you." God help him, he still did. And far too much, he feared.

A rose-hued blush stained her cheeks, and he gripped Midnight's reins to keep from touching her. "You . . . that night . . . it was my first kiss, you know," she said.

Something inside Nathan seemed to expand. "No, I didn't know for certain, but I suspected as much."

Her cheeks reddened further and her gaze slid from his. "My inexperience must have bored you."

He could only stare. Surely she was joking. Bored him? *If only it had.* Yet her blush and clear embarrassment indicated she was in earnest. While his common sense told him it was wiser to let her believe what she wanted, his conscience simply couldn't allow her to harbor such a gross misapprehension. Reaching out, he touched two fingertips under her chin. Even that infinitesimal contact with her soft skin sizzled heat through him. When she met his gaze, he said softly, "You didn't bore me, Victoria. You . . ." *Intoxicated me. Bewitched me. Enchanted me. Captivated me. Rendered yourself irrevocably unforgettable with a single kiss.* ". . . were delightful."

He swore he caught a flash of relief in those eyes that were the same vivid azure as the sea. The hint of a smile trembled on her lips. "I could perhaps say the same about you."

"You could . . . or you are?" His tone was lightly teasing, but he suddenly realized he very much wanted her answer.

"Are you certain you really want to know the answer, Nathan?" she asked in a matching teasing tone, mimicking the question he'd asked her more than once.

Slipping his fingers from beneath her chin, he grinned. "Actually, being the master spy I am, I already know the answer. Your enthusiastic response indicated you found the encounter as delightful as I did."

She inclined her head in a gesture of acquiescence, then shrugged. "I've learned that men who are well versed in the art of kissing are accustomed to enthusiastic responses."

He narrowed his eyes, but she didn't notice as she turned to watch a pair of twittering birds dancing on a nearby branch. What the hell had she meant by *that*? Jealousy, searing hot and undeniable, shot through him. Why did he even need to wonder? Obviously there was only one way she could have learned such a thing—by kissing. Men. Men who weren't him.

Damn it, last night he'd suffered through sleepless hours tormented by such thoughts. Well, not the entire night. Part was spent indulging in erotic fantasies of touching her, kissing her, making love to her a dozen different ways, exploring every inch of her soft, fragrant skin with his hands and mouth and tongue. But part was also spent fighting back tormenting images of her sharing such intimacies with another man. When she returned to London she would choose a husband. One of her bloody earls. Or worse, Gordon or Colin, both of whom were clearly attracted to her. The real problem, however, was his own painful, ever growing, and extremely unfortunate attraction to her.

She turned to him. "Did my father believe you innocent?"

"He said he did."

She nodded slowly. "If it makes any difference, I believe you innocent."

His heart jumped in that ridiculous way, and with those simple words, she touched something deep inside him. Her belief in him shouldn't make a difference. He didn't want it to make a difference. But . . . it did. "Thank you."

"I also believe my father innocent," she continued, making it clear she understood the implications of believing Nathan innocent of wrongdoing. "There must be another explanation. And I'm determined to find out what it is. The answer lies in the jewels. So, shall we begin our search?"

"Yes," he agreed, although he was beginning to suspect that he'd already found a treasure he hadn't even suspected existed.

After nearly three hours of unsuccessfully searching a dozen rock formations in the first grid square, they arrived at a gurgling stream.

"This marks the northern boundary of the estate," Nathan said. "I suggest we stop here to eat and allow the horses to drink and rest."

"All right," Victoria said, hoping she didn't sound as grateful as she felt. Tired, sore, hungry and thirsty, she was more than ready to take a break.

Nathan swung from the saddle, removed the worn leather bag holding their picnic meal, then gave Midnight a gentle pat on the rump. The gelding immediately headed toward the stream. Nathan then walked to Victoria and lifted his arms to assist her. Flutters tickled her stomach, but his touch was impersonal, and the instant her feet touched the ground, he released her, leaving her oddly disappointed. Indeed, he'd spoken little during the past three hours.

Setting her hands on her lower spine, Victoria arched her back to relieve the stiffness and winced. Nathan looked up from where he crouched beside the saddlebag.

"I should have suggested we stop earlier," he said in an apologetic tone. "Why didn't you say something?"

"And have you accuse me of being a wilting hothouse flower? No, thank you. Not only that, but we were getting along so well in our silence, I hated to disrupt our accord. Besides, I didn't want to stop searching. We've a great deal of ground to cover." She looked around her, taking in the tall trees and vast landscape. "I didn't realize how much."

"It's a huge estate." He pulled two apples from the saddlebag and tossed them lightly up to her. "Why don't you give Midnight and Honey a snack while I set up our picnic?"

"All right." Apples in hand, Victoria walked to the edge of the stream, where the two horses were still drinking the crystal clear water. While she waited for them to finish, she removed her riding gloves and surveyed her surroundings. Sunlight glinted stripes of gold through the leaves, while fluffy clouds floated lazily against a dazzling blue backdrop. Lush greenery interspersed with patches of colorful wildflowers and uneven rocks lined both sides of the stream. The gentle gurgle of water running over time-smoothened rocks provided background music to the twittering of birds and the rustling of leaves from a breeze cool enough to offer relief from the sun's warmth without providing a chill. Victoria drew a deep breath, enjoying the faint scent of the sea that lingered in the air even though they weren't near the shore.

Honey lifted her head, and Victoria fed the mare her treat, while patting her neck and murmuring soothing words. Midnight nudged her, clearly wanting the same attention. With a laugh, Victoria awarded him his apple and bestowed an equal amount of pats and murmurs. Finished with her task, she rinsed her hands in the chilly water, then turned toward Nathan.

He stood in the shade of a soaring elm next to a colorful quilt upon which was spread a massive variety of food. He offered a low bow then grinned. "Your meal awaits, my lady."

"Heavens," she said, walking toward him, surveying the array of cheeses and tarts, meats and biscuits, fruits and bread. "How did all this fit in one saddlebag?"

"Cook is an expert at packing."

Looking down at the blanket, she laughed. "There's enough food here for half a dozen people. Are we expecting guests?"

"No. It's just the two of us."

Her head snapped up and their eyes met. Yes, it was indeed just the two of them. Her heart skipped a beat.

"Cook informed me that she doesn't want any food left over. That we cannot return until it's all gone."

Good lord, that could take . . . hours. Another skipped heartbeat. Pulling in a calming breath, she smiled. "Then we'd best get started."

She walked to the blanket, then sat in the place he indicated, arranging her skirts around her. He lowered himself next to her, folded his longs legs in front of him, and proceeded to prepare her a heaping plate. After preparing one for himself, he filled two pewter mugs with cider. Raising his mug, he pinned her with a look she couldn't decipher but that rolled a wave of heat through her just the same. "Here's to finding what we're looking for."

"Yes," she murmured, touching her mug to his. She took a grateful sip, welcoming the coolness on her dry, parched throat. The food looked delicious, and since she was famished, she dug in with gusto. Nathan, she noted, did the same, and for several minutes they simply ate, surrounded by the sun-dappled shade and the sounds of the outdoors.

After helping himself to another thick slice of bread, Nathan pulled in a long, deep breath then exhaled. "God, I love the smell here. That bit of the sea that's always in the air. Much as I love Little Longstone, it doesn't smell like this. Neither does London." He glanced at her and gave an exaggerated shudder. "How can you stand spending so much time there?"

"There're the shops."

He shook his head. "Crowds."

"The fabulous parties."

"Tedious conversation with tiresome strangers."

"The opera."

"People singing indecipherable songs in languages I don't understand."

She laughed. "I'm afraid we'll have to agree to disagree. What about you? How can you stand to spend all your time buried in the country? Don't you find it desolate?"

"No. It's peaceful."

"There's no excitement."

"Tranquil."

"No Regent or Bond streets."

"Thank God."

"Lonely."

He paused at that, a small frown burrowing between his brows. "Sometimes," he said quietly. "But I have my books and my animals and my patients."

"No woman anxiously awaiting your return?" She tossed out the question with a lightness that was in complete contrast to the hard thumping of her heart.

"No one." One corner of his mouth quirked upward. "At least that I know of. Perhaps I have several secret admirers who are pining away for me even as we speak." He popped a bit of cheese into his mouth. After he swallowed, he said, "I imagine Branripple and Dravensby eagerly anticipate your return to London."

God help her, she almost asked *Who*? before her inner voice chimed in to remind her, *Your earls. One of whom you're going to marry.*

Were they eagerly awaiting her return? Most likely they were busy attending the whirlwind of parties associated with the Little Season. Where, given their eligibility, they would be much sought after by a bevy of marriage-minded young women. Who would fawn over them. Flirt with them. Dance with them. Perhaps even share kisses with them. The thought of which . . .

Didn't bother her at all.

A frown yanked down her brows. Surely that *should* bother her. Surely she should feel *something* at the thought of another woman capturing Branripple or Dravensby's attention. Some fissure of concern. A twinge of annoyance. A pang of jealousy. Yet she felt . . . nothing.

But then she turned to Nathan, who was regarding her with heated intensity, and suddenly she did feel something. A sizzling *whoosh* of something that curled her toes inside her leather riding boots. And it hit her in a lightning flash of realization that the thought of another woman kissing *this* man made her stomach cramp. Made her want to break something. Made her want to slap the other woman so hard that the lips that had dared to kiss Nathan fell off. Onto the ground. Where she could then grind them into the dirt with the heel of her shoe.

"Are you all right, Victoria? Your expression looks quite . . . ferocious."

Victoria blinked away the image of a slapped, lipless woman and beat back the claws of jealousy that were as undeniable as they were confusing. What on earth was wrong with her?

"I'm fine," she said, taking a hasty sip of cider.

"Good." He set aside his empty plate, then patted his stomach. "Delicious. But now comes the best part of a picnic."

"Dessert?"

"Even better." He slipped off his jacket, folded it—none too neatly—then lay back, using the bundle as a makeshift pillow. "Ahhhh . . ." The deep sigh of contentment pushed from between his lips, and his eyes slid closed.

Victoria sat perfectly still and stared. Well, perfectly

still except for her eyeballs, which performed a thorough downward ogle, er, survey. Skeins of sunlight illuminated burnished streaks in his mussed hair and cast his face into an intriguing pattern of golden light and smoky shadows. Snowy linen, marked with wrinkles from his jacket, stretched across his broad chest and shoulders. His hands rested on his abdomen, his long fingers loosely linked just above the waist of his fawn breeches. Ah, yes . . . those fawn breeches that hugged his muscular legs in that fascinating, speech-robbing way. The breeches disappeared just below his knees into well-worn black riding boots. The picture of utter relaxation was complete with his casually crossed ankles.

Good Lord, had she just claimed she was fine? She must be mad. The man was spread before her like a banquet feast. A feast from which she desperately wanted to partake.

When precisely had the male form become so fascinating? Clearly the blame rested on the explicit descriptions of a man's anatomy in the *Ladies' Guide*. While she'd always possessed a natural curiosity, she'd never felt anything like *this*. Neither Branripple nor Dravensby had ever inspired this desperate compulsion to touch. To explore. To remove their clothing.

With her eyes riveted on him, she had to swallow twice to locate her voice. "Wh-what are you doing?"

"Enjoying the last phase of a picnic."

"I don't think taking a nap here is a very good idea, Nathan." Heavens, she sounded prim. If only she felt prim, as opposed to feeling like an overly ripe peach about to burst from its too tight skin.

"I'm not napping. I'm relaxing. You should try it. It's very good for the digestion."

"I'm perfectly relaxed, thank you." Yes. And if liars caught on fire, she'd be incinerated on the spot. Nervous words gathered in her throat, and she knew she was about to start babbling. "Tell me, what made you want to become a doctor?" The words came out in a breathless rush, but she heaved an inward sigh of relief that at least they made sense.

"I was always drawn to healing, even as a boy. Birds with broken wings, dogs with mangled legs, that sort of thing. That, combined with my love of science and my curiosity for the workings of the human body, and there was never any question in my mind what path I would follow."

She'd watched, as if in a trance, his beautiful mouth form each word, and her fingertips tingled with the overpowering need to touch his lips. To prevent herself from succumbing to the temptation, she raised her knees, wrapped her arms tightly around her legs and gripped her hands together. There. Now she was saved from making a fool of herself. "And if you hadn't become a doctor? What profession would you have chosen?"

"A fisherman."

"You're joking."

"What is wrong with being a fisherman?"

"Nothing. 'Tis just not a very . . ." Her voice trailed off and suddenly she felt foolish.

"Not a very what?"

"Gentlemanly pursuit."

"Perhaps not, but it's honest work. Certainly more useful than the gentlemanly pursuits of gaming and running foxes to the ground. But then I've always made my own rules. I never understood why I should spend my life doing things I didn't enjoy simply because it was what was expected of me. I think I'd have made a fine fisherman.

Mount's Bay is good fishing ground and offers protection even when the seas turn rough, as they often do. I've always enjoyed fishing, any time of year, but summer was by far the best. Every July, I eagerly awaited the annual excitement of the great catch of the pilchard."

"What is that?"

"The Cornish pilchard, a local fish. Men in boats launch massive nets that form an enormous circle around the entire group of fish, called a shoal. The procedure is comparable to the way sheep are herded into pens. Dozens of people, myself included, waited on the shore, where we hauled the tremendous nets filled with thousands of fish onto the beach. We then piled those thousands of fish into every available container, basket, and bucket. It was exhausting and exhilarating and the most anticipated event of the season."

"What did you do during the rest of the summer?"

"Walked the beaches. Collected shells. Read. Raised mischief with Colin. Studied the stars. Enjoyed picnics. Caught crabs and lobster."

"You caught them yourself?"

"Yes." He peeked one eye open at her and grinned. "They hardly walked onto the dinner plates of their own volition, you know."

Victoria smiled in return and an image materialized in her mind, of a handsome tousle-haired youth, tanned golden from the sun, scooping up crabs, walking along the sand, his hair blowing in the brisk sea breeze. The image was then replaced with one of her, as a young girl, and the contrast was jarring.

"While you were doing all those things, I was learning how to dance and embroider and speak French. You spent your time here, by the sea, while I was raised in London.

Even our country home is only a three-hour journey from Town. You enjoyed the company of your brother, while my brother would have rather been shot than spend time with me. You grew up knowing you wanted to be a doctor, I grew up knowing I would have to marry well to ensure my future. How different our lives have been."

"Surely your father and brother will see to your future."

"My father will ensure my financial security, but my brother, sadly, cannot be depended upon for anything. And even if he could, I want a family of my own. Children."

He rolled onto his side, propped the weight of his upper body on his forearm and regarded her through serious eyes. "If you could have been something other than an earl's daughter, what would you have been?"

"A man," she answered without the slightest hesitation.

She'd expected him to smile, but his gaze remained steady and serious. "What sort of man? An earl? A duke? A king?"

"Just a . . . man. So I could have choices. So my destiny wasn't determined by my gender. So I, too, could choose if I wanted to be a doctor or a fisherman or a spy. You have no idea how fortunate you are."

His gaze turned thoughtful, then he nodded slowly. "I never thought of it quite like that. What was your childhood like?"

Victoria rested her chin on her upraised knees and considered. No one had ever asked her such a thing. "Lonely. Quiet. Especially after my mother died. If I hadn't possessed such a deep love of reading, I might have gone mad. I envy you having a sibling you could talk to. Share things with. Edward is ten years my senior. For all the time we spent together, I might as well have been an only child."

"I can't imagine not having had Colin. But given our

different interests—Colin thinks science is synonymous with torture and he'd prefer to put his head on a chopping block rather than study Latin, and the fact that he had to learn the responsibilities that come with the title—I spent a great deal of my time alone as well." He studied her for several long seconds, then said, "It seems we might actually have something in common."

Victoria pretended to look scandalized. "How shocking. Although, I must tell you, I've never wanted to be a fisherman."

"Just as well. Those rough ropes would wreak havoc with your soft hands." His glance slid to her hands, gripped lightly together around her legs, and her fingers tightened involuntarily. Then he raised his gaze back to hers. "I must tell you, Victoria, while I understand your reasons for wishing you were a man, I'm extremely glad that you're not."

"And why is that? Afraid I would best you at billiards?"

"Not at all. I'm an unsurpassedly excellent billiards player."

"I thought we'd agreed 'unsurpassedly' wasn't a word."

"I thought we'd agreed it should be. But no matter. The reason I'm glad you're not a man is because if you were, I wouldn't do this. . . ." He reached out and brushed a single fingertip over the back of her hand, stopping her breath. Her fingers loosened and he gently clasped her hand and brought it to his lips.

"Nor would I do this," he whispered, his warm breath caressing her skin. He pressed a gentle kiss against the back of her fingertips.

How was it possible that with all this air surrounding them, her lungs had ceased to function? Before she could find an answer, he released her hand and sat up. His face was a mere foot from hers, and the heat simmering in his eyes mesmerized her. The scent of sandalwood mixed with the subtle hint of shaving soap teased her senses, flooding her with an unbearable desire to touch her lips to his cleanly shaven skin, which looked so warm and firm.

"Certainly I wouldn't think of doing this. . . ." Reaching out, he lightly stroked the pad of his thumb over her cheek, then sifted his fingers into her hair, brushing over her nape to cup the back of her head. Somehow a breath must have found its way into her lungs because she let out a long sigh of pleasure.

He leaned forward, his hand gently coaxing her closer, until only a paper thin space separated their lips. "And this would be completely out of the question." His mouth feathered across hers, once, twice, a whisper of a touch that only served to tease. But rather than satisfy her, he instead kissed his way across her jaw, softly, barely touching her. His tongue flicked over her earlobe, eliciting a quick intake of breath, then his warm lips nuzzled the sensitive skin behind her ear. "Roses," he whispered, the single word awakening a barrage of tingles that skittered down her back. "How is it that you always smell so perfectly of roses?"

Her eyes drifted closed and she stretched her neck to give him better access. "My bath. I scent it with rosewater."

He leaned back, and she barely swallowed her groan of disappointment. Dragging her eyes open, she stilled at the heat burning in his gaze. "So you smell of roses . . . everywhere."

It wasn't a question, but a statement uttered in a husky rasp that ended on a groan. Whatever response she might have hoped to make evaporated when his fingertips lightly grazed her features. The fire in his gaze mixed with a baffled expression, as if he were trying to solve a perplexing puzzle. "You must be told at least a dozen times a day how beautiful you are."

A short, breathless laugh escaped her. "Hardly. Although I cannot deny I've been told."

"Has anyone told you today?"

"Not so far."

His index finger grazed her lower lip. "You're beautiful."

"Thank you. Although . . ."

"What? You prefer exquisite? If so, I'll oblige you."

"No. It's just that . . . it doesn't really mean anything."

"What doesn't?"

"Being beautiful. Or at least it shouldn't."

"What do you mean?"

"It's not something a person has any control over. It certainly isn't any great accomplishment—like being a doctor. It didn't require any special talent or effort on my behalf. It doesn't make one kind or decent. Yet, it seems to be what I am most admired for. Perhaps _all_ I am admired for. Well, that and my family's fortune—but again, that is something over which I have no control, nor is it an accomplishment. No special talent or effort required."

His expression turned even more mystified. "I am surprised to hear you say this. I would have thought you'd place great importance on beauty."

She inwardly sighed at her tendency to babble. Would she never learn to keep her lips closed? Since she'd come this far, she saw no point in stopping now. "I cannot deny I enjoy pretty clothes and looking my best, which I suppose is fortunate since, given my position, it is expected of me. But I carry in my heart an image of my mother . . . my mother who was so beautiful people couldn't help but stare at her. Yet for all her beauty, she wasn't truly happy."

The image rose in her mind of her stunning dark-haired mother who laughed gaily in front of guests then cried in her bedchamber. "After I was born, she miscarried two babies. It sent her into a melancholy from which she never recovered. When she died, she was barely forty. And still beautiful. But of what use was that? As for me, all I wanted was my mother. I didn't care if she was gorgeous or a hag. I would have traded anything I owned, all my supposed 'beauty,' for one more day with her. One more of her rare smiles." Moisture pushed behind her eyes and she blinked to dispel it. A self-conscious sound escaped her. "I suppose all I'm saying is that outward beauty is really rather . . . useless."

He was looking at her with an odd expression—as if he'd never seen her before—and embarrassment swept through her. Good lord, once again her mouth had run amok.

"You continue to surprise me, Victoria," he said slowly, his gaze searching hers. "And I don't particularly care for surprises."

She blinked, and then her eyes narrowed. "Why, thank you. I don't know when I've heard such heartwarming words. Truly."

He shook his head as if to clear it. "I'm sorry. I didn't mean that the way it sounded." Reaching out, he brushed a curl from her cheek. "Forgive me?"

As quickly as her irritation had flared, it evaporated. He sounded so sincere, and looked so serious and earnest, yet . . . baffled. Troubled. Perhaps there was a woman somewhere in the kingdom who could resist his softly spoken query, but she was not that woman. "Forgiven," she whispered.

His gaze flicked to her lips, and her body quickened in

anticipation of another kiss. Instead, he abruptly stood. "It's time we headed back."

She looked at the ground so he wouldn't see her disappointment. Her common sense applauded the decision. Sitting on a picnic blanket, sharing kisses and confidences with Nathan, was clearly not prudent. Her heart, however, yearned to spend the rest of the day right here.

These feelings were simply not part of her plan, yet she was at a loss as to how to stop them. Had it been only two days ago that she'd thought she could walk away from here, free of Nathan and unaffected by their encounter? Yes. Yet here she sat, after such a short time, already feeling anything but free and most definitely affected. If he could wreak such havoc with her plans in a mere two days, what on earth would he do in two weeks' time?

God help her, she didn't know if the possibilities more frightened her or thrilled her.

Fourteen

Today's Modern Woman must understand that men often say one thing and mean another. For example, "Would you like to accompany me for a moonlight stroll" means, "I want to kiss you." However, when a man says, "I want you," there can be no mistaking his meaning. The only question is whether or not the lady will want him as well.

A Ladies' Guide to the Pursuit of Personal Happiness and Intimate Fulfillment by Charles Brightmore

Three hours after arriving back at Creston Manor and leaving Victoria in the drawing room with her aunt, Nathan still paced the confines of his bedchamber, his thoughts knotted like a hopelessly tangled ball of yarn. He should be concentrating on figuring out where the jewels might be hidden. Should actually be out looking for them. But he'd given his word not to conduct any searches without Victoria, and spending more time in her company right now was simply not a good idea. Not when his command over himself teetered so close to the edge. Bloody hell, she'd set him on fire. Simply by sitting on a blanket. Watching her eat had proven an exercise in torture, requiring a monumental effort not to fling their meal aside and simply snatch her into his arms. He'd thought that lying back, closing his eyes so he couldn't see her would help, but his reclined position had only served to make him burn to pull her on top of him.

He raked his hands through his hair and blew out a long breath. Damn it, he'd known lust before, but *this* . . . this aching desire for her, this intense passion she inspired, was unlike anything he'd ever experienced. He'd always considered himself a man of control, finesse, and patience. But Victoria somehow stripped him of all three. He didn't want to kiss her, he wanted to devour her. He didn't want to slip her gown from her shoulders, he wanted to tear it from her body. With his teeth. He didn't want to slowly seduce her, he wanted to push her against the nearest wall and simply bury himself in her. Make hot, sweaty, mindless, searing love to her. Then turn her over and start again. If she knew even half the things he wanted to do to her, with her, she'd most likely never recover from the shock.

When the need to have his hands on her, to kiss her, had finally become unbearable, he'd given in, but had forcibly restrained himself, barely touching her. He'd succeeded, but the effort had cost him. He'd desperately wanted to remain by the stream with her, prolong their outing, but he knew his limits, and he'd reached them. One more touch, one more kiss, would have snapped his tenuous control.

He paused by the window, looking down at the expanse of lawns, the soaring trees, and the slice of white-capped blue water visible in the distance. The sight had always soothed him. But not now. Every nerve and muscle pulled with tension, and a sense of frustration such as he'd never known prowled through him. And damn it, it was all her fault.

Dragging his hands down his face, he groaned. Had he actually believed he could resist her? Yes, he had. And perhaps he might have been able to if his attraction had remained purely physical. He'd at least had a prayer of standing his ground against a woman who was merely beautiful. An even better chance if she proved shallow, superficial, and annoying, as he'd assumed Victoria ultimately would.

But how could he withstand the allure of a woman who was not only beautiful, but exhibited so many other facets that he found irresistible? He'd desired her the moment he'd set eyes on her, but each moment spent in her company revealed another unexpected layer of her personality, which only increased his hunger for her.

She'd proven herself unafraid to stand up to him. She was amusing. Witty. Intelligent. She'd offered him sympathy, kindness, and understanding. Believed him innocent of wrongdoing. Tried to befriend his ducks. She liked his cat. His dog. His cat and dog liked her in return. In spite of all her possessions, she'd suffered loneliness, and the fact that she would have given up all those possessions, her beauty, for one more day with her mother . . .

Damn it, he hadn't expected her to be . . . vulnerable. Hadn't anticipated her touching his heart. Hadn't wanted to care about her like this. In this heart-tugging, gut-wrenching, mind-numbing way. A woman who would never be his. A woman who, within a matter of weeks, would be engaged to another man.

"Augh!" He pressed the heels of his hands against his eyelids to blot out the torturous image of her lifting her face for another man's kiss. Enough. He needed to clear his mind of her. Erase the taste and feel and scent of her. Had to start concentrating on the things he should be thinking about. The jewels. So he could either find them or be convinced there was no hope of finding them so he could then pack up his belongings and animals and return to his peaceful life.

A swim. A long, brisk swim in the cold water would set him back to rights. Cool this unwanted ardor and force his thoughts back on the proper path.

Relieved to have a plan, he quickly exited his bedchamber. When he entered the foyer, he asked Langston in an undertone, "Where is everyone?"

"Your brother rode into Penzance with instructions to not expect him until late," the butler reported in a hushed tone. "Your father, Lady Victoria, and Lady Delia are having tea on the terrace."

Excellent. He could easily avoid the terrace. "If anyone asks, you haven't seen me. I'll return for dinner."

"Yes, Dr. Nathan."

Breathing a sigh of relief, Nathan left the house.

Victoria stirred a lump of sugar into her third cup of tea and nodded absently at whatever Aunt Delia was saying. Not that it mattered that she wasn't paying attention to the conversation about some party Aunt Delia and Lord Rutledge had both attended over a decade earlier, as she was convinced that her presence was quite forgotten. There hadn't been a break in the lively chatter between her aunt and Lord Rutledge since they'd sat down to tea an hour earlier. She'd considered excusing herself, but she couldn't resist the lure of the gorgeous late afternoon weather. And if she remained indoors, she would be alone with her thoughts—not something she cared to contemplate. There'd be plenty of time for that during the long night ahead.

Besides, it was a pleasure to see her aunt so animated and thoroughly enjoying herself. There were a number of gentlemen with whom Aunt Delia occasionally attended the opera, and she never lacked for partners at a ball, but she insisted those men were merely friends of long standing.

Never had Victoria seen her aunt blush. A becoming pink flush colored her face as she laughed at something Lord Rutledge, who was also clearly enjoying himself, said.

A muffled tapping on the flagstones behind her caught Victoria's attention and she turned. B.C., head held regally high, trotted across the terrace toward her. Upon his arrival, he bumped his massive head against her thigh. With a quiet laugh, she scratched behind his ears while he lifted his nose and sniffed the air.

"Smell biscuits, do you?" she murmured. The eager look in his intelligent dark eyes clearly indicated he did. She broke off a piece of her biscuit and offered the morsel to B.C., who, after eating it, rested his head on her lap and gazed up at her adoringly.

"Hmmm. I suppose I'm to think this attention springs from gratitude, but I suspect it's because you want more."

For an answer, B.C. stood at attention, licked his chops, then sent a pleading glance toward the remaining biscuit on her plate. "And I suppose you expect me to share the rest of my last biscuit with you?"

B.C. instantly plopped onto his bottom and raised his right forepaw.

Victoria laughed. "That seems to be your all-purpose answer. Lucky for you, it is quite irresistible." Breaking the biscuit into several pieces, she'd just offered B.C. the last bit when a flash of white caught the corner of her eye. Turning, she saw a man walking into the woods behind the stables. In seconds he disappeared from sight, but there was no mistaking that it had been Nathan. She shot up from her seat as if ejected from a catapult.

"Heavens, are you all right, Victoria?"

She jerked her gaze from the spot where the forest had swallowed him to look at her aunt. "Yes, I'm fine. A . . . uh, bee startled me." She flapped her arms around for good measure. "It's gone. But now that I'm up, I think I'll take a walk. If you don't mind."

"Not at all, my dear," Aunt Delia said.

"By all means, enjoy this lovely weather," Lord Rutledge said with a smile. "Although the sun will set soon. Take care to return before dark."

After assuring them she would, Victoria didn't hesitate another second. Recalling her promise not to wander off alone, she whistled softly for B.C. to join her. The dog fell into step alongside her and she steamed across the terrace like a ship under full sail, determined to find out exactly what Nathan was up to. Oh, yes, it was possible he was just innocently strolling through the forest, but there'd been something distinctly furtive in his manner. Hurrying along with his head down, as if not wanting to be seen. She wouldn't accuse him again without proof of searching for the jewels alone, but she was determined to do a bit of spying of her own to make certain such proof did not exist.

She shot B.C. a grim smile. "You'd best hope your master isn't skulking about looking for treasure without me, because if he is . . ." Her voice trailed off as she was unable to think up a punishment dire enough. "If he is, he'll have proven himself a liar. Dishonorable. A man of no integrity who does not keep his word."

Yet, perhaps that would be best. If he were dishonorable, that would surely kill her unwanted attraction to him. She would never remain drawn to a man of poor character, no matter how handsome or charming. She quickened her pace. "Come along, B.C. Let's find out what the master spy is up to."

When they entered the forest several minutes later, Victoria moved swiftly along the well-worn path. As they approached the fork, she slowed and looked down at B.C.

"Any idea which way he went?"

B.C. sniffed the air, then headed down the path leading to the lake. Her lips pressed into a grim line, Victoria followed the dog, scanning left and right, looking, listening. But she saw nothing save the trees and greenery, heard only the chirping of birds and the rustling of overhead leaves courtesy of the breeze. Long shadows fell across the trail with the waning rays that harkened to the coming twilight. They were nearing a curve in the path when B.C. broke into a run and galloped around the corner. Seconds later she heard a distinct crashing in the underbrush.

"B.C.," she whispered as loudly as she dared. Where had that dog dashed off to? Probably after a rabbit or squirrel. Or perhaps he'd located Nathan? Botheration, she had no desire to be discovered by Nathan, as she was supposed to be the one doing the spying. Of course, if he found her, she could simply claim she was out for a walk with the dog. Perfectly true.

She rounded the corner and saw a slender path that led off to the right. As that was the direction in which she'd heard B.C., she followed the trail, trying to step gingerly so as to make the minimum amount of noise. A minute later she caught a glimpse of the lake through the trees. The trail cut sharply to the left, and when she turned, she came upon B.C., who sat, tongue lolling, tail wagging, next to an oddly shaped dark mass she prayed wasn't the remains of some poor animal he'd hunted down.

"There you are," she murmured, approaching cautiously, leaning forward, casting a suspicious eye on the strangely shaped thing that showed no signs of life. Her stomach tightened with dread. "Please don't be a rabbit. Or a squirrel. Or a—"

Boot.

Victoria straightened as if a plank had been shoved down her drawers. Hastening forward to investigate, she discovered it was not a single boot, but a pair of boots. Lying atop a sloppily folded pile of clothing. There was no doubt to whom it all belonged. She'd recognize Nathan's worn boots and fawn breeches anywhere. And if his clothes were here, that meant he was . . .

Naked.

Whoosh. A flash of heat engulfed her. He'd told her of his fondness for swimming in the lake. Clearly he'd done so, for she sincerely doubted he was searching for the jewels while . . .

Naked.

Crouching down, she peered through the dense foliage toward the lake. The water resembled a sheet of blue glass, absorbing the brilliant orange and red reflections of the setting sun on its pristine surface. No sign of him. Drat! Er, excellent. She could scamper off undetected. Her gaze fell to the pile of clothing and she pursed her lips. Hmmmm . . .

She cast a quick look all around, verifying she was alone, then looked again at his clothing, which seemed to silently chant *Take me, take me.*

Oh, but she couldn't. Could she? Some imp inside her

told her she most certainly could. He was accustomed to such games—indeed he'd confessed to playing them during his youth. When on earth would she ever be presented with such an opportunity again? Never. Practically chortling with glee, she quickly gathered up the bundle, then stood. After casting one last look toward the lake to make certain Nathan wasn't approaching the shore, she turned. And froze.

Nathan stood before her. Nathan, dripping wet, his skin glistening, rivulets of water trailing down his body—

Holy. Saints. Above.

Look at his face. Look at his face. But her disobedient gaze did not heed. Instead it riveted on his torso with the stupefied zeal of a thief who'd unexpectedly happened upon a sack filled with money. Beads of moisture meandered down the muscled wall of his chest, clinging to the swatch of dark hair that narrowed into a silky ribbon as it bisected his ridged abdomen . . . then spread again to cradle his—

Holy. Saints. Above.

She could only stare and be grateful her jaw was attached to her face so it didn't flop onto the ground at her feet. Dear God, he was . . . magnificent. While she had nothing to compare him to, there was no doubt Nathan was exquisitely and, er, generously made. Undoubtedly the rest of him—his arms and legs—were exquisite as well, and she'd verify that the instant her eyeballs recalled how to move. She inanely wondered if the Official Spy Handbook addressed this situation: female clothing poacher struck dumb, reduced to drooling, insensate mass with freakishly paralyzed eyeballs by sight of magnificent, exquisite naked wet man.

"Rather like 'Puss in Boots,' don't you agree?"

The sound of his deep, amused voice jerked her from her stupor, and her gaze snapped up to meet his. A devilish gleam danced in his eyes. A witty response would most likely come to her in a year or two. Perhaps three or four. Right now she said the only word she could manage.

"Huh?"

" 'Puss in Boots.' The fairy tale. Except there isn't a king here to offer me his robe. Only you." He raised one dark brow. "I don't suppose you'd care to remove your dress?"

Dear God, she'd love nothing better. Especially since it was so *hot* out here. She felt as if she were roasting from the inside out. Sanity, however, prevailed, and she lifted her chin. "Certainly not." Egad, was that squeaky noise her voice?

"Not even in the name of good sportsmanship? It would certainly even the playing field, don't you agree?"

"I don't see how both of us being naked would even the playing field at all."

"No? Well, I'd be delighted to show you."

"I believe I've seen . . ." *Not nearly enough.* ". . . quite enough, thank you."

"Perhaps you could explain what you're doing here? You gave me your word you wouldn't wander off alone."

"I wasn't alone. I was with B.C. . . ." Her voice trailed off as she realized the dog no longer stood beside her. She glanced quickly around, but he was nowhere to be seen. *Humph.* Wretched deserter. See if he ever got another biscuit from *her.* ". . . who was here just a moment ago, I assure you. But in any event, I knew I wouldn't be alone once I found you."

A smile that could only be described as wolfish curved his lips. "So you came in search of me. I'm flattered. Had you hoped to join me for a swim?"

"Of course not. I saw you stealing off into the woods and—"

"And once again you suspected me of searching for the jewels without you?"

Another wave of heat, this one guilt-induced, crept up her neck. "Not exactly. It was more a case of wanting to prove that you *weren't* searching without me."

"Ah. Well, as you can see, I was not."

"Right. You were swimming. Isn't the water rather cold this time of year?"

"As a matter of fact, it's very cold."

"You like cold water?"

"Not at all."

"Then why were you swimming?"

"Are you certain you want to know the answer?"

Good lord, she wasn't certain of anything, least of all why she continued to stand as if nailed in place and converse with him while he was still naked. And wet. And naked.

She swallowed. "Why do you continually ask if I want to know the answers to my questions?"

"Because I suspect you may not *really* want to hear the answer. Or be prepared for it. The unvarnished truthful answer, that is. As opposed to the sugarcoated drivel your Society acquaintances would offer you."

"I assure you, I am perfectly prepared to hear why you were swimming."

"Very well. I couldn't stop thinking about you. The thought of touching you, kissing you, making love to you, was driving me to distraction. I'd hoped a swim in the cold water would take the edge off my ardor. As you might have noticed, it didn't." He looked pointedly downward and Victoria's gaze followed his.

Holy. Saints. Above.

"You're blushing, Victoria."

Her gaze jumped back up to his. "Am I? Yes, I suppose I am. I've, er, never seen a naked man before."

"Yet why should that embarrass *you*? If anyone at this impromptu party felt the need to be embarrassed, surely it would be the person who was naked."

"*Are* you embarrassed?"

"No. Embarrassed isn't what I'm feeling. Obviously."

Obviously. "Well. That's good. Because as far as I can tell, you have, um, nothing to be embarrassed about."

"Thank you. Neither do you. I told you there's no need for you to ever be embarrassed around me, Victoria."

Yes, he'd told her. But her embarrassment had nothing to do with his reaction and everything to do with her own. With the fact that instead of turning away, she couldn't stop staring at him. She wanted to touch him so much she actually trembled. How would all that beautiful male skin feel beneath her hands? Her lips? She'd always considered herself a lady, but there was absolutely nothing lady-like about what she wanted to do to him. What she wanted him to do to her.

Her skin felt tight, hot, beneath her gown, which was suddenly far too restrictive, constricting her breathing until her breaths came in shallow puffs. Her nipples hardened into aching points, and the flesh between her thighs grew heavy, pulsing in tandem with her rapid heartbeat.

"Are you all right, Victoria?"

She moistened her lips. "Are you?"

"There you go, answering a question with a question again."

"Which I normally never do. It is all your fault. You

make me—" She pressed her lips together to stem the flow of words.

He took a step toward her and her heart stuttered. "I make you what?"

Tremble. Ache. Want things I shouldn't. "Say things I normally wouldn't say. Do things I normally wouldn't do."

"Perhaps that is good. Perhaps you're discovering new aspects of your nature. Or freeing traits you've kept hidden, knowingly or unknowingly."

"Why would I do that?"

"Any number of reasons. The constraints of Society. Because your past experiences haven't allowed you enough freedom to *know* your true nature. Therefore you just do what's expected of you rather than what your heart desires. Speaking your mind, acting on your impulses, they can be very liberating."

"One can't simply say or do whatever they want."

"Not very often," he agreed, "and not with all people. But sometimes . . . sometimes you can." He took another step closer. "Feel free to say anything you want to me." Another step. "Or do anything you want."

A half-dozen things she wanted to do to him instantly crowded into her mind, firing more heat into her face. His gaze drifted over her flaming cheeks and a wicked gleam glittered in his eyes. "Any chance you'd make a similar offer to me, my lady?"

Yes, please. "No, thank you."

"That is . . . disappointing. But my offer stands." He took three more steps forward. Now less than an arm's length separated them. "One of the things I've come to admire about you is your courage. There's nothing to be afraid of. This place is completely private. So tell me, Victoria . . . what do you want?"

Dear God, he made her want so many things. But really, it all came down to just one. "I want to touch you."

The words came out in a rush. Without hesitation he plucked from her grasp the forgotten bundle of his clothes she still clutched to her chest then tossed the items aside. Before she had a chance to even draw a breath, he clasped her wrists and settled her hands in the center of his chest. "Then touch me."

The fire burning in his eyes dissolved her thoughts. Melted her modesty. And ignited her courage. Heat seeped into her palms and her gaze dropped to her hands, pale against the golden tan of his skin. He released her wrists, lowering his hands to his sides, and she experimentally splayed her fingers. Warm. He was so warm. And firm. Smooth. Like toasted satin over iron.

She slowly dragged her palms outward, flattening the beads of water that still clung to his skin, his silky rough chest hair curling between her fingers.

"Your heart is pounding," she whispered. *Nearly as hard and fast as mine.*

"Surely that doesn't surprise you."

She shook her head. At least she thought she did. She meant to, but every ounce of her attention was focused on watching her hands again glide across his chest. His quickened breathing left no doubt that he liked that, encouraging her to grow bolder. Smoothing her hands upward, she followed the line of his broad shoulders, then down over his powerful arms to his elbows.

"You're very strong," she murmured.

He emitted a rough, humorless sound. "Normally I'd agree," he said in a deep rasp. "Right now, however, my armor is feeling decidedly . . . *aahhhh* . . ." Her fingertips brushed over his nipples. ". . . dented."

His muscles jumped beneath her gentle touch, and a wave of feminine satisfaction such as she'd never known rushed through her. Emboldened, fascinated, transfixed, she dragged her hands slowly downward, absorbing the texture of his flat, ribbed abdomen, and the shudder that ran through him. Shifting her hands outward, she skimmed down the vee of his waist, then over his hips until she couldn't reach any lower without bending her locked knees, and rested her palms on his hair-roughened thighs. His manhood rose between them. Fascinating. Beckoning. He seemed to have stopped breathing, and she looked up.

The raw intensity in his gaze shook her. Any doubts she may have harbored that she affected him as profoundly as he did her vanished with that single look. Keeping her gaze locked on his, she brushed the back of her fingers over his arousal.

His eyes snapped closed and his nostrils flared as he pulled in a sharp breath. Again she trailed her fingers over him, stunned at how hot he felt. This time he rewarded her with a low groan. With her own breaths coming in erratic puffs through her parted lips, she looked down and watched herself caress the hard length of him, first with one hand, then with both, his groans growing more guttural with each pass of her fingers over his silky, hot flesh. His hands remained clenched in a white knuckle grip at his sides, and she could see the muscles in his legs, his arms and shoulders, his jaw and neck flexing, straining with the effort he expended to remain still. Spellbound, she wrapped her fingers around him and gently squeezed.

"Victoria . . ." Her name ended on a low moan. She squeezed him again, then brushed the pad of her thumb over the velvety engorged head.

"Done." The word was a tortured groan that sounded wrenched from his throat. He grasped her wrists and pulled her hands from him. "Damn it, *done*. Can't take any more."

Before she could so much as draw a breath, he yanked her against him and crushed his mouth to hers. But no breath would have been deep enough, no preparation thorough enough, for the onslaught of this kiss. Where during their picnic he'd barely touched her, now he seemed to touch her everywhere, head to toe, his arms clasping her to him so tightly she could feel his heat, his strength, through her clothing all the way down to her feet. He kissed her as if he wanted to devour her, and she clung to his shoulders, ready, willing, desperate to be devoured, reveling in every nuance of his tongue exploring her mouth with such fevered, passionate perfection.

With a moan of pure pleasure, she wrapped her arms around his neck and held on. He kissed her again and again, drugging meldings of lips, breath, and tongues, reducing her to a tiny boat adrift in a fierce storm, desperately trying to stay afloat in the sea of sensation drowning her.

Utterly lost, she strained closer to him, plunging her fingers through his still damp hair, pressing her aching breasts against his chest, overheated, burning. Wanting. Needing.

She squirmed against him and he changed tempo, gentling their wild, frantic exchange to a slow, deep, languid seduction that pulled her deeper into the vortex of dizzying need. His hands roamed freely down her back, up her sides, then between them to caress her breasts. She arched into his palms, a silent plea he instantly answered. One warm hand slipped into her bodice, his fingers, his magical fingers, stroking one aching nipple, then the other, shooting fire straight to her womb.

Abandoning her lips, he kissed his way down her neck, then also deserted her bodice, skimming his hands down her back. Cool air touched her overheated limbs and she realized he'd lifted her skirt, the material bunched around her waist. With nothing but her linen drawers now between them, he insinuated one knee between hers and she willingly spread her legs wider, seeking to press her aching feminine flesh against him. Cupping her buttocks, the heat of his palms branding her through the thin material, he urged her higher, tighter against him, guiding her hips in slow circles against his hard thigh.

Victoria's head fell back and a long moan of pure pleasure vibrated in her throat. She was vaguely aware of him kissing her neck, of her hands gripping his bare shoulders, but all her focus narrowed to the throbbing flesh between her legs. To the incredible sensations jolting through her with each circle of her hips from his guiding hands. He increased the pace, and her breath became ragged, choppy, her hips undulating, pressing harder against him, more desperate, seeking relief, moving closer to the precipice of something . . . something . . .

And then it was as if she soared over the edge and dove into a whirlpool of sensation. Pleasure spasmed through her, dragging a surprised cry from her lips that melted into a low growling sound as the tremors tapered off, then subsided. Weak with a delightful, boneless languor, she leaned forward, grateful for the support of his strong arms around her. Closing her eyes, she rested her forehead in the curve where his neck and shoulder met and drew a deep breath. Her head filled with the scent of his skin—a warm, delicious, heady scent she couldn't describe other than to know that it intoxicated her. And that she would never forget it.

When her breathing evened and she felt able to move, she lifted her head. And stared into his serious gold-flecked hazel eyes. Dear God, the way he'd made her feel . . . she'd read about a woman's pleasure in the *Ladies' Guide,* but the description in no way did justice to what she'd just experienced. And he'd given her that pleasure without even intimately touching her. What on earth would it be like if he had? How much more incredible could it be?

She felt a pressing need to say something, to acknowledge what had just happened to her, but for the life of her, she couldn't think of any words befitting the occasion. No doubt in a week or two she'd think of something brilliant, but right now all she could find to say was, "Nathan."

His expression softened and the ghost of a smile touched his lips. "Victoria." He gently tucked a stray curl behind her ear. "Are you all right?"

She briefly closed her eyes and released a long, feminine sigh. "I'm . . . marvelous. Except for my knees. I seem to have misplaced them."

His grin flashed, then he brushed the pad of his thumb over her lips. "I didn't hurt you?"

"No." She rested her palm against his cheek. "You . . . dazzled me. Stole my breath."

"As you stole mine. And dazzled me." After dropping a quick kiss to the tip of her nose, he said, "I'll get dressed so we can look for your knees." He gently released her, and her upraised skirts unfurled like the curtain coming down after the opera. When he bent to retrieve his clothing, Victoria knew she should turn away to afford him some privacy, but she simply couldn't tear her gaze from him. And surely she should feel some remorse, a flicker of shame, but all she felt was exhilaration. If she felt bad about anything, it was that this interlude was over.

As she watched him pull on his breeches, she couldn't help but notice his still aroused state. Clearing her throat, she said, "You allowed me great freedom with your body."

"It was my pleasure."

"And mine as well."

He shrugged into his shirt and smiled. "I'm glad."

"You, um, didn't take the same degree of liberties with me."

"An effort that cost me greatly, I assure you."

"May I ask why you . . . made such an effort?"

He halted in the act of fastening his shirt, and his gaze sharpened. "Are you asking me why I didn't make love to you?"

Warmth flooded her cheeks. "I'm wondering why you didn't touch me as I touched you."

"It's the same question, because if I had touched you in that way, we absolutely would have made love."

"And you didn't want that."

His brows shot up. "On the contrary, I believe it was painfully obvious that I did. Not making love to you was solely a result of me considering you, not myself." Leaving his shirt flapping open, he erased the distance between them. Lightly clasping her upper arms, his gaze searched hers. "Victoria, surely you realize that if we were to make love, I risk nothing, whereas you risk everything. Regardless of what else you may think of me, I am not a man to simply take pleasure without thought to the consequences. And to be brutally blunt, the time to ponder such decisions is not when one is sexually aroused or basking in the afterglow of pleasure." His fingers flexed on her arms. "Something happens to me when I touch you . . ." He shook his head. ". . . hell, something happens to me when I'm in the same room as you. You impair my control. My good judgment."

A thrill ran through her at his admission. "There is no point in me denying that I suffer from the same 'something' as you."

Any thought that her admission would please him vanished with the troubled look in his eyes. "Then there is much for you to consider. And it's best that we return to the house now."

Releasing her, he stepped away to finish dressing. With a start she realized that it had grown quite late, the shadows of the approaching dusk an obscuring gray under the dense cover of trees. She brushed the wrinkles from her gown and repaired as best she could the havoc his hands had wreaked on her hair. When they both finished, he extended his arm with a courtly flourish, indicating she should precede him on the narrow trail leading back to the main path. As she moved past him, however, he reached out and snagged her hand, raising it to his lips. Although the light kiss he brushed over the backs of her fingers could be described as proper, there was nothing proper about the wicked gleam in his eyes.

"Just so you know, Victoria," he said, his warm breath caressing her skin, "regardless of what other decisions might be made, I fully intend to have my revenge for the sweet torture I endured this afternoon at your hands. And I shall have it when you least expect it."

Whoosh. Good lord, she needed to carry a bucket of water about so as to douse the flames this man ignited. He started down the narrow path, clearly expecting her to follow, no easy task when he'd reduced both her mind and knees to porridge with his announcement. But the encroaching darkness snapped her from her stupor and she hurried after him. The trail veered, and as soon as she rounded the bend, she saw him standing in the path ahead, clearly waiting for her. Her gaze narrowed on his face and she moved forward. *Humph.* Obviously he thought he could just toss out provocative statements then saunter away. Well, she'd show him that—

"Victoria!"

Nathan's shouted warning came just as she was grabbed from behind by a muscled arm that trapped her against a hard chest. She saw the silver glint of a knife just as the blade was pressed against her throat.

Fifteen

In her pursuit of intimate fulfillment and adventure, Today's Modern Woman may find herself in a situation that could be deemed dangerous. In that case, she must remain calm and stay focused on her objective: extricating herself from said situation. If all attempts at diplomacy fail, a well-placed kick will usually do the trick.

A Ladies' Guide to the Pursuit of
Personal Happiness and Intimate Fulfillment
by Charles Brightmore

"*O*ne sound, one movement out of you," the man growled next to Victoria's ear, "and you'll seal your own fate."

Terrified, she clamped her lips shut and ceased struggling, her gaze searching out Nathan.

Nathan started forward but skidded to a halt when the man jammed the knife tighter against her throat. His gaze flicked to hers and he shot her a look that clearly indicated she should listen to the madman with the knife.

"One more step and I'll slit her ear to ear," the man

threatened in a tone that slithered dread down her spine.

"Let her go," Nathan said in a frigid, steel-edged voice Victoria had never heard from him before.

"Happy to oblige ye, after I get what I want."

"I'll give whatever you want. *After* you let her go."

" 'Fraid it don't work like that, seein' as how I'm the one holdin' the blade to her throat. Now, speakin' of blades, I want ye to slip yours out of yer boot, real nice and slow, then toss it in the bushes. You make any fast moves, Doctor, and the lady'll suffer."

"You know who I am," Nathan stated in a deadly voice.

"Who ye are *and* who ye were." He jerked Victoria tighter against him. "Do as I said."

Scarcely able to breathe with the blade pressed so tight against her throat, she watched Nathan, his gaze never shifting from the man's face, slowly slip a knife from his boot, then toss it lightly toward the bushes. "Now let her go."

"As soon as ye hand over the letter."

"What letter?"

With the flick of his wrist the man nicked the skin beneath Victoria's jaw and she gasped. Warm wetness trickled down her neck and black spots danced before her eyes at the realization that it was her own blood.

"Yer stupid question just gave the lady a scar. If ye ask another, it'll cost her an ear. If ye claim ye don't have what I want, she'll lose her life. Understand?"

A brief pause, then Nathan said, "Yes."

"I want the letter that was in the lady's bag. *Now*. Hand it over, nice and slow, and I'll be on my way."

Dear God. She was going to die. Nathan didn't have the letter *here*. She knew he'd try to save her, but what could he possibly do with no weapon and no letter? Her life was going to end. Here. Now. At the hands of this horrible man. Who would probably kill Nathan, too. Stark terror at the realization edged black around her vision.

"How do I know you'll let her go once I give you what you want?"

"Guess ye'll just have to take my word for it." The evil chuckle next to her ear raised prickles all over her clammy skin. "Don't worry, Doctor. My word's as good as yours. Honor among thieves, you know."

Drawing what was surely her last breath, she watched Nathan slowly reach down again, this time pulling a folded piece of ivory vellum from his boot. Shock trembled through her. The letter. He had it. Hope flooded her, pushing aside the fear that had momentarily crippled her.

But surely Nathan wouldn't really give the letter, the map, to this brigand. Surely any second he would utilize some ingenious spy tactic to disarm and capture this thief. Instead, he slowly straightened and extended his arm, holding the note between his thumb and index fingers.

"Toss it," her captor growled. "So it lands right nice near my feet. If it don't, the lady will pay."

The note sailed through the air. With her chin pointing nearly toward the sky, Victoria couldn't see where the letter landed, but since her throat remained uncut, she assumed Nathan's aim had been true.

"Now, on the ground, facedown," the man ordered Nathan.

All right, any second now Nathan would employ one of his spy tricks to save them and disarm the man. She kept her gaze trained on his face, waiting for some sort of signal, some indication of what he wanted her to do, but his gaze never wavered from the man holding her. She watched, every nerve alert. Nathan lowered himself to the dirt path as instructed.

"Hands behind your head, Doctor."

Nathan clasped his hands behind his head.

A fury unlike anything she'd ever before experienced erupted in Victoria. Damnation, he was going to get away with this!

"Now, little lady," her captor said, his hot breath by her ear, "you're going to walk over to the doctor and lie face-down with yer hands behind your head, just like him. Make a sound or do anything other than that and I'll sink this blade right between yer shoulder blades. And the doctor will be next."

She'd never felt so helpless or filled with rage in her life. She longed to scream, struggle, but she feared he'd carry out his threat. Raised up on her toes as she was, she had no leverage to even stomp on his foot. But something inside wouldn't allow her to do *nothing*. Perhaps if she could shove the note out of the thief's reach, it would give Nathan a chance to act. In a blind attempt to do so, she kicked her leg to the side.

But at that precise instant her captor released her, shoving her roughly away from him. She stumbled forward, her boot catching on the hem of her gown. With an involuntary cry, she pitched forward, falling hard on her knees, breaking her fall with her hands. She skidded forward, landing on her stomach with a jarring thud, knocking the breath from her lungs.

She'd barely realized what had happened when gentle hands grasped her shoulders and turned her over. She looked up into Nathan's face, his expression stark with worry.

"Victoria," he said in a low, urgent voice, his gaze riveting on her throat while he yanked off his shirt. She touched her fingers to the stinging spot and felt warm stickiness.

"I'm bleeding."

"Yes, I know. I need to see how badly."

"Where is—"

"He's gone."

"But he has—"

"Shhhh. It doesn't matter. Don't worry."

"But you must—"

"Take care of you. Don't talk. Just tilt your head this way a bit for me . . . that's it." She felt him wipe something soft . . . must have been his shirt . . . against her stinging throat. "The cut is small," he said in a calm voice tinged with relief. "I'm going to apply pressure to it to stop the bleeding. Stay still and relax."

She remained still, although how she was supposed to relax remained a mystery, and watched him fold over a section of his shirt, which he gently but firmly pressed to the skin beneath her jaw. Holding the material in place with one hand, he turned his attention to the rest of her, examining the scrapes on her palms, then lifting her skirt to gently probe her sore knees. He then ran his hand over her, pressing here and there, asking if this or that hurt. This was an aspect of him she'd never seen—his professional side. His touch was that of a doctor seeing to a patient—tender, skillful and impersonal.

"Nothing serious," he reported, giving her a reassuring smile. "You'll be sore for a day or two, but I have some salve that will help." His gaze shifted to her neck. "Now, let's take another look at that cut."

After slowly releasing the pressure, he removed the makeshift bandage. "The bleeding has nearly stopped." He refolded his shirt then settled the material back against her neck. Taking her hand, he set it on the bandage. "Do you feel strong enough to apply pressure to that?"

"Of course. I'm not the hothouse flower you think I am." She'd meant to sound firm, but to her mortification her bottom lip quivered and hot moisture pushed behind her eyes, both made worse by the tender smile he gave her.

"My darling Victoria, you are the bravest girl I've ever met."

"I tried to be—"

"You were magnificent."

A fat tear hovered on her lashes, blurring her vision then dribbling down her cheek. "I don't know what's wrong with me. I'm not at all a weepy sort of female." Another tear overflowed and she sniffled. "Really, I'm not."

He brushed away the moisture with gentle fingers. "I know, sweetheart. You're a warrior. But even warriors get the sniffles after a tough battle."

"They do?"

"Absolutely." And with that, he scooped her up into his arms.

"Wh-What are you doing?"

"Bringing you back to the house." He started briskly down the path. "Hold on."

Victoria wrapped her free arm around his neck, her hand settling on his warm, bare skin. "I can walk," she felt compelled to protest.

"I know. But it makes me feel better to hold you, so humor me. Please."

"Well, as long as you said 'please.'" She sighed and snuggled closer to him, resting her cheek against his strong, warm shoulder. Her eyelids drooped, and suddenly she felt as if all her strength evaporated, leaving her exhausted. But not so exhausted that she couldn't ask, "That man knew you. Did you know him?"

"No."

"How do you suppose he found out about the letter?"

"I don't know. And quite frankly, right now I'm more concerned with getting you properly seen to than I am about wondering about the bloody bastard who injured you. We can discuss this after I've treated you and you're safely ensconced by a warm fire. For now, just concentrate on keeping pressure on that cut."

She vaguely noted his ungentlemanly use of an obscenity, but since she felt so drained, she decided not to take issue with him.

When they arrived at the house, they were greeted by a stunned Langston. After assuring the wide-eyed butler that she wasn't seriously injured, Nathan said tersely, "I need hot water, clean linen strips, and brandy delivered to my bedchamber immediately." He then headed up the stairs.

"*Your* bedchamber?" Victoria said in a scandalized whisper. "You cannot bring me to *your* bedchamber."

"The hell I can't. It's where my medical supplies are, and I'm not leaving you to fetch them."

"I would be perfectly fine alone for a few moments."

"No doubt. But I wouldn't be. And there's no point in arguing since we've already arrived."

Nathan dipped his knees to open the door, which he purposely left ajar for propriety's sake. Not that he cared a jot about propriety, but he didn't want to cause Victoria any undue stress. Swiftly crossing the blue and maroon Axminster rug, he strode directly to his bed, where he gently lowered her to the counterpane.

"Keep the pressure on just a bit longer," he said, keeping his features perfectly composed as he touched his fingers to her hand, which held his folded shirt to her neck. His shirt that bore crimson streaks of her blood. "I'm just going to get my medical bag and wash my hands."

He walked to the ceramic pitcher and basin set in the corner next to the massive cherrywood wardrobe where he'd stored his medical bag. Although he hated to take his eyes off her for even a second, he kept his back to her while he poured water into the basin and scrubbed his hands with soap. God knows he needed a moment to compose himself.

Bloody hell, if he lived to be one hundred he would never forget the sickening sight of her with that knife held to her neck. The only time he'd ever come close to feeling such naked fear was when he found Gordon and Colin shot. And even that didn't seem to compare with the stark terror he'd experienced watching that madman materialize seemingly from nowhere, detaching himself from the shadows behind her, that flash of lethal steel as he grabbed her. Her blood trailing down her neck to stain her gown.

His fault, damn it, *his* fault. He'd been too far away to protect her. Why had he let her out of his sight for even an instant? He'd thought she was right behind him. When he turned and discovered she wasn't, he should have gone back. But he'd seen her in the next instant, walking toward him, and he stood and watched her approach, loving the way she moved. The look of her. And then the shock of that moving shadow—

He squeezed his eyes tightly shut to banish the nauseating image. Later. He could dwell on it later, along with the retribution he would hand that bastard when he found him. And he had every intention of finding him. Right now she needed a doctor.

A knock sounded and he turned to see Langston enter

carrying a huge tray bearing a basin of steaming water, linen, and brandy. "On the bedside table, Dr. Nathan?"

"Yes." Drying his hands, Nathan asked, "Where is Lady Delia?"

"In the drawing room with your father."

"Good. I've no wish to alarm them, especially given the nonthreatening nature of Lady Victoria's injuries. Give me a quarter hour to clean and dress her cuts, then I'll come down and tell them myself."

"Yes, Dr. Nathan." Langston cleared his throat. "You might wish to don a shirt before you do so."

Nathan looked down at his bare chest, nonplussed. "Good idea. Thank you."

With a nod, the butler quit the room, leaving the door ajar. Nathan opened the wardrobe, grabbed his medical bag in one hand and a folded, clean shirt with the other, then crossed to the bed. He looked down at Victoria's pale face, and his chest constricted at the sight. Summoning his professional mien, he set his medical bag on the floor next to the bed and offered her his best doctorly smile.

"How are you feeling?" he asked, shrugging into his shirt.

"A bit sore," she admitted with a wan smile. "Thirsty."

After hastily tucking in his shirttails, he poured her a generous finger of brandy. Hoisting a hip onto the edge of the bed, he held the glass to her lips. "Sip this."

She obediently sipped, then wrinkled her nose. "*Blech.* That is absolutely wretched."

"Actually, given my father's taste in brandy and the fact that I, um, found numerous cases of Napolean's finest, I suspect it's really excellent brandy."

She raised a brow. "*Found?* Where does one *find* cases of French brandy?"

He shrugged and adopted his most innocent expression. "Oh, here and there,"

"Hmmm. Well, if this is the finest Napolean could do, no wonder he was exiled."

A laugh rumbled in Nathan's throat, a welcome relief from the tension gripping him. "It may not be to your taste, but it will help relieve your aches and pains, so sip."

She shot him a potent glare, but obeyed. When the glass was empty, she said, "That vile stuff will burn a hole in my stomach."

"How lucky that I'm a doctor and can cure you."

"*You're* the one who caused the problem by making me drink it."

"And never let it be said that I don't fix any affliction I've caused." He set the empty glass aside and soaked a handful of linen strips in the steaming water. "Now, if you'll cooperate and let me do my job, I shall be most appreciative."

She eyed him with a sudden combination of suspicion and trepidation. "How appreciative?"

"Appreciative enough to arrange for a dinner tray and a hot, soothing bath in your bedchamber. How does that sound?"

"Lovely. It's just that . . ."

He squeezed the water from the linen strips. "What?"

"I don't much care for doctors." The words came out in a rush.

He nodded gravely. "Oh, neither do I. Nasty old men with cold hands who jab and prod exactly where it hurts."

"Precisely!"

"How fortunate for you that I am neither nasty nor old, my hands are never cold, and I would throw myself into the Thames before I would ever hurt you."

A bit of the tension left her eyes, but she still looked nervous. "I'm not certain how comforting that is, given your obvious predilection for splashing about in the water."

"Lake water, yes. Thames River water? Absolutely not." He gently removed her hand from the soiled linen she still pressed to her neck. "What happened to my brave, fierce warrior woman of the forest?"

"Perhaps she's not as brave as you thought."

"Nonsense. She is courage personified." As he spoke, he gently bathed away the dried blood, relieved to see that the bleeding had completely ceased. "And she has my permission to cosh me with the decanter if during the course of my duties I displease her in any way."

"Agreed."

"And very quickly agreed, I see. However, no coshing until my duties have been completed. Now tell me your thoughts about the ruffian who absconded with our note."

"Absconded? I'm not certain that correctly describes what happened. It seemed you gave up the note very willingly." Her tone sounded faintly accusatory.

"I most certainly did. Seeing as how his knife could have cut through your neck in an instant, I thought it best." After applying salve to her cut, he turned his attention to her scraped hands.

"I didn't know you carried the letter with you."

"I wanted to keep it safe."

An unladylike snort escaped her. "Clearly you should have picked a different spot."

He cocked a brow and dabbed at her palms. "Are you upset with me?"

"Do you really want to know?"

"Of course."

"Well then, yes, I am upset. Or at least disappointed.

You did nothing to stop that man! I thought spies knew all sorts of tricks and maneuvers to disarm and outwit their opponents. Yet you simply did everything he asked and now he has the note and map."

"And your head is still attached to your shoulders. Which would you think is more important to me?"

She instantly looked chastened. "It's not that I'm ungrateful. I'm just concerned that he'll find the jewels before we do."

"I don't think so. At least not with the letter and map *he* has."

"What do you mean?"

"I mean that the letter and map he possesses will send him on what is fondly referred to in the Official Spy Handbook as 'The Wild Goose Chase.'" He eased her skirts up to bathe her knees.

"But . . . but how?"

"I wrote a false letter containing wrong information. Drew a fake map clearly depicting the Isles of Scilly, which lay twenty-eight miles off the coast of Lands End." He shrugged. "That should keep him far enough away from here until we conclude our investigation using the real note and map, which are perfectly safe, by the way."

She stared at him, clearly taken aback, then her expression changed to a combination of admiration and pure chagrin.

"Oh," she said in a small voice. "It would appear I owe you an apology."

"Well, if you *really* feel it's necessary—"

"Oh, I do." Gazing up at him, she said softly, "I'm sorry, Nathan. I should have known you'd be unsurpassedly brilliant."

"Hmmm. Yes, you should have." He smiled and lightly massaged the healing ointment into her palm.

"I feel like a complete fool. The reason I tripped was because I was attempting to kick the note out of his reach. I thought that might give you the opportunity to retrieve your knife or somehow subdue him. I didn't know you had everything under control."

He barely swallowed the humorless laugh that rose in his throat. Under control? He'd never felt more helpless in his life.

"Of course, you might have *told* me about the fake note in the boot ploy," she said. "But regardless, you saved my life." She brought his hand to her lips and kissed his knuckles. "My hero. Thank you."

He brushed his fingertips lightly over her jaw. "You're welcome. Glad to know you're not disappointed I beat the enemy with my brain rather than my brawn. But mark my words, when I see that bastard again, he will pay dearly for touching you. For hurting you."

A shudder ran through her. "I hope never to see him again. I've never been so frightened in my life."

Never been so frightened? That makes two of us. He lowered her skirts to cover her knees. "I'm finished with my treatments. How do you feel?"

"Finished? Already?" She flexed her hands, bent her knees, and wiggled her jaw. "I feel very much improved."

"Excellent."

Her eyes narrowed, but amusement glittered in her gaze. "You tricked me."

He adopted an expression of innocent shock. "I?"

"You distracted me from your ministrations by urging me to talk."

"Did I? It's been my observation that you seem to require very little encouragement to chatter away."

"Hmmm. Very clever. And effective. My aunt told me she thought you'd have an excellent bedside manner. I shouldn't have doubted her, as she has always proven to be uncannily correct in her assessments."

"Then I thank you both for the compliment," he said lightly. "As for the rest of your treatment, you're to allow the salve I applied to soak in for the next two hours, during which time you will remain in bed and eat dinner. Then you shall have your promised warm bath, after which the salve needs to be reapplied. Then it's off to bed for you. Agreed?"

"Yes, Doctor."

"Excellent. A docile patient."

"I'm nothing of the sort. I'm simply pretending to be to repay your kindness."

"I see." He put his supplies away, then firmly closed his medical bag. The instant he'd done so, he reached for the brandy decanter.

Victoria shook her head. "Oh, no. Not again. I'm not drinking any more of that foul brew."

"Not to worry. This one is for me." He poured himself two fingers and tossed it back in a single gulp. Closing his eyes, he savored the fire heating its way to his belly and allowed his tense muscles to relax. When he opened his eyes, he set aside the glass. Lightly clasping her shoulders, he looked steadily into her eyes.

"Now that my doctor duties have been completed, I want you to know that there is no kindness for you to repay. The fact that you were injured is entirely my fault."

"It is nothing of the sort—"

"*Entirely* my fault, Victoria. Your father sent you to me to protect. I failed today. But I give you my word I will not fail again."

Her gaze softened and she pressed her palm against his cheek. "You didn't fail, Nathan."

"That you are lying in that bed proves otherwise. Just as this episode proves that someone is desperate to find those jewels. And they'll do anything to succeed." He laid his hand atop hers then turned his head to lightly kiss her abraded palm. "Promise me you will not venture anywhere outside the house alone." He hadn't meant to sound so harsh, but the scare he'd suffered still lurked within him.

"I promise."

With a nod, he rose. "I'm going to tell your aunt and my father what happened. Then I'll send your aunt to you so she can settle you in your bedchamber and help you change clothes."

Because he couldn't stop himself, he leaned down and brushed his lips against her brow. Then he quit the room. As he walked down the corridor, his lips pressed into a grim line. He didn't know who was responsible for this, but unlike three years ago, he wasn't going to walk away this time. This time he'd have his answers. And the person responsible would pay.

Sixteen

While Today's Modern Woman should seek out her own life experiences at every opportunity, it is always wise to listen to other women who, through their own daring, have already gained knowledge of intimate matters. Time spent talking to those well versed on such subjects can prove comforting, enlightening, and offer helpful guidance. Besides, it is always more fun to have a partner in crime.

*A Ladies' Guide to the Pursuit of
Personal Happiness and Intimate Fulfillment*
by Charles Brightmore

$\mathcal{V}$ictoria set aside her silver dinner tray, then leaned back against the bed pillows with a satisfied sigh. "That chowder was delicious." She smiled at her aunt who, after helping her get settled and changed into a fresh linen night rail, had had a dinner tray sent up as well. "Do you suppose the cook would share the recipe?"

"Well, if she won't give it to us, surely Dr. Oliver could charm it out of her." She regarded Victoria over the edge of her crystal wine goblet. "I believe if anyone other than he had brought me the news of your frightful experience, I would have quite fainted away. Dr. Oliver, however, has . . . a way about him. He's very confident. And reassuring."

"Yes, he is." *And so many other things*. Things that excited and delighted her. Yet confused and unsettled her.

"And so devilishly attractive," Aunt Delia continued. "And strong. He carried you all the way back to the house!" She made a fanning motion with her napkin. "Clearly he's most vigorous. And so concerned for you, Victoria."

Heat crept up Victoria's face from beneath the neckline of her nightgown. "Naturally he was concerned. He is a doctor. He is concerned for all his patients."

Aunt Delia set down her teacup with a decided click. "My dear girl, you've adroitly sidestepped the subject of Dr. Oliver all through dinner, and it's time to stop." Her eyes filled with concern. "Dearest, if you think that his concern is only that of a doctor for his patient, then you are in need of a stronger restorative. Surely you can see he is deeply attracted to you. And a blind person could see that you are attracted to him as well."

She inwardly winced at her apparent transparency. "Given his good looks, I'm sure most women would find him attractive."

"Yes. But you are the only one I am worried about." Aunt Delia rose from her wing chair and resettled herself on the edge of Victoria's bed. "I can see you are troubled, Victoria. Why don't you talk to me about what's distressing you?"

Victoria plucked at the counterpane. The need to share with someone the plethora of conflicted feelings overwhelmed her. But she couldn't confide to her aunt the sensual nature of those feelings, of her encounters with

Nathan. Couldn't share the scandalous desires, the heat, the needs he inspired in her. Her poor aunt would swoon from shock. Even worse, such an admission would certainly mean her aunt would no longer allow her any time alone with Nathan. While her inner voice said that was surely for the best, her heart did not agree. Besides, how could she hope to discuss something that she didn't herself comprehend?

Forcing a smile, she said, "I appreciate your offer, Aunt Delia, but I'm fine."

"I see. You think that I will wilt from shock, but I assure you such is not the case." She laid a sympathetic hand over Victoria's. "I understand completely, my dear. You have always been a planner. Even as a child you planned your tea parties, and as a young girl, your ensembles down to the last detail. Planned the next ten books you intended to read. During the Season, you've planned precisely which parties you wanted to attend, which gentlemen you would partner for each dance. You've planned exactly the sort of man you should marry and know precisely the sort of wedding you want—plans to be put into action immediately upon your return to London. You came to Cornwall with a definite plan in your mind—to endure this visit your father insisted upon for the shortest amount of time possible, then return to London and decide upon a husband. And now you're completely out of sorts because the devastatingly attractive Dr. Oliver and the unexpected feelings he inspires have thrown all your fine plans into total disarray."

Her aunt's assessment of the situation was so accurate, Victoria could only stare. "How did you know that?"

"Two reasons. First, my intuition is—and I say this with the utmost modesty—formidable. And second, because you and I are very much alike, and that is precisely the way I would react in your situation. I think you're learning that the problem with plans is that they lack spontaneity."

"I don't like spontaneity."

"On the contrary, I think you're discovering, much to your dismay, that you like it very much. You only think you don't like it because you've never known it before. It's rather like saying that you don't care for blueberry pie when you've never tasted blueberry pie." Her gaze searched Victoria's for several heartbeats. "Neither Branripple nor Dravensby affect you this way."

There was no point in denying it. Indeed, it was a relief to admit it. "No. And I can't understand *why*. Both are handsome. Certainly I'm much more suited to either of them than I am to Dr. Oliver."

Aunt Delia's brows shot upward. "Are you?"

"Of course. Lords Branripple and Dravensby are not only superior matches socially, I have much more in common with them."

"Really? You don't find them . . . boring?"

Dead boring, she realized. However, instead of helping, this conversation confused her even more. "I don't understand. I would have thought you'd warn me against a man like Dr. Oliver."

"A warm, handsome man who is clearly besotted with you and who puts that sparkle in your eye?"

"A man who does not possess a title. Who lives in a modest cottage, earns a modest living, and eschews Society."

"None of which make him *un*suitable, my dear. He may not be the heir, but he is still the son of an earl."

"But what of securing my future? Marriage to either Branripple or Dravensby would make me a countess. Guarantee my position in Society. The decisions I make now will affect the rest of my life."

"That is true." Aunt Delia gently squeezed her hand. "But surely you know your father wouldn't leave you financially destitute."

"Father expects me to marry well."

"Of course he does. But by 'well' I'm sure he means that he wants you to be happy." Her aunt drew a breath, then continued, "What of Lords Sutton and Alwyck? You have a viscount and an earl right here at your fingertips, and 'tis clear from the two evenings we've just spent in their company that they both find you attractive. I would be hard pressed to choose who was the handsomer, as they are both extraordinarily comely."

"Yes, they are." But neither made her pulse jump or her heart stutter. Neither made her want to be near him just so she wouldn't miss one of his smiles or a single word he uttered. Neither made her fingers tingle with the overwhelming need to touch him. Nathan did all those things simply by . . . being. "But both of their estates and lives are here in Cornwall. While this hasn't proven the dreadful place I'd envisioned, I could never live so far from Town. From civilization. Besides, I barely know either gentleman, whereas I've been acquainted with Branripple and Dravensby for years."

"You haven't known Dr. Oliver very long, either," Aunt Delia said softly, "which just goes to show that the length of the acquaintance is not an accurate measure to one's feelings." Her gaze shifted toward the fire and her eyes took on a faraway expression. "Sometimes a person we've just met can ignite a spark, a desire, a yearning that someone we've known for years has never lit."

She blinked twice, then seemed to recall herself and turned back to Victoria. "I'm certain that either Branripple or Dravensby would make polite, acceptable husbands who would give you little trouble. But search your heart,

Victoria. Life can be staid and boring, or it can be a grand adventure. Life with a staid, boring man will be just that. On the other hand, life with someone who makes your heart soar . . ." She heaved a dreamy sigh the likes of which Victoria had never heard from her. "That life will be a glorious adventure."

"Perhaps. But one must *eat* while on this great adventure."

"True. Though one need not feast on the richest cuisine every day to appease the appetite."

"It is not enough to be physically attracted to someone. I have nothing in common with Dr. Oliver."

"Really? His father has told me a great deal about him, and from what he's said, you share a number of similar interests."

"Such as?"

"A love of reading. A passion for knowledge. A fondness for fairy tales. You both like animals."

Victoria looked toward the ceiling. "He does not keep everyday, ordinary animals."

Her aunt shrugged. "He is not an everyday, ordinary man. You're both intelligent, and clearly he recognizes that trait in you and admires it. A smart woman would certainly impress a man like Dr. Oliver."

"Perhaps I don't want to impress him."

"*Pshaw.* Any woman who draws breath would want to impress that divine man. Do you want to know what I think?"

Even though she wasn't sure, Victoria nodded. "Of course."

"I think you're afraid to impress him. That you're trying to keep some distance between you, to keep in place whatever barricades you've managed to erect."

"Surely given our situations, that is for the best. When I return to London, I am going to choose another man to marry. And I am not at all the sort of woman Dr. Oliver wants. He believes me a hothouse flower."

"He may not *want* to want you, but he most emphatically does want you." Aunt Delia pursed her lips and studied her for several seconds, then what looked like satisfaction flashed in her eyes. "He's kissed you."

Fire scorched Victoria's cheeks. Before she could reply, her aunt said briskly, "I can see quite clearly that he has. And that he knows how to kiss a woman."

Bemused at this frank talk from her aunt, Victoria shook her head. "You're not shocked? Scandalized?"

"My dear, I would be shocked to learn that he hadn't. And frankly disappointed in him. 'Twould be a shame for a man not to deliver on the promise hinted at by that devilish gleam in his eye." But then her gaze turned searching. "And now your feminine curiosity has been awakened."

Victoria bit her bottom lip and nodded, forcing back the image of a wet, naked Nathan from her mind. "Jolted wide-awake, I'm afraid."

"Has he spoken of his feelings for you?"

"No."

"As he strikes me as most forthright, 'tis then clear he is as befuddled as you."

"More likely because there are no feelings to speak of."

Aunt Delia waved away the words with a flick of her wrist. "He finds himself enamored of a woman I'm certain is nothing like his usual sort."

An image exploded in Victoria's mind . . . of Nathan, naked, aroused, lowering his head to kiss a woman. A woman who wasn't her. White-hot jealously speared through her.

A slow smile curved Aunt Delia's lips. "That must vex him dreadfully. And the thought of you marrying another—that would not please him one bit." Her smile disappeared and she fixed her gaze on Victoria. "The question is, what do you intend to do about this attraction? What is your plan?"

Plan? She had no plan. Her revenge scheme to give Nathan a kiss that would haunt him and then simply walk away now seemed ridiculously naive. Which left her, for the first time since she could remember, without a plan. She was simply a feather adrift on tempest-roiled seas, tossed about with abandon, no destination in sight.

Victoria cleared her throat. "I'm afraid I haven't yet formed a plan. Indeed I'm . . . rather at a loss."

Aunt Delia nodded thoughtfully. "Believe it or not, Victoria, I have found myself in circumstances precisely like this. And you are correct—the decisions you make now will affect the rest of your life. Therefore it is imperative you choose wisely." She rose. "There is something I have in my bedchamber I must show you. I'll return in a moment."

She departed the room. Victoria hadn't even begun to try to assimilate the stunning turn of this conversation, the unexpected things her aunt had said, when she returned, carrying a maroon satin satchel closed by a tasseled drawstring top.

"What is that?" Victoria asked as her aunt again sat on the edge of the bed.

In answer, her aunt loosened the drawstring ribbon and reached into the bag. She withdrew an ornate gold ring set with diamonds. "My wedding ring."

Victoria recognized the piece but hadn't seen it in years. "You don't wear it anymore."

"I removed it from my finger the day Geoffrey died, and I've never worn it since."

Sympathy pulled at Victoria at her aunt's flat tone. Uncle Geoffrey had been a dour, humorless man with a penchant for drinking and, according to rumor, brothels. Aunt Delia rarely mentioned him.

She looked at the ring resting in her aunt's palm. She supposed some women might have liked it, given its obvious value, but it wasn't at all to her own taste. "Why do you show it to me?"

"Because I want to explain to you what it represents to me. It is a contradictory symbol, embodying all that I thought I wanted and everything I came to deplore. When I look back, when I realize how utterly naive I was when I married Geoffrey . . ." She shook her head. "I knew nothing. Nothing of the world. And as it turned out, nothing of myself. I was innocent in every way, and when I agreed to a marriage I believed was in my best interest, I thought that my innocence would serve me well."

She looked at Victoria, a wealth of experience and sadness in her blue eyes. "It did not serve me at all. When I now reflect upon my marriage, all I can think is, 'If I knew then what I know now . . .' "

"What?" Victoria finally asked softly when the silence continued, broken only by the ticking of the mantel clock. She held her breath, afraid to say anything else, afraid she would break the mood, making her aunt reconsider sharing these deeply personal confidences.

Her aunt's expression turned from bleak to fierce. "I would not have made the same choices, Victoria. I would have known to search my heart, my soul, to determine my *true* desires—not simply those which I just thought I wanted because my plans, my likes, had never been challenged. Then, once I'd determined what I *truly* wanted, what was *truly* important to me and my happiness, then I would have made my choices based on what *I wanted*. Not on what anyone else expected of me. Based on what would please me—not anyone else. And regardless of what battle I chose to wade into, I would have made certain I was well-armed and knew what to expect. Thomas Gray purported in his poetry that 'ignorance is bliss,' to which I can only say the man was a fool. As far as I am concerned, a lack of knowledge does not bring bliss—it is a breeding ground for disaster." She handed the silk bag to Victoria. "I want you to have this."

Puzzled and curious, Victoria reached into the bag and pulled out a slim book. She stared at it and went perfectly still. She wasn't certain if she were more shocked that her aunt possessed the volume or that she had given the book to her. She traced unsteady fingers over the discreet gold lettering on the brown leather cover. *A Ladies' Guide to the Pursuit of Personal Happiness and Intimate Fulfillment* by Charles Brightmore.

"You know of it, of course," Aunt Delia said. "Everyone does. It's been the talk of London for months. And with good reason, as its provocative advice steps far beyond what anyone would consider proper. But it offers direction and information I dearly wish I'd had at my disposal as a young woman. It's filled with information I want *you* to have, Victoria. That you *need* to have. So that you do not make the same mistakes I did. So that you have the knowledge to choose wisely. This trip to Cornwall has provided you with the chance to learn about yourself, far away from Society's prying eyes. It is an opportunity I dearly wish I'd had, and one I refuse to do anything to deny you."

Victoria tore her gaze away from the book to look up. Aunt Delia's blue eyes were filled with love and concern. Now she understood why her aunt had not been more diligent in her chaperoning duties. Without a word, Victoria slipped the book into the silk bag and handed it back to her aunt.

"I cannot accept it."

A blush stained Aunt Delia's cheeks. "I've shocked you. I'm sorry. It's just that—"

"Because I couldn't possibly deprive you of your copy when I already have one of my own." She cleared her throat. "A much read copy."

Aunt Delia blinked, then quickly recovered her aplomb. She offered Victoria a gentle smile filled with such understanding, it brought a lump to Victoria's throat. "Then have your adventure, darling. Live your life to the fullest. Do not allow your gender to determine your destiny. Rather, let Fate's hand caress you. Leave something to Chance. Follow your heart and see where it leads. You will always have my unwavering support." She pressed the silk bag containing the book to her chest and a look of determination came over her features. "Follow your heart," she reiterated softly. "I intend to."

"What do you mean?"

"I mean I want my heart, my soul, to sing. I deserve the grand passion, the happiness I was denied as a young woman, and should I have the opportunity, I'll not be denied again. You deserve that passion and happiness as well, my dear."

Victoria could scarce believe what she was hearing. Surely Aunt Delia wasn't suggesting that she . . . But it certainly seemed she was encouraging her to . . .

Take Nathan as a lover.

Whoosh. The mere idea speared fire through her that threatened to turn all her good intentions to ash. She hadn't allowed the idea to take root in her mind for fear of it overwhelming her. But now the thought was firmly planted. And growing at an alarming rate.

A knock sounded, startling both of them. "Come in," Victoria said.

The door opened to reveal Nathan. Victoria's heart shifted into a different beat. Harder, faster. His gaze swept over her, intense, searching, stealing her breath. Dressed in black breeches, white shirt, and an ivory waistcoat, he looked strong and masculine. And utterly beautiful. A shock of dark hair she knew felt like silk tumbled over his forehead, something that might have looked boyish on another man, but nothing about the man crossing the room could be described as boyish.

"Good evening, ladies," he said, his gaze taking in both of them. Then his attention focused solely on Victoria. "How are you feeling?"

Breathless. And it's all your fault. "Much improved. Dinner was delicious."

He smiled. "I'm glad you enjoyed it. I confess this isn't strictly a social call—I'm here as your physician."

Aunt Delia stood. "Shall I leave?"

"Not at all. Indeed your presence would serve as a distraction for my patient, who has expressed an aversion to doctors. Please, continue your conversation."

Victoria's gaze flew to her aunt's, whose eyes gleamed with unmistakable deviltry and mirth.

"Very well. Now what was it we were discussing, Victoria?" She adopted a puzzled expression and tapped her chin. "Ah, yes. Books we've recently read. What was the title you were recommending to me?"

Victoria coughed to disguise the bark of shocked laughter that rose in her throat. Heavens, when had Aunt Delia turned into such a minx? Praying the heat she felt in her cheeks wasn't as visible as it felt, she said in a repressive tone, "*Hamlet*."

Aunt Delia was all bafflement. "Are you certain? I thought you said—"

"*Hamlet*," Victoria broke in hastily, torn between horror and hilarity. "Definitely *Hamlet*."

Aunt Delia batted her eyes behind Nathan's broad back. "And here I though it was *A Midsummer Night's Dream*."

Nathan lifted one of Victoria's hands and gently examined her scraped palm. "So that is what ladies chat about amongst themselves?" he asked in an amused voice. "Shakespeare?"

"Yes," Victoria said quickly, before Aunt Delia could act upon the mischievous twinkle in her eye.

Nathan smiled. "And here I thought you talked about men."

"Shakespeare *was* a man," she said in an arid tone, valiantly trying to ignore the tingles of pleasure his touch invoked while he tilted up her chin to peer at her cut.

"I meant living, breathing men."

"Oh, we talk about them, too," Aunt Delia chimed in.

"Among other things," Victoria said with a quelling look at her aunt.

"My father and I missed you ladies at dinner this evening," Nathan said, lowering the counterpane then smoothing up her night rail just enough to look at her knees. His touch and demeanor were completely impersonal, but there was nothing impersonal about the heat the brush of his hands ignited on her skin.

"Your brother did not dine with you?" Victoria asked, appalled at how breathless she sounded.

"No. He traveled to Penzance earlier today and isn't expected home until late." He lowered her gown and covered her again with the sheet. Then he rose and smiled down at her. "Your bumps and cuts and scrapes are all looking fine. And you're no longer pale." His gaze touched her cheeks and a frown creased his brow. "In fact, you look rather flushed." Reaching out, he laid his hand against her forehead. Good Lord, how to tell him that his touch would only serve to brighten her coloring?

"No fever," he said with unmistakable relief, removing his hand.

"I feel fine. Truly. The ointment you used seemed to absorb the stinging."

"Good. Still, you will experience some soreness tomorrow. But your warm bath will help that." His gaze wandered across the room to the big brass tub that two footmen had set near the fireplace earlier. "I'll arrange for the water to be sent up. And when you're finished bathing, it's into the bed for you. You need your rest."

He turned toward Aunt Delia. "May I escort you downstairs, Lady Delia? My father is in the drawing room, hoping for a backgammon partner." He leaned toward her and said in a stage whisper, "He does not like to play me because I always beat him."

"I would be delighted to beat him as well," Aunt Delia said with a laugh. She leaned over Victoria and pressed a kiss on her cheek. "Think about what I said, darling," she whispered in her ear.

Nathan escorted her aunt across the room. Before closing the door behind them, he turned around and his gaze sought Victoria's. A long look passed between them, and her heart pounded, wondering what he was thinking. Something flashed in his eyes, then he said softly, "Enjoy your bath." And then he was gone.

But very much not forgotten.

Seventeen

If Today's Modern Woman should ever decide to grab hold of her destiny and tell the object of her affections "I want you" (and she is certainly encouraged to do such grabbing), she'd best be very certain because it is extremely unlikely the gentleman will turn down her invitation.

A Ladies' Guide to the Pursuit of
Personal Happiness and Intimate Fulfillment
by Charles Brightmore

With the catlike grace that had served him well during his service to the Crown, Nathan let go of the windowsill of the unused room on the floor above Victoria's bedchamber. He landed lightly on her balcony, then moving quickly into the shadows where the moonlight didn't reach, peered through the French windows. And stilled at the sight he beheld.

Victoria reclined in the brass tub, her silhouette glazed by the golden glow of the crackling fire. Her dark, shiny hair was piled on her head in artful disarray, several long tendrils trailing along her neck and cheeks. Curls of steam spiraled around her, glossing her cheekbones with dewy heat.

She held a book in front of her and appeared deeply engrossed in her reading, nibbling on her bottom lip. As he watched, an intriguing smile that seemed filled with secrets tilted her lips, and he found himself hoping it was thoughts of him that inspired such a look.

She slowly closed the book, setting it on the small round table that had been placed next to the bathtub to hold a pair of thick snowy towels. Then her eyes slid closed.

With an ease born of much practice, he soundlessly opened the French windows and made his way on silent feet across the room, carrying a single, long stem red rose. When he stood next to the tub, he looked down. Her head rested on the polished brass lip, exposing her elegant, damp neck. His gaze riveted on the red mark where the knife had nicked her and his jaw tightened. Forcing his attention away from the cut, he continued his perusal. Steamy water lapped at her shoulders, forming tiny pools in the delicate indents of her collarbone. Beneath the surface that shimmered gently with her breathing, full breasts topped with rosy nipples glistened. His gaze drifted over her stomach, the triangle of dark curls at the apex of her thighs, then along the line of her shapely legs. The tub was shorter than Victoria, and to compensate, she'd rested her crossed trim ankles on the other edge, leaving her calves and feet exposed to the air. Her feet were small, her instep a high curve his fingers itched to trace.

"Are you enjoying your bath, Victoria?"

Her eyes snapped open and she gasped. Water sloshed over the side of the tub as her feet slapped below the surface and she simultaneously crossed her legs and folded her arms across her chest. "Wh-What are you doing here?"

"I came to see if you were enjoying your bath." He held out the rose. "For you."

Her startled gaze skipped between him and the proffered flower. Then she reached up and took the stem, bringing the bloom to her face and burying her nose in its velvety petals. Looking at him over the top of the rose, she took in his attire, then asked, "Why are you dressed all in black?"

"So as to avoid detection from anyone who might be lurking outdoors while I swung down onto your balcony."

She looked quickly toward the French windows, then back at him. Although she still appeared stunned, there was no mistaking the flare of interest in her eyes. "You came in through the balcony? How?"

"Jumped down from the window on the floor above."

Her eyes widened. "You did not."

"I did."

"Are you mad? If you'd fallen, you could have been seriously injured."

"Dead, most likely," he corrected with a grave nod. "How fortunate I am sure-footed."

"Have you never heard of a *door*?"

"Too predictable, especially given that I wanted the element of surprise in my favor. Besides, I ran a far greater risk of discovery entering your bedchamber from the corridor. And what if the door had been locked? While I could have picked the lock, I risked discovery doing so. Nor did I have any wish to knock, for if I did, you might have been compelled to exit the tub and don a robe to open the door. Then I would have missed seeing you in the bath, and my darling Victoria, allow me to assure you, it is not a sight to be missed."

Crimson to rival the rose he'd given her stained her

cheeks. "So you jumped out of a window and landed on my balcony."

He shrugged. "It is the way of us spies. Although I admit I'm relieved I didn't injure any pertinent body parts. I'm a bit out of practice with the maneuver, I'm afraid."

"And you're here to examine my scrapes?"

"Not exactly," he said, crossing the room. When he reached the door, he turned the key in the lock. The soft click seemed to reverberate in the air. While walking slowly back to her, he rolled up his shirtsleeves to his elbows, noting how carefully she watched him, the alertness and awareness simmering in her eyes. When he reached the tub, he lowered himself to his knees and rested his forearms on the edge. The tips of his fingers gently stirred the water.

"I would of course be delighted to check on your injuries," he said, his gaze riveted on hers, "but in the interest of fair play, I must warn you, I am here not as a doctor but as a man. A man intent upon . . ." His voice trailed off and he reached out to slowly drag a single fingertip along the delicate line of her collarbone.

She looked at him with wide, luminous eyes. "Upon what?" she asked in a breathless voice. "Seduction?"

"Seduction," he repeated slowly, savoring the word like a fine, rich claret. "Now that is a tantalizing, arousing idea. And one I will certainly ponder. Next time."

Confusion flickered in her eyes. "Next time?"

"Yes." He arranged his features into a mask of regret. "As delightful as seduction would be, I'm afraid *this* visit is for revenge."

Without giving her a chance to reply, he stood and smoothly whisked her towels from the small table. Then he moved to the far end of the fireplace, well out of reach, and casually rested his shoulders against the white marble mantel.

Her gaze shifted from the empty table to the towels he held, then swept the room. Her night rail and a robe lay across the foot of the bed. The nearest thing to cover herself with were the towels he held. She looked at him and pursed her lips.

"I understand," she said, nodding. "This is your revenge for what happened at the lake. I saw you naked and wet, so now you shall see me naked and wet."

"'Tis only fair. And I did warn you I would seek retribution. But you seeing me naked and wet isn't all that happened at the lake." A slow smile curved his lips. "And I fully intend to retaliate."

He was deeply gratified by the unmistakable flare of interest in her gaze. Without breaking their eye contact, she leaned forward, laid her folded arms along the edge of the tub and rested her chin on her stacked hands.

"What if I don't get out of the tub?"

"You'll eventually have to." He smiled and crossed his ankles. "I'm prepared to wait as long as it takes."

"Hmmm. And if I refuse?"

"Then I suppose I shall be forced to climb into the tub with you."

"Would you really do that?"

"Is that an invitation?"

Her lips twitched. "No. It's a question. I'm weighing my options and need an answer."

"In that case, my answer is yes, I would. In a heartbeat."

"I see. Well, I shall need a moment to reflect upon this and plan. To decide what to do."

"Take your time," Nathan said with a magnanimous sweep of his hand. He bent down to set the towels on the edge of the hearth rug and realized he'd scooped up her book along with the towels. Plucking it from the top of the pile, he read the title and raised his brows.

"Ah, the infamous *Ladies' Guide*," he said, straightening. He opened to a random page and read:

" '*There are countless ways Today's Modern Woman can seduce the gentleman she desires. She is hindered only by her imagination. Suggest a moonlit stroll with the intention of veering off onto a private path for an outdoor tryst. He won't be able to resist a note, unsigned but scented with your fragrance, upon which you've written only a time and place.*' "

Looking up, he nodded approvingly. "Yes, either of those would work very nicely for me. Shall I continue?"

"If you like. I believe the next suggestion involves the lady discreetly stroking her gentleman through his breeches."

Nathan glanced down and silently read the next two lines. "It does indeed." He couldn't decide if he was more intrigued or disquieted by her choice of reading material. He found the thought of her using any knowledge gained from the book on *him* highly arousing. The thought of her using it on anyone else shot white-hot jealousy through him. He closed the book and set it on the mantel, noting she regarded him with an unreadable expression.

"What are you thinking?" he asked.

"Do you really want to know?"

"Yes."

"I'm wondering how it is that you manage to set me on

fire even while you stand two dozen feet away and I'm submerged in water."

Before he could decide which surprised him more—her reply or the smoky voice in which she delivered it—she cut off any hope of him speaking by slowly rising. Water sluiced down her body, a shimmering waterfall cast in gold by the firelight. His gaze meandered down the length of her and desire hit him low and hard.

He had to swallow twice to find his voice. "I'm not certain if 'rise from a steaming pool like an enchanting water nymph' was listed in your *Ladies' Guide* as a seduction method, but if so, I commend you, as you've quite got the hang of it."

"It's not listed, but I'll make a note in the margin." She gracefully stepped from the tub then walked slowly toward him, her hips gently swaying, bewitching him with each step, with the half bold, half shy look gleaming in her eyes. She halted when only an arm's length separated them. Everything in him craved to yank her against him, crush her to him with all the randy fervor of a green lad. He pulled in a slow, deep breath to calm his hammering heart, but that only served to fill his head with the delicate scent of roses.

"I thought you said it was into the bed for me," she whispered. "That I needed to rest."

"It is into the bed for you. But not quite yet." His gaze moved over her with a hunger he fiercely fought to tamp down. Their eyes met, and his heart tripped at the arousal he read there. A touch of shyness, yes, but his Victoria was no coward.

His Victoria . . .

Dangerous, unsettling words. For she wasn't his. Would

never be his for more than a few stolen moments. But for these stolen moments she was, so he'd worry about that later. "The proverb claims that 'Revenge is sweet,'" he said in a rough whisper. "Let's see if it really is."

Clasping her hand, he led her toward the far corner of the room, stopping in front of the oval, full-length cheval glass. Standing between her and the mirror, he brushed his fingers over her smooth, flushed cheek. "I want to touch you, Victoria." Even as he said the words, it struck him that this wild, urgent turbulence roaring through him was more than simply a "want" to touch her. It was a *need*. Beyond anything he'd ever before experienced.

He stepped around her to stand directly behind her. "I want you to see me touch you." *So you can see how much I want you. So I can see you wanting me.*

Victoria stood perfectly still, scarcely daring to breathe as she took in the sight of herself, naked, and Nathan standing behind her. The vision simultaneously shocked and aroused her. She made an unconscious move to cover herself, but he caught her hands from behind and shook his head. "No," he whispered against her temple. "Don't hide from me. Or yourself."

A full-body blush engulfed her and she locked her knees to keep her balance. She'd stood naked before her bed-chamber mirror on numerous occasions, studying her form, running her hands experimentally over her body, her curiosity burning. What would it feel like to be touched by a man? And not just any man. *This* man. Who had captivated her imagination from the first time she'd set eyes on him three years ago. Her heart jumped with anticipation of finally discovering the answer.

He reached up and gently pulled the pins from her hair,

letting them fall to the carpet. Her haphazard pile of curls unfurled, falling over his hands and her shoulders, rippling down her back to her waist. Lightly clasping her upper arms, he leaned forward and buried his face against her hair. "Roses," he whispered.

Somehow she found her voice. "It's my favorite scent."

His gaze met hers in the mirror. "It's now mine, as well."

The warmth of his hands on her skin, the heat emanating from his body, enveloped her like a velvet cloak. Heart pounding, breaths coming in choppy pants, she struggled to maintain some semblance of outward calm, but her efforts proved futile. Dear God, the way he was looking at her . . . no man had ever looked at her like this before. She supposed because she spent all her time in polite society, and there was nothing polite about the intensely carnal desire glittering in Nathan's eyes.

Dressed all in black, his face cast in starkly contrasting panes of shadow and light from the fire, he looked like the swashbuckling pirate she'd once imagined him—devastatingly attractive, wholly masculine, and just a bit dangerous. God help her, she couldn't wait to see, to feel, what he planned next.

He brushed her hair aside with one hand, exposing the back of her neck, while his other hand stole around her waist and pressed her gently back, erasing whatever space had remained between them. His body touched hers, from shoulder to knee, the hard ridge of his erection nudging against her buttocks. Heat emanated from him, infusing her with a flood of warmth. Bending his head, he kissed the back of her neck.

She watched, transfixed, as his fingertips settled on her neck then slowly dragged downward, dipping into the shallow hollow at the base of her throat, which quivered in betrayal of her rapid pulse. He'd barely begun and already she was lost.

Settling his palms on her shoulders, he skimmed his hands down to hers and entwined their fingers. Then he lifted her hands up and back, around his neck. "Hold on," he said, his voice rough velvet. She did as he bid, clasping her fingers together at his nape, grateful for something to hold on to.

He settled his warm lips against her temple, then slowly trailed his fingers down her upraised arms. A thousand pleasurable tingles shot over her skin, and she leaned her head back against his shoulder, watching his clever, long-fingered hands, so dark against her much paler skin, embark upon an agonizingly slow exploration, as if he meant to memorize every pore, every freckle, building an unbearable need in her.

He splayed one hand on her chest and whispered against her temple, "Your heart is pounding."

The same words she'd said to him, she realized. "Surely that doesn't surprise you," she said, mimicking the response he'd given her.

She felt his smile, but her attention was riveted to the sight, the feel, of his hands, slipping lower, lightly brushing over her breasts. Her breath caught and her eyes slid closed.

"Don't close your eyes," he said, his warm breath brushing by her ear. "Watch how beautiful you are." She watched his large hands cup her breasts, teasing her nipples into aching points, rolling the aroused peaks slowly between his fingers. A long purr of pleasure vibrated in her throat. Unclasping her hands, she combed her fingers through the thick dark silk of his hair and arched her back, offering more of herself, an invitation he immediately took advantage of.

His lips wandered down her neck, alternating between lazy kisses and velvety strokes of his tongue. Indeed, all of his caresses were languid, indolent, a shocking contrast to the sharp-edged need spearing through her.

"Nathan . . ." She breathed out his name in a long sigh and squirmed against him, impatient, wanting. He sucked in a sharp breath and pressed himself closer against her back, nestling the hard length of his erection more firmly between her buttocks.

"Patience, love," he rasped against her ear.

While one hand continued to caress her breasts, his other hand continued its breathtaking descent, over her stomach, learning the curve of her waist, circling, then dipping into the sensitive hollow of her navel. Then lower, his fingertips grazing the triangle of dark curls at the apex of her thighs.

"Spread your legs for me, Victoria."

She obeyed, then watched, breathless and entranced as his fingers dipped lower and caressed her feminine folds. That first touch stunned her, then it was as if the floodgates of sensation opened, saturating her in awareness of her own body, her muscles straining closer to him, her hips undulating against his hand. His fingers slid over an exquisitely sensitive spot, pulling a deep moan from her throat. She didn't recognize the woman in the mirror who stared out of eyelids drooped heavy with arousal, her pale skin entwined by strong, sinewy, golden brown forearms and relentless, magical fingers. The woman looked wanton and carnal. Voluptuous. Wicked.

His fingers dipped lower, caressing her with a slow circular motion that threatened to drive her mad. "I told you," he said in a husky rasp against her neck, "that me kneeling before you was a sight you would never see. Do you remember?"

Dear God, surely he didn't expect her to be able to answer questions? "Yes," she managed, the word ending on a breathless sigh of pleasure.

"You said, 'Never say never,' and you were right." He slid his hands from her body and a groan of protest rose in her throat. But the groan turned into a moan when he moved in front of her. Their lips met in a lush open-mouthed kiss, tongues mating, while his hands skimmed down her back, then forward to cup her breasts. Breaking off their kiss, his lips blazed a hot trail down her neck, then lower, to her breasts. He drew her nipple into the silky heat of his mouth, a delicious tug that elicited an answering pull deep in her womb. Immersed in sensation, she gripped his shoulders, searching for an anchor, then let her head drop limply back.

After lavishing the same attention to her other breast, he slowly sank to his knees, his tongue tracing a line down the center of her torso then dipping into her navel. He kissed his way across her belly, and she heard him pull in a deep breath, then softly say, "Roses."

His hands circled around her ankles, then slowly moved up her legs, caressing her thighs, then cupping her buttocks, lightly kneading her flesh. He feathered kisses along her abdomen, then lower, until his lips, his tongue, caressed her as his fingers had. Her grip on his shoulders tightened in direct proportion to her knees weakening. A gasp escaped her at the stab of shocking pleasure. He insinuated his shoulder between her thighs, spreading them wider. Her legs trembled, but his strong hands on her bottom supported her, urging her hips to move against him. The pleasure built to an unbearable pitch then exploded, dragging a cry from her throat as tremors pulsed through her. As the shudders waned, they stole her strength, leaving her sated, satisfied, and utterly limp.

Without a word he rose and scooped her up in his arms. He carried her to the bed, depositing her on the turned-back bedding with a gentle bounce. She looked up at him, expecting mischief in his gaze, but he regarded her through very serious eyes. After pulling up the sheet to cover her, he hitched his hip on the mattress and tucked a curl behind her ear with fingers she noticed weren't quite steady.

"Revenge is indeed sweet," he murmured.

Her heart skipped. Something in his tone, in the way he'd covered her, made it seem as if he intended for their interlude to now end. Summoning her courage, she said, "But surely you're not done."

Something flashed in his eyes. "You wish to continue?"

"Don't you?"

"You're answering a question with a question. Have you thought on the matter?"

"Extensively. And not while I was, as you put it, sexually aroused or basking in the afterglow of pleasure."

"You've considered *all* the ramifications?"

"Yes. Under normal circumstances I would perhaps not enter into an affair, however, there are extenuating factors here."

"Such as?"

"Our location. It would be difficult to maintain discretion in London, but no one knows me here. I've no intention of ever returning here, and it's not as if any of my Society acquaintances are in the area."

"If we were discovered, there isn't any distance great enough to protect you from the scandal. Then there is also the matter of pregnancy."

"There are ways to prevent such an occurrence," she said. "Surely as a doctor you know that."

"Of course I do." His eyes narrowed. "I wasn't aware you did."

"I've gleaned an enormous amount of knowledge from my reading of the *Ladies' Guide*."

"Ah, yes, the *Ladies' Guide*. Clearly it is a cornucopia of information. I must admit I found the snippet I read quite titillating."

"It isn't merely titillating," she said, driven to defend the book that had come to mean so much to her. "It provides information to women that we would otherwise most likely not be privy to."

"Such as how to touch a man? Seduce a man?"

She raised her chin. "Among other things, yes."

"Hmmm. In that case, I believe I owe the author a note of thanks. However, there are other things to consider as well. Even if an affair wasn't discovered here, now, the fact that you'd engaged in one will be revealed on your wedding night, lending the evening a dubious outcome. I suspect that neither Branripple nor Dravensby would be pleased to learn their bride had had a lover."

"The *Ladies' Guide* suggests several ways to handle such a situation—a situation which the author firmly asserts is none of the gentleman's business, by the way. Certainly men are not expected to come to the marriage bed virgins."

"Perhaps not. But I am all curiosity. How does the author suggest you handle the situation?"

"My personal choice is enthusiasm. The *Guide* states that if a bride is an active, willing participant in the wedding night lovemaking rather than simply an inert mass, her groom will be so enthralled he won't have the presence of mind to question the, er, details."

His expression was unreadable, but a muscle ticked in his jaw. "I see," he said in a neutral tone.

"I cannot see why the outcome of my wedding night would concern you."

Something flashed in his eyes, but was gone before she could decipher it. "I'm concerned because I wouldn't want you to be hurt. In any way."

A frown formed between her brows. "Thank you. I appreciate your concern. But . . ."

"But what?"

She huffed out a breath. "Well, for a man who claims he desires me, you are frustratingly reluctant to become my lover. And unfortunately, in my numerous readings of the *Ladies' Guide*, I do not recall any mention of how to deal with an unwilling gentleman."

"Unwilling?" His eyes darkened and he stood. Pinning her with his gaze, he slowly unfastened his shirt. "My darling Victoria, I am most assuredly not unwilling. I simply wanted to make certain that you knew full well what you're getting into."

He shrugged out of his shirt and dropped it carelessly on the floor. Her gaze tracked over his chest, resting on the silky whorls of dark hair that narrowed to an ebony ribbon, bisecting his flat, ridged belly. His arousal was clearly outlined beneath his snug breeches. *Oh, my.* There was nothing about him that looked unwilling.

"And what would I be getting into?" she asked, her pulse leaping.

"A lover who won't be satisfied to simply have you once. I'll expect our liaison to continue for the duration of your stay in Cornwall."

"I see." She sat up, pushing the sheet off her, then rolled onto her knees. Reaching out, she trailed a single fingertip down that fascinating ribbon of hair. "Then, in the interest of fair play, I'd best warn you that you, too, will be taking on a lover who won't be satisfied to simply have you once. I also shall expect our liaison to continue for the duration of my stay in Cornwall."

She trailed her finger around the skin just above the waistband of his breeches. His muscles jumped beneath her light touch. "A hardship I shall endeavor to bear with a smile."

"Of course, if you don't think you have the stamina . . ."

One dark brow climbed up. "You doubt my vigor?"

"If I say yes, will you prove me wrong?"

"I'm afraid it would indeed compel me to rise to the challenge."

"Yes," she said without hesitation.

Eighteen

Today's Modern Woman should choose a gentlemen who will be a generous, thoughtful lover, a man who will make certain to see to her pleasure. It is equally as important that she always see to his pleasure. And realize that by doing so, she will increase her own.

*A Ladies' Guide to the Pursuit of
Personal Happiness and Intimate Fulfillment
by Charles Brightmore*

𝒩athan didn't hesitate. He already felt as if he'd waited forever to hold her skin-to-skin. The thirty seconds it required him to remove the rest of his clothing was an exercise in frustration, an interminable time when his usually steady hands trembled and his fingers fumbled. He couldn't recall ever feeling this unraveled. Undone. Not in control of his passions.

The instant he stepped out of his breeches, he joined her on the bed, pressing her back against the mattress, covering her with his body. Absorbing the exquisite feel of her beneath him, he plunged his fingers into her satiny hair and kissed her deeply, his tongue seeking entrance into the heated silk of her mouth. His rapidly diminishing control slipped another notch when she wrapped her arms around his neck and met the demanding thrust of his tongue with one of her own.

Desire pumped through him and he fought to regain the command over himself that this woman stripped him of with a glance. A single touch. Slow. He had to go slow this first time. But bloody hell, it was nearly impossible, with the taste of her in his mouth, the feel of her squirming beneath him. His body tightened, and his erection, pressed against her soft belly, jerked in response. With an agonized groan, he reared up and knelt between her thighs.

She reached for him, but he shook his head, beyond words. Hooking his hands beneath her legs, he raised her knees and spread her thighs wide. The sight of her glistening sex dragged a ragged groan from his tight throat. Reaching out, he teased the plump, slick, velvety folds. Her thigh muscles tensed, but he gently stroked her, aroused her. When her hips undulated in a silent plea, he eased first one, then two fingers inside her. She was so tight. So wet and hot. And ready. And God help him, he couldn't wait any longer.

He lowered his body onto hers, his weight on his forearms, and looked down as he slowly entered her. She stared up at him, her blue eyes brimming with wonder and a shade of trepidation. "Give me your hands," he said, his voice rough with want.

She slipped her hands into his, and he clasped them, entwining their fingers. Then, with his gaze fixed on hers, he thrust.

Her eyes widened and her fingers tightened on his, and he fought to remain still. "Did I hurt you?"

She slowly shook her head. The silky wet heat of her body gripped him in a velvet fist, and he gritted his teeth against the pleasure, against the desperate need to thrust.

The half minute that passed felt like a century, then her eyelids drooped and her lips parted with a breathy sigh. "Your body on mine . . . in mine . . . it feels . . . delicious."

She lifted her hips, embedding him deeper, and his war with his control was lost. With a groan, he withdrew nearly all the way from her body, then slowly slid deep. Again. Again. Over and over, faster and harder, feeling each breath ripped from his lungs, need clawing him with ever sharpening talons. Her eyes slid closed and she arched her back, pushing her hips up to meet each thrust. Her breathing turned choppy and her hands gripped his tighter. A cry escaped her, and he felt her climax overtake her, pulsing around him. The instant he felt her relax beneath him, he withdrew from her and buried his face in the warm curve of her neck, his erection pressed tightly between them. His release shuddered through him, dragging her name from his throat in a guttural rasp.

For several long seconds he remained perfectly still, breathing in the delicate fragrance of roses warmed with the musk of arousal. Then he lifted his head and looked down into her beautiful face. Her skin was flushed with the afterglow of pleasure, her moist lips plush and red from their passionate kissing, her eyes awash with sensual discovery. She slid her hand from his loosened grasp and laid her palm against his cheek.

A tiny smile trembled on her lips, then she whispered, "Nathan."

A warmth, a tenderness like nothing he'd ever known, ambushed him. His gaze steady on hers, he gently kissed her scraped palm. "Victoria."

Her smile bloomed fuller, her eyes slid closed, and she stretched beneath him. His gaze followed the graceful line of her cheek and froze on the red mark marring the pale skin beneath her jaw. An image exploded in his mind, of the knife against her throat, nicking her flesh. She could have been killed. He could have lost her. A sense of fury and loss burned through him, leaving in its wake a single awareness that blazed with undeniable clarity.

He loved her.

The realization walloped him like a blow to the temple, and he shook his head as if to clear it of the notion. But there was no budging the thought from his mind now that it had rooted itself there.

Bloody hell. Surely he wouldn't be that stupid. To fall in love with a woman who was so utterly wrong for him. As he was for her. A woman who planned to soon choose a husband—a man who would never be him. She wanted a Society fop with a title and money and estates and a love of Town life. The sort of man who would escort her to the opera and soirees, and who could afford to shower her with jewels. That man was definitely not him.

Oh, he wasn't poor by any means, yet neither was he wealthy, nor did he aspire to be. Three years ago he'd thought money important enough to risk everything, and the result had cost him dearly. Had nearly cost Colin and Gordon their lives. Now his riches came in the form of his peaceful, modest life in Little Longstone. Victoria's world existed in an orbit far above and beyond his—an orbit that did not intersect his at any point. Yet, still the words echoed through his mind and heart: *I love her.*

Double bloody hell. He loved her. Her wit and charm. Her smile and determination. Her courage, intelligence, and kindness. The way she challenged him. The way she made him feel. She'd captivated him the instant he saw her three years ago, and he'd spent the intervening time convincing himself that she was nothing more than a spoiled hothouse flower. That the chemistry he'd felt between them had merely been a figment of his imagination. Now, with the passage of only two days, she'd knocked aside his perceptions, proving not only that there was much more to her than he'd supposed, but that the chemistry he'd imagined between them had been no mistake. If she could do that to him in a matter of days, what havoc might she wreak upon him in a matter of weeks?

Good God. This was *not* supposed to happen. He was supposed to fall in love with a demure country chit who enjoyed the same simple things he did, the same modest lifestyle. Not a Society diamond who thrived in the glittering world he eschewed. A woman who would return to her fancy life in London and leave him behind with nothing more than memories and a broken heart.

Surely he'd simply taken temporary leave of his senses. He brightened at the thought. Yes, an aberration, that's all this madness was. A post coital quirk that would clear up as soon as he put some distance between.

"Nathan . . . are you all right?"

Her soft voice yanked him from his thoughts. She was looking up at him with a concerned, confused expression.

No. "Yes. I'm fine." *I'm anything but. And it's entirely your fault.* He eased off her, then strode to the hearth to pick up the forgotten towels. At the wash basin he quickly cleansed himself, keeping his back to her. Fifteen feet now separated them. He pulled in a deep breath, relieved when he felt his self-possession seep back into his veins. Excellent. Just as he'd suspected, all he needed was to put a bit of distance between them. How could he possibly be expected to think properly while she lay naked beneath him? He couldn't. But now he could. A distraction—that's all she was. A beautiful, rose-scented distraction. Relief suffused him. Thank God everything was once again back in perspective.

After wringing the excess water from the towel, he turned back. His gaze met Victoria's from across the room, and his relief and perspective vanished like a poof of smoke in a windstorm.

He loved her.

Bloody hell.

With a calm he was far from feeling, he walked back to the bed with the dampened towel. Resting one hip on the mattress, he gently bathed away the evidence of their spent passion. He forced himself to concentrate on the task and not look into her eyes, for fear she'd read his feelings, discover what his heart longed to proclaim but could not: *I love you.*

A fissure of annoyance at himself edged through him. Damn it, during his years in service to the Crown, he'd perfected the art of lying. Hiding his emotions behind an unreadable mask. It wouldn't be difficult to call upon those skills again. *You're not that man anymore*, his inner voice whispered. No, he wasn't. And he never wanted to be that man again. But for however long she remained in Cornwall, he'd have to pretend to be.

Setting aside the used towel, he drew up the sheet around her. Only after her pale naked beauty was covered did he dare look at her. And everything inside him stilled.

Her eyes were wide with distress and glistened with unshed tears. Her lower lip quivered, delivering a blow to his heart. "I've displeased you," she whispered.

He lightly clasped her fingers, stilling them from fidgeting with the counterpane and inwardly cursed himself for giving her the wrong impression. "No. God, no."

She lifted her chin in that way of hers he found so endearing, but even that show of bravado couldn't hide the hurt and confusion in her gaze. "I'm not blind, Nathan. If I've done something to disappoint you, I want you to tell me what it is."

"Nothing," he said, bringing her hands to his lips and pressing a fervent kiss against the backs of her fingers. "I swear it. If anything you pleased me *too* much." He forced a crooked smile. "You quite unraveled me, my dear, which I fear surprised me."

A bit of the worry faded from her eyes with dawning comprehension. "And you don't like surprises."

"I confess I find them . . . unsettling. But in this particular case, I found it enchanting."

There was no mistaking her relief. "I could say the same, you know."

"You could—or you are?" he teased.

She laughed, and he felt as if the sun emerged from behind the clouds. "Was that a shameful bid for a compliment?"

He blew out an exaggerated put-upon sigh. "I'd force myself to listen to any accolades you might wish to toss my way."

"Very well. I believe I now know what it is you do best."

"Do you?"

"Yes. And I'd very much like for you to show me again."

He turned over her hand and kissed her palm. "What if I told you that I still hadn't demonstrated what I do best?"

The way her eyes widened and darkened fired pure lust through him. She sat up and the sheet fell away, exposing her breasts. "Then I most definitely am anxious to discover what it is you *do* do best."

Reaching out, he teased his fingers over her rosy nipples, watching them tighten, his body experiencing the same pull of want. "I certainly know what you do best, Victoria."

She arched into his hand and sighed. "What is that?"

"You captivate—by simply entering a room. You fascinate—with your unexpected facets. You enchant—with a single smile. You seduce—with nothing more than a look."

"That's four things," she said in a breathy whisper.

"And you excel at all of them."

She sifted her fingers through his hair then urged his head toward hers. "Kiss me," she said, an impatient edge to her voice.

Biting back a smile, he allowed her to pull him closer. He brushed his lips over hers, then traced the fullness of her lower lip with his tongue. "You're very demanding, you know."

"I've decided it's far more effective than being demur."

He instantly recalled their first kiss and her impatient one word response: *Again.* "Were you ever demur?"

She leaned back and a look of confusion passed over her features. "I don't know. I know I am expected to be. But tossing out demands—I like it. Before I started doing so, I was simply patted on the head and relegated to the corner like an ornamental object." Her gaze dropped to his mouth and she leaned forward. "Again."

"It would be my pleasure." But even as his lips met hers and he pressed her back onto the mattress and covered her body with his, he knew that the pleasure they'd share in the days to come would leave him with the pain of a broken heart.

Nineteen

If Today's Modern Woman is in a situation where she must choose between two or more gentlemen, she will likely find the practical nature of her mind at war with the emotional nature of her heart. In such cases she must ask herself, is it best to choose based on financial and social considerations or to follow the desires of her heart?

A Ladies' Guide to the Pursuit of
Personal Happiness and Intimate Fulfillment
by Charles Brightmore

Victoria hurried down the corridor toward her bed-chamber, filled with a giddy, heady sense of anticipation. By previous agreement, Nathan had retired shortly after dinner, while she remained with Aunt Delia and Nathan's father in the drawing for a quarter hour, after which time she, too, retired. But sleep was definitely not in her plans.

Nathan . . . Had an entire week passed since that first night he'd come to her room? It seemed the time had gone by in a blink—time during which they'd been unsuccessful at locating the jewels, but had in every other way proven fulfilling beyond her wildest dreams.

Using the grid map Nathan had devised, they spent the days systematically inspecting each section, exploring dozens of rock outcroppings, searching in crevices and small caves, looking for a shape that resembled the picture she had drawn. As each square on the map was eliminated, Victoria's hopes that they'd locate the missing cache faded a bit more. Further hindering their attempts, they'd as yet received no response from her father to Nathan's letter, but given the distance to London, that was to be expected.

Nathan never strayed far from her side during their outings, always wary of them being set upon again. At his insistence, he'd hidden a small lady's pistol for her protection in the tool bag containing their hammers and chisels. The fact that there were no further instances renewed their optimism that the brigand who'd stolen the fake note and map was indeed far away on a wild goose chase and had not deduced that he possessed erroneous information.

Those hours spent searching for the jewels were also hours together with Nathan. Laughing, learning, talking, discovering new facets of him and of herself. She brought him to the gardens and taught him to make a mud pie— then led him to a dark corner in the conservatory and had her wicked way with him. He brought her to the beach and taught her to make a sand castle—then led her to the crystal cave and had his wicked way with her. He took her for a ride on the lake in his small boat and taught her to row. She learned not only how to work the oars but that standing up in a rowboat is not wise if one wishes not to capsize. That directly led to her discovery that the tem-

perature of a chilly lake is gloriously forgotten while
making love in the water—and instantly recalled once the
heat of passion is spent.

Nathan showed her how to catch crabs, kissed her finger when one pinched her with its claws, then applauded
when she caught a dozen of the feisty crustaceans on her
own. They'd proudly delivered their catch to Cook, who
prepared them for dinner that night, a meal they shared
with Aunt Delia and Nathan's father, who, it was plain to
see, were getting on extremely well together. For the past
seven days, it had been just the four of them sharing meals
and retiring to the drawing room after dinner. Nathan's
brother had not returned from his excursion to Penzance,
sending a note that business required him to stay away,
and Lord Alwyck had not made a return visit.

One morning, to her delight, Nathan brought her to the
kitchen and helped her realize her childhood dream by
having Cook teach her to bake a pie. She'd burned part of
the crust, but Nathan ate it anyway, declaring it delicious.
That evening after dinner, while her aunt and Lord Rutledge played backgammon, Nathan brought her to the billiards room and taught her to play—or rather, he tried to,
as she proved quite hopeless at it, a fact she blamed on the
distracting nature of her instructor. They then retired to
the music room, where she attempted to teach him a song
on the pianoforte. For a man with such talented fingers, he
possessed no aptitude for music—but an amazing skill for
insinuating his talented fingers under her skirt.

Yet even though she reveled in the sensual delights and
discoveries they shared, she enjoyed his company just as
much while doing nothing more exciting than drinking
tea. What struck Victoria the most was the way he talked
to her. Listened to her. How he sought her opinion on a

wide spectrum of topics. How he didn't make her feel foolish if she didn't know something, and how intently he paid attention when she did. The gentle way he teased her, challenged her, encouraged her to think about things to which she'd previously given little consideration, such as politics.

He fascinated her with his personal theories on medicine and healing, a number of which were in direct opposition to currently accepted methods. They spent hours debating the works of Shakespeare and Chaucer, Byron's poetry and Homer's *Iliad*. It seemed that they grew closer every day, and she realized that in addition to being her lover, he was also her friend. A friend who could set her blood on fire with a mere look.

And then there were the seven glorious nights she'd spent in Nathan's arms. Making love, exploring each other's body, enjoying the countless intimacies lovers share. Sometimes their mating was a soft, slow dance, other times a fast, furious race. He helped her discover what pleased her and urged her to discover what pleased him, although as far as she could tell, he was very easily pleased. And now, hurrying the last few steps to her bedchamber, where she knew he awaited her, her heart skipped in anticipation of the sensual delights tonight would hold.

Breathless from a combination of her quick pace and the thought of what awaited her, she opened her bedchamber door. And stilled on the threshold at the sight that met her eyes. As if in a trance, she slowly entered. After closing and locking the door, she leaned back against the oak panel and stared. The room was awash with roses. Dozens of blooms ranging from the purest white to the deepest scarlet spilled from a silver bowl set on her dresser. A trail of petals led from the door to the center of the room, where the path split into two directions. One ended near the fireplace, where a petal-strewn blanket and a picnic basket awaited. The other trail veered toward the bed, its ivory counterpane dotted with crimson blooms. Nathan stood at the juncture of the paths holding a single long stem rose.

The look in his eyes, that intoxicating concentration of heat, of want and need, stole her breath. She approached him slowly, stopping when less than two feet separated them. He reached out and traced her jaw with the flower's velvety petals. "I offer you a choice, Victoria," he said softly, his eyes serious, his gaze intent upon hers. "Which do you want?"

"I want them both," she answered without hesitation.

The next morning, Victoria stood at the window of her bedchamber, looking down at the garden and lawns bathed in a diffused haze of early morning sunshine. It had rained most of the night, but the azure sky dotted with fluffy white clouds promised a day of fair weather. A day of adventure as their search for the jewels continued. Another glorious day to be spent with Nathan.

Her eyes slid closed and she recalled last night. How after she'd told him she wanted both paths, he'd instantly obliged her, swooping her up in his strong arms and carrying her to the bed, where their lovemaking had been wild and frantic, as if they hadn't touched in months. Then later, after a light repast of bread, wine, and cheese, they'd made slow, luxurious love on the blanket in front of the fire.

The memory faded and she opened her eyes. Looking down at the sunlight sparkling on the dew-laden grass, she asked herself the question that invaded her mind with increasing frequency as each day passed: How was she going to say good-bye to him when it came time to leave and return to her normal life? And, as it did every time, the mere thought brought a lump to her throat and a strange, uncomfortable hollow to her chest. So, as she did every time, she roughly shoved the question away. When it came time to leave, she would simply . . . leave. And go on with her life. As he would go on with his.

Turning from the window, her gaze wandered to the bed and fell upon the single red rose he'd left on the pillow next to hers. To her dismay, moisture filled her eyes. A beautiful flower from a beautiful man who she greatly feared was coming to mean far too much to her. A man who, despite her best efforts to keep at an emotional arm's length, was finding his way into her heart. When she awoke that morning, she'd been alone, all evidence of their sensual petal-strewn picnic gone, except for that solitary bloom.

She walked to the bed, picked up the rose and buried her nose in its soft center. Again vivid images of the previous night permeated her mind's eye. Nathan looming over her, buried deep inside her body, then her astride him, his hands everywhere as they made love in the rose-scented haven he'd created for her. She would never be able to separate the scent of roses from those sensual images, which was problematic, as she couldn't recall a day since she was a child that she hadn't surrounded herself with the fragrance of her favorite flower.

But she wouldn't worry about that now. She would have plenty of time to lock away her memories when this interlude ended. Until then, she would treat each day as a gift and enjoy her passionate adventure to the fullest.

With that in mind, she pulled the bell cord to summon Winifred, then walked to the wardrobe to choose a dress for the day. But before choosing, she pulled her copy of the *Ladies' Guide* from the portmanteau and carefully pressed the rose Nathan had left her between the book's pages.

After emptying a sack filled with kitchen scraps into the trough in the animal pen—much to the delight of Daisy, Reginald, and Petunia—Nathan collected his hens' daily offering of eggs. He gave them to Hopkins, who, with a nod of thanks, headed across the lawns toward the kitchen with his prize. Then, with B.C. at his heels, Nathan walked the short distance to the copse of elms nearest the stables, a favorite boyhood spot. Sitting on the ground, he leaned back against the sturdy trunk's rough bark, stretched his legs out in front of him and crossed his ankles. B.C. flopped down next to him, rested his massive head on Nathan's boots, and breathed out a sigh of canine contentment.

"Don't even think about making a snack out of these boots," Nathan said, scratching behind the dog's ears. "They're my favorite pair."

B.C. sent him a reproachful look, as if to say that he would never in a million years chew Nathan's favorite pair of boots—but any other pair was fair game.

Resetting his back against the tree, Nathan absorbed the quiet serenity of the early morning and watched his animals enjoy their breakfast. If only his thoughts were as serene as his surroundings. . . .

Reginald left the animal pen, and catching sight of Nathan sitting under the tree, the pig trotted toward him. B.C. lifted his head, and after the two animals, who were well used to each other, had exchanged a friendly smelling of each other's breath, Reginald flopped down on Nathan's other side and plopped his head on Nathan's knee.

"Looks as if it's just us boys this morning," Nathan said. "No women." He blew out a sigh. "Do yourselves a favor my good men, and do *not* fall in love. But at least if you're going to fall in love, make certain that you fall in love with someone you can have." B.C. licked his chops and shot Nathan a mournful gaze. Nathan nodded, grateful for the obvious canine show of sympathy. "Yes, that's precisely how I feel. It would be as if you fell in love with a cat instead of a dog, B.C. Of course you could love the cat, but it would only lead to heartbreak. You're too different, live in two different worlds, for it to ever work. Trust me when I say that falling in love is a tremendous pain in the arse. Not to mention the heart."

"Good morning, Nathan," came a familiar deep voice behind him.

Nathan turned and saw his father approaching from the direction of the house. "Good morning, Father."

"I thought I'd find you out here."

Over the past week, some of the tension between them had dissipated. Of course, Nathan thought that could have been because they hadn't been alone together. Having Lady Delia and Victoria join them for meals, after-dinner whist, and conversation, had unmistakably thawed a bit of the chill.

"You were looking for me?"

"Yes. Mind if I join you?"

"Not at all. B.C., Reginald, and I were just having a little man-to-man chat.

Father nodded. "You always were fond of talking to

your pets." His father surveyed the area around the tree with a frown, then pulled a snowy handkerchief from his pocket, which he set on the ground. To Nathan's amazement and amusement, Father then gingerly settled his bottom on the linen square. It required a bit of careful shifting about, but he finally found what was obviously a comfortable spot, then leaned his back against the tree.

After several seconds of companionable silence, his father asked, "You'll continue your search for the jewels today?" He'd given his father a sketchy briefing of how he hoped to find the missing cache.

"Immediately after breakfast, yes."

"I would offer my assistance," Father said, sounding uncomfortable, "but I cannot go off and leave Lady Delia alone all day, nor would it be proper to subject her to such arduous outings."

"I completely understand." Actually, he was grateful, as he had no desire to include anyone on those precious hours he spent alone with Victoria.

"Of course, having Lady Victoria accompany you without her chaperone—"

"I promised her father I would protect her. I cannot do that if she remains behind."

"I suppose not. And you are out in the open—it's not as if you're in a closed carriage together."

"Exactly." Nathan noted his father hadn't suggested that Victoria remain home with him and her aunt, which piqued his curiosity as to precisely what they did during the hours he and Victoria were away from the house. He'd noticed that they seemed to be getting along very well together.

"What are your plans for today?" he asked his father.

"I promised Delia—I mean Lady Delia—a visit to Penzance."

"An outing I'm certain she'll enjoy. She is a very nice woman. Intelligent. Amusing and vivacious."

Out of the corner of his eye he noted ruddy color rush into his father's face. "Yes, she is all those things. I would say her niece very much takes after her in those respects."

"I agree." Indeed, Victoria was all those things and more. She was rare. Extraordinary. Unlike anyone else. Every day, he learned something new about her, and each new layer he uncovered only served to deepen his love and admiration for her. Bloody hell, he even found her faults endearing. The way she babbled when nervous. Her streak of stubbornness. The way she insisted upon retelling Shakespeare's darker tales so they had fairy-tale endings. His reminder that the titles were *The* Tragedy *of Hamlet* and *The* Tragedy *of Romeo and Juliet* fell on deaf ears. All the things that made her imperfect that somehow managed to make her seem all the more perfect.

Silence stretched between them, then Father said, "You care for her."

"We've formed a friendship."

"Your feelings run deeper than mere friendship, Nathan."

"What makes you say that?"

"I'm not exactly in my dotage, you know. I see the way you look at her."

Nathan forced a nonchalant shrug. "If my feelings run deeper, I cannot see why that would concern you. I'm more than capable of keeping my own counsel."

"Which is precisely what concerns me."

"Why? Do you fear me making a fool of myself?" he asked, unable to disguise the hint of bitterness underlying his words.

"No. I fear you suffering from a broken heart. 'Tis a

pain like no other and a fate I would wish on no man, let alone my son."

Heavy silence engulfed them for several heartbeats while Nathan fought to hide his surprise at his father's words. Apparently he wasn't entirely successful, for Father added softly, "I can see that you think I don't know what I'm talking about, but I assure you I speak from experience." He turned and looked briefly toward the gardens then returned his gaze to Nathan. "If you think it didn't break my heart when your mother died, you are very much mistaken. I loved her deeply. She captivated me from the first moment I saw her."

A sentiment which, thanks to Victoria, Nathan could well understand. "I'm afraid that when Mother died I was so immersed in my own grief, I gave little thought to your loss. I'm sorry."

His father nodded. "My point is that a broken heart is a pain like no other. I therefore encourage you to do whatever is necessary so it doesn't happen to you."

Confusion assailed Nathan. He'd never shared a conversation even remotely like this with his father, and he was quite frankly at a loss. Finally he said carefully, "Are you suggesting that if there was perhaps a woman I cared for, I should consider confessing my feeling to her?"

"Bloody hell, Nathan, if you danced around it any more you'd be turning pirouettes on the lawn. I've reached an age where I'm not so inclined to waste time. I'm suggesting nothing about some hypothetical woman. I'm stating outright that if you care for Lady Victoria you should tell her."

Nathan's brows shot upward. "Are you not the same man who only a week ago stated that my brother or Gordon or those two fops in London—or hell, anyone with a title and an estate—were far more suitable matches for her?"

"Actually, no, I'm *not* the same man I was a week ago."

"What does that mean?"

"That means that over the past week I've come to some important and, quite frankly, unexpected realizations about myself. My life. What I want. For the first time in a long while I feel . . . invigorated. Rejuvenated."

And suddenly Nathan realized he'd indeed seen evidence of this over the past week. His father had seemed more relaxed. He'd laughed, smiled, and told amusing stories, and Nathan enjoyed the lessening of unease between them. He'd noticed the changes, but with his attention focused on Victoria, hadn't dwelled on them. "To what do you attribute this rejuvenation?"

"A great deal of soul searching, which is the result of the friendship I've formed with Lady Delia. Having people in the house again made me realize how . . . lonely I've been, and having someone my own age to talk to has been delightful. Lady Delia knows *everyone*, and it turns out we share an enormous number of acquaintances. You know I don't keep up with the comings and goings of the *ton*, and she's brought me up to date on the lives of people I haven't seen or heard from in years. I was shocked to learn of the number of peers I know—men my age or younger—who are in poor health. Or dead."

Father shook his head. "I have to tell you, it gave me a chilling sense of my own mortality, and made me appreciate what I have, including my health. Life is too precious and far too short to allow opportunities to be missed. Or to allow wrongs to go unrighted."

He drew a deep breath then continued, "I want this estrangement between us to end, Nathan. I now realize that I never allowed you to offer an explanation for your actions the night Colin and Gordon were shot. Rather, I fired questions and accusations at you. In my own defense, I can only say that I was shocked—not only by the shooting, but to discover my sons were spies for the Crown. I showed no faith in you, and even though we haven't always agreed, knowing the sort of man you were, I should have known better than to believe you would act dishonorably."

Those quietly spoken words hit Nathan hard, and for the first time in three years the hurt and sense of betrayal that had bound his heart loosened. He looked at his father, who regarded him through serious eyes and continued, "I attempted to apologize by letter, but I admit it was a half-hearted effort. So now, even though it's coming three years after the fact, I wish to offer my heartfelt apology and ask for your forgiveness." He extended his hand.

A lump lodged in Nathan's throat and he swallowed to clear it away. Reaching out, he clasped his father's hand in a firm grip. "I owe you an apology as well, Father, for allowing the gulf between us to grow so wide. I can't deny it was a crushing blow to realize that my father *and* brother *and* best friend all doubted me. At the time I was bound by an oath of secrecy and couldn't offer an explanation."

"I shouldn't have needed one."

The admission warmed any remnants of chill Nathan might have harbored. "I fear my pride has kept me from offering an explanation since my return—an error in judgment I'd like to correct if you'd like to listen."

"I'd like that very much."

After drawing a bracing breath, Nathan repeated the same story he'd told Victoria, finishing with, "The irony of the entire thing is that I'd intended the jewels to be my last mission—the one that would afford me financial security. Instead it stripped me of everything I held dear—my reputation, my family, my home."

"You had no need to go searching for financial security, Nathan. I would have given you whatever amount you needed."

"Yes, I know. And while I appreciate your generosity, I don't want things given to me. I prefer to earn them."

"An aspect of your character I never understood," Father said, shaking his head. "If there is ever anything you need—"

"I would let you know. Believe me, I've no desire to live in poverty, and while I know you think I *do* live in such a state, I assure you I don't. My home may not be a grand palace, but I live very comfortably. And in spite of the occasional nonmonetary compensation I accept for my services, I am well paid."

"What will happen if you don't find the jewels?"

"I'll have no choice other than to get on with my life. But I'm determined to find them. Three years ago I didn't stay and fight to clear my name. I won't give up so easily this time. Someone betrayed the mission, and I want to know who. Someone hurt Victoria, and I want to know who. I want to recover the jewels and turn them over to the Crown so the mark on my reputation is wiped clean." He clasped his father's shoulder. "But no matter what happens, knowing that you believe me innocent of wrongdoing means a great deal."

"Too bad Colin isn't here for this meeting of the minds," Father said.

"Yes, it is," Nathan said thoughtfully.

"My instincts tell me he won't be away much longer. Most likely his 'business' is a curvaceous beauty he'll soon tire of."

"Yes, you're most likely right," Nathan said. Unfortunately, however, his instincts were telling him something different.

Late that afternoon, after another unsuccessful search of another craggy rock formation, Nathan leaned against the trunk of a stately elm, consulted his grid map and drew an X across another square. Only five more squares remained. Would they need to search all five areas—or would the jewels be found perhaps tomorrow? Or the next day? Even if it proved necessary to search all five squares, he still felt the pressure of time. Once the search was over—either having found the jewels or admitting defeat—his time in Cornwall would draw to a close.

Surely he would hear from Victoria's father within the next week regarding his letter, hopefully providing additional information that could aid in the search for the jewels. But might Lord Wexhall also ask that his daughter be sent back to London?

No matter how Nathan looked at it, he felt his magical time with Victoria dwindling, like grains of sand trickling inexorably through his fisted hands.

After refolding the map and slipping it into his boot, he looked at Victoria, who crouched two dozen feet away, gathering a small bouquet of purple wildflowers. The sun caught at her hair, coaxing burnished highlights from the silky skeins. Bloody hell, she was so beautiful. And he loved her so much. Wanted her so badly. His father's advice echoed in his mind, and Nathan realized he was right. He had to tell her how he felt. But how? When? *Wait,* his inner voice cautioned. *Give her more time. 'Tis obvious she cares about you—perhaps she'll fall in love with you.* A humorless sound escaped him. Or perhaps she'd break his heart.

She stood, then glanced over at him. His desire must have shown in his eyes because an answering heat kindled in her gaze. With a siren's smile playing about her lips, she slowly walked toward him.

"You're looking rather pensive," she said as she approached.

"Just admiring the view."

Her gaze boldly raked over him, resting pointedly on his groin before returning to meet his again. "Yes, the view is fascinating."

He swallowed the rueful laugh that rose in his throat at the ease with which she aroused him. She halted two feet from him and extended the bouquet. "For you," she said.

Touched at the simple gesture, he took the flowers, brushing his fingers against hers as he did. "I've never been given flowers before."

She smiled. "I've never given flowers before. I realize they pale in comparison to the magnificent roses you gave me, but—"

"No, they don't. It's not the sort of flowers you receive, but who gives them to you that's important." He brushed his lips against her soft cheek. "Thank you."

"You're welcome."

"As it just so happens, I have a present for you as well. I'll be right back." He pushed off from the tree and crossed to where Midnight and Honey stood tethered in the shade of a huge weeping willow. After putting his flowers in Midight's saddlebag, he removed a small leather pouch then returned to Victoria. "For you," he said, handing her the small gift.

There was no mistaking her surprised pleasure. "What is it?"

"Only one way to find out."

He watched her pull open the drawstring top of the pouch and spill the contents into her palm. Suddenly, doubts assailed him. What the hell was he doing, giving her something so lacking in monetary value when she was accustomed to and deserved the most expensive, extravagant of jewels? She lifted the slender black velvet cord from which hung a single white glossy seashell.

She studied the shell for several seconds, then said, "I recognize this shell. You found it near the shore the first day you brought me to the beach." Her gaze shifted from the necklace to him. "The first day you showed me the crystal cave."

"Yes," he said, unable to deny his pleased surprise that she remembered. "How did you know?"

Unmistakable tenderness filled her eyes. "Nathan, I'm not likely to ever forget *anything* about that day." After setting the leather pouch on the ground, she lifted her arms and drew the velvet cord over her head. She then held the delicate shell up to the sun and examined it. "How did you make it so shiny?"

"A dozen coats of clear lacquer. It makes it glossy and strong." He cleared his throat. "I wanted you to have something by which to remember your time here. I know it isn't much, but—"

She touched her fingers to his lips, halting his words. "You're wrong, Nathan. This necklace is . . . lovely. And thoughtful. In every way. Just like the man who gave it to me. Thank you. I'll treasure it always."

Taking her hand, he backed up a few paces, gently tugging her along, until his back rested against the tree trunk. Spreading his legs, he slowly drew her closer until she leaned against his body in the vee of his thighs. "I'm glad you like it," he said, bending his head to touch his lips to the sensitive rose-scented skin behind her ear.

A delicate shudder ran through her, and her arms stole around his neck. Leaning back in the circle of his arms to look at him, she said, "Speaking of liking something—I think my aunt likes your father."

"Excellent news, as I think my father likes your aunt." He trailed his fingers over her petal-soft cheek. "I think his son likes her niece."

She raised her brows. "Oh? Which son? He has two."

He knew she was teasing; still, a fissure of jealousy seeped through him. "I meant me."

"Ah. Likes her, hmmm? Does that mean he wishes to be friends?"

"No."

"No? Why not?"

"Because friends don't do this." He palmed her breasts, teasing her nipples through the fine material of her riding gown. "Nor do they do this." Leaning forward, he pressed a heated kiss against her neck.

Her head dropped limply back and a pleasure-filled sigh escaped her. She insinuated her hand between them and stroked her palm over his erection, dragging a groan from his throat.

"I suspect friends don't do that, either?" she asked in a smoky voice.

His fingers set to work undoing the buttons on her gown. "I'm not certain . . . do it again and I'll let you know."

She stroked him again, then teased the head of his arousal with her fingertips. "No," he said in husky rasp. "They don't do that, either."

"Not even if they are the very best of friends?"

"Not even then." Finished with the buttons, he pushed her gown and chemise down her arms in one motion.

"What else don't friends do?"

He drew a lazy fingertip around her pebbled nipple. "Are you certain you want to know?"

"Yes." The word ended in a hiss of pleasure as he bent his head and drew her nipple into his mouth. She breathed his name, and all the pent-up frustration of wanting her, loving a woman he feared he could never have, burst, flooding him with a desperation unlike anything he'd ever known. He yanked her gown, chemise, and drawers roughly down over her hips, then simply lifted her and kicked the material aside, leaving her clad in only her stockings and ankle-high riding boots. With his breaths pumping from his lungs like a bellows, he snagged one hand under her thigh and lifted her leg against his hip while his other hand skimmed down her bare back, over her round buttocks, then lower, to stroke the plump folds of her sex. That she was already wet for him snapped the last vestiges of his control.

Kissing her deeply, he slipped two fingers into her moist heat, his tongue stroking her in the same smooth rhythm as his fingers stroked inside her body. Her arms tightened around his neck and she strained against him. He broke off their kiss, relentlessly stroking her body, and watched her pleasure overtake her while she pulsed around his fingers.

The instant the tremors subsided, he scooped her up in his arms and sat her on top of her discarded gown. Dropping to his knees between her splayed thighs, he yanked open his breeches with impatient, unsteady hands, and freed his erection. Now, damn it. He needed her *now*. Sitting back on his heels, he grasped her hips and settled her over him, astride his thighs. She clasped his shoulders and slid down as he thrust upward. He tried to go slow, to savor the exquisite glide into her velvety heat, the erotic pull of her tight passage gripping him, but slow was beyond him. Clenching her hips in a viselike hold, he gritted his teeth and thrust, hard, fast, beads of sweat forming on his brow. And just like his thrusts, his release came upon him hard and fast. With a guttural groan that sounded more like pain than pleasure, he withdrew and crushed her against him, his face buried in the warm fragrant valley between her breasts. The instant the passion-induced fog cleared from his brain, guilt smacked him. Damn it, what the hell had come over him? He never lost control like that. He'd taken her without a thought to her pleasure. He lifted his head, fully prepared to apologize and beg her pardon, but found her looking at him with a flushed, sated, slumberous expression.

"Oh . . . my," she whispered, resting her forehead against his. "Just when I think I've finally discovered what you do best, you prove me wrong."

Relieved that she'd found as much pleasure as he, he dropped a kiss on her nose. "You still haven't discovered it."

"Oh . . . my," she whispered again. She glanced down at her naked breasts pressed to his chest. "I'm guessing that friends don't do this, either?"

"Are we friends, Victoria?" He tossed out the question lightly, but found himself tensing, awaiting her reply.

"I like to think so."

"Well, in that case, I guess friends do *do* this."

"Hmmm. How long do you suppose it would take friends to do this again?"

He smiled. "Let's find out."

Twenty

If Today's Modern Woman is in a situation where she must end a love affair, the best way is to make a clean, fast break. Of course, this is more easily accomplished if her heart isn't involved.

A Ladies' Guide to the Pursuit of
Personal Happiness and Intimate Fulfillment
by Charles Brightmore

*L*ate that night, Nathan paced the confines of his bedchamber. When he approached the fireplace, he glared at the mantel clock. Less than a minute had past since he'd last glowered at the enamel timepiece, which meant that not only did his most potent frown not make time pass any quicker, but that he still had to suffer through another quarter hour for midnight to arrive. Until he left his bedchamber and joined Victoria in hers.

Swiping his hands through his hair, he strode back toward the window, the silk of his robe flapping against his bare legs. What the hell had he been thinking, agreeing to wait until midnight to go to her? He'd retired twenty minutes ago, leaving Victoria, Lady Delia, and his father in the drawing room. It had taken him all of ten minutes to undress, wash, and don his robe. And so he'd commenced pacing, frustrated at his lack of sangfroid, as he'd always considered himself a very patient man. But there was nothing patient about the need, the want, to be near her, touching her, that clawed at him.

He paused at the window and looked down at the gardens bathed in a silvery glow of moonlight. He was about to turn away when a movement below caught his eye. As he watched, a dark clad figure carrying a sack emerged from the shadows and moved stealthily across the lawn toward the dense forest. For an instant the moon shone directly on the figure and Nathan froze in recognition. Seconds later the darkness swallowed the furtive form, and Nathan, mind spinning with questions, stared at the spot where he'd disappeared.

What the hell was Colin up to?

There was no point giving chase——he'd never find his brother in the forest in the dark. But that didn't mean he didn't intend to look for answers. Grabbing the oil lamp from his end table, he exited his bedchamber and headed down the corridor. When he reached Colin's bedchamber, he entered, closing the door behind him.

Raising the lamp, he walked slowly around the darkened room, surveying the area through narrowed eyes. Little had changed since he'd last seen the room three years ago. The same cherrywood furniture, the same dark green patterned Axminster carpet and heavy velvet drapes. At first glance everything seemed in perfect order, but upon close inspection, he noticed the fringe on one end of the hearth rug was mussed, something the maid would not have left uncorrected.

He approached the round mahogany table near the wardrobe, where a decanter of brandy and a crystal snifter rested on a silver tray. Lifting the snifter to his nose, Nathan inhaled. The scent of potent liquor lingered in the glass. Holding the glass up to the light, he noted the drops of pale gold still in the bottom. *A quick bracer for the dash across the lawn, Colin?*

Crossing to the French windows, Nathan noted with a grim smile that they were locked from the inside. "But you're an expert at locking doors from the other side," he murmured. "And unlocking them, for that matter, as I suspect you didn't waltz in the front door and come up the stairs."

He opened the doors and stepped onto the balcony. Walking to the stone balustrade, he raised the lantern and minutely examined the stone. Directly in the center of the railing he found what he was looking for—bits of rope fiber. "Now I know how you got in—but what were you looking for?"

Lowering the lamp, his gaze swept the stone balcony and halted on the pale object near his feet. He crouched down and picked up the folded ivory vellum. A sense of dread rushed through him as he slowly unfolded the paper, hoping he wouldn't see what he suspected he would. Seconds later his worst suspicions were confirmed.

It was the fake letter and map he'd drawn. The same fake letter and map that had been stolen from him.

Bloody hell. Filled with foreboding, he hurried back to his own bedchamber. After entering the room, he went immediately to the wardrobe and pulled out the pair of riding boots in the far corner. Grabbing the heel of the left boot, he gave a deft twist then felt in the hidden compartment. As he'd suspected, it was empty.

* * *

"The letter and map have been stolen," Nathan said the instant he closed the door to Victoria's bedchamber behind him. "Our grid map as well."

Victoria stared at his sternly set features, her heart sinking in dismay at the news. "When?"

"Must have been during dinner this evening." He raked his hands through his hair. "I should have suspected, should have considered he'd do this, but I didn't want to believe he'd be so foolish."

"Who?"

Victoria went still at the tortured look in his eyes. "Colin," he said, his voice laced with anguish. "He was here. Tonight. I saw him on the lawn, heading toward the forest. When I searched his bedchamber, I found this."

She took the vellum he held out to her and frowned at the unfamiliar words and drawing. "What is this?"

"It's the fake note and map that was stolen from us."

She felt her eyes go wide as the implications showered down on her. "That means Colin—"

"Is involved. There are only two ways he could have that note. One—if he hired that bastard to steal it; or two—if Colin stole it from that bastard."

She searched his gaze. "And which do you believe?"

"That Colin stole it from our thief," he said without hesitation. "My brother, in addition to his many other talents, is a formidable pickpocket. Very useful during his spy days. Apparently still useful."

Pieces clicked in Victoria's mind as she stared at the vellum. "So you believe," she said slowly, "that Colin somehow crossed paths with our thief, stole the letter and map from him, and has been trying to find the jewels himself—only using the wrong information. . . ." She looked up and met Nathan's gaze. "Except now, he not only has the real letter and map and therefore the correct information, but our grid map showing the areas we've already searched."

His taut features relaxed a bit and unmistakable admiration shone in his eyes. Reaching out, he clasped her hand and brought it to his mouth, pressing a warm kiss to her fingers. "My darling Victoria, have I told you that I love your ability to cleave through even the thickest fog and get right to the heart of the matter?"

Her breath caught at the intensity burning in his gaze and she shook her head. "I don't believe you've ever mentioned it."

"Consider it mentioned." After pressing another brief kiss to her fingers, he released her hand and paced in front of her.

She watched him in silence for a full minute, his expression so troubled, her heart hurt for him. The next time he passed in front of her, she reached out and laid her hand on his arm, stopping him. "You're thinking that Colin had something to do with the failure of the mission three years ago," she said softly. She gently squeezed his arm in a sympathetic gesture. "I'm sorry."

He shook his head, looking mildly surprised. "Actually, no, I'm not thinking that at all. Whatever faults Colin might have, he is a man of honor and integrity. Unfortunately, he also tends to be daring. I'm thinking that he somehow stumbled onto the truth of what happened three years ago and instead of telling me, he's decided to take matters into his own hands."

"But why wouldn't he tell you? Enlist your aid?"

A muscle ticked in his jaw. "I can only guess, but I'd surmise that it's because three years ago he doubted me. I think that over the past three years, as much as he wanted to believe I was innocent of any wrongdoing, that kernel of doubt remained. When he discovered what really happened, and realized I hadn't betrayed the mission . . ." He blew out a long breath. "I'm sure he was seized with guilt. Knowing him as I do, I think he's acting on his own as some sort of self-imposed penance. A way to make up for his lack of faith in me. He wants to find the jewels, expose the traitor, and clear my name."

She searched his gaze. "You feel this way because that's exactly what you would do for him."

"Yes, I would."

"I'm barely acquainted with your brother, so as an objective observer I feel the need to point out that while you could be right—and for your sake I pray you are—it is equally as possible that you're wrong. That Colin is responsible for everything that has happened."

"The chances may be equal, but I'm not wrong. Which means Colin could be in grave danger." Clasping her hand, he drew her toward the mahogany slant-top desk near the window. "I'm going to recreate the decoded letter and grid, and I want you to redraw the map. Then we're going to study them until we figure out what we've missed. Figure out the best place to search next. My every instinct warns me that time is short. I don't think we have the time to search all five of the grids left on the map."

For the next thirty minutes the only sound in the room besides the crackle of snapping wood burning in the fireplace was the scratching of their quills on vellum. Victoria then spent the next two hours minutely studying the series of squiggles she'd drawn. They looked like gibberish. She slowly turned the vellum, looking at the lines from all angles until her eyes felt gritty.

"I've tried a dozen different codes, but can't decipher anything further," Nathan said, his voice filled with frustration. "Anything from the map?"

"No . . . although an idea just occurred to me." Sitting up straighter, Victoria stared at the lines. "All along we've assumed that based on the words 'rock formation' in the letter, this drawing depicted the particular formation where the jewels were hidden. But what if it depicts something else?"

"Like what?"

"I don't know. Perhaps a patch of tall sea grass?"

Nathan scooted his chair closer to hers and peered at the drawing. "If it's sea grass, we've either missed the jewels or Baylor's information was wrong." He slid over the grid map he'd recreated and pointed to the still unexplored areas. "All of the five remaining squares are inland, too far away for the sea grass to grow. But I think you may be right about this not being a drawing of the actual rock formation."

They both studied the lines, and she mused, "What if it's a series of trails, or paths?"

He nodded, then pointed to a spot where the lines intersected. "It could be three trails that converge here."

Victoria looked at him with a growing sense of excitement. "Do you know of such a place on the property? Where three trails converge near a rock formation?"

He rose and paced across the room, his brows bunched in a frown. Forcing herself to remain silent so as not to interrupt his thoughts, she could almost see the wheels turning in his mind as he mentally scanned the estate's abundant acreage.

"Near the north corner," he muttered, then shook his head. "No, no rocks there." He paused at the desk and again studied the grid map. "There are so many trails," he said, shaking his head in frustration. "But nothing is coming to mind. I'll need to think on this—" He stopped abruptly and stared at the squiggles she'd drawn. "Water," he said. "Not dirt trails, but water. Streams." He repeated the word "streams" a half-dozen times, each time sounding more excited. Then he pointed to one of the squares they hadn't yet searched on the grid map, the square covering the farthest northwest end of the property.

"Here. There are three streams that converge here. It marks the boundary between my family's property and the Alwyck estate."

"Is there a rock formation there?"

His gaze met hers. "There are the ruins of a small stone cottage. Just three crumbling walls, no roof . . . by God, I think that must be it!" There was no mistaking the excitement in his voice, in his eyes. Taking her face between his hands, he pressed a hard, fast kiss to her lips then let out a short, triumphant laugh. "You're a genius."

"Me? You're the one who figured it out."

"But you provided the idea. The inspiration." He brushed his thumbs over her cheeks. "I'd say we make an unsurpassedly marvelous team."

Something in his tone, in the sudden seriousness of his gaze, curled heat through her, robbing her thoughts. Next week she would think of an outstanding reply, but for now she simply nodded. *Next week you'll most likely be on your way back to London,* her inner voice whispered. At the unwanted reminder, her entire body tensed.

Clearing her throat, she asked, "Shall we leave immediately for this abandoned cottage, or do you wish to wait for daybreak?"

His brows snapped down in a frown. "Victoria, I want you to stay here."

She stepped back and his hands slipped from her cheeks. Planting her hands on her hips, she glared at him. "Stay here? While you recover the jewels by yourself? I'm afraid not."

He reached for her, but she stepped back again, eluding his grasp. "Victoria, I need to know you're safe—"

"And I need to know *you're* safe."

"Now that the real letter and map are no longer in my possession, anything could happen. I can't risk having you in the middle of a possibly dangerous situation." This time when he reached out, he caught her shoulders. "After what happened with that knife-wielding bastard . . ." He briefly squeezed his eyes shut and swallowed. "Your father swore me to protect you, and I won't fail again."

Lifting her hands, she clasped his strong forearms. "You didn't fail the first time, Nathan. As far as I'm concerned, the safest place for me is with you. I've come this far on the search, I refuse to be denied seeing it through to the end. We've been partners all along and shall remain as such. Besides, with both of us looking, the search will go twice as quickly." When he seemed about to argue further, she added, "You might as well agree, because if you don't, I'll simply follow you. So the only question that remains is whether you think it better to depart now and conduct our search under cover of darkness or wait until dawn."

"I'm surprised you've deemed to leave that decision up to me," he muttered in a disgruntled tone.

She cast her gaze demurely downward. "You're much more experienced in these matter than I."

"Yes, I am. Which is why—"

"You'll choose when it's best for *us* to depart."

A muscle ticked in his jaw. "Have you always been this headstrong?"

"I think I must have been, but until recently I've kept the trait hidden."

"I think you should have kept it hidden a bit longer."

"No you don't. You told me that discovering new aspects of my nature was good. I recall precisely what you said—that my past experiences haven't allowed me enough freedom to *know* my true nature. That I've done what's expected of me rather than what my heart desires. That speaking my mind, acting on my impulses, can be very liberating. And that I should feel free to say anything to you that I wish."

He muttered something under his breath that sounded like "hoist on my own petard," and she bit the insides of her cheeks to keep from smiling at his displeased expression.

"You will not, for any reason, wander away from me."

"I swear. And let's not forget the lady's pistol in our tool bag. I wouldn't hesitate to use it if necessary," she said, praying that was true.

That reminder didn't cheer him nearly as much as she thought it should. Indeed, his frown deepened. "But you might not be able to get to the pistol in time, and I don't want you to actually carry it on your person. You might shoot someone."

"Wouldn't that be the point?"

"I meant like yourself. Or me."

"Oh. Well, then I'll just load my reticule with rocks and keep it at the ready."

He pinched the bridge of his nose and shook his head. "A *reticule*? Filled with *rocks*?"

She raised her chin. "Yes. Surely there's something about such a thing in your Official Spy Handbook."

"I assure you there is not."

"Well there should be. A reticule is small, easy to handle, and looks nothing like a weapon. And I won't hesitate to cosh any brigands, believe me." She hiked up a brow. "Hopefully you won't make me start with you."

She fancied she heard his teeth grinding in annoyance. "We'll depart at dawn," he said in a voice that resembled a growl.

"That would have been my choice as well."

"How delightful that we agree on *something* this evening."

"I'd wager that we could agree on something else."

"I wouldn't be too certain. I'm not feeling especially agreeable."

She slid her arms around his neck. Raising up on her toes, she pressed herself against him and lightly bit the side of his neck. "I'd wager we could agree that there are more interesting ways to pass the hours before dawn than arguing. Do you not think so?"

His hands slid to her waist, the heat of his palms warming her through the thin satin of her robe. "I don't know." A low groan rumbled in his throat as she nibbled on his earlobe. "I'm going to need some more convincing."

She skimmed one hand down his chest, over his abdomen, then lower, to boldly fondle him through his silk robe. He sucked in a quick breath, his eyes glowing like twin braziers.

"Better than arguing?" she whispered, stroking his hardening length.

"I'm convinced," he said, and crushed her to him.

They silently left the house just as the first mauve smudges of dawn touched the sky. Her heart pounding in anticipation, Victoria hurried along next to Nathan, who held her hand in a warm, comforting grip. In her other hand she carried her dark blue velvet reticule—filled with rocks.

"We'll walk rather than take the horses," he said in a hushed tone as they bypassed the stables. "That way we can more easily survey the area surrounding the ruins without risking detection."

Victoria nodded her agreement, and then concentrated on the path in front of her. They moved along rapidly, passing the lake then continuing on a trail that veered off to the right. She judged a half hour passed before Nathan slowed their pace. Sullen gray streaked the sky, and the air felt cool and heavy with approaching rain. She could hear the sound of water gurgling over rocks, indicating a nearby stream. He pulled her behind a huge elm and, keeping one arm firmly around her shoulders, pointed. "The ruins," he whispered next to her ear.

Peering through the trees, she saw the crumbling trio of roofless walls. She could feel his tension, knew his every nerve was alert as his gaze carefully scanned the area. Finally, clearly satisfied they were alone, he led her toward the cottage.

They stepped into the U shape formed by the three remaining tumbledown stone walls. Nathan slowly surveyed the area, then pointed toward the remains of the fireplace in the center wall. "Let's begin there," he said, pulling their chisels and hammers from the tool bag. "The stones are set in a more irregular pattern, making it easier to conceal any that might be out of place." He handed her the tools with a grim smile. "You take the right side and I'll take the left—and good luck."

For more than an hour the only sounds besides the usual birdcalls and the gurgling of the stream were the *chinks* of hammers striking chisels. A heavy gray mist saturated the air, dampening their clothes. Victoria noticed that Nathan had stopped hammering and she looked over at him. He'd turned so his back was to the fireplace. His gaze, narrowed and alert, scanned around them. Her stomach jittered at his tense expression.

"Is something amiss?"

"No. I just don't like this heavy mist. I don't think the rain will hold off much longer. Another hour or two at the most."

"I'm not afraid of getting wet, Nathan."

He looked at her and gave a small smile. "I know, my brave warrior. But rain would make us vulnerable. Make it easier for anyone to sneak up on us."

"Well, then let's just find the jewels and leave before anyone does." Without waiting for his reply, she turned back to the fireplace. A quarter of an hour later, kneeling on the ground, she tapped her chisel into a bit of mortar surrounding a stone close to the ground and the plaster crumbled differently than before.

"Nathan," she said in an excited whisper. "I think I've found something. The mortar around this stone feels softer."

He dropped to his knees beside Victoria and looked at the stone she indicated. "And the mortar is a slightly different color," he said.

Together they chiseled around the stone. When they'd loosened it, Nathan worked his fingers into the narrow side openings and pulled, rocking the stone back and forth, up and down. Slowly, slowly, he inched the heavy stone forward until it landed on the ground with a dull thud. He reached his hand into the dark opening, and Victoria held her breath. When he withdrew his hand, he held a dirt-encrusted, battered leather satchel.

She exhaled her pent-up breath in an awed gasp. "Are the jewels inside?"

He loosened the drawstring top and their heads bumped as they both looked into the bag. Even the gray mist couldn't dull the sparkling glitter of the contents. Reaching in with an unsteady hand, she reverently lifted the first thing she touched—an exquisite strand of creamy pearls. Delving back in, she lifted an emerald necklace, tangled with a sapphire bracelet.

She tilted her hand so the jewels slid back into the bag then looked at Nathan. "Even though I'm seeing this with my own eyes, I can scarcely believe it."

"Neither can I. But we can dwell on that later." He pulled the drawstring closed, then tucked the cache under his arm. "Let's gather our things and get out of here."

While Nathan hastily shoved the hammers and chisels into the tool bag, Victoria scanned the ground for her rock-filled reticule. Spying it several feet away, near Nathan's feet, she was about to reach for it when a familiar voice behind her said, "Victoria."

Before she could so much as blink, she found herself shoved behind Nathan, who held his small pistol in front of him.

"Nathan, *stop*," Victoria cried, darting around him. "Father," she said, staring in stunned amazement at the gray-haired man standing a dozen feet away. Before she could utter another sound, a shot rent the air.

Victoria watched in horror as her father crumpled face-down to the ground.

Twenty-one

Today's Modern Woman must realize that not every love affair will have a happy ending.

A Ladies' Guide to the Pursuit of
Personal Happiness and Intimate Fulfillment
by Charles Brightmore

*N*athan was aware of Victoria dashing to her father, falling to her knees beside him, but his attention was riveted on the wooded area beyond the ruined cottage. A slight movement behind a thick tree trunk alerted him. Dropping to one knee to make himself a smaller target, he aimed his pistol at the tree. "Stay down, Victoria," he ordered in a low voice.

"Drop your weapon, Nathan." The command came from behind the tree. For an instant Nathan froze at that familiar voice. Then white-hot anger and betrayal shot through him. *You bastard*. Before he could reply, the voice continued, "I have a pistol aimed right at her head. If she moves, I'll kill her. If you don't follow my directions to the letter, I'll kill her. Now set your pistol on the ground and push it away."

Nathan's gaze flicked to Victoria, who was pressing the hem of her gown against her father's bleeding wound. She looked up at Nathan with wet, horrified eyes. "Keep as much pressure on his wound as you can," Nathan said in a terse undertone, "but *don't move*."

Moving slowly so as not to be perceived as making any sudden moves, Nathan set his pistol on the ground then shoved it aside.

"Good," came the voice. "Now do the same with the knife in your boot. Don't bother to pretend you do not have it, especially as I'm the one who gave it to you. For your birthday five years ago, as I recall."

Nathan slid the knife from his boot and shoved it aside.

"Now stand up and put your hands on your head."

After he'd obeyed, Nathan said in a mocking voice, "Brave enough to show yourself now?"

Nathan remained still as a statue, his gaze burning into the man who stepped out from behind the tree. Holding a pistol in one hand, his other hand resting on the hilt of a sheathed knife tucked into the waistband of his breeches, Gordon approached.

"Very kind of you to locate the jewels for me, Nathan," Gordon said in a conversational tone, his gaze flicking down to the worn leather sack at Nathan's feet. "I knew if I followed you, you'd eventually lead me to them. You cannot imagine what an inconvenience it's been trying to locate them for the past three years."

Nathan's mind whirled. Damn it, he needed time, a diversion, yet if there was any hope of saving Lord Wexhall, he couldn't stall for long. "You betrayed us three years ago," Nathan sneered. "Why? Why risk everything when you already had everything?"

Stark hatred burned in Gordon's eyes. "Everything? I had *nothing*. My father had gambled away everything—my entire inheritance—except the entailed property. He left me with a half-dozen homes I couldn't afford to maintain and that I couldn't sell due to the entailments. I needed money—a lot of money—and quickly."

"Because of your greed, my brother could have been killed."

Gordon's face twisted. "Your brother was supposed to have been killed. And I was only supposed to have been grazed."

Understanding dawned and Nathan's eyes narrowed. "And I was supposed to remain uninjured, thus thrusting the guilt upon me. How much did you pay Baylor to betray the mission?"

"Too much. And the bastard ruined everything. He got away with my money and the jewels. Once I recovered from my gunshot wound, I searched everywhere for him. I'd given up hope of ever finding him or the jewels until you showed up. When I learned Wexhall was sending his daughter to Cornwall, I knew something was afoot."

"You searched Lady Victoria's belongings."

"Yes. Sadly, I didn't find what I was looking for."

"And you hired that thug who robbed us in the woods."

Gordon chuckled. "Very clever of you, Nathan, having a false note with you. Clever, but exceedingly annoying. I wasted a week chasing false clues."

Nathan's gaze shifted briefly toward Victoria, who stared at him through solemn eyes. "That bastard you hired nearly killed Lady Victoria."

Unfortunately, Gordon didn't follow his gaze, as Nathan had hoped he would. "If it makes you feel any better, he'll never hurt anyone again."

"A tremendous load off my mind," Nathan murmured. "You cannot possibly hope to get away with this."

"On the contrary, I'm confident I shall. No one will gainsay the word of the Earl of Alwyck."

"I will."

An unpleasant smile curved Gordon's lips. "Dead men can't tell tales, Nathan. Now give me the jewels."

"If you're going to kill me anyway, why should I?"

"Because if you do as I say, I'll allow your father to live. If not, I fear he shall meet with a tragic accident. Now pick up the jewels very slowly and toss them to me. After you do, your hands go back on top of your head. You'll have *one* chance to make a nice, gentle toss I can catch. If you fail, Lady Victoria will have drawn her last breath."

Nathan picked up the leather satchel and nimbly tossed it to Gordon, who caught it in his free hand. He lifted the cache up and down several times, testing its weight, and a slow smile curved his lips. "Finally," he said. "And now—"

"There was no need to shoot Lord Wexhall," Nathan said quickly, clasping his hands on his head.

A look of utter disgust passed over Gordon's features. "He got exactly what he deserved. God only knows what he was doing here today. Looking out for you, no doubt. You always were his favorite of the three of us. Never understood why. Never understood why he gave *you* the chance to recover the jewels."

Nathan shrugged. "He thought I could use the money. If he'd known your financial difficulties, I'm sure he would have given you the opportunity."

"It makes no difference now. I have the jewels."

Nathan flicked his gaze toward the ground. "Um, yes. Yes, you do." He made a tiny sideways kick with the toe of his boot.

Gordon's gaze dropped to the ground and riveted on the dirty blue velvet drawstring bag near Nathan's boot.

"What is that?"

"Nothing," Nathan said a shade too quickly.

A gasp came from Victoria. "No, Nathan," she said in a low hiss. "Not those, too."

Gordon's eyes narrowed on Nathan. "Holding out on me, Nathan?"

"No."

"Another bag of gems?"

"Those stones are *mine*," Victoria said in a shaky voice.

"How greedy you are, Lady Victoria," Gordon said, making a *tsking* sound. He tucked the leather cache under his arm then pointed toward the blue velvet bag. "I'll take those as well, Nathan. Nice and slow, just like before."

Nathan slowly bent his knees, reaching down, never taking his gaze from Gordon. Just as he rose, an unearthly wail of distress came from Victoria. Distracted, Gordon's gaze shifted to her. It was all Nathan needed. With lightning speed he hurled the blue velvet rock-filled reticule at Gordon. The weighted bag struck him on the temple with a sickening thud and he went down like a tenpin. Nathan ran forward, ripping off his cravat. "Keep the pressure on the wound, Victoria. I'll be right there."

Using the cravat, he quickly tied Gordon's hands tightly behind his back in case he regained consciousness. Then grabbing Gordon's pistol, he turned to Victoria and her father.

"Are you all right?" he asked her, dropping to his knees.

"I'm fine. But Father . . ."

"Let me look," he said, gently moving her pressing hands away from her father's shoulder. "I need you to bring me my knife. Then I want you to gather up the jewels and our tools."

She scrambled to her feet and seconds later returned with Nathan's knife. He gently rolled her father onto his back and checked his pulse. Strong and steady. He used his knife to cut away the bloodied jacket and shirtsleeve. Probing the oozing wound on his shoulder, Nathan breathed a sigh of relief. "Flesh wound." He looked at the purple bruise on Lord Wexhall's forehead. "Looks like he's unconscious from knocking his head on the ground."

"He's going to be all right?" Victoria asked, kneeling beside him, her arms filled with their belongings.

"Yes. His wound is little more than a scratch, and he has the hardest head of anyone I've ever met. I suspect he'll have a devil of a headache for the next day or so."

As if to prove his words, Wexhall groaned. They both looked down. "Ooooh, I've a devil of a headache," he murmured. He blinked several times then attempted a smile at his daughter. "Victoria," he whispered.

"I'm right here, Father," she said, a catch in her voice.

Nathan heard the pounding of horses' hooves. Retrieving his gun, he peered around the corner of the crumbling wall. Seconds later Colin rode into view, followed by a man Nathan recognized as the local magistrate.

"Am I too late?" his brother asked, dismounting before he'd even fully reined in.

Nathan smiled. "You're right on time."

Several hours later Victoria stood next to her father's bed, holding his hand. Father, propped up on a mound of fluffy pillows, glared at the assembled group standing around the bed.

"I wish you would all stop staring at me," he grumbled. "I'm perfectly fit." The impatience in his voice let Victoria know more than his words that he was telling the truth. "If you don't believe me, ask my doctor," he continued, indicating Nathan with a bob of his chin. "I've been bathed and bandaged within an inch of my life, and have been told that I have to take a nap. My injuries only look serious because of all these blasted bandages wrapped around me. A sling for my arm, linen strips around my head, why 'tis ridiculous. I sustained a scratch on my shoulder and bump on my head."

"*I* think the bandages make you look rakishly handsome," she teased. "And rather . . . helpless."

"Just how I wish to be viewed," Father grumbled.

"Consider yourself fortunate that I do, lest I'd be tempted to lay you low for not confiding in your daughter about your secret life as a spy."

"Or your sister," Aunt Delia said with a sniff.

"Now see here, Victoria, Delia, I couldn't very well tell you something like that. It was imperative my identity remain secret." He sighed. "Of course, the cat's out of the bag now. Looks like I'll be retiring."

"I realize you couldn't tell, Father." Victoria leaned over to kiss his cheek. "I'm very proud of you."

Color rushed into his pale cheeks. "Thank you, my dear. As I'm proud of you. A father couldn't ask for a better daughter." When Aunt Delia cleared her throat, Father hastily added, "Or a better sister."

Everyone chuckled, then Nathan's father said, "Well I for one am anxious to know exactly how this all came about."

"I think perhaps Colin should begin," Nathan said. "I'd be very interested to know the details of how he came by this." He pulled a piece of ivory vellum from his waistcoat pocket and dangled it in front of his brother.

Lord Sutton's brows shot upward. "Where did you find that?"

"On the balcony of your bedchamber. You must have dropped it during last night's nocturnal visit."

A sheepish look crossed Lord Sutton's face, then he grinned. "Rather careless of me."

"Yes. Who did you steal it from?"

Nathan and his brother exchanged a long look. Then Lord Sutton said softly, "You never doubted that I stole it from someone? Never believed I'd arranged to have it stolen from you?"

"No."

"Your faith in me is more than I deserve."

"I disagree, but we can argue about that later. Now, from whom did you steal it?"

"A man named Oscar Dempsy. A week ago, I visited a tavern in Penzance where I heard this brute at the next table bragging about stealing a treasure map from 'a doc and a little lady' which he planned to sell for a large price. Being the incredibly clever gent I am, I suspected he meant Nathan and Lady Victoria. I bought the man several rounds, heard the story of how he cornered them in the woods and gave the little lady a nick for a souvenir. During his tale I relieved him of his ill-gotten gains. I briefly excused myself, claiming, um, personal needs, and quickly copied the note and map. When I rejoined him, I slipped his copy back in his pocket without him ever being the wiser."

"Very ingenious," Nathan murmured.

"I thought so. I'd intended to follow Dempsy to see who

he sold the letter and map to, but unfortunately one of those tavern brawls broke out and in the melee I lost him. I practically haunted the tavern for the next four days, but he never returned."

"He's dead," Nathan said in a cold, flat voice. "Gordon killed him. Probably not ten seconds after getting the letter from him." He looked at his brother. "Why didn't you come to me with this information?"

Lord Sutton met his brother's gaze. "As soon as I learned that it was indeed you he'd robbed and Lady Victoria he'd hurt, I realized I'd made a terrible mistake ever doubting you. Why would you hire someone to rob you? And I knew, without a doubt, you would never do anything that might endanger Lady Victoria. I decided then and there that I had to make amends for the terrible disservice I'd done you."

Nathan's gaze flicked to Victoria and she nodded. He'd been absolutely right about his brother's motives. "Go on," Nathan said.

"After deciding Dempsy wasn't coming back, based on the information in the letter and map I'd copied, I took a boat to the Isles of Scilly and did a bit of searching, but turned up nothing. I was surprised to run into Gordon there, especially since he suffers from seasickness and hates the boat crossing to the islands. We chatted, but I found him evasive, and of course, I was equally so. He returned to Penzance with me, and although we parted amiably, my suspicions were aroused. I decided to come back to the house last night and do a bit of eavesdropping to see what I could find out. I wanted to know if you'd located the jewels, or were close to doing so."

"Clearly you heard something that prompted the search of my bedchamber," Nathan said.

"Yes. I heard you mention a grid map. When I discovered it in your boot heel—nice hiding spot, by the way— along with the letter and map, I realized that I'd been on a wild goose chase."

"What was in the sack you were carrying as you skulked away from the house?" Nathan asked.

Lord Sutton grinned. "Clean clothes."

"Hmmm. And what happened after you eavesdropped then stole my belongings?"

"I returned to the inn in Penzance and pored over that drawing all last night, yet I couldn't figure out where to search next. But then Fate stepped in, in the form of Lord Wexhall. I'd just finished breakfast this morning when he strolled into the dining room. He was as surprised to see me as I was him."

Victoria's father picked up the story from there. "I'd arrived in Penzance last night with the thought in mind of doing a bit of snooping around the area before making myself known."

"Once a spy . . ." Nathan said with a smile.

Her father smiled. "Yes, old habits die hard. Anyway, after some discussion, Sutton filled me in on his plan to recover the jewels and clear Nathan's name. I pulled out the replica of the map I'd hidden in Victoria's luggage—" He glanced up at her and gave a sheepish grin. "Sorry, my dear." After clearing his throat, he continued, "Sutton showed me the letter and map and grid he'd taken from Nathan's room. It was immediately apparent that for some reason his map was noticeably different than mine."

Nathan's gaze shot to Victoria and heat crept up her face. "I did say that I wasn't an artist," she said in her own defense. "And it was *your* goat who ate the original."

"Goat?" Father asked, raising a brow.

"I'll explain later," Victoria said. "Continue."

"Sutton studied my map," her father went on, "and Nathan's grid map. With the proper drawing, it didn't take him long to figure out that the sketch depicted three streams. And that he knew of such a place that wasn't already marked off on the grid map. We compared thoughts and theories and realized that since neither of us had betrayed the mission and neither believed Nathan did, that only left one person who could have—Gordon."

"That realization pushed us to act," Lord Sutton said. "We rode here to tell Nathan and Lady Victoria what we'd learned, but they weren't here. We realized they must be searching for the jewels, and since they'd apparently left very early, we surmised they might have figured out the correct place to search. Since we didn't know where Gordon was, and we needed to find Nathan and Lady Victoria right away to warn them, Lord Wexhall and I split up. I went to Alwyck Manor to confront Gordon, and I told Lord Wexhall how to get to the ruins by the stream. When I discovered Gordon wasn't at home, I went immediately to fetch the magistrate, then we went to the ruins. We were nearly there when we heard the most god-awful, inhuman-sounding wail." He looked at Victoria and winked. "Nicely done."

"Thank you." She turned to Nathan. "And very nice throw of my *reticule* filled with *rocks*."

With a sheepish look, he inclined his head in thanks. "I shall personally pen an addition to the 'useful weapons' chapter in the Official Spy Handbook. You are unquestionably a genius." He coughed modestly. "Of course, my aim is unsurpassedly excellent."

"I agree. And it was no less than he deserved. I did tell him those stones were *mine*."

Nathan smiled at her. "Indeed you did. And I must commend you on your fine performance. You picked up on my ruse perfectly."

"Where is Lord Alwyck now?" asked Aunt Delia.

"Magistrate took him away," Nathan said. "He'll never see the outside of a prison cell again." He turned to Victoria's father. "And now, since you know everything, as your physician, I must insist that you rest."

"Yes, yes, all right," Father said with grudging acceptance. "I agree I need to rest, especially since I wish to leave tomorrow."

It seemed all the air was sucked out of the room at his words. "Tomorrow?" Victoria repeated weakly.

"Tomorrow?" Aunt Delia and Lord Rutledge said in unison.

"Tomorrow," her father repeated firmly. "My doctor has already given me permission to travel."

Victoria's gaze flew to Nathan, who regarded her with an unfathomable expression. "Is this true?" she asked. "Is it really safe for him to travel? Surely it would be better if we were to wait."

"I agree it would better," Nathan said, "but his injuries are minor enough that traveling won't impose any danger to him."

"I must return to London as soon as possible and deliver the jewels to His Majesty," Father said. His gaze shifted between Victoria and Aunt Delia. "We'll plan to depart directly after breakfast. Agreed?"

"Agreed," Aunt Delia whispered. Not trusting her voice, Victoria merely nodded.

"Well, now that that's settled," Nathan said, "I must ask everyone to leave so my patient can rest."

"I'd like a private word with my daughter, Nathan."

Nathan's gaze met Victoria's, and again she couldn't

read his thoughts. "Of course," he said. He was the last to leave the room, and quietly closed the door behind him.

Father turned his head on the pillow and searched her gaze. "Have you enjoyed your time here?"

Warmth instantly flooded Victoria's cheeks. "Yes."

"But you didn't expect to."

"To be perfectly honest, no. But I've been pleasantly surprised."

"Suspected you might be. Always good to have a change of scenery before making any huge decisions."

"Huge decisions?"

"Like who to marry. I saw Branripple and Dravensby the night before I departed London. Both wished to be remembered to you."

Lords Branripple and Dravensby. Good heavens, she hadn't thought about them in days.

"You seem to have formed a friendship with Nathan," Father said.

Victoria studied him, but his eyes were as innocent as his tone. "Yes."

"Glad to know it. He's one of the finest, bravest men I've ever known. Deuced brilliant when it comes to deciphering codes. Impressed me the first time I laid eyes on him."

I know precisely what you mean. "He's been very kind to me," she said, inwardly cringing at the inadequate words.

"And what of his brother, Lord Sutton? Another very fine man. Has the mien of a gentleman and the hands of a thief. Excellent combination for a spy."

"Lord Sutton was away during much of my visit, but I enjoyed his company while he was here."

"Well, good. I know you didn't want to come here, my dear, but I knew it would be good for you." He patted her hand. "A father knows best about these things."

Before she could ask what "these things" were, he added, "Happy you enjoyed your visit, but I imagine you're anxious to return to London. Get back to the Little Season and the business of considering marriage offers."

"I . . . yes, of course."

"I'd wager I'll be seeing my girl betrothed before the month's over."

Victoria's stomach performed a lurching tumble. Unable to voice an agreement, she simply nodded.

"Excellent. Well, you get a good night's sleep, my dear. I'll see you at breakfast."

Feeling as if she were in a daze, Victoria leaned down and kissed her father's cheek. After bidding him goodnight, she quit the room.

She walked swiftly to her bedchamber, her pace increasing until she was running down the corridor. After closing the door behind her, she leaned back against the oak panel. With her chest constricted and her breathing labored, she closed her eyes.

She was leaving tomorrow. To go back to her life in London. Her suitors. Her soirees and shops. To choose a husband. She should be filled with happiness. Anticipation. Relief. Instead, she was filled with a horrible sense of loss. A feeling of sick dread. A desperate ache that had her pressing her hand to the suddenly hollow spot where her heart belonged.

All the confused emotions simmering beneath the surface that she'd ruthlessly ignored and shoved aside for the past week gripped her in a vise she could no longer disregard. This feeling of desolation had nothing to do with where she was, but at the thought of leaving here. Leaving Nathan.

The realization that she didn't want to leave this place where she so vehemently had not wanted to come stunned her. And right on its heels came the truth her heart could no longer deny.

She'd fallen in love with Nathan.

Twenty-two

Today's Modern Woman should refrain from mak-
ing any life-altering decisions "in the heat of the
moment." She should step back from the situation
and give herself ample opportunity to carefully
review the situation from all angles so as to make a
decision she will not later regret.

A Ladies' Guide to the Pursuit of
Personal Happiness and Intimate Fulfillment
by Charles Brightmore

$\mathcal{D}$inner that evening seemed a somber, tense affair to
Victoria, although she wasn't certain if it was indeed that
way or simply a reflection of her own mood. Certainly
there was little conversation. Only Lord Sutton seemed animated, and he soon fell quiet when all his attempts at small
talk withered. As soon as the interminable meal ended,
Victoria excused herself to see to her packing. No sooner
had she arrived in her bedchamber than she heard a knock
on the door. Was it Nathan? Heart pounding, she called,
"Come in," but it was only her maid Winifred to assist her.

After everything was packed except her night rail and the

clothes she would wear tomorrow, Winifred left. Walking to the window, Victoria looked down at the moonlit lawn. Her fingers clasped the lacquered shell hanging around her neck. She hadn't had a chance to speak privately to Nathan, but surely he would come to her tonight. Her last night.

A quiet knock sounded at the door and her heart leapt. Crossing the room at a near run, she pulled open the door. Aunt Delia stood in the corridor.

"May I speak to you, Victoria?"

"Of course," she said, guilt pricking at her for her disappointment. "Please come in." After closing the door, Victoria asked, "Are you all right? You look . . . flushed."

"I'm fine. Indeed, I'm marvelous. And most assuredly flushing. From happiness." Reaching out, she clasped Victoria's hands. "I want you to be the first to know, darling. Lord Rutledge has asked me to marry him and I've accepted."

Victoria stared at her aunt in stunned amazement. "I . . . I don't know what to say."

"Say you're happy for me. Say you wish me years of joy."

"I do. Of course I do. I'm just surprised. You haven't known each other very long."

"True, but I know everything I need to. I know he's honorable and kind. Generous and loving. He makes me laugh. He loves me. And I love him. He is everything I did not have in my first husband, and I feel blessed to be given this opportunity for happiness and companionship at this stage of my life." She squeezed Victoria's hands. "It may seem like we've only known each other a short time, but my dear, it only takes the heart a single beat to know what it wants."

Moisture warmed Victoria's eyes and she pulled her aunt into a snug embrace. "Dear Aunt Delia. I'm delighted for you both." Pulling back, she asked, "Have you decided upon a date?"

"Yes. One month from today. Here, in Rutledge's parish."

"But that's an enormous amount of traveling for you. . . ." Victoria's words trailed off as understanding dawned. "You're staying here. You're not leaving with me and Father tomorrow."

"No. I wish to remain here. Become better acquainted with this lovely house, this quaint area which shall become my new home."

Victoria blinked. "But what of your love for Society and London? Your life there?"

Aunt Delia laughed. "Don't look so stricken, darling. Rutledge has agreed to spend the Season in Town if I wish." Her expression turned thoughtful. "And as for my love of Society and London, I can only say that my love for Rutledge far exceeds any fondness I have for city life." She gave Victoria a searching look. "Have you spoken to Dr. Oliver this evening?"

"Not privately, no." To her mortification, hot tears pushed behind her eyes. "I don't know how I'm going to say good-bye to him," she whispered.

Her aunt's eyes grew troubled. "Your heart will tell you the right thing to say, Victoria. The right thing to do. Listen to what it tells you." It appeared she wanted to say something more, but instead she merely brushed a quick kiss against Victoria's cheek. "I'll leave you now, my dear. I'll see you in the morning before you leave." With no further explanation, her aunt quit the room.

Victoria stood frozen in place, staring at the closed door. A myriad of emotions ambushed her, hitting her with such force she staggered to the nearest chair, an overstuffed chintz settee set in front of the fireplace, and sat down with an unladylike plop.

Aunt Delia's announcement of her decision to marry

Lord Rutledge had stunned her. Literally left her breathless. Dazed. Happy. But underneath all that, there was something else. Something she feared looking at too closely because it felt suspiciously like . . .

Envy.

A single tap sounded at the door. Before she could rouse herself to answer, the door opened and Nathan walked in. Their gazes met and Victoria's throat swelled with emotion. God help her, she loved him so much she ached. How had she allowed this to happen? Was there any chance he felt the same way about her? He'd never said so. Yet even if he did, what did it matter? Their lives were so drastically different.

But what if he had fallen in love with her? What if, like his father had offered her aunt, Nathan intended to offer her marriage? The mere thought brought on a sensation she couldn't define. Was it elation—or fear? None of this—Nathan, falling in love with him—had been in her plans. How could she consider giving up everything she'd planned her entire life based on a weeklong affair?

An affair based on a spark that was lit three years ago, her inner voice whispered slyly. But perhaps she had nothing to worry about. He hadn't said he loved her. Or wanted her in any way beyond what they'd already shared. If she'd been capable of doing so, she would have laughed at her own conceit. Here she was fretting about a proposal that he'd never given any indication he intended to offer. A proposal she wasn't prepared to hear. Still, if she became all choked up just looking at him, how would she be able to say good-bye to him tomorrow?

After closing and locking the door behind him, he walked slowly toward her, his gaze riveted on hers. He carried a wrapped parcel in one hand and a single red rose in the other. He rounded the settee, then sat next to her, setting his package on the floor. He held out the rose to her. "For you."

She touched the velvety petals. "Thank you."

"I checked on your father. He's doing well. Exceedingly well if one judges health by the level of complaints coming from the patient."

She smiled weakly. "He dislikes inactivity."

"Indeed? I hadn't particularly noticed. I also spoke to my father and your aunt. They told you their news."

"Yes."

He studied her face. "You're not pleased?"

"Yes, of course I am. No one deserves joy more than Aunt Delia. It's just that I'm . . ."

"What?"

Envious of their happiness. Of my aunt's daring. "I'm just surprised," she finished lamely. "Aren't you?"

"Actually, no. I had a conversation with my father that made it clear he cared deeply for your aunt. It's good to see him so happy. Good to see them both so happy." His gaze searched hers. "When I opened the door, you looked pensive. What were you thinking?"

"Are you sure you want to know?"

A faint smile touched his lips. "Yes."

"I was wondering how I was going to say good-bye to you."

His gaze turned troubled. "I've been wondering that very same thing with regards to you."

She had to press her lips together to keep from asking if he'd come up with a solution. Reaching down, he picked up the package he'd set on the floor and handed it to her.

"After much thought, I decided this was the best farewell I could give you."

Placing her rose on the mahogany end table, she laid

the package on her lap and carefully unwrapped the layers of tissue paper. When she looked down at the book nestled in the wrappings, her breath caught. Reverently, she brushed her fingertip over the title.

"*Histoires ou contes du temps passé, avec des moralités: Contes de ma mère l'Oye,*" she whispered. "*Tales of Mother Goose.*" She turned to the first page and saw the publication year: 1697. "It's a first edition," she said, awed. "Wherever did you find one?"

"I didn't have to look very far, as it was in my traveling trunk. That is my copy."

Victoria's head snapped up from admiring the book and she stared at him. "The copy you said you wouldn't consider selling for any sum? The copy that was the last gift you received from your mother before she died?"

"Yes."

Her heart began a slow, hard beat. "Why would you give me something so valuable to you?"

"I wanted you to have something to remember me by."

The tiny flame of impossible, ridiculous hope inside her that had been struggling to stay lit was suddenly extinguished. He indeed intended to say good-bye.

She should be glad. Relieved. It was for the best. And surely as soon as she didn't feel so enervated, so numb, she would feel all those things.

I wanted you to have something to remember me by. Dear God, as if she would ever, could ever, forget him. "I . . . don't know what to say."

"Do you like it?"

She looked into his eyes, so serious, so beautiful, and a sob rose in her throat. She attempted to cover it up with a laugh, but the effort failed miserably, and to her mortification, hot tears pushed at her eyes. "I love it." *And I love you. And I desperately wish I didn't because nothing ever has hurt this badly.*

Should she tell him? Tell him he owned her heart, and that it was breaking at the thought of leaving him? *No!* her inner voice screamed, and she realized she'd be a fool to tell a man who was clearly determined to say good-bye that she loved him.

Blinking back her tears, she straightened her spine and offered him a smile. "Thank you, Nathan. I'll treasure it always."

"I'm glad. Since I cannot give you the fairy-tale ending you've always planned, I at least wanted to give you the fairy tale."

"Will I ever see you again?" she asked, her voice shaking and barely above a whisper.

Framing her face between his hands, he studied her through serious eyes. Finally he said, "I don't know. That is up to . . . Fate. All I do know is that we have this one last night together. And I want to make it unforgettable." He leaned forward and softly touched his lips to hers. When he started to lean back, a sense of desperation unlike anything she'd ever known flooded her. Wrapping her arms around his neck, she pulled him back toward her.

"Again," she whispered against his mouth. "Again."

And as he had the first time she made that demand of him three years ago, he obliged her.

And when she awoke the next morning, she was alone.

"Are you all right, Victoria?"

Her father's voice penetrated the fog of despair enveloping her. She pulled her gaze from the window of the coach that with every turn of its wheels sent her farther away from Nathan.

"I'm . . ." looking into her father's concern-filled eyes, she couldn't bring herself to lie and say she was fine. "Tired." God knew that was the truth.

Father frowned and his jaw moved back and forth, as it always did when he puzzled over something. Offering him the best smile she could muster under the circumstances, she returned her gaze to the window. How long ago had they left Creston Manor? An hour? It felt like a lifetime. And as much as she loved Father, she dearly wished she were alone. To mourn the end of her affair in private. To shed the tears that hovered so close to the surface. To hold the book Nathan had given her against her heart.

Dear God, how was it possible to feel so much pain when she felt so utterly dead inside? Her eyelids slid closed and instantly a dozen images danced in her mind's eye—of Nathan smiling. Laughing. Making love to her. Saying good-bye at the carriage this morning as if they were nothing more than polite acquaintances—

"Damn it all, you're crying. That does it."

Victoria's eyes flew open at her father's fierce words, and to her mortification she realized that tears had indeed silently leaked down her cheeks. Before she could reach for her handkerchief, Father pressed his into her hand. Then, with a fierce scowl, he reached into his waistcoat pocket and withdrew a folded piece of vellum.

"I was instructed not to give this to you until after we'd reached London, but since I never actually gave my word that I would wait, I'm not going to." He held out the vellum, which was sealed with a blob of red wax.

"Instructed by whom?"

"Nathan. He gave it to me last night and asked that I hold it until we were resettled in London. To give you some time to think. To reflect. About what you want. But a blind man could see that you're heartbroken and miserable, and I can't bear to watch it a moment longer. If there's even the slightest chance that whatever he's written might make you feel better, I'll risk his displeasure."

Victoria reached out an unsteady hand and took the vellum. After breaking the seal, she slowly unfolded the thick ivory paper and, with her heart pounding, read the neatly scrawled words:

My dearest Victoria,

Here is a story to include in the Tales of Mother Goose, entitled "The Ordinary Man Who Loved a Princess":

Once upon a time, there was a very ordinary man who lived in the country in a small cottage. The man went through each day thinking his life was very fine and good until one day he met a beautiful princess from the city from whom he stole a kiss. As soon as he did so, he regretted it because from that moment on, no other kiss but hers would do, which was very bad because very ordinary men have nothing to offer princesses.

The memory of that single kiss lived in the man's heart, burning like a candle he couldn't extinguish. Then, three years after that kiss, he saw the princess again. She was even more beautiful than he remembered. But by then the princess was destined to marry a wealthy prince. Yet even though he knew a princess wouldn't marry an ordinary man, even though he knew his heart would be broken, he couldn't help but fall in love with her, for she was not only beautiful, she was kind and loving. And brave. Loyal. Intelligent. And she made him laugh. So even though he was far too ordinary for a princess, he had to try to win her love, for he couldn't give her up without a fight. He therefore offered her the only things he could—his heart. His devotion. His honor and respect. And all his love. And then he prayed that the moral of the story would be that even an ordinary man could win a princess with the riches of love.

> *My heart is yours, now and always,*
> *Nathan*

Victoria's vision blurred and she blinked back the tears hovering on her lashes. Then she raised her gaze to her father, who regarded her with a questioning expression.

"Well?" he asked.

A half laugh, half sob burst from her. "Let's get this carriage turned around."

Nathan stood at the shore, staring at the white-capped waves that pounded relentlessly at the rocks and sand. The wind was picking up, warning of an approaching storm, and the somber gray sky perfectly matched his mood.

Had she only left two hours ago? Had it only been one

hundred and twenty short minutes since it felt as if his soul had been ripped out? Bloody hell. His heart felt . . . gone. As if the only thing holding up his head were his lungs—and they hurt.

He dragged his hands down his face. Damn it, he'd done the right thing for her by letting her go. But that didn't make it hurt any less.

"Nathan."

He whipped around at the sound of her voice and stared, dumbfounded. She stood not ten feet away, clutching a piece of folded ivory vellum marked with his seal in red wax to her chest. But it was the look in her eyes that simultaneously stilled him and roared hope through him. A look filled with so much longing and love that he was afraid to blink lest he discover this was some sort of wishful dream.

Rooted to the spot, he watched her approach. When less than a foot separated them, she reached out and laid her hand against his cheek.

"There is absolutely nothing ordinary about you, Nathan," she said in a shaky whisper. "You are extraordinary in every way. And I've known that since the first moment I set eyes on you three years ago."

He turned his face and kissed her palm, then took her hand and clasped it between his. "Your father gave you my note."

Still clutching the vellum, she wrapped her arms around his neck. "You can thank him later."

"I wanted you to have time to think—"

"I've had plenty of time. I've done nothing *but* think. I know what I want."

"And what is that?"

"Are you sure you want to know?"

"Very sure."

"You," she whispered, her gaze steady on his. "You."

All the spaces inside him that less than a minute ago had seemed so desolate and empty, now filled to overflowing. Taking her hands from around his neck, he held them between his. "I once told you that I would only marry for love."

"I remember."

He dropped to one knee before her. "Marry me."

Her chin quivered and her eyes flooded. Tears slipped silently down her cheeks and plopped onto their joined hands.

Nathan stood and frantically patted his waistcoat in search of his handkerchief. Finding the square of white linen, he dabbed at her wet cheeks. "Don't cry. God, *please* don't cry. I simply can't stand it." He swore softly and continued to dab as her tears fell unabated. Finally he gave up and simply brushed his thumbs over her wet cheeks.

"I'm not a rich man, but I'll do everything in my power to make sure you're always comfortable," he vowed, hoping his words would comfort her. "We'll spend part of our time in London—I'll proudly escort you to the opera, even though I'm quite sure 'opera' is Latin for 'death by unintelligible music.' I'll attend whatever soirees you wish, then make love to you during the carriage ride home. And again once we arrive home. I don't have much to give, but everything I have I offer to you. And I'll love you every day for as long as I live."

Victoria looked into his eyes and saw everything she'd never known she always wanted. Probably next week she'd come up with a brilliant reply to his lovely words, but for now all she could do was speak her heart. "I've come to realize that it doesn't matter where I am, as long as I'm with you. And I've even grown fond of your menagerie. I already adore B.C. and Boots, and I'm certain Petunia and I can come to an understanding about what she can and cannot eat." She blinked back a fresh wash of tears. "I love you, too. So very much. It would be my honor to be your wife."

"Thank God," he muttered, pulling her close. His lips captured hers in a long, deep, lush kiss that left her spinning.

When he finally lifted his head, she said in a breathless voice, "You know, I *do* come with a dowry."

"Do you? I'd quite forgotten."

And that, Victoria decided, was the loveliest gift a woman who'd always known she'd be married for her money could have received.

Epilogue

While Today's Modern Woman should refrain from making any life-altering decisions "in the heat of the moment," she should also recognize that some decisions require no thought at all because there is clearly only one answer.

A Ladies' Guide to the Pursuit of
Personal Happiness and Intimate Fulfillment
by Charles Brightmore

Six weeks later

𝒩athan stood at the altar in the small parish church his family had attended for generations and watched his beautiful bride walk slowly toward him. Dressed in a simple pale blue gown with a modest square neckline and puffed sleeves, carrying a bouquet of pastel roses, she took his breath away. When she reached him, he smiled.

"You look beautiful," he whispered.

"So do you," she whispered back with an answering smile.

The vicar cleared his throat and shot them a frown.

The ceremony proceeded without incident until the vicar intoned, "If there is anyone present who knows of any reason why these two people cannot be joined in holy wedlock, speak now or forever hold your peace."

Nathan cleared his throat. "I have something I need to say."

The vicar's brows shot up to his hairline. "You do?"

"Yes." He turned to Victoria. "I need to tell you something."

She paled. "Dear God," she whispered. "This can't be good."

"It seems quite obvious to me that you have every intention of seeing this ceremony through to its conclusion," he said.

"That was my plan, yes."

"Excellent. Then in the spirit of making a full disclosure before we're officially man and wife, I want you to know I'm, um, no longer of modest means."

"What do you mean?"

"I mean His Majesty has given me a very handsome reward for the return of the jewels."

"How handsome?"

He leaned closer and whispered in her ear. "One hundred thousand pounds." He leaned back, enjoying her look of utter shock. "And then there's the house."

"House?" she repeated weakly.

"In Kent. About three hours outside London. Just a modest estate, according to His Majesty. Probably no more than thirty or so rooms. Lots of space for your soirees, lots of acreage for my animals."

She gaped at him. "How long have you known about this?"

"Your father told me only moments ago—just before he escorted you down the aisle."

Her mouth opened and closed twice without any sound coming out. Finally she said, "You've known about this windfall for six minutes?"

"Approximately."

"And you didn't tell me?"

He shrugged, then grinned. "I wanted to make sure you weren't marrying me for my money."

For several seconds she said nothing, then she gave a quick laugh. "I must say, this is unsurpassedly good news."

"There's no such word as unsurpassedly."

"There is now." And then she started talking so fast he could barely understand her. He risked a glance at the vicar, who looked as if he were about to suffer from apoplexy.

"Victoria," Nathan whispered. When she continued to chatter, he shut her up the only way he knew how. Pulling her into his arms, he kissed her.

"Good heavens," the vicar said in an outraged voice. "Not yet! I haven't yet pronounced you man and wife!"

Breaking off the kiss, Nathan turned to the scarlet-faced man. "If I hadn't kissed her, believe me, you never would have had the chance to do so."

He returned his attention to Victoria, who looked flushed and well-kissed.

"Heavens," she said, "you kissing me to shut me up—that is just how we started."

"It is indeed."

"And now I suppose it marks that this is the end of our courtship."

Nathan brought her gloved hand to his mouth and pressed a kiss against her fingers. "No, my love, this is, in every way, just the beginning."

The end.

IT'S AMAZING! IT'S ASTONISHING!
MAYBE HE REALLY _IS_ INTO YOU!

WELCOME TO THE WORLD
OF THE AVON ROMANCE SUPERLEADERS . . .
A SURPRISING AND UNUSUAL PLACE,
WHERE MEN ACTUALLY DO WHAT THEY SAY . . .
AND ACT ON THEIR FEELINGS!

———————

We hear it all the time on television,
read about it in books . . .
we have been trained to know the signs.
When a man isn't into you,
he lets you know.

But surely there must be
some men out there who _are_ interested!
Who are these men?
And how can you tell what they're up to?

Now, in the next four
Avon Romance Superleaders,
you will learn to spot the true heroes
around you—or, at least, in the pages
of the best romances in the marketplace today!

The first sign a man is into you

He gets nervous at the thought of being around you!

In Jacquie D'Alessandro's September 2005 release, *Not Quite A Gentleman*, Nathan Oliver, the youngest son of an earl, comes face-to-face with the arrival of Lady Victoria Wexhall. On the surface they have *nothing* in common: he's content as a country doctor; she's considerably put-out at having to leave fashionable London Society for some pretty scenery and farm animals. But then she can't help but notice Nathan's strong arms and tempting ways . . .

Colin waved his hand in a dismissive gesture. "Perhaps it was a table in the drawing room. How did Lord Wexhall put it in his letter? Oh, yes. 'I expect you to take care of Victoria and see that no harm comes to her,'" he recited in a sonorous voice. "I wonder what sort of harm he believes might befall her?"

"Probably thinks she'll wander off and fall from a cliff. Or overspend in the village shops."

Colin cocked an eloquent brow. "Perhaps. Note how he said *you*. Note how I was not mentioned *at all*. The chit is completely *your* responsibility. Of course, if she's as lovely as I recall, I perhaps could be persuaded to assist you in looking after her."

Nathan blamed the heat that scorched him on the unseasonably warm afternoon. Bloody hell, this conversation was bringing on the headache. "Excellent. Allow me to persuade you. I'll give you one hundred pounds if you'll watch over her," Nathan offered in a light tone completely at odds with the tension consuming him.

"No."

"Five hundred."

"No."

"A *thousand* pounds."

"Absolutely not." Colin grinned. "For starters, given the fact that you're routinely paid with farm beasts, I doubt that you have a thousand pounds, and unlike you, I've no wish to be paid with things that make 'mooing' sounds. Then, no amount of money would be worth giving up seeing you do something you so clearly do not wish to do, as in acting as caretaker to a woman you think is a spoiled, irritating twit."

"Ah, yes, the reasons I stayed away for three years all come rushing back."

"In fact," Colin continued as if Nathan hadn't spoken, "I'll give *you* a hundred pounds—in actual currency—if you're able to carry out your duty to Lady Victoria without me witnessing you fighting with her."

Well accustomed to Colin's tricky nature, Nathan said, "Define fighting."

"Arguing. Exchanging words in a heated manner. Verbal altercations. I'm assuming you would not enter into any physical altercations."

"I've no intention of getting within ten feet of her," Nathan said, meaning every word.

"Probably for the best. She's unmarried, you know."

He stilled. No, he hadn't known. Not that it mattered. He shrugged. "Can't say as I'm surprised. I pity the poor bastard who finds himself leg-shackled to that puffed-up bit of talkative goods."

The second sign a man is into you

His mission is to tempt you to leave your own party!

In Stephanie Bond's October 2005 release, *In Deep Voodoo*, Penny finds herself with a deadbeat ex-husband who soon turns into a dead ex-husband! Some people think that she's to blame, and it sure seems like she's being followed by a handsome, rough-around-the-edges, but oh-so-sexy P.I. But does he want to apprehend her for the crime—or capture her for his own pleasure?

"Is this a private conversation, or can anyone join in?"

She swung her head around and the mystery man was standing there, still smoking, although she guessed he'd killed at least a half a dozen cigarettes since she'd last seen him. And he was still breathtakingly sexy . . . all muscles and male, leather and Levi's. Her gaze strayed to his left hand and noted it was ringless.

"I, uh . . ." Her brain was pickled.

He looked at the flyer she'd been studying. "Do you know her?" His smooth Cajun cadence made him sound as if his jaw was double-jointed.

"No. I was just . . . wondering what might have happened to her."

He took a drag on his cigarette and exhaled, still reading. "Looks like a good kid; I hope she's found safe."

"Or not."

He arched one eyebrow. "You hope she isn't found?"

She shrugged. "She's seventeen—maybe she doesn't want to be found."

He pursed his lips. "Is that the voice of personal experience? Do you have secrets, Penny?"

Her mouth went dry as his gaze bored into hers. One minute in and he was already too close for comfort. "No," she croaked.

"Ah. So it's the cynicism of someone newly divorced." He grinned and took another drag off his cigarette, then dropped it into an abandoned glass of ice. "You left your own party?"

"I just stepped out for a few minutes."

"I'm ready to leave, too. So why don't we leave together?"

She blinked, wondering if she'd misheard him, but the sexy glint in his eyes and the curve of his mouth was unmistakable—he wanted to get busy . . . with her. A tug on her midsection answered his call, and her breasts tingled, but her good-girl training kicked in. "I don't even know your name."

"It's B.J.," he said. "And don't worry—I'm not a serial killer."

She smirked. "I'll bet that's what all the serial killers say."

He laughed, a pleasant noise that stroked her curiosity. "I promise that as long as you're with me, nothing will ever happen to you . . . that you don't want to happen."

She swallowed hard. Strangely, she believed him, trusted him . . . with her body, anyway.

He leaned forward. "You smell good."

"Thanks . . . it's, um, almond oil."

"Really? Smells like doughnuts."